fur

bla

J. G. BALLARD: QUOTES

J.G. BALLARD: QUOTES

Editor/Publishers: V. Vale, Marian Wallace
Assistant Editor for project: Mike Ryan
Transcriptions/Proofreading: M.H. Beebe, Sandra Derian, Joe Donohoe, Toby Levin, Mary Ricci
Interns: Bruce Townley, Kim Romero, Yoshi Yubai, Ann Kaplan
Photographers/Artists: Ana Barrado, S.M. Gray, Mike Ryan, Charles Gatewood, Julie Glanville
Design: Brian MacKenzie, Seth Robson, Marian Wallace, Eric Nordhauser
Lawyer: David S. Kahn
Design Advisors: Andrea Reider, Judy Sitz, Chris Cobb, Catherine Wallace, Scott Alexander, Peter M.
Research Staff: Nix, Gary Chong, Marian Wilde, Adrienne Cardwell, Douglas Currie, Alan Coe, Mark Pauline, John Sulak, Christopher Trela (NYC)
Founding Benefactors: Allen Ginsberg, L. Ferlinghetti, D. & C. Hamby, K. Acker, Geoff Travis, Betty Thomas, Scott Summerville.
THANKS TO ALL J.G. BALLARD INTERNET LISTEES who helped! Also Valerie Kunz.
Inside cover photos (pp. 1 & 416) and back cover photos: Ana Barrado
Photo p. 415: Charles Gatewood
Cover design: Brian MacKenzie
Cover art: ©1950 Super Science Stories

Novels & collections by J.G. Ballard

Please note: many quotes in this project were spoken by fictitious characters in the below listed books, not directly by "the author."

The Wind from Nowhere 1962
The Drowned World 1962
The Drought 1965
The Crystal World 1966
The Atrocity Exhibition 1970
Crash 1973
Concrete Island 1973
High-Rise 1975
The Unlimited Dream Company 1979
Hello America 1981
Empire of the Sun 1984
The Day of Creation 1987
Running Wild 1988
The Day of Creation 1987
The Kindness of Women 1991
Rushing to Paradise 1994
A User's Guide to the Millennium (Nonfiction) 1996
Cocaine Nights 1996
Super-Cannes 2000
The Complete Short Stories 2001
Millennium People 2003

ISBN: 1-889307-12-2 (paperback)   Library of Congress:

THIS BOOK DEDICATED TO:
David Pringle, J.G. Ballard's archivist (a labor of love & exactitude) since 1972.

RE/Search Publications 20 Romolo #B San Francisco CA 94133
tel: 415-362-1465 fax: 415-362-0742
www.researchpubs.com   email: info@researchpubs.com

Printed in Hong Kong by Prolong Press, Ltd.

2   4   6   8   10   9   7   5   3   1

TABLE OF CONTENTS

IN today's dense communications environment, where the average New Yorker experiences 14,000 branding messages *each day,* one needs to continually *make sense* of a bafflingly complex, constantly changing environment. Brief, succinct quotes can quickly produce clarity amid moral murkiness—like a torch illuminating a dark forest ahead.

Why "moral"? Because life is a journey through an increasingly criminal world, where CEOs, Presidents, prestigious art auctioneers and celebrities are blatantly committing felony crimes against society.

Why J.G. Ballard? For five decades the U.K. writer (*Crash, Empire of the Sun*) has most accurately predicted the future. Provocative, witty and unafraid of embracing contradiction, Ballard especially illuminates anything taboo involving sex, death, technology, power, and media.

Why quotations? The quotation is the most useful form of philosophy, giving insight. Some of our favorites date from 300 B.C. with Lao-Tzu, Lieh-Tzu and Heraclitus, and even earlier—from the Egyptian texts presented by Rene and Isha Schwaller de Lubicz. Other favorite quotations derive from Hegel, Goethe, Gracian, Lichtenberg, Schopenhauer, Nietzsche, de Chazal, Duchamp, Dubuffet and Warhol, as well as from the complicated schools of Surrealism and Situationism.

This book is especially aimed at all who have to work for a living. It is our hope that many a commute may be mollified by this quotations book, which is easy to carry and use—just one minute at a bus stop may yield an inspiration sufficient to set one's imagination reeling. This is one of the few books published today which has no hidden profit-motive and agenda, except to expand and illuminate the reader's consciousness as rapidly as possible. You need something you can *trust!* Consider yourself a Chosen One to have even *found* this independently-published, limited-edition **Handbook for Deciphering the Future.**

RE this project: Philosopher-Poet-Imaginative Fictionalist J.G. Ballard himself sent us many books, as well as xeroxed interviews, articles, and stories used herein (sadly, some lacked credits), giving us full permission to extract anything of use from all of his works.

Happy reading, and thinking!—V. Vale

(V. Vale is the founder of *Search & Destroy* [1977] and *RE/Search* magazine [1980]. His newest venture is *Real Conversations,* a cable TV show to be available on DVD.)

THE FUTURE

■ Does the future still have a future? [*Daily Telegraph,* 1993]

■ The advanced societies of the future will not be governed by reason. They will be driven by irrationality, by competing systems of psychopathology. [letter, 2003]

■ People as a whole really aren't interested in the future any longer. [*Frieze,* 1996]

■ Some people have suggested that mental illness is a kind of adaptation to the sort of circumstances that will arise in the future. As we move towards a more and more psychotic landscape, the psychotic traits are signs of a kind of Darwinian adaptation. [BBC Radio, 1998]

■ Yet I can remember when people throughout the world were intensely interested in the future, and convinced that it would change their lives for the better. In the years after the Second World War, the future was the air that everyone breathed. Looking back, we can see that the blueprint of the world we inhabit today was then being drawn—television and the consumer society, computers, jet travel and the newest wonder drugs transformed our lives and gave us a powerful sense of what the 20th century could do for us once we freed ourselves from war and economic depression. In many ways, we all became Americans. [Introduction to *Myths of the Near Future,* 1994]

■ It was an excess of fantasy that killed the old United States, the whole Mickey Mouse and Marilyn thing, the most brilliant technologies devoted to trivia like instant cameras and space spectaculars that should have stayed in the pages of Science Fiction . . . some of the last Presidents of the U.S.A. seemed to have been recruited straight from Disneyland. [*Hello America,* 1981]

■ The future is probably going to be something like Las Vegas. [*Friends,* 1970]

■ Whereas the 20th century was mediated through the *car,* the 21st century will be mediated through the *home,* and ... *home means work.* [*Spike,* 2001]

■ The ultimate concept car will move so fast, even at rest, as to be invisible. [*Atrocity Exhibition,* 1990]

■ The ultimate crime-based society is one where everyone is criminal and no one is aware of the fact. [*Cocaine Nights,* 1996]

■ The most perfect crime of all: when the victims are either willing, or aren't aware that they are victims. [*Cocaine Nights,* 1996]

■ We live in unheroic times. [letter, 2003]

■ Our governments are preparing us for a future without work, and that includes the petty criminals . . . The psychopath, with his inward imagination, will thrive. He is already doing so. [*GQ,* 1996]

■ Sadly, at some point in the 1960s our sense of the future seemed to atrophy and die. Overpopulation and the threat of nuclear war, environmentalist concerns for our ravaged planet and unease at an increasingly wayward science together made everyone fearful of the future. [Introduction to *Myths of the Near Future,* 1994]

■ We're moving into a high-technology era centered on the proliferation of communications devices of every conceivable kind— which will transform just about everything. [*Thrust,* 1980]

■ Nobody is interested in the future at all. I think the future has been annexed into the present. Occasionally a futuristic image is trotted out, ransacked like an image of the past and absorbed into the ongoing continuum that represents present-day life. [*C21,* 1991]

■ Probably the first casualty of Hiroshima and Nagasaki was the concept of the future. I think the future died some time in the '50s—maybe with the explosion of the hydrogen bomb. [ZG, n.d.]

■ One of the reasons we've turned our backs against the future at present is that we unconsciously sense that the logics that will dictate our lives in the next 20, 30, 40, 50 years will be completely unlike those which rule our lives today and have ruled our lives in the past. We may move into a very indeterminate, seemingly dangerous and chaotic era where all the old certainties and the social cement that held society together will have gone. [C21, 1991]

■ The Arab world, the Moslem world, may well take the place of the Communist world as the great bogeyman of the future. [JGB News, 1993]

■ There is going to be an energy crisis, obviously. The supply of oil is finite, and the whole notion that the essence of the good life resides precisely in its abundance and in a casually spendthrift approach to everything, is going to have to be revalued. There's no question about that. [Thrust, 1980]

■ A titanic battle is about to begin, a Darwinian struggle between competing psychopathies. Everything is for sale now—even the human soul has a barcode. [Super-Cannes, 2000]

■ People are capable of the highest morality in certain areas of their lives, but of complete blanks in others. [Mississippi Review, 1991]

■ An institutionalized paranoia seems a bleak future for the human race. [letter, 1967]

■ We now live in the present, unconsciously uneasy at the future, and this short-term viewpoint does have dangers. We know that, as human beings, we are all deeply flawed and dangerous, but this self-knowledge can act as a brake on hope and idealism. [intv Hans Obrist, 2003]

■ On the whole, people had shown less resourcefulness and flexibility, less foresight, than a wild bird or animal would. Their basic survival had been so dulled, so overlaid by mechanisms designed to serve secondary appetites, that they were totally unable to protect themselves. They were the helpless victims of a deep-rooted optimism about their right to survival, their dominance of the natural order which would guarantee them against everything but their own folly, that they had made gross assumptions about their own superiority. [*Wind From Nowhere,* 1962]

■ These days one needed a full-scale emergency kit built into one's brain, plus a crash course in disaster survival, real and imagined. [*Concrete Island,* 1985]

■ How do you run a society where a large proportion of people will never work? [unknown]

■ The superheroes of the future will be people who'll challenge this condominium of boredom, and we'll find that our Bonnies and Clydes will emerge to challenge the suburban values. [*JGB News,* 1993]

■ We're driven by bizarre consumer trends, weird surges in the entertainment culture, mass paranoias about new diseases that are really religious eruptions. How to get a grip on all this? We may need to play on deep-rooted masochistic needs built into the human sense of hierarchy. [*Super-Cannes,* 2000]

■ I've always suspected that the Soviet Union was the last of the old style authoritarian tyrannies. The totalitarian systems of the future will be obsequious and subservient, plying us with drinks and soft slippers like a hostess on an airliner, adjusting our TV screen for us so that we won't ask exactly where the plane is going, or even whether there is a pilot on board. [intv Zinovy Zinik, 1998]

■ I've always said that the totalitarian system of the future will be ingratiating and subservient, rather than using the jackboot.

It will be the simpering smile of Ken Livingstone, with his "Congestion Charge" zone and its hundreds of cameras watching everything you do. The whole thing is Orwellian and no one protests—there seems to be a passive strain in the English psyche. [*Independent,* 2003]

■ I've long said that the totalitarian systems of the future will be subservient and ingratiating, the false smile of the bored waiter rather than the jackboot. We see this subservient Stalinism in London mayor Ken Livingstone's plans for controlling central London traffic. Hundreds of spy cameras, an army of wardens, a computerized surveillance system out of [Jean-Luc Godard's] *Alphaville*—in short, an Orwellian nightmare come true, but disguised as a public service. Of course, there should be no parking or traffic restrictions of any kind. What we need are more roads, a huge system of overhead freeways on the Los Angeles pattern, But we are too brainwashed to demand this. [intv Hans Obrist, 2003]

■ In a sense, we're policing ourselves and that's the ultimate police state, where people are terrified of challenge. [1997]

■ Such is mankind's innate optimism, our conviction that we can survive any deluge or cataclysm . . . confident that some means will be found to avert the crisis when it comes. [*Crystal World,* 1966]

■ There is a deep underlying unease about the rate of social change, but little apparent change is actually taking place. [*Atrocity Exhibition,* 1990]

■ I'm not against internationalism. Cooking is a good analogy. This mixing of cuisines is more common nowadays. Western chefs cook with lemongrass and ginger, elements of Oriental cooking. What I'm against is nothing but McDonald's. [*The Face,* 1987]

■ People realize that they're living in a totally valueless world—that morality is coming to an end, in the sense that the moral institutions that have underpinned society and given it some sort of fleeting purpose are being dismantled. [*21C,* 1997]

■ Lifestyle: Don't want one. Haven't had one for thirty years. We don't seem to *need* a lifestyle. [*Millennium People,* 2003]

■ There is a terrific volatility in mass psychology nowadays. Strange little obsessions become huge lava flows and threaten to smother common sense. [*Guardian,* 1989]

■ We seem to be in the trough of a wave; there's a huge wall rushing towards us with a white crest, and I just hope that we can ride to the top of it and maybe see something—a larger, more interesting world—on the other side. On the other hand, we may be swamped. We're living in very interesting times but, at the same time, deeply uncertain ones. [*21C,* 1997]

■ Only one thing is left which can rouse people, threaten them directly and force them to act together: crime, and transgressive behavior. [*Cocaine Nights,* 1996]

■ How do you energize people, give them some sense of community?. . . [By] all activities that aren't necessarily illegal, but provoke us and tap our need for strong emotion, quicken the nervous system and jump the synapses deadened by leisure and inaction. [*Cocaine Nights,* 1996]

■ It's no coincidence that religious leaders emerge from the desert. Modern shopping malls have much the same function. A future Rimbaud, Van Gogh, or Adolf Hitler will emerge from their timeless wastes. [*Atrocity Exhibition,* 1990]

■ Lovable psychopaths occur right throughout all of my fiction. I'm not talking about someone like Adolph Hitler, but nowadays our world is so conformist, we need these crazy ogres, a dangerous personality to bring about change. All of my psychopaths are socially integrated. And they're benevolent! [*Sub Dee,* 1997]

■ The Adolf Hitlers and Pol Pots of the future won't walk out of the desert. They'll emerge from shopping malls and corporate business parks. [*Super-Cannes,* 2000]

■ There are hints that a benign version of a Sadeian society is still emerging, of tormentors and willing victims. [*Literary Review,* 2001]

■ I wrote a short story called "The Intensive Care Unit" about a world where people never meet. They simply make contact via TV; marriage is conducted hundreds of miles apart. And in my story I visualize a man who actually decides to meet his wife and children in the flesh. Of course, it's a disaster. They just cannot bear the sensory overload. On a mere neurological level, they can't bear to be together—rather in the way that we can't bear to be too close to strangers. So I can believe that, in the future people won't be able to bear to be in the same room as others. Or even on the same street. Of course, it's very difficult to read these kinds of aspects of the future. [*ZG,* n.d.]

■ You've got to set something like *Crash* against what I think of as the normalizing of the psychopathic—something that's been happening for most of this century, but has really gathered force during the past 30 or 40 years, annexing more and more kinds of deviant behavior into the realm of the acceptable. Particularly in the sexual field, where people are now tolerant of sexual deviance in ways they weren't in my parents' generation. [*Frieze,* 1996]

■ We live in a world which is now entirely artificial, almost as though we were living inside an enormous novel. You have dozens of little machines in your kitchen, in your living room. The range of machinery that surrounds us is quite incredible. [*Fineline Features Online,* 2002]

■ Three bikers in metallized boots and Mad Max leathers sat at the outdoor tables. They formed a feral presence in the hypermodern complex, like carrion-birds on a skyscraper cornice, filling an unplanned niche in the ecology of the future. [*Super-Cannes*, 2000]

■ People want to save the whale and the seal because they know that sooner or later the human being is probably going to be next on the list. [*Mississippi Review*, 1991]

■ I think the main threat in the future is not to personal relationships, which will thrive despite easier divorce and the breakdown of the extended family, etc. I think the danger our children and grandchildren face lies in the decline and collapse of the public realm. Politics, the Church, the monarchy are all slowly sinking back into the swamp from which they rose in the first place. We stand on the shore, watching as they wave their rattles and shout their promises, while the ooze sucks at their feet. When the clamor at last subsides we will return to our suburbs, ready to obey the traffic lights and observe the civic codes that keep the streets safe for children and the elderly. But a small minority will soon be bored, and realize that in a totally sane society madness is the only freedom. So random acts of violence will break out in supermarkets and shopping malls where we pass our most contented hours. Surprisingly, we will deplore these meaningless crimes but feel energized by them. [*Literary Review*, 2001]

■ Bourgeois life—in the sense of suburban norms—will be completely maintained. Yet at the same time there will be huge dislocations that will come from any quarter. They might be terrorist outrages that paralyze the motorway network of the whole of Western Europe. They might be social in the sense that some fanatical pressure group will man the barricades and disrupt ordinary life; or aesthetic—a decision to embrace a new kind of fashion. A preference for the color blue rather than the color red may have huge planetary consequences we can't conceive of at the moment. [*Blitz*, 1984]

■ There were times in its history when the United States came close to suggesting what a utopian project might be, but the less appealing sides to American life now seem to be in the ascendant—there's a self-infantilism strain that gives America the look of Peter Pan's Never-never land. However, the future may well be a marriage between Microsoft and the Disney Company—an infantilized enter-tainment culture imposed on us by the most advanced communica-tions technology. [intv Hans Obrist, 2003]

■ If the future is a marriage between Microsoft and the Disney Corporation, what can the rest of us do about it? [*New Statesman*, 2002]

■ People seem to enjoy being infantilized. The future before us is a nightmare marriage between Microsoft and the Disney company, the

most juvenile fantasies brought to us by the most advanced communications technology. [letter, 2003]

■ Adults look back to the depression of the '30s and look to an end of the crisis, while the younger generation see it as a permanent state. [*New Musical Express,* 1985]

■ What I fear for my grandchildren is a benign dystopia of ever-present surveillance cameras watching us for our own good, a situation in which we will acquiesce, all too well aware of our attraction to danger. [intv Hans Obrist, 2003]

■ Think of the universe as a simultaneous structure. Everything that's ever happened, all the events that will ever happen, are taking place together . . . Our sense of our own identity, the stream of things going on around us, are a kind of optical illusion. ["Myths of the Near Future," 1994]

■ We may see ourselves at the turn of the century, each of us the star of a continuous television drama [webcam?—ed], soothed by the music of our own brain waves, the center of an infinite private universe . . . Childhood, marriage, parenthood, even the few jobs that still need to be done, will all be conducted within the home. [*Vogue,* 1977]

■ This is the trouble, always: enlightened legislation or enlightened social activity of whatever kind does play into the hands of people with agendas of their own—with secret agendas . . . If you legalize euthanasia, you provide a field day for people who like killing other people . . . and they'll find plenty of reasons for doing so. [*KGB,* 1995]

■ Every year planes were doubling their speed, and then after the war we had antibiotics, computers, motorways being laid down. People were constantly predicting what life was going to be like in ten or fifteen years, and all those vast futurama exhibitions were sources of enormous pride. [Now] people really aren't interested in the future any longer. That's the baffling thing. [*Frieze, 1996*]

■ There will be extraordinary unpredictable outbursts, a sort of volatility, largely driven by extremist cults of one sort or another . . . That's what we have to look forward to—that, plus the Internet and Virtual Reality. People will retreat into these electronic hideaways. [*KGB, 1995*]

■ We're looking at the situation where bourgeois society is controlling everything, without exception. One looks at certain publications [that] interview young designers, artists, photographers. It asks them what they want and they say money and fame. Someone of 19 who can only sum up his own ambition in terms of money and fame—for god's sake that's *the end*, that's *the death of the spirit*. [*New Musical Express, 1985*]

■ Come the year 2000, if not sooner, the past will disappear and the future will go next. [*Friends #17, 1970*]

■ Leisure societies lie ahead of us, like those you see on this coast. People will still work—or, rather, some people will work, but only for a decade of their lives. They will retire in their late thirties, with fifty years of idleness in front of them. A billion balconies facing the sun. [*Cocaine Nights, 1996*]

■ You won't find who was responsible by looking for motives. In Estrella de Mar, like everywhere in the future, crimes have no motives. [*Cocaine Nights, 1996*]

■ "A User's Guide to the Millennium" would be a good title for my work as a whole. Picturing the psychology of the future is what it's all been about. [*Independent,* Nov 10, 2001]

■ The future will be a struggle between huge competing systems of psychopathology. [*Independent,* 11-10-2001]

■ The world's turning into a madhouse, one half of society gloating righteously over the torments of the other. Most people don't realize which side of the bars they are. ["The Insane Ones," 1962]

■ The chief role of the universities is to prolong adolescence into middle age. [*Pretext*, 2004]

■ The totalitarian systems of the future will be docile and subservient, and all the more threatening for that. [*Kindness of Women*, 1991]

■ No longer will it be Orwell's vision of a boot stamping on a human face. We'll have something highly subservient and ingratiating, where the *tyranny is imposed for our own good* . . . The New Totalitarians come forward, smiling obsequiously like headwaiters in third-rate Indian restaurants, and assuring us that everything is for our benefit . . . So one gets this smiling tyranny, which is something my characters rebel against. [*Independent on Sunday*, 2003]

■ In the future everyone will need to be a *film critic* to make sense of anything. [*Kindness of Women*, 1991]

■ If one had to categorize the future in one word, it would be that word "home." Just as the 20th century has been the age of mobility, largely through the motor car, so the next era will be one in which instead of having to seek out one's adventures through travel, one creates them, in whatever form one chooses, in one's home. The average individual . . . will have all the resources of a modern TV studio at his fingertips, coupled with data processing devices of incredible sophistication and power. [*Penthouse*, 4/1979]

■ I would sum up my fear about the future in one word: boring. And that's my one fear: that everything has happened; nothing exciting or new or interesting is ever going to happen again. . . the future is just going to be a vast, conforming suburb of the soul. [*RE/Search #8/9*, 1984]

■ We have increasing flashes of racism, homophobia and irrational antipathy towards Europe. As we search for a new identity, our dark side emerges, creeping out of its sewer. [*Spectator,* 2000]

■ The English middle class ... are rebelling simply because they feel ruthlessly exploited ... Look in the papers and you see polls of doctors—one of the great pillars of society—in which 50% of doctors would like to do something else—would like to give up medicine... There's a huge dissatisfaction in this country, across the board. [*Independent on Sunday,* 2003]

■ I think we're all perhaps innately perverse, capable of enormous cruelty, yet paradoxically our talent for the perverse, the violent, and the obscene may be a good thing. We may have to go through this phase to reach something on the other side. *It's a mistake to hold back and refuse to accept one's nature.* [Atrocity Exhibition, 1990]

■ People are expected to package themselves, their emotions and sexuality in attractive and instantly appealing forms. [*Atrocity Exhibition,* 1990]

■ The fact is, we're novelty-seeking creatures. Novelty is as important as Vitamin C. [*Independent,* Sep 14, 2000]

■ I think relationships in the future will be far more ambiguous and far more uncertain than they seem to be now. ["Unlimited Dream Company" film, 1983]

■ The future is ceasing to exist, devoured by the all-voracious present. We have annexed the future into the present, as merely one of those manifold alternatives open to us. [Introduction to *Crash,* 1995]

■ I see the future as being abstract, geometric—the landscape of the moon seems to me to be a good image of the future landscape for Earth. [*Transatlantic Review,* Spring 1971]

■ A drastic increase in a wide range of plant diseases was noticed in the southern states of America and in the Kazakhstan and Turkmenistan republics . . . All over Florida there were outbreaks of blight and mosaic disease, orange plantations withered and died, stunted palms split by the roadside like dried banana skins, saw grass stiffened into paper spears in the summer heat. Within a few years the entire peninsula was transformed into a desert. ["The Cage of Sand," 1962]

■ The worldwide drought now in its fifth month was the culmination of a series of extended droughts that had taken place with increasing frequency all over the globe during the previous decade. Ten years earlier a critical shortage of world foodstuffs had occurred when the seasonal rainfall expected in a number of important agricultural areas had failed to materialize. One by one, areas as far apart as Saskatchewan and the Loire valley, Kazakhstan and the Madras tea country were turned into arid dust basins. After two years these farmlands were totally devastated. [*The Drought*, 1965]

■ Covering the offshore waters of the world's oceans . . . was a thin but resilient mono-molecular film formed from a complex of saturated long-chain polymers, generated within the sea from the vast quantities of industrial wastes discharged into the ocean basins during the previous fifty years. This tough, oxygen permeable membrane lay on the air-water interface and prevented almost all evaporation of surface water in the air space above. [*The Drought*, 1965]

■ Millions of tons of highly reactive industrial wastes—unwanted petroleum fractions, contaminated catalysts and solvents—were still being vented into the sea, where they mingled with the wastes of atomic power stations and sewage schemes. Out of this brew the sea had constructed a skin no thicker than a few atoms, but sufficiently strong to devastate the lands it once irrigated. [*The Drought*, 1965]

■ Fish? There isn't a single fish alive on the entire planet. The whole zoological class died out ten years ago. ["Deep End," 1961]

■ The planet's mineral, energy and agricultural resources have been efficiently, and even ruthlessly, exploited. . . They have harnessed the energy of the atom, deciphered the molecular codes that oversee their own reproduction . . . Despite these achievements the peoples of this planet have in other respects scarcely raised themselves above the lowest levels of barbarism. The enjoyment of pain and violence is as natural to them as the air they breathe. War above all is their most popular sport, in which rival populations, and frequently entire continents, attack each other with the most vicious and destructive weapons, regardless of the death and suffering that follow. These conflicts may last for years or decades. Nations nominally at peace devote a large proportion of their collective incomes to constructing arsenals of lethal weapons . . . ["Report From an Obscure Planet," 1992]

■ It's always been assumed that the evolutionary slope reaches forever upwards, but in fact the peak has already been reached, the pathway now leads downwards to the common biological grave. It's a despairing and at present unacceptable vision of the future, but it's the only one. ["The Voices of Time," 1960]

■ Women have always been suppressed, and never given the chance to flourish intellectually. When the first female Darwin or Freud appears it will have an astonishingly liberating force, and could change the world in an almost religious way. Perhaps this is the messiah we're unconsciously waiting for. [*Literary Review*, 2001]

■ Perhaps the future belongs to magic, and it's we women who control magic. [*Rushing to Paradise*, 1994]

■ Bourgeois life is crushing the imagination from this planet. In due course this will provoke a backlash, since the imagination can never be wholly repressed. A new Surrealism will probably be born. [*S.F. Eye*, 1991]

■ The consumer conformism—"the suburbanization of the soul"—on the one hand and the gathering ecological and other crises on the other do force the individual to recognize that he or she is all he or she has got. And this sharpens the eye and the imagination. The challenge is for each of us to respond, to remake as much as we can of the world around us, because no one else will do it for us. We have to find a core within us and get to work. Don't worry about worldly rewards. Just get on with it! [*Rolling Stone*, 1987]

■ A place of real promise: a city without street signs, laws without penalties, events without significance, a sun without shadows. [*Millennium People*, 2003]

■ Already we can see, a little sadly perhaps, the beginnings of a world without play. [*Guardian*, July 31, 2004]

THE PAST

■ Do you realize that since the death of Einstein in 1955 there hasn't been a single living genius? From Michelangelo, through Shakespeare, Newton, Beethoven, Goethe, Darwin, Freud and Einstein there's always been a living genius. Now, for the first time in 500 years we are on our own. ["The Overloaded Man," 1967]

■ The twentieth century criminally misspent itself. [*Rushing to Paradise*, 1994]

■ The twentieth century ended with its dreams in ruins. The notion of the community as a voluntary association of enlightened citizens has died forever . . . . People find all the togetherness they need in the airport boarding lounge and the department-store lift. [*Super-Cannes*, 2000]

■ The 20th Century . . . lingers on. It shapes everything we do, the way we think. There's scarcely a good thing you can say for it. Genocidal wars, half the world destitute, the other half sleep-walking through its own brain-death. We bought its trashy dreams and now we can't wake up. All these [supermarkets] and gated communities. [*Millennium People*, 2003]

■ The vast war crimes committed during the 20th century remain its greatest mystery, a moral and psychological black hole that swallows all pity and remorse, and leaves behind a void that will haunt the next millennium. [*New Statesman*, 2002]

■ During their long advance across the Pacific, the American armies liberated only one large capital city, Manila. A month of ferocious

© ANA BARRADO

fighting left 6,000 Americans dead, 20,0000 Japanese and over 100,000 Filipinos, many of them senselessly slaughtered, a total greater than those who died at Hiroshima . . . During the fierce struggle for Okinawa, an island close to Japan, nearly 200,000 Japanese were killed, most of them civilians. ["The End of My War," 1991]

■ China's greatest political leader and ideologue, Mao Tse-tung, brought an end to decades of devastation and civil war under the corrupt rule of Chiang Kai-shek but in turn Mao, his wife and henchmen brought equally appalling cruelties to the Chinese people . . . With Mao's conquest of the country, and the flight of Chiang to Formosa, a new and fairer China seemed waiting to be born. But mind-numbing sessions of public "self-criticism" began to occupy much of the revolution's time. Everything was now politicized, as the regime suppressed the last vestiges of spirit and independence . . . Cleanliness was regarded as unproletarian, ignorance was celebrated as freedom from bourgeois thinking, and constant meetings left no time for inward reflection, virtually eliminating the private sphere. [*Sunday Times,* 1992]

■ One suspects Mao's real achievement was to allow the Chinese, a supremely stoic and unemotional people, to express emotion fully for the first time. [*Sunday Times,* 1992]

■ In the 1920s rising prosperity turned Americans from a nation of producers to a nation of consumers. This simple shift has convinced all Americans to this day that they are middle-class. [review of "Working-Class Hollywood," 1997]

■ By the 1970s, as far as the public was concerned, the Space Age had ended, and with it died the greatest dream of the future yet conceived. The next 20 years were a timeless limbo, where past and future were annexed into the present. The past became little more than an attic of old trunks to be rummaged through for the latest nostalgia fad. ["Anything Could Happen," 1996]

■ The past is just a kind of anthology of design statements that one dips into as the mood takes you. It doesn't have any real validity; you don't have the sense of a road stretching behind us in the rearview mirror of life. [*Blitz,* 1984]

■ I think the past was the first casualty in World War II. People simply became uninterested in the past. Now they are only interested in the past in a sort of theme-park-like way—they ransack the past for the latest design statement. There's no sense of a continuity to which one owes a certain sort of obligation or duty or feels one's self shaped by; one just sort of picks and chooses what elements of the past one wants to exploit for one's purposes. The second casualty possibly—I don't know if you can date it—is the death of the future. It might be connected with the Kennedy assassination. It's quite possible that Kennedy was in some way an avatar of the notion of radical change, of a new world recovering from the threat of thermonuclear war in the '50s. Had he lived and served two full terms, he might have energized this planet. I don't mean that I approve of Kennedy. I'm talking about a media construct by and large, but he might have—the media construct which we call J.F. Kennedy—might well have energized the planet and thrown it into a forward motion, as he did, to his credit, with the space race. [*C21,* 1991]

■ Three immense forces, [Robert] Heilbroner contends, transformed the Distant Past into Yesterday—science, capitalism and *the revolutionary belief that people might become masters of their own fates.* For the first time, mankind saw the future as a beckoning prospect. The growth of technology and science, in particular, rapidly transformed the world for the better—a process that everyone assumed would stretch forever into the future. ["Anything Could Happen," 1996]

■ Science, economics and mass political movements still rule our world, but they now appear threatening, if not actively malign. Our faith in science was shaken by the nuclear bombs that destroyed Hiroshima and Nagasaki . . . ["Anything Could Happen," 1996]

■ The future may belong to neither work nor leisure, but to a violent and ultra-competitive form of play—hinted at in American football and the Olympic Games—where Virtual Reality will make its marriage with psychopathology, and the Marquis de Sade will find his ultimate home in the domestic video-sensorium. ["Anything Could Happen," 1996]

■ The Sixties were a time of endlessly multiplying possibilities, of real selflessness in many ways, a huge network of connections between Vietnam and the space race, psychedelia and pop music, linked together in every conceivable way by the media landscape. We were all living inside an enormous novel, an electronic novel, governed by instantaneity. In many ways, time didn't exist in the Sixties, just a set of endlessly proliferating presents. Time returned in the Seventies, but not a sense of the future. The hands of the clock now go nowhere. Still, I've hated nostalgia, and it may be that a similar hot mix will occur again. [*Paris Review*, 1984]

■ It's very easy to forget how the world has changed over the last 30 years. Even on the domestic level, our homes are just loaded with consumer electronics which have changed our lives to a considerable degree—TV sets, CD players, video cameras, microwave ovens, freezers and all the other gadgets which have changed our lives and, indeed, our sense of ourselves. If anything, these changes are accelerating. [*C21*, 1991]

■ Obsession with the past is a sign of English failure. [BBC News Online, 2002]

■ The 20th Century has been a huge manufacturer of what I call predictive mythologies . . . One of the greatest is the notion of space travel, the idea that one day mankind will leave this planet and move outwards into the solar system, colonizing other planets, and then beyond the solar system into the universe as a whole . . . Other [predictive mythologies are] classic Wellsian: society perfected by science. It's the dream one saw laid out in Aldous Huxley's *Brave New World,* countless novels and films. The notion that science sensibly applied to social problems will solve most of them and that we can all live in a kind of Corbusier world where tensions are defused by enlightened social legislation, and so on . . . hasn't really worked out. Human beings perhaps haven't evolved sufficiently to be able to enjoy living in high rise blocks or something like Corbusier's radiant city . . . We seem to need a certain element of street level chaos in our lives. We aren't as enlightened as we'd like to be, but that's another great predictive mythology. [BBC Radio 3, 1998]

■ I suspect that within a few years there will be a widespread rejection of the 20th century, its horrors and corruptions. Despite huge advances in science and technology, it will seem a barbarous time. My grandchildren are all under the age of four, the first generation who will have no memories of the present century, and are likely to be appalled when they learn what was allowed to take place. For them, our debased entertainment culture and package-tour hedonism will be inextricably linked to Auschwitz and Hiroshima, though we would never make the connection. I hope that a wave of idealism will move through their lives—not the weird mix of New-Age slogans and [teleprompter] sincerity that is our own substitute for high-mindedness, but a level-headed decision to put the planet to rights. [*New Statesman,* 1999]

■ Russia was very late in developing a middle class, so that until the start of the 20th century there was almost nothing between the aristocracy and the rural and urban working class, a set-up that stops the clocks, as you can see in any banana republic or oil-sheikhdom . . . [intv Zinovy Zinik, 1998]

■ Looking up at the ancient impassive faces [of the iguanas], Kerans could understand the curious fear they roused, rekindling archaic memories of the terrifying jungles of the Paleocene, when the reptiles had gone down before the emergent mammals, and sense the implacable hatred one zoological class feels towards another that usurps it. [*Drowned World,* 1962]

■ ...an aboriginal half-man prowling in dim bewilderment over the ruins of a futuristic city lost in an inversion of time. ["Venus Hunters," 1963]

■ The past, in social and psychological terms, became a casualty of Hiroshima and the nuclear age. [Intro. to *Crash,* 1995]

■ Fifty years ago a degree guaranteed you a job for life and a certain standard of living. But that's not true anymore. People in middle management are forced into early retirement and the polls reveal huge levels of dissatisfaction. The traditional privileges of the middle classes are no longer there. [*Telegraph,* 9-23-03]

■ The past will disappear and the future will go next. People will soon be living only in the present and will not be interested in the future at all. The possibility of maximizing our own pleasures, our own intelligent pleasures, will be so great, given the worldwide application of computer systems ... The present will be so rich; the future will not exist as a possibility. One will be able to lead a completely quantified life; the present will contain its own limitless future ... A child going into an amusement arcade does not think, "What will I do and where will I play in five minutes?"—he is merely in the flux of alternatives. Life is like that. [*Friends,* 1970]

■ What most struck me about England when I arrived in 1946 was how detached the whole country was from reality. It had an intense nostalgia for a vanished past, it was deeply class-ridden, and it had no awareness of its very reduced place in the world. In fact, it took some thirty years before it finally came to terms with its own reality. [BBC Online Live Chat, 2002]

■ Inmates of Lunghua camp [in *Empire of the Sun*] are a metaphor for the inhabitants of Britain today. They're selfish, they squabble amongst themselves, because the myth of the British cooperating in the adversity of the prison camp is something entirely created by wartime films like *The Great Escape*—in fact it was very much a matter of every man for himself. Also they have this strange sense of security which the boundaries of the camp give them—they're reluctant to look outside and they're even more reluctant to let anybody else in. [*New Musical Express*, 1985]

■ It seems to me that more and more people have come to terms with the past, declaring a private moratorium on their own past failures and experiences, and are becoming more and more fascinated by a future that presents itself in terms of uncertainty, opportunity, and the brilliant illumination of the chance encounter . . . the strange logic of the chance encounter, the fusion of apparently irreconcilable images that is the stuff of poetry. [*JGB News*, 1993]

■ I'm old enough to remember the 1930s and '40s when people were intensely interested in the future; when popular magazines and newspapers were saturated with news of the fastest train in the world, the longest bridge, the fastest plane, land-sea records, deep-sea penetration dives—people were fascinated by the future. Schools of architecture and design like Art Deco and the Modernist movement were engines running forward into the future. There was immense optimism and immense confidence in the ability of science to deliver the future and a better world with it. Now, that ended by the '70s. Nobody was interested in the future and, to this day, nobody cares tuppence half-penny about some new scientific development. I mean, people have no sense of what the world three years from now will be like, whereas people in the '30s and '40s had a sense that the future had been marked out clearly. One knew that—

I mean one would see actual diagrams in newspapers stating that 10 years from now such-and-such will come into existence and then we can expect television in all our homes and then video-telephones and so on. Now all that's over. [C21, 1991]

■ The automobile culture that Americans have had since the 1920s really arrived in Europe in the 1960s . . . dating and sex in cars suddenly became a part of the global way of life. [*Seconds,* 1996]

■ Everything happened during the Sixties. The Kennedy assassination was the key event/the catalyst that got it all moving. Thanks to TV, mass communications, and all the rest, you got strange overlaps between the assassinations and Vietnam and the space race and the youth pop explosion and psychedelia and the drug culture. It was like a huge amusement park going out of control. And I thought, "Well, there's no point in writing about the future—the future's here. The present has annexed the future onto itself." [*Heavy Metal,* 1982]

■ Young people of Western Europe since the Sixties have grown up in a remarkably uniform environment, both in terms of the postwar architecture of high rises and motorways and shopping malls, and also in terms of fashion in clothes and pop music, beach holidays in Spain and Greece, and their attitudes to society as a whole and their place in it. [*Paris Review,* 1984]

■ One sees a generation which finds itself living in sane, just, and largely humane societies—the welfare-state social democracies, and is deeply suspicious of them, while in fact sharing all the values for which those societies stand. [*Paris Review,* 1984]

■ I think the prosperity in the '60s and '70s induced a kind of infantilism. People stopped dealing with a time scale that lay outside of their immediate present. They began to have no sense of what had happened yesterday or of what would happen the day after tomorrow. So people became immersed in the fulfillment of their own needs and their own satisfactions. They literally lost interest in the future. But by the same token, they also lost interest in the past. These days most people's idea of the past is a rerun of *Casablanca*. They have very little idea of history nowadays. So time has dismantled itself. [ZG, n.d.]

■ The stream of retinal images reaching the optic lobe is nothing more than a film strip. Every image is stored away, thousands of reels, a hundred thousand hours of running time. ["Zone of Terror," 1960]

■ The streets had died twenty or thirty years earlier; plate-glass shopfronts had slipped and smashed into the roadway, old neon signs, window frames and overhead wires hung down from every cornice, trailing a ragged webwork of disintegrating metal across the pavements. Stacey drove slowly, avoiding the occasional bus or truck abandoned in the middle of the road, its tires peeling off their rims. ["Chronopolis," 1960]

■ Most people have declared a moratorium on the past; they are just not interested. One is constantly meeting people who have only a hazy idea of their parents, and who have changed their lifestyles since their childhood in every possible way. In a genuine way they have transformed themselves. It's rather like Los Angeles, where people can adopt any role they like and be convincing in that role... There is going to be a stupendous renaissance. [*Friends,* 1970]

■ The biological phase of intelligent existence may be only a brief one belonging to the more primitive epochs. [*S.F. Eye,* 1991]

Photo: S.M. Gray

9 - 11

■ September 11 changed America, one of the few countries in the past century that has never been bombed from the air. I feel that the U.S. is still trapped in the 20th Century, and is still trying to solve its problems by 20th Century means—carriers, field armies and bomber groups. Of course, writers should speak out. [intv Hans Obrist, 2003]

■ **The attack on the World Trade Center in 2001 was a brave attempt to free America from the 20th Century. The deaths were tragic, but otherwise it was a meaningless act.** [*Millennium People,* 2002]

■ The World Trade Center has gone, but the shadows of the twin towers seem to lengthen, pointing to the coming war in Iraq, and beyond that to Saudi Arabia and even, who knows, to an uncooperative European state. On the one side lies a fanaticism unrestrained by reason, and on the other a religiose and self-important America, determined to remake the world in its own image, a comic-book culture driven by ruthless technologies. [*New Statesman,* 2002]

■ **Anguished Americans responding to 11 September 2001 described the attacks as cowardly and the product of envy, a huge misjudgment, I suspect. The Al Qaeda terrorists despise, not envy America, and no coward could fly an aircraft into the side of a skyscraper or carrier.** [*New Statesman,* 2002]

■ The wartime newsreels that show waves of suicide pilots diving into aircraft carriers near Okinawa uncannily evoke the images of Al Qaeda terrorists flying their hijacked Boeings into the World Trade Center. There are the same horrific fireballs, and the same mystery of how human beings—so intelligent, gifted and far-sighted—could lock themselves into such insane confrontations. [*New Statesman,* 2002]

■ I suspect that one reason for our out-of-sync response to September 11 is that, after a similar attack, we Europeans would react numbly and do virtually nothing, whereas Americans grieve fiercely but in an upbeat way, while warming up the F-16s. One of the unnerving things about Donald Rumsfeld, the U.S. defense secretary, is that he merges seamlessly into the kind of super-patriotic naval commander played by Gene Hackman in *Behind Enemy Lines,* who is ready to destabilize the entire Balkans and trigger a world war in order to rescue a downed pilot. [*New Statesman,* 2002]

■ One has to assume that there will be other suicide attacks on the US mainland, and that the American response will be ever more decisive, and, sadly, ever more provocative. [*New Statesman,* 2002]

■ [9-11] was a scene that had been rehearsed again and again, in U.S. comic books and disaster movies—images of skyscrapers and aircraft flying into them. Whether intentionally or not, the 11 September hijackers were using our own deepest dreams of self-destruction . . . Crashing two planes into skyscrapers in the heart of the American capitalist system, and bringing them down so easily, was enough to shock America into launching a couple of nasty wars. Had plane Number Four succeeded in hitting the White House, I really believe America would have gone nuclear. You can see there's an unconscious need on the part of the present American government to nuke the rest of the world. [*Independent on Sunday,* 2003]

■ 11 September, in addition to the enormous human tragedy, was a raid on the collective unconscious of the Western mind. [*Independent on Sunday,* 2003]

■ If you look at the 11 September footage, you feel something quite different inside your brain—a kind of tremor . . . It's like watching a video game in an arcade. Very scary. [*Independent on Sunday,* 2003]

■ The destruction of the World Trade Center on 9-11 has not yet been repackaged into something with more consumer appeal. [*Pretext,* 2004]

■ What is so disturbing about the 9-11 hijackers is that they had not spent the previous years squatting in the dust on some Afghan hillside with a rusty Kalashnikov. These were highly educated engineers and architects who had spent years sitting around in shopping malls in Hamburg and London, drinking coffee and listening to the muzak. There was certainly something very modern about their chosen method of attack, from the flying school lessons, hours on the flight simulator, the use of hijacked airliners and so on. The reaction they provoked: a huge paranoid spasm that led to the Iraq war and the rise of the neo-cons, would have delighted them. [*Pretext,* 2004]

■ Americans, rightly, mourned the 9-11 attack on the World Trade Center. . . The horrific newsreels are effectively the greatest disaster movie to date. . . My fear is that in due course the "remake" of 9-11, with the ultimate in special effects, will inspire Americans to *more than revenge.* [*Guardian,* May 14, 2004]

■ We might think that the U.S. had enough problems coping with Iraq, where the abuse of prisoners has given a spin of *sexual perversion* to its drive towards world domination. . . Self-destructive urges [lurk] alongside the hamburger and comic-book culture we all admire. As the nation infantilises itself, the point is finally reached where the abandoned infant has nothing to do except break up its cot. [*Guardian,* May 14, 2004]

■ A real revolution, as 9-11 was in its way, will always come out of some unexpected corner of the sky. [*Pretext,* 2004]

Photo: Charles Gatewood

POLITICS/ECONOMICS REVOLUTION

■ The overriding power of the global economy threatens the autonomy of the nation state, while the ability of politicians to intervene as an equalizing force has faded. Huge disparities of income and property now exist in the developed world, visible on the TV sets of every shantytown on the planet. [unknown, 1996]

■ The world is ruled by vast commercial empires who shift gigantic cash balances from one side of the globe to the other at the speed of light. This governs the planet. [*Seconds*, 1996]

■ Before the [Iraq War], my feeling was one of great anxiety. Now, I think we still have yet to discover if the war was justified, given the huge damage done to the U.N., to Britain's relations with Europe and to the West's relations with the Arab world. If the near-mythical weapons of mass destruction are found, then the war will have been justified. I fear however that Britain and America will pay a fearsome price when the Arab world takes its revenge. [*Observer*, 2003]

■ You see it in Iran and in the East—the West is being rejected. [*The Face*, 1987]

■ Invisible technologies rule our lives, transmitting their data-loads at the speed of an electron. Vast cash balances move around the world's banking systems, bounced off satellites we never see, but whose electromagnetic footprints bestride continents and form our real weather. ["Impressions of Speed," 1998]

■ Consumer capitalism is now taken for granted, and in effect is a public utility. [*Literary Review*, 2001]

■ The middle class is the new proletariat, clinging to antiquated notions such as the belief that *education matters,* just as the old working class believed in the *sanctity of the job.* [*New Statesman,* 2001]

■ Professional qualifications are worth nothing—an arts degree is like a diploma in origami. As for security, it's nonexistent. Some computer at the Treasury decides interest rates should go up a point and I owe the bank manager another year's hard work. [*Super-Cannes,* 2000]

■ People here may be middle-class, but they're little more than an indentured coolie force. [*Millennium People,* 2003]

■ Work is the new leisure. Talented and ambitious people work harder than they have ever done, and for longer hours. They find their only fulfillment through work—the last thing they want is recreation. [*Super-Cannes,* 2000]

■ We were driving along the shore of a large ornamental lake, an ellipse of glassy water that reflected the nearby mountains and reminded me of Lake Geneva with its old League of Nations headquarters, another attempt to blueprint a kingdom of saints. [*Super-Cannes,* 2000]

■ Tactlessly, [Nancy Reagan] announced the purchase of a $200,000 china set on the same day that the President cut school lunches and declared that ketchup would be counted as a vegetable in the federally subsidized program. [*Guardian,* 1991]

■ In terms of economics [Mrs. Thatcher is] an old fashioned *laissez-faire* liberal. But she has a very powerful sexual and mythological aura. Like all great leaders, she promises not just a better future, but a more dangerous one! [*The Face,* 1987]

■ The middle classes are as poorly paid, housed and entertained (allowing for a modest advance in living standards) as the working class of fifty years ago. Their disposable incomes are really very small, and there is virtually nothing of value for them to spend them on—cheap holidays, poisonous food, vastly overpriced housing. Their educations no longer buy them security. Most of them, earning say £60,000 a year, would be unable to afford a house in London or educate their children privately. Anyone earning less than £300,000 a year scarcely counts, or so it seems. The new monied class, largely but by no means only based in the City, has already begun to distort life in London, as it has in New York. I assume this state of affairs will worsen, and the middle class may wake up one day and rebel. [*Literary Review*, 2001]

■ I suppose there just hasn't been room for political statements in my fiction. You could take a novella like "The Ultimate City"—*that* makes a number of what I suppose you could call implicit political points, about conservation on the one hand and the pitfalls of limitless opportunist capitalism on the other. [*Thrust #14*, 1980]

■ Adolf Hitler's shrill scream, as he proclaims "The day of individual happiness is over . . . a new age of magic interpretation of the world is coming," has a nightmare ring that resonates long after . . . [*Telegraph Weekend*, 1992]

■ Dictators always step into an open jackboot. [*Super-Cannes*, 2000]

■ Politics are a pastime for a professional caste. [BBC Radio, 1998]

■ I think we've now gone beyond politics into a new and potentially much more dangerous realm where non-political factors will pull the levers of power—these may be vast consumer trends, strange surges in the entertainment culture that dominates the planet, quasi-religious eruptions of the kind we saw at [Princess] Diana's death, mass paranoia about new diseases, aberrant movements in popularized mysticism, and the growing dominance of the aesthetic (which I prophesied 20 years ago). The only ballot box common to all these is the cash register, an extremely accurate gauge of consumer preference in the very short term but useless beyond the next five minutes. All this leaves the human race extremely vulnerable to any master manipulator. [intv Zinovy Zinik, 1998]

■ The consumer and entertainment landscape dominates everything, but it's nothing but wallpaper. The real problem is that it (the consumer and entertainment landscape) is the *only* wallpaper—every other form of competition for people's attention and imaginations has been vanquished. [intv Zinovy Zinik, 1998]

■ Where socialist systems endure for decades, as in China and the Soviet Union, they do so because people unconsciously want things to get worse, rather than better. [*Ibid*]

■ Sadly, I think that the notion of a utopia died at some point in the 20th Century—two vast utopian projects, Soviet Russia and Nazi Germany, turned into the greatest nightmares the human race has ever experienced, and people now are understandably skeptical about any future utopia. We're still living in the aftermath of an extremely dangerous century. People today are rightly skeptical about any proclaimed intentions to build heaven on earth. [intv Hans Obrist, 2003]

■ Presumably the Soviet system delivered more than people give it credit for—the whole country organized like a vast internment camp, with all the boredom and dulling of hope and enterprise, but an underlying sense of security. [intv Zinovy Zinik, 1998]

■ Orwell's *1984* confirmed one's fears that tyrannies can play upon people's deep-rooted masochistic needs. One could see the Soviet Union as a kind of Sadeian society of torturers and willing victims. In the same way the Nazis seem to have exploited the latent docility of their victims. [*Ibid*]

■ What do we see? All over the world chemicals are pouring into rivers, effluents are fouling our beaches and poisoning our children. Just for once, let's assume it was deliberate. [*Rushing to Paradise*, 1994]

■ The rest of the world, busy with its own survival, has largely forgotten about America—a nation whose destruction began with its bungling of the energy crisis in the 1980s. Nearly a century has passed since General Motors declared itself bankrupt; an attempt to revive the nuclear power industry (after all those conscientious anti-nuclear lobbies) was tried and failed. . . and a complete evacuation—a kind of reverse migration—caused American colonies to crop up all over Europe, Asia and Africa. [dust jacket notes, *Hello America*, 1981]

■ What could they conceivably find in that landscape of ash and clinker, in those empty cities that required more fuel to run them in a day than the whole planet now consumed in a month? [*Hello America*, 1981]

■ Most professional people work in offices. It's an extraordinary world that we all take for granted. We all assume that everybody who works in an office switches off the mind when they walk in through the front door. All those competitive instincts and animal obsessions and drives are thought to have been left behind. It's not true. I think [Francis] Bacon caught how appalling office life can be. [*Art Newspaper*, 1999]

■ Working in an office for a great many years can be one of the most crucifying experiences. You are forced to repress your biological need to kill everyone around you. [*ibid*]

■ Today we scarcely know our neighbors, shun most forms of civic involvement and happily leave the running of society to a caste of political technicians. [*Super-Cannes*, 2000]

■ The 1990s was a low, dishonest decade, the era of focus groups and cash-filled envelopes. [*New Statesman*, 2000]

■ Twenty years ago the notion that a second-rate film actor could become President (which I like to say I anticipated in 1967 in my "Ronald Reagan" piece) remained strictly within the pages of avant-garde Science Fiction. [This] was laid down by the media explosion of the '60s, the way in which people like Kennedy were admired for their television images, *for their style rather than their substance*. Nixon in part was rejected because he was an old-style Tammany Hall-type politician, with a stubble at eleven o'clock in the morning, who didn't fit into the TV age. [*Interzone*, 1987]

■ Buying a Citroen or an Hermès scarf was a sin equal to the destruction of ten acres of rain-forest or the murder of a hundred albatross. [*Rushing to Paradise*, 1994]

■ A giant multinational like Fuji or General Motors sets its own morality. The company defines the rules that govern how you treat your spouse, where you educate your children, the sensible limits to stock-market investment. The bank decides how big a mortgage you can handle, the right amount of health insurance to buy. There are no more moral decisions than there are on a new superhighway . . . We can rely on their judgment, and that leaves us free to get on with the rest of our lives. We've achieved real freedom, the freedom from morality. [*Super-Cannes*, 2000]

■ As long as one-tenth of one percent of the population are catered for, everybody's happy . . . But God help the other 99.9 %. [*Wind From Nowhere*, 1962]

■ In order to keep us happy and spending more as consumers, capitalism is going to have to tap rather more darker strains in our characters, which is of course what's been happening. . . American football, wrestling, boxing, and of course the most violent entertainment culture of all, the Hollywood film—all these have tapped into the darker side of human nature in order to keep the juices of appetites flowing. ["Prophet with Honour," n.d.]

■ Consumer capitalism has a voracious appetite—it needs to keep us buying . . . Now, how do you keep the whole system energized? . . . There's one big resource they can tap . . . the latent psychopathy of the human mind. [*Independent,* Sep 14, 2000]

■ Nothing frightens them more than the thought of a real middle-class revolution . . . The French revolution was started by the middle class. [*Millennium People,* 2003]

■ Many of the transformations made in our lives by science and technology are not visible ones. [*Thrust #14,* 1980]

■ They're in the grip of some bizarre ideas. Abolish the 20th Century. Ban tourism. Politics, commerce, education—all corrupt. [*Millennium People,* 2003]

■ It may be that the main engine of revolution, even within a Marxist interpretation, will no longer be provided by economics, but by *aesthetics.* [*RE/Search #8/9,* 1984]

■ Inexplicable and senseless protests were the only way to hold the public's attention . . . Action groups had attacked a number of "absurd" targets—the Penguin pool at London Zoo, Liberty's, the Soane Museum and the Karl Marx tomb at Highgate Cemetery . . . The public was unsettled, aware of a deranged fifth column in its midst, motiveless and impenetrable, Dada come to town. [*Millennium People,* 2003]

■ I don't think that radical change can come from political means any longer. I think it can only come from the confines of the skull—by imaginative means, whatever the route may be. [*RE/Search #8/9,* 1984]

■ Revolutions in aesthetic sensibility may be the only way in which radical change can be brought about in the future. . . It may be only from *aesthetic* changes of one sort or another that one can expect a radical shift in the people's consciousness.

[*RE/Search #8/9*, 1984]

■ It's a myth to think that the middle classes are incapable of violence. They're just very patient and they need to be sufficiently provoked before they explode. [*Telegraph*, 9-23-03]

■ Blow up the Stock Exchange and you're rejecting global capitalism. Bomb the Ministry of Defense and you're protesting against war. But a truly pointless act of violence, shooting at random into a crowd, grips our attention for months. [*Millennium People*, 2003]

■ The struggle between capitalism, fascism and communism was a struggle between competing psychopathies. [*Independent*, 9/14/2000]

■ In any industrial society there is usually one social revolution each century . . . In the eighteenth century it was the urban proletariat, in the nineteenth the artisan classes, in this revolt the white collar office worker, living in his tiny so-called modern flat, supporting through credit pyramids an economic system that denied him all freedom of will or personality, chained him to a thousand clocks. ["Chronopolis," 1960]

■ We've studied the TV commercials put out by Governor Reagan of California. You can see that all this fierce right-wing stuff is the complete oppposite of his reassuring body language. But people believe the *body language*. [*Kindness of Women*, 1991]

■ In the struggle for a better world, no one was more disposable than a friend. Unless friends were prepared to betray each other, no revolution would ever succeed. [*Millennium People*, 2003]

■ Huge disparities of income and property now exist in the developed world, visible on the TV sets of every shanty town on the planet. [*Times*, 1996]

■ Salaries have plateaued. There's the threat of early retirement. Once you're forty it's cheaper to hire some bright-eyed graduate clutching her little diploma. [*Millennium People*, 2003]

■ **Politics is a branch of advertising.** [The Imagination on Trial, 1981]

■ Is the election actually taking place? . . . Candidates roam the television studios, and the party political broadcasts keep our remote controls busier than ever. But it all seems strangely unread, a muddled and overlong melodrama whose cast have left their scripts on the bus. [*New Statesman,* 2001]

■ **Elections are now held as a public information service, like the VD and drunk-driving campaigns of old, to maintain the necessary illusion that politics matters.** [New Statesman, 2001]

■ The trouble with Marxism is that it is a social philosophy for the poor. What we need is a social philosophy for the rich. [*Friends #17,* 1970]

■ **The multinational companies? All they do is turn money into more money.** [Super-Cannes, 2000]

■ Readers say that *Millennium People* made them laugh aloud, which is wonderful news, but then there is something inherently funny about the idea of a middle-class revolution. But perhaps that in itself is a sign of how *brainwashed* the middle-classes are. The very idea that we could rebel seems preposterous. [*Pretext #9,* 2004]

■ **A vicious and genuinely mindless neo-fascism, a skillfully aestheticized racism, might be the first consequence of globalization.** [*ibid*]

■ The time span between the "rebel"—the "revolution"—and total social acceptance is getting shorter and shorter . . . In the future, you'll get some radical new idea, but within 3 minutes it's totally accepted, and it's coming out in your local supermarket. [*Search & Destroy #10,* 1978]

Photo: S.M. Gray

VIRTUAL REALITY

■ Electronic images are the air we breathe, and Virtual Reality merely represents the end-point of a logic laid down when the first electric current was put through a light filament. [C21, 1991]

■ Space Age II will probably have to wait until the Virtual Reality systems can recreate the mystery and excitement of space travel in the domestic living room. [S.F. Eye, 1991]

■ A huge inward migration is taking place at the moment; people are retreating from the outside world into the inner world. When Virtual Reality arrives, it won't be necessary to go anywhere. [Seconds, 1996]

■ Thanks to Virtual Reality, we will soon be moving into a world where a heightened super-reality will consist entirely of *action replays,* and reality will therefore be all the more rich and meaningful. [*Disturb,* n.d.]

■ One must remember the brain is itself a Virtual Reality machine. The illusion we have of the real world, of factories and streets and office blocks and other people talking to us is itself a Virtual Reality simulation generated by our brains. [BBC Radio 3, 1998]

■ If Virtual Reality systems actually begin to be installed in people's homes and are effective in their illusion of reality, this will represent the greatest event in human evolution. For the first time, mankind will be able to deny reality and substitute its own preferred version. [*Blitz,* 1984]

■ Human intercourse, like the exchange of social signals in the street and office, and even the elaborate cues between mother and baby, may one day seem of minor importance when compared with the infinite riches of the Virtual Reality universes that the modem will bring to us. ["Impressions of Speed," 1998]

■ When the first true Virtual Reality systems become available, and contain more visual information and are more visually convincing than ordinary reality, the temptation for the human race will be to enter this Virtual Reality system and close the door behind it. I mean, I think there's a danger there because one will really be able to enter into a fantasy world which, unlike all fantasies in the past, would be more convincing than everyday reality ... When people enter their Virtual Reality world, where they can play games with their own psychopathologies—if they want to they can assume the role of any character in history or any imaginary character. If they want one day to be a Nobel Prize winning physicist and the next day play a concentration camp commandant, they'll be able to step beyond the sort of conventional bounds of morality all together. One would be morally free to play with one's own psychopathology as a game. That's rather dangerous, putting it mildly. [BBC Radio 3, 1998]

■ Technology defines the conventions by which we recognize the world. In a future version of *Point Blank* we will *be* Lee Marvin, feel his anger and sadness rather than observe them. In *Sunset Boulevard*, we will stagger as Norma Desmond's bullets shatter our ribs, and taste the icy water with our lips as we die in her pool. Heightened by all the skills of future Roegs and Scorseses, film will be more visceral, more poetic, more emotionally rich than anything in real life. And perhaps as exhilarating but as empty as a roller-coaster ride. [*Sight & Sound,* 1996]

■ What we have seen coming down the road in terms of Virtual Reality and the like, is a much more rigorous filtering system that doesn't allow a Billy Wilder or a Jean Cocteau or an Orson Welles to set out his pitch. That's the fear. The [Rupert] Murdochs of the future who control the Virtual Reality of studios may not be as catholic. [*Index,* 1997]

■ The domestic equivalent [of Virtual Reality], when it comes, will transform the world. There is nothing else to look forward to. [*S.F. Eye*, 1991]

■ Reality is just a stage set that can be pushed aside, and a very different set of rules can then apply. [BBC Radio 3, 1998]

■ The fantasy that dominates our world, the enormous novel we live inside, is the new reality. A giant billboard image of Drew Barrymore lying across an unmade bed is a more real landscape than the Sahara desert. [letter, 2003]

■ Ordinary reality is too messy and confusing—why not construct a replica to satisfy all your instant needs for heritage? There's no litter, it's comfortable and if somebody has a heart attack, an ambulance disguised as the Fairy Queen will sweep them away. But this isn't reality, it's not even a dream. It's sort of a halfway house between the two. [*Sub Dee*, 1997]

■ When we can, in some virtual playground, play at being a concentration camp guard or any one of a thousand other grisly roles—for example, acting out the parts of Fred and Rosemary West, the English couple who raped and murdered their children—I think the human race will really face a threat. You see elements of all this pushing at the door all the time, just waiting for the technology to facilitate all its possibilities. [*21C*, 1997]

INTERNET

■ I think [the Internet is] a whole series of private universes that are paraded across the screen in an absolutely riveting way. It's a form of self-publishing that is obviously just in its infancy now. [BBC Radio 3, 1998]

■ The modem may become our most important interface with external reality. [letter, 2003]

■ The Internet, which I relish for the unlimited information it provides, and the unlimited possibilities. Large sections of it strike me as remarkably poetic. It may turn out to be more important and more innovative than television. It's a kind of collective lucid dreaming. [intv Hans Obrist, 2003]

■ The Internet is our confession box. [*Millennium People,* 2003]

■ [The Internet] is an incredible medium of information, communication, and most important of all, the expression of the imagination. How it evolves in the coming years is one of the most fascinating subjects there is. [BBC Online Live Chat, 2002]

■ The Internet offers an unprogrammed picture of the world, closer to the book and newspaper-dominated era before radio and then TV came along. [*Literary Review,* 2001]

■ The loss of freedom in the surveillance society is balanced by the huge gain in freedom and possibility found in the Internet. [intv Hans Obrist, 2003]

■ The world we live in now—the Internet, heart transplants, genetic manipulation, the *politics of psychopathy*—makes sense if seen through a Science-Fiction lens. In fact, Science Fiction is so all-pervasive that most of us fail to realize we are living inside a Science-Fiction novel. [*Literary Review,* 2001]

■ In my secretary's office that morning I had scanned the e-mail summaries of the papers. The confident claims for the new corporate psychology seemed to float above the world like a regatta of hot-air balloons. A vicious boredom ruled the world, for the first time in human history, interrupted by meaningless acts of violence. [*Millennium People,* 2003]

■ There's a website by people at a bird sanctuary in Norfolk who [*www.ospreys.org.uk*] have been tagging ospreys with radio transmitters. They've been tracking their flights to and from their winter ground, an island off Ghana or somewhere, and they show maps of the routes taken by each bird flying across Europe and the Mediterranean. Some of them detour for years before returning to this bird sanctuary. Watching all this is deeply moving. It lets another dimension into your life. [*Spike*, 2000]

■ [On the Internet you can see] a disused American nuclear silo [*www.xvt.com/users//kevink/silo/silo.html*]. It's wonderful! You're taken on a tour and you can choose alternatives: "Would you like to look at the missile control room?" [*Spike*, 2000]

■ Human beings today display a deep and restless violence, which no longer channels itself into wars but has to emerge in road rage, Internet porn, contact sports like hyperviolent professional rugby and US football, reality TV, and so on. [intv Hans Obrist, 2003]

■ The fax machine and the e-mail seem to threaten the old-fashioned printed word, at a time when a reader who owns no books has access to an entire university's database, and when a diligent browser will hunt out from the world's newspapers and magazines those topics that most keenly interest us. But books and newspapers survive and even prosper, suggesting that we need the fortuitous and contingent, and that our imaginations have evolved to scan the silent margins of our lives for any intriguing visitors or possible prey. ["Impressions of Speed," 1998]

■ We are surrounded by invisible technologies and a change in social and psychological attitudes. The changes you had in the '60s were all up front; now they're much more difficult to read and in a way much more threatening. [*New Musical Express*, 1985]

■ There is a sort of desire for anonymity these days. People [accept] alienation in a way that one would never have imagined. We rub shoulders in traffic jams and on airport escalators. I don't know whether the Internet leads to more alienation or not. It's wonderful to have the Harvard University Library database sort of just sitting there waiting; every scientific journal can be downloaded onto your PC. That seems wonderful to me—I've never had enough information. [letter, 1999]

■ It's the role of the artist to illuminate the real world for the ordinary person—the new world which technology and communications have created. [*Studio International*, 1971]

■ McLuhan's dreams of a global village have pretty well come true. What he never predicted is the nervousness of the viewer's response to all this. [*Interzone*, 1987]

■ Marshall McLuhan was right to talk about the global village, thanks to the communication networks that wrap themselves around the planet. He didn't anticipate, however, the enormous volatility of everything, the way in which financial, political, social typhoons can sweep across the world . . . Huge cash balances can move from one side of the planet to another with the press of a computer key, destabilizing entire economies. The Gulf War is an example of a gigantic conflict in terms of the military forces engaged, which began and was over almost before one noticed it. There is a possibility that an all-out nuclear confrontation in World War III could last about seven minutes, and we might not even notice it. [*Blitz*, 1991]

■ We see emerging now new patterns of social behavior and a new volatility in things that may have been laid down years ago. I'm thinking of the instability of world financial markets created by prosperity (which has generated a vast amount of spare cash) and by the international communications-satellite nets. These shift immense balances from one side of the world to the other at the speed of an electron and introduce the most incredible jitters and instability, and do have an effect on commerce and industry and on political events. [*Interzone*, 1987]

■ In the near future aesthetic and cultural shifts in the planetary consciousness will move around the globe with the force and pace of *tsunamis,* replacing the slow, ancestral drift of politics and religion in the years before the information age. ["Impressions of Speed," 1998]

■ I'm waiting for the first new religion on the Internet—one that is unique to the Net and to the modern age. It'll come. [*Spike,* 2000]

■ Twenty years ago no one could have imagined the effects the Internet would have: entire relationships flourish, friendships prosper . . . there's a vast new intimacy and accidental poetry, not to mention the weirdest porn. The entire human experience seems to unveil itself like the surface of a new planet. [*Pretext,* 2004]

■ My dream would be to download the entire Harvard University database, or to consult every psychiatric journal ever published. However, I'm terrified that if I do get the modem working, I'd never do anything else! [*Sub Dee,* 1997]

MEDIA LANDSCAPE

■ The climate of our planet now consists of a set of very strange dreams that are swimming across the surface of our minds like weird clouds. [*Blitz,* 1991]

■ If people were alert and critical of their consumer environment, there would be some hope that they might wake up. But there is no conspiracy. This leaves people in the valueless world, wandering like aimless Saturday crowds through the great supermarket of life. [intv Zinovy Zinik, 1998]

■ The media is now the reality that most people inhabit. [*The Face* #96, 1988]

■ The links between the media and politics are now hardwired. [*Pretext*, 2004]

■ We need to look *beyond* the worlds of consumer goods and mass iconography. [*Studio International*, 1971]

■ Is there any mechanism known by which the simultaneous hypnosis of large groups of people could occur? ["The Watch-Towers," 1962]

■ I think there's an information starvation at present [1971] and technology will create the possibility of knowing everything about everything. [*Studio International*, 1971]

■ Normality: the next special effect? [*ZG*, 1985]

■ The whole entertainment world we inhabit is a tyranny of blandness. One reason why the *Big Brother* series were so popular is that for a few weeks, people briefly got a glimpse of what reality was—a whole lot of louts lying scratching themselves, and looking bored. That was genuinely something new! [*Independent on Sunday*, 2003]

■ The 1960s had effortlessly turned the tables on reality. The media landscape had sealed a technicolor umbrella around the planet, and then redefined reality as itself. [*Kindness of Women*, 1991]

■ The central nervous system is nature's Sistine Chapel, but we have to bear in mind that the world our senses present to us... is a ramshackle construct which our brains have devised to let us get on with the job of maintaining ourselves and reproducing our species. What we see is a highly conventionalized picture, a simple tourist guide to a very strange city. We need to dismantle this ramshackle construct in order to grasp what's *really* going on [*Kindness of Women*, 1991]

■ The dream machine that produces our "lifestyle" right now: fictions like TV, radio, politics, the press, and advertising. [*Books and Bookmen*, 4/1971]

Photo: S.M. Gray

■ We're living in a consumer society that is one vast shopping mall. [*Independent,* Sept 14, 2000]

■ A huge volume of sensational and often toxic imagery, much of it fictional in content, inundates our minds. How do we make sense of this ceaseless flow of advertising and publicity, news and entertainment? [*Atrocity Exhibition,* 1990]

■ Our environment today, by and large a media landscape, is over-saturated by aestheticizing elements (TV ads, packaging, design and presentation, styling and so on) but impoverished and numbed as far as its *psychological depth* is concerned. [*Pretext,* 2004]

TELEVISION

■ Far more dangerous: TV crews, journalists, publishers' agents. Unlimited destructive power at every finger-tip. [*Rushing to Paradise,* 1994]

■ The carefully edited, slow-motion, action replay of a rugby tackle, a car crash or a sex act has more significance than the original event. [*Disturb,* n.d.]

■ People have willingly lobotomized themselves with the aid of TV, with consumerism. [*Rolling Stone,* 1987]

■ We're living in a landscape of enormous fictions, of which television is a major supplier. [*Twilight Zone,* 1988]

■ There's no yesterday in television. Nobody remembers what they saw on television a year ago, or scarcely even a week ago. [*21C,* 1997]

■ Reality now is a kind of huge advertising campaign, selling television's image of what life is about. [*Twilight Zone,* 1988]

■ A politician's lies are the new truth. Mental disease is the new health. TV wars are the new peace. Alienation is the new together-ness. Nothing is true. Nothing is untrue. [letter, 2003]

■ Television today is electronic gossip. [review of *Working Class Hollywood*, 1997]

■ *Our addiction to television, our addiction to the image*: if anything, this is the century of the image, whatever its source, and we're infatuated—we're image-makers as much as we are great engineers. *Electronic images are the air we breathe.* [*21C, 1991*]

■ I find "Reality TV" absolutely fascinating. I think people are so desperate to find what they believe to be "reality," that they will happily watch programs of CCTV [closed circuit TV] footage filmed in underground car parks, rainy shopping malls and motorway junctions . . . in a sense, the drabber the better. [BBC Online Live Chat, 2002]

■ The danger with TV is that it predigests and pre-empts any kind of original response by the viewer. It just feeds the viewer a kind of reality. (It has become in fact the new reality, just like processed food has become the staple diet of many people in the West.) This force-feeding makes us rather like a lot of bullocks in a pen. [*Twilight Zone*, 1988]

■ As a successful television celebrity, she had mastered a good-natured blandness that audiences especially prized. [*Millennium People*, 2003]

■ Yes, [I can imagine a world without television]. The Internet hints at it. It offers an unprogrammed picture of the world, closer to the book and newspaper-dominated era before radio and then TV came along. Television certainly doesn't have the influence or authority it had thirty years ago. Already there is a post-TV generation that spends its free time on other recreations and hobbies. [*Literary Review, 2001*]

■ There should be *more* sex and violence on television; I don't think there's anywhere near enough. I think sex and violence are powerful catalysts for change; they are powerful energizers of the imagination. [*Spin,* 1989]

■ The environment is so full of television, party political broadcasts and advertising campaigns that you hardly need to *do* anything. [*Observer,* 2002]

■ Television is the perfect medium for the age of paranoia. We can venture into its simulation of the world without ever being seen, and a switch will turn down those strange voices inside our heads. TV domesticates reality, filters out its harder tones and shows us only what the less ambitious of us want to see and hear. It has done far more to make a fairer society than Marx or American consumerism. ["Impressions of Speed," 1998]

■ Strange dreams have come out of Africa for centuries. What's happening now is that TV is imposing its own, mythologized view of the Third World and of Africa in particular. [*I-D,* 1987]

■ Truth doesn't come from experience anymore. Culture comes from the local supermarket. That's another danger: the TV landscape that now suffocates the world. [*The Face,* 1987]

■ TV does my traveling for me. [*I-D,* 1987]

■ We are in the situation where elements of psychopathology have been annexed into normal life and neutralized. TV is the biggest influence on that, of course—the blurring of poetic images of earthquakes, cheek by jowl with commercials for cars and whatever. It seems to me that the progress of the 20th century has been the greater accessibility of states of psychopathology. The doors of a great many cages have been unlocked and all the armatures that hold upright the systems that we live in; the franchises and dealerships of our consumer-goods transactions have a very high degree of tolerance for what would previously have been regarded as rather perverse and reprehensible sets of values. [*New Musical Express,* 1985]

■ TV produced a set of sustaining myths which kept this nation going. I think there will be a kind of inward collapse. But that's when things might start to get interesting. It's quite possible that deregulation of the airwaves will lead to a deregulation of the imagination. [*I-D,* 1987]

■ I know people who were so gripped by *Big Brother* [TV program] that they watched every available second, even though the contestants were the sort of faddish young men and women they would avoid like the plague if they were living in the next holiday villa. It illustrates the desperate hunger people feel for reality, however tedious. We're all suffocated by the consumer society and its entertainment culture, where everything is an image or imitation of something else. We're so starved of the real (as we think of it) that we'll happily watch CCTV [closed-circuit TV] footage of motorways, rain-swept precincts and corner shops. [*Literary Review,* 2001]

■ We live in this all-pervading, all-dominating present. Television did that, and this was of course followed by the creation of the huge worldwide communication network that has linked everything from banking to shopping to the transfer of information of every conceivable kind—all of which creates an instantaneousness, a kind of perpetual present. [*21C,* 1997]

■ There is a brain-rotting aspect to TV that's much more evident than it was. [*Interzone,* 1987]

■ Television promised to bring us a high-speed monarchy, fit for the age of the soundbite and the peak-hour commercial. But the institution has proved to have all the inertia and flexibility of Stonehenge. ["Impressions of Speed," 1998]

■ TV is no longer an innovative medium . . . Every program

should have the word "entertainment" in front of it, because that is its real goal. The BBC nine o'clock news is the BBC Entertainment News. A documentary on camels in the Kalahari desert is an *entertainment documentary*. Nothing is included which isn't going to entertain the audience, nothing that will distress or bore the audience or that the audience may find difficult. [*Interzone*, 1987]

■ He turned down the sound, not out of boredom with these documentaries and situation comedies, but because they were meaningless. Even the commercials, with their concern for the realities of everyday life, were transmissions from another planet. [*High Rise*, 1975]

■ The general level of French television is a lot lower than ours [England's]: it's a nonstop stream of entertainment programs, but it's so much the better for that because you know where you stand. It's a trashy medium, and it has been allowed to float down to its own true level, not artificially maintained by a huge government-financed BBC/ITV monopoly. [*Interzone*, 1987]

■ A large number of the ills that beset British life can be laid at the door of television—the vast repertory of myths and national delusions that it creates. [*Interzone*, 1987]

■ Most television is remarkably good, bearing in mind that it is a popular entertainment medium, but Melvyn Bragg poses a problem of his own making. The *South Bank* show is a classic example of dumbing down: most television trivializes the already trivial, but the *South Bank* show trivializes the serious, which is far more dangerous . . . I watch arts documentaries, Parkinson, the news, and I also enjoy *The Bill*. [*Guardian*, 1999]

■ I always loved *Hawaii Five-0*—which I often watched *with the sound turned down*, in the belief that it didn't matter what the plots were about . . . I love *Miami Vice* [too] because it takes it even further. As many people have said, *it's entirely about style*, the style of the young men and women who appear in it, their clothes, the decor. There are some wonderful Art Deco settings. It's like leafing through the pages of a chic and sleek fashion magazine, where you see the models against a series of artfully-contrived backdrops, an international airport or a marina or a nightclub, which give the impression that some sort of narrative is unfolding but in fact the backdrops are merely decorative. And the story lines in *Miami Vice* are purely decorative, which only carries to the nth point a tendency evident in most TV drama. [*Interzone,* 1987]

■ What I really like about television is the points of intersection you get where one is watching a documentary about brain surgery, which is intercut, at the flick of a switch, to a quiz show. In a half-subliminal way, one suspects that one's brain is taking in the idea of a quiz show about brain surgery . . . The medley of this media city that TV creates is interesting. It's defining the sort of logical connections and operating formulae that govern our passage through consciousness. [*Blitz,* 1991]

■ You're not using up any vital resources sitting in front of a TV tube. Probably the most economically beneficial act you can perform on behalf of society at large is to watch *Hawaii Five-0!* [*Thrust,* 1980]

■ Television is running out of lies. [*Blitz,* 1991]

■ [Referring to the trend of heavily-illustrated books tied to TV programs/series] Are books becoming another form of television? [*New Statesman,* 1978]

■ Everything's going to be coming off your TV [and computer] screen over the next ten years, whether you like it or not. We're going to be drowning in electronic possibilities—the *tsunami* of possibilities heading towards us two miles high. [*Thrust,* 1980]

■ I've always believed that ultimately every home will be transformed into its own TV studio. We'll all be simultaneously actor, director and screenwriter in our own soap operas. People will start screening themselves. They will become their own TV programs. [*I-D*, 1987]

■ I've referred in the past to the tendency to transform the home into a TV studio, with everybody playing star, director and audience of their personal *Coronation Street*. I don't mind that as long as the script is provided by the individual himself—too many people have accepted other people's scripts, they're living out a script provided—well, not by Saatchi & Saatchi but by J. Walter Thompson, which is rather more sinister in a way, representing all those big, American-based multinationals . . . Where it begins to become dangerous is when people's ideas about education, technology, medicine, and cultural values, are taken from advertising. [*NME*, 1985]

■ Film and television are saturated with a stylized violence that touches our imaginations but never our nerve endings. [*Index*, 1997]

■ TV is theme-parking and sterilizing greater and greater areas of experience. [*Blitz*, 1987]

■ TV monoculture [is] dissolving the last barriers between fantasy and reality. [*Guardian*, 1991]

■ TV in a way has failed. It had huge promise 20–30 years ago . . . TV is now electronic gossip; it reduces everything to the level of gossip. [ICA conversation, 1998]

■ With a lot of TV, I watch it with the sound turned down. What is interesting about it is the latent content as opposed to the manifest or apparent content. On the manifest level, it's a cops 'n' robbers show. On the latent level, it's very interesting how the program stylizes reality to create something that touches our emotions . . . touches our imaginations. [*Blitz*, 1987]

■ TV is like a flagging piece of nervous tissue—you need a bigger and bigger charge to get a kick out of it. [*I-D,* 1987]

■ Surveys, it seems, show that "Coke" is the second most recognized word in the world. The first is "Okay." The genius of Coca-Cola is that it has made the two mean much the same thing. [review of Mark Pendergrast's *For God, Country and Coca-Cola, Daily Telegraph,* 1993]

■ Walt Disney must be the most famous brand name of the twentieth century, stamped onto the happiest memories of countless childhoods . . . Far from being the world's favorite uncle, [Walt] Disney was a vicious anti-Semite and hater of Communists, who for 25 years was a Hollywood spy for J. Edgar Hoover's FBI . . . The theme of abandonment that runs through so many Disney films may have been rooted in his sense of his own lost childhood. [review of Marc Eliot's *Walt Disney: Hollywood's Dark Prince, Daily Telegraph,* 1994]

■ At the end of the day after writing all day, my eyes are too tired to read, so I like to see what's going on in the world. Is [watching TV] a good way of finding out? . . . TV is not very interesting at present and I wouldn't say I have a lot of favorites. [*Blitz,* 1987]

■ By the Sixties, one was beginning to see live events transmitted simply because the camera happened to be there. Zapruder just happened to have a movie camera pointing at Kennedy's car when he was shot, and the murder of Oswald was shown, I think, virtually live. So we were on the cusp of this transfer from the old print media, which tended to be retrospective in the sense that it was yesterday's news . . . to the electronic media, where we live in an instantaneous world. This was very significant, because it abolished the past and the future, condensing everything into the present. [*21C,* 1997]

■ Our TV sets provided an endless background of frightening and challenging images—the Kennedy assassination, Vietnam, the Congo civil war, the space program—each seeming to catalyze the others, and all raising huge questions which have never been answered. Together they paved the landscape of the present day. [*Atrocity Exhibition,* 1990]]

■ The only frightening people I met were the police and television crews. The police were morose and unpredictable, paranoid about any challenge to their authority. The television reporters were little more than *agents provocateurs,* forever trying to propel the peaceful protests into violent action. [*Millennium People,* 2003]

■ I believe there should be *more* sex and violence on TV, not less. Both are powerful catalysts for change, in areas where change is urgent and overdue. [*Atrocity Exhibition,* 1990]

■ Many activists package their campaigns for the media, and the death of the Mark Bracewell character in *Rushing to Paradise* was part of an attempt to examine that. In the world today you can't do anything without having a camera crew arrive in five minutes, and that changes the nature of the events being recorded. [*Disinfo.com,* 2000]

■ The Kennedy assassination of '63 could be regarded as a detonator. We moved from a pre-electronic world, in imaginative terms, into an electronic world. TV really arrived here, color TV in particular, at that time. You saw things live on television in the mid-to-late '60s. You saw the Vietnam War virtually live. Oswald was shot dead *live* on TV. [*Blitz,* 1991]

■ What actually happens on the level of our unconscious minds when, within minutes on the same TV screen, a prime minister is assassinated, an actress makes love, an injured child is carried from a car crash? Faced with these charged events, prepackaged emotions already in place, we can only stitch together a set of emergency scenarios, just as our sleeping minds extemporize a narrative from the unrelated memories that veer through the cortical night. [*Atrocity Exhibition,* 1990]

■ We're desperate for excitement of some kind. That's the drawback to living in an entertainment culture—the entertainment begins to pall after a while. It's like spending too long at a theme park—you begin to long to get out of it. And when you realized that there's nowhere to get out to, that it's all like this, that the theme park now circles the planet and that's all there is—that makes for desperation. [*Frieze*, 1996]

■ If you are going to find out what's going on in the world, on TV you have better insight into what is going on than in probably any book you can read. Simply because TV sets the agenda and defines how the world sees itself—but I have a tendency to exaggerate. [*Index*, 1997]

■ Today nothing is real and nothing is unreal. We live in an artificial environment, dominated by advertising and consumer mythologies, but these are the closest we will ever get to reality. You will be much more successful, and make more sense of your lives, if you believe what the TV advertisements tell you than if you are skeptical of them. The only eternal truths and realities lie now inside our own heads, but these are difficult to access. The imagination is the best means for exploring that inner space. [intv L. Tarantino, 1994]

■ Most people I know seem to live inside an enormous novel or a TV commercial. [intv Claire MacDonald, n.d.]

■ For him everything turns into television. [*Rushing to Paradise*, 1994]

■ Reality? That's a public service channel. [*Rushing to Paradise*, 1994]

■ Everyone says there's too much violence on TV but secretly they want more. [*Kindness of Women*, 1991]

■ "Nothing matters anymore. Jackie Kennedy, Vietnam, flying to the Moon—they're just TV commercials." "And what are they selling?" "Everything you need—pain, fun, love, hate." [*Kindness of Women*, 1991]

■ The sort of distinction that Freud made between the latent and manifest content of a dream, one now has to apply to external reality. What is going on? [*NME*, 10/23/1983]

■ We're living in a wholly synthetic environment where it's very difficult to separate the strands; very difficult to define what is real. A major advertising campaign for a new kind of motorcar, hairspray or washing powder may be the only kind of reality we have now. What you and I do as we walk around our living rooms or make scrambled eggs in the kitchen, how we carry on relationships with other people, might be fantasy by comparison ... might be a kind of illusion of reality. [*Blitz*, 1991]

■ I accept that [*The Day of Creation*] is a fiction in the same continuum as those which it describes. It's part of the process of what used to be called falsification, but can't be called that now because there is nothing left to falsify. The false is now the reality, so that it's better to adopt Freud's distinction between the latent and manifest content. These are now reversed and the external world, so-called, is now almost wholly a fiction. One saw this process in 1969 when Armstrong landed on the moon and there was a camera there. [intv Claire MacDonald, n.d.]

■ You have to make a distinction between latent and apparent content—Freud's old distinction. I go to Juan Les Pins with my lady friend for the sun. But it's more *real* to see it on TV. [*The Face,* 1987]

■ People have made the leap between viewing the fictions that surround them as fictions and the present situation where they are willing co-conspirators. They accept complicity in this re-evaluation of reality. That is a fundamental revolution and will be perceived as such by social historians in the future. Reality in its traditional mode died in the 1960s. Once the global telecommunications umbrella was in place it redefined reality as itself and has been accepted as such—that is what's interesting. If you look at the main activities that take place in the large megastructures, large cities and housing complexes, they are all perceived as satisfying fictional goals. [intv Claire MacDonald, n.d.]

■ We have these prudes who have succeeded in censoring the news—if there's a terrible plane crash, with a hundred people killed, you won't see a single body. [*Fineline Features,* n.d.]

■ Across the communications landscape, thermonuclear weapons systems and soft drink commercials coexist in an over-lit realm ruled by advertising and pseudo-events, science and pornography. Paolozzi's role in providing our most important visual abstracting service should not be overlooked. Here the familiar materials of our everyday lives, the jostling iconographies of mass advertising and consumer goods, are manipulated to reveal their true identities. [His] "General Dynamic F.U.N." is a unique guide to the electric garden of our minds. ["General Dynamic F.U.N.," n.d.]

■ I'm interested in psychological roles, not character. The media landscape we inhabit is filled with powerful archetypal figures with the characteristics of heroes and heroines—if there were any—of Greek legends. They bestride the media lands like Andromeda and Persephone. [intv Claire MacDonald, n.d.]

■ *The Atrocity Exhibition* was about the way that the media landscape has created something very close to a gigantic art gallery with a lot of very lurid paintings on exhibition—this was in the '60s—and the way in which psychopathic strains which are normally either ignored or suppressed were beginning to use the media landscape to express and reveal themselves. It's still going on, but one saw it particularly in the '70s with the TV coverage of the Vietnam war, and the reduction of all events to pure *sensation*. [*NME*, 10/23/1983]

■ A hundred years ago one has the impression that people had made a clear distinction between the outer world of work and of agriculture, commerce and social relationships—which were real— and the inner world of their own minds, daydreams and hopes. Fiction on the one hand; reality on the other. This reality which surrounded individuals, the writer's role of inventing a fiction that encapsulated various experiences going on in the real world and dramatizing them in fictional form, worked. Now the whole situation has been reversed. The exterior landscapes are almost entirely fictional ones created by advertising, mass merchandising, and politics conducted as advertising. It is very difficult for the writer. [*Friends*, 1970]

■ I feel that the balance between fiction and reality has changed significantly in the past decade. Increasingly their roles are reversed. We live in a world ruled by fictions of every kind—mass merchandising, advertising, politics conducted as a branch of advertising, the instant translation of science and technology into popular imagery. The increasing blurring and intermingling of identities within the realm of consumer goods, the pre-empting of any free or original imaginative response by the television screen. For the writer in particular it is less and less necessary for him to invent the fictional content of his novel. The fiction is already there. The writer's task is to invent the reality. [Introduction, *Crash,* 1995]

■ The global telecommunications umbrella finally wrapped itself completely around us by the end of the 1960s, and it then redefined reality as itself. That was a remarkable development in its own right, but the extraordinary thing—and I think it will be regarded by future historians as a significant moment—is that the public at large accepted this distinction, it accepted that the fictions of the mass media are reality. I notice that nobody ever uses phrases like "advertising stunt" or "publicity stunt" anymore. People in the '40s and '50s did use them; if some big balloon floated by in the shape of a hamburger, people said, "Oh, it's a publicity stunt"—but they don't any longer. [*Omni,* n.d.]

■ Science is now the greatest producer of fiction . . . particularly the "soft sciences"—the psychological sciences, the social sciences. [*Friends,* 1970]

■ We move through a landscape composed of fictions; our own minds, the postures of our bodies, the world of our senses, is the only reality. Given this position, one's own personality becomes the yardstick by which one constructs the architecture of any kind of possibility; the word "subjective" no longer has the pejorative overtones it used to have. Quite the opposite. [*Friends,* 1970]

■ Given that reality is now a fiction, it's not necessary for the writer to invent the fiction. The writer's relationship with reality is completely the other way around. It's the writer's job to find the reality, to invent the reality, not to invent the fiction. The fiction is already there. [*Speculation,* 1969]

■ It's becoming more and more difficult to distinguish between fiction and reality in modern life. More and more of our lives have been invaded and are now ruled by fictions of one sort and another. By fiction I mean anything invented to serve someone's imaginative end, whether it's an advertising agent's, a novelist's or a prostitute's. [*Transatlantic Review*, 1971]

■ It seems to me that the main points of reality are those points at which the various levels of public fantasy—Vietnam, the Congo, the assassinations of public figures, and so on—cross the level of our own private fantasies and the third level of our private lives. Where these three levels intersect you find the only valid points of reality, the new reality which we all inhabit. [*Transatlantic Review,* 1971]

■ *The Atrocity Exhibition* sets out to find a new reality. It says everything about depraved public tastes being created by the overlay of public violence and private fantasy. Just as sex is the key to the Freudian world, so violence is the key to the external world of fantasy that we inhabit. There's this clash between what we all believe to be true, such as that violence is bad in all its forms, and the actual truth, which is that violence may well serve beneficial roles— much as we might deplore it. [*Transatlantic Review*, 1971]

■ The sorts of things that take place, particularly where politics and advertising meet, the world of pseudo-events, are accepted as the real world now. You see this in the presidency of Ronald Reagan—people were quite happy to have as President a man who was a complete construct of image-making. At the start of his Presidency people remarked on the way he seemed to confuse reality and fiction, to the extent of referring to old World War II movies as if they had actually taken place, but I noticed that the critics of Reagan soon shut up because they discovered that *the public were quite happy to accept him on the terms that* he'd *defined*. And that applies to large sections of life. People

Photo: S.M. Gray

accept that the fictions of publicity campaigns and the like are the new reality. That's a huge shift. [*Omni,* n.d.]

■ In 20th century media terms, it's the accumulated picture of Beirut or Tokyo that constitutes the reality of that particular place. The media is now the reality that most people inhabit. It shapes their lives and governs their truths. [*The Face,* 1987]

■ More and more, everything around us is fictional. That is, it's invented to service somebody's imaginative ends, whether it's a politician's, or an advertising agent's, or our own. It's particularly prominent in the field of politics, but even an airline flight from, say, London to New York is almost entirely a fictional experience created by advertisers, designers, market researchers. In our time, science, especially so-called behavioral science, is the largest producer of fiction. [*Evergreen Review, 1973*]

■ The only mode of reality now is inside our own heads—that's the only thing we can trust. And surrounding us on all sides is this massive bank of fiction. Even the English countryside and most of the countryside in the Western world is totally artificial, what with factory farming, landscaping, concrete cows at Milton Keynes, and color-coordinated nature trails. To a large extent it's impossible to say that the external landscape is anything but a fiction. [*New Musical Express,* 1985]

■ Home to me is really a kind of virtual country inside my head. [BBC Online Live Chat, 2002]

■ What I call the media landscape has transformed ordinary reality into a huge dream that needs to be analyzed if any sense is to be made of it. I've used the basic formulas that I learned as a child during the war to understand what is called "peace." [*Omni,* n.d.]

■ The *Day of Creation* is an allegory about the nature of creation, the creative process. It's all about the different levels of creation, acts of imagination, that take place today. Any experience is seized upon and overlaid by the mass media. [*Interzone,* 1987]

■ The universe presented to us by our senses is a kind of ramshackle construct that happens to suit the central nervous system of an intelligent bipedal mammal with a rather short conceptual and physical range. We see rooms and people and have perceptions—but it's all a construct. And I see the role of the imaginative writer as an attempt to get through this neuro-psychological construct into something closer to the truth. [*Rolling Stone,* 1987]

■ Modern communications has usurped and hijacked everyday reality—it gets between us and any kind of *original response* by imposing its own myths and fictions on us all. [*Spin,* 1989]

■ We are at a significant turning point, which I would describe as the *death of the real,* using real in the traditional sense of an external, self-verifying realm. The worrying question is: how far is the human central nervous system trained and able to cope with an external environment that is fictional and no longer self-authenticating? [intv L. Tarantino, 1994]

■ The death of affect is inseparable from the sort of media landscape we inhabit and the way in which our lives are completely dominated and structured by communication systems. They are just so dominant. So much of the input into the central nervous system now is profoundly distant from any kind of firsthand experience. It's filtered through not just the mass media of various kinds but through all the selection and fictionalizing processes of major TV companies, film organizations, advertising and the like. I don't mean that human beings aren't capable of responding on a sort of human and emotional level—they are; there is no question about that. But they are not given that much *opportunity* certainly as groups, except when there is some sort of disaster. Take Lockerbie—when a plane fell out of the sky, people rallied around to rescue everyone. Likewise, you get these big media events like the Band Aid/Geldof Famine Relief Project of some years ago which raised huge sums of money from a public only too willing to give. The trouble is that the tap is turned on and off by the mass media, manipulated by the mass media. You get a kind of moral tourism: "Today we will all go to Bangladesh and feel concerned for the poor who are starving to death there and perhaps we will give." I mean, the whole thing is odd. I'm all for giving money to the poor of Bangladesh, but when that becomes a media stunt—! It tends to diminish all those human impulses that it's playing upon. [*C21*, 1991]

■ Electronic aids, particularly domestic computers, will help the inner migration, the opting out of reality. Reality is no longer going to be the stuff out there, but the stuff inside your head. It's going to be commercial and nasty at the same time. [*Heavy Metal*, 4/1982]

■ With its passive and unobtrusive despotism, the camera governed the smallest spaces of our lives. Even in the privacy of our own homes we had all been recruited to play our parts in what were little more than real-life commercials. . . The medium of film had turned us all into minor actors in an endlessly running day-time serial. [*Kindness of Women*, 1991]

■ Technology in terms of videotape machines and so on may make it possible to have a continuous alternative to direct experience— and I mean any alternative. You can have this played back in slow motion, or do you want it in infra-red, or do you want this, or that— take your pick, like a jukebox. [*Studio International*, 1971]

■ I drove Jane into Cannes. We drank too many Tom Collinses, ate seafood from metal platters, wandered tipsily around the Vieux Port, and I remade Jane's lipstick before showing her off. I knew we were very happy, but at the same time I felt that we were extras in a tourist film . . . [*Super-Cannes*, 2000]

■ "They're launching some kind of ship." "It's Heyerdahl's papyrus ship—*Ra*. We published the book." ... The mock-papyrus superstructure, assembled from molded plastic and fiberglass, was bolted onto a sturdy steel hull. "It's the *replica of a replica* ... They must be using it in a film." [*Kindness of Women*, 1991]

■ Given that external reality is a fiction, the writer's role is almost superfluous. He does not need to invent the fiction because it is already there. [*Friends*, 1970]

■ I think people perceive that life is probably meaningless, that we're an accident of fate biologically, and that societies that we inhabit, far from being social structures that reflect deep, enduring needs, are in fact gim-crack, almost extemporized sets of rules that someone in charge of a lifeboat might impose on survivors sitting around him; so many biscuits per day and half a pint of water. And that society's just a set of opportunistic conventions that we accept in order to facilitate ordinary life, just as we accept that we drive in this country on the left side of the road; and we all know that that doesn't reflect some deep pre-existing meaning within our lives. [BBC Radio 3, 1998]

■ We live in an almost infantile world where any demand, any possibility, whether for lifestyles, travel, sexual roles and identities, can be satisfied instantly. [Introduction to *Crash*, 1995]

■ I think we are moving into extremely volatile and dangerous times, as modern electronic technologies give mankind almost unlimited powers to play with its own psychopathology as a game. [*Disturb*, n.d.]

ADVERTISING: THE CORPORATE PLANET

■ You can almost regard advertising as another art. [*Index*, 1997]

■ We live in a world of complete fictions; so much of what used to be an internalized psychological space within an individual's head—his hopes, dreams and all the rest of it—has been

Photo: S.M. Gray

transferred from inside our individual skulls into the corporate sensorium represented by the media landscape. [*Fineline Features Online,* 2002]

■ I think most people realize that what they think of as everyday reality is a kaleidoscope of competing fictions, created by giant commercial and entertainment conglomerates. We think we're free agents, comparatively speaking, but our tastes have been imposed on us by years of conditioning from all that advertising. There's almost no reality anywhere in the external world. [BBC Radio 3, 1998]

■ [While watching television,] hidden agendas . . . subtexts begin to write themselves into the script. Inevitably you see images of an actress making love followed by an injured child being carried from a crashed car, followed by some African prime minister being shot down, followed by an advertisement for a martini. On the unconscious plane, what sort of scenarios are we stitching together out of these events? [*Mississippi Review,* 1991]

■ The better life which advertising has been trying to convince us of is a complete mythology, as complete as anything the ancient Greeks came up with. And it's extremely potent, only most people half-believe it. In fact you can say today that we live entirely on a whole system of predictive mythologies that actually are all we have to give our lives any meaning. [BBC Radio 3, 1998]

■ Taking out an advertisement [is] a completely virgin continent for the creative writer. Troubadours used to sing for their girls. Now they should take out an advertisement. [unknown]

■ Thhe whole transformation of society has been proceeding apace in a largely invisible way. I'm thinking particularly of the developments in computers, data-processing devices, communications satellites, which are changing the character of life, our whole relationship to what is real and what is not. [*Thrust #14,* 1980]

■ Royal sat down in the high-backed oak chair at the head of the dining table. The candlelight flickered over the silver cutlery and gold plate, reflected in the silk facings of his dinner jacket. As usual he smiled at the theatricality of this contrived setting, like a badly rehearsed and under-financed television commercial for a high-life product. [*High Rise,* 1975]

■ [In the concentration camp] There were so few books or magazines, that an unfamiliar brand name had all the mystery of a message from the stars. [*Empire of the Sun,* 1984]

■ Parked behind the Jaguar was a low-slung Japanese confection with huge wing mirrors, grotesque spoiler and air intakes large enough for a ramjet. To my puritan eye the car was an anthology of marketing tricks, and I refused even to identify its manufacturer. [*Super-Cannes,* 2000]

■ All these ads for aquaparks and swimming pools . . . they're the real enemy. They subvert everything. [*Super-Cannes,* 2000]

■ The unconscious collisions between the primary psychic drives are now transferred into the world of consumer design. The car, of course, has to embody contradictions between safety and fashion. [*Frieze,* 1996]

■ Human beings have an almost limitless capacity to absorb the psychologically perverse, because it's all so buffered by the electronic media that stand between us and the images. Plus there's a process at work that I call the "normalizing of the psychopathic." More and more of what used to be regarded as aberrant or perverse activity is now accepted as more or less conventional behavior. We're almost infinitely tolerant of human behavior of any kind, as long as it's consensual. [*Artforum,* 1997]

■ Advertising is here to stay. We've no real freedom of choice, anyway. We can't spend more than we can afford; the finance companies soon clamp down. ["The Subliminal Man," 1963]

CELEBRITY

■ The nature of celebrity has changed: it is perceived today as rather false and synthetic and therefore the famous are not seen as worthy of the assassin's attentions. By contrast, innocent bystanders, by virtue of their innocence and anonymity, seem all the more desirable. Their very anonymity makes them a special kind of celebrity. [*S.F. Eye*, 1991]

■ Celebrity is a unique element in the 20th-century consciousness, simply because we live and breathe in a media landscape. It's not that celebrity has arisen naturally as a consequence of all these different portholes having opened onto the world of the rich and powerful, but that the media itself has created celebrity in order for it to remain a powerful mechanism of general dissemination. Celebrity is the fuel needed to run the media machine. [*Frieze*, 1996]

■ We used to admire people like Kennedy; now we're running around paying a ludicrous amount of attention to people like Paula Yates and Elizabeth Hurley. I mean—*Elizabeth Hurley?!* . . . Obviously the system is entropic, energy is running down. It may be that we're nearing the end of celebrity. [*GQ*, 1996]

■ Reagan was the first politician to exploit the fact that his TV audience would not be listening too closely, if at all, to what he was saying, and indeed might well assume from his manner and presentation that he was saying the exact opposite of the words actually emerging from his mouth. [*Atrocity Exhibition*, 1990]

■ Margaret Thatcher tapped all sorts of dreams that every Englishman has of going to bed with Nanny. [*JGB News*, 1993]

■ Many pop stars define how people lead their lives. They set their social and moral values, whereas when politicians try to become pop stars, they try to create a kind of entertainment culture. [*JGB News,* 1993]

■ The presence of the mass media, particularly the sight of television newsreel cameras, does incite people to more extreme behavior than they would if the cameras were absent. [*JGB News,* 1993]

■ Celebrity uncontaminated by actual achievement has enormous lift-off capacity. It can float instantly into the air and we all stand back in amazement. This puzzles us and triggers a curiosity about the real nature of these people whose fame you can't justify. Fantasy then rushes in to fill the vacuum, which is a very different thing from the way fame operated in the past. I don't suppose the average Londoner living through the Blitz had any fantasies about Winston Churchill. [*Frieze,* 1996]

■ Martyrdom waited in the wings of her ambition, ready to bestow stardom. [*Millennium People,* 2003]

■ The President of the United States bears about as much relationship to the real business of running America as does Colonel Sanders to the business of frying chicken. [*Index,* 1997]

■ [J.F.] Kennedy was speed reconfigured in terms of style. The quick wit, the slim-shouldered English suits, the streamlined hairdo and cortisone-smooth face, the decision-making perceived as an aspect of gesture politics, the instant rapport with an audience eager to be enraptured, together formed the model for government in the space age he launched. ["Impressions of Speed," 1998]

■ I see Kennedy's death as a kind of catalyst of the media planet that exists now. There was something about the way in which this young President (who was himself a media construction) was dismantled by the same media landscape that created him, that generated a kind of supernova that's still collapsing. [*Twilight Zone,* 1988]

■ The curious thing about the Zapruder film [of the J.F. Kennedy assassination] is that it's so like a car commercial. The only drawback is that the passenger gets his head blown off! [*LA Weekly*, 1997]

■ [The Cannes Film Festival] measured a mile in length, but was only fifty yards deep. For a fortnight the Croisette and its grand hotels willingly became a facade, the largest stage set in the world. Without realizing it, the crowds under the palm trees were extras recruited to play their traditional roles. As they cheered and hooted, they were far more confident than the film actors on display, who seemed ill at ease when they stepped from their limos, like celebrity criminals ferried to a mass trial. [*Super-Cannes*, 2000]

■ [Madonna and Michael Jackson] lack magic. Where is the look that pierces walls? [*S.F. Eye*, 1991]

■ In each questionnaire the subject was given a list of celebrities from the worlds of politics, entertainment, sports, crime, science and the arts, and invited to devise an imaginary car crash in which one of them might die. [unknown]

■ On the one hand, a character is displayed on an enormous billboard as a figment in some vast CinemaScope epic. On another level, he's an ordinary human being moving through the ordinary to-and-fro of everyday life. On a third level, he is a figment in his own fantasy. [*England Swings SF*, 1968]

■ Caught with their smiles switched off, the great screen actors and actresses seem as uneasy and hungry for fame as any auditioning hopeful. ["All the World in its Humour and Chaos," n.d.]

■ The bodies of [Mae West, Marilyn Monroe and Jayne Mansfield] form a kit of spare parts, a set of mental mannequins that resemble Bellmer's obscene dolls. As they tease us, so we begin to dismantle them, removing sections of a smile, a leg stance, an enticing cleavage.

The parts are interchangeable, like the operations we imagine per-
forming on these untouchable women, as endlessly variable as the
colors silkscreened onto the faces of Warhol's Liz and Marilyn.
[*Atrocity Exhibition, 1990*]

■ The planes of their lives interlocked at oblique angles, frag-
ments of personal myths fusing with the deities of the *commercial cosmologies.* [unknown]

■ I've always found Howard Hughes a terrifically sympathetic character. I absolutely endorse his climbing into the penthouse suite of
an hotel in Las Vegas and closing the door on the rest of existence.
I admired him for doing that. He's a wonderfully enigmatic figure. He
embodies all the great myths of the 20th century in his character
and in his life. This young aviator ace was also a great explorer and
inventor; bought himself movie studios and airlines; and was
extremely rich but untouched by the trappings of wealth. Then there
was his obsession with germs. He sort of died of AIDS (not the real
AIDS but the imaginary, symbolic AIDS) before his time. He really
sums up so many of the obsessions and paranoias of this century.
And he was totally American too, in a very attractive way; an utterly democratic man. One can imagine him eating at McDonald's when
he was younger—something no European millionaire would ever
do! [*ZG*, n.d.]

■ As we watch celebrities interviewed on television, or see
them in close-up on cinema screens . . . we can explore every
detail of their makeup. We can see, the incipient mole that is
appearing on Charlotte Rampling's right cheek . . . Our imaginations begin to play over these stellar figures. We can't help
but dismantle them in our minds. Their bodies are tantalizing-
ly close, almost closer to us than our own bodies. [*Artforum*, 1997]

■ A kind of banalization of celebrity has occurred. [*Atrocity Exhibition*,
1990]

■ [Celebrity culture] is a very important part of the mass imagination. We see Princess Di interviewed on television and we see the little pimple she's got on her chin. We're as close as we would be if we were sharing a bathroom with her, practically! Both the celebrity and the car have changed all our relationships with each other, and with ourselves. [*Fineline Features*, n.d.]

■ The relationship between the famous and the public who sustain them is governed by a striking paradox. Infinitely remote, the great stars of politics, film and entertainment move across an electric terrain of limousines and bodyguards, private helicopters and state func-

Photo: Mike Ryan

tions. At the same time, the zoom lens and the interview camera bring them so near to us that we know their faces and their smallest gestures more intimately than those of our friends ... Caught in the glare of our relentless fascination, they can do nothing to stop us exploring every blocked pore and hesitant glance, imagining ourselves their lovers and confidantes. The most intimate details of their lives seem to lie beyond an already open bathroom door that our imaginations can easily push aside. [*Atrocity Exhibition*, 1990]

■ Fame and celebrity were again on trial, as if being famous was itself an incitement to anger and revenge . . . [*Millennium People*, 2003]

■ There's a logic today that places a greater value on celebrity the less it is accompanied by actual achievement. [*Pretext*, 2004]

■ [Ronald] Reagan's real threat is the compelling example he offers to *future* film actors and media manipulators with presidential ambitions . . . [*Atrocity Exhibition*, 1990]

CELL PHONES

■ The mobile phone can be seen as a fashion accessory and adult toy as well as a break-through in instant communication, though its use in restaurants, shops and public spaces can be irritating to others. This suggests that its real function is to separate its users from the surrounding world and isolate them within the protective cocoon of an intimate electronic space. At the same time phone users can discreetly theatricalize themselves, using a body language that is an anthology of presentation techniques and offers to others a tantalizing glimpse of their private and intimate lives. ["Impressions of Speed," 1998]

Photo: Julie Glanville

THE ARTS

WRITING

■ We're just drowning under manufactured fiction, which satisfies our Need For Fiction—you scarcely need to go and read a novel. [*Observer,* 2002]

■ Do novels today have any real influence on our lives, in the sense of radically changing our behavior and political beliefs? ["Book of the Century," 1998]

■ Sadly, I don't think the novel has any influence on life today, which was not true even 50 years ago. In the first half of [the 20th] century, novelists had a very real impact on the way people saw the world. I think something like George Orwell's *1984* did influence the way people saw political forces at work in the post-war era. *Catch-22* changed people's attitudes towards not just war, but the huge governmental bureaucracies that now control so much of our lives. But I can't think of a single novelist today who has any influence on anything. [*Frieze*, 1996]

■ The novel is still largely a 19th-century form which has completely excluded, I think it's fair to say, any consideration of the impact of science and technology on human beings from the main body of its work. One can see a writer like Kafka as having much in common with Science Fiction, being a cousin of George Orwell who wrote *1984* and the Huxley who wrote *Brave New World*. You could say that Kafka was the writer of the technology of bureaucratic totalitarianism, and indeed there are one or two others one could cite. I think Jorge Luis Borges has many affinities with Science Fiction. But, by and large, most so-called mainstream 20th-century novelists are still working with a 19th-century form that's concerned not with dynamic societies but with static societies where social nuance is all important. [*C21*, 1991]

■ In the mid- to late 1950s the "Angry Young Men" arrived on the scene—John Osborne's *Look Back in Anger*, Kingsley Amis's *Lucky Jim*, Alan Sillitoe, all the rest . . . I felt they were a totally parochial phenomenon, they didn't shake the literary establishment in any serious way whatever. They were all soon annexed into it. [unknown]

■ We're now so mentally lazy. I think if Borges were published for the first time now, people would say it's far too literary and too complicated. It's a good thing he established his reputation in the late 1960s when people were still prepared to make a bit of an effort . . . I think critical judgments were sharper then. [*Dream Makers,* 1980]

■ When I was thinking hard about becoming a writer, I could look up to Greene, Waugh, Orwell and Aldous Huxley, and to Hemingway and Faulkner in America, Camus and Genet in France. There's no one remotely comparable working today, but this could change. I suspect that the great writers of the future will be out-and-out mavericks, like Genet and Burroughs—genuinely people of the fringe. Our perception of "serious fiction" may have to change. [*Literary Review,* 2001]

■ Most people don't like imaginative fiction—though, paradoxically, it is imaginative fiction that survives the best. [*Thrust,* 1980]

■ American novels who have a high literary reputation—let's say, that school of writers like Roth and Vonnegut . . . are middlebrow writers who don't stretch their readers' imaginations in any way whatever. [*Dream Makers,* 1980]

■ Most of the mainstream novelists we now regard as holding center stage will vanish into oblivion. They won't be remembered fifty years from now. [*Index,* 1997]

■ *J.G. Ballard book recommendations:*

1. *The Outsider* aka *The Stranger* by Albert Camus: "The story of a beach murder, one of the century's classic novels. Blood and sand."

2. *Hitchcock's Secret Notebooks,* ed. by Dan Auiler: "Look over the master's shoulder as he plans his films. Fascinating to see how painstaking he was."

3. *Easy Riders, Raging Bulls* by Peter Biskind: "How Coppola, Scorsese, Lucas and Spielberg created the new Hollywood. Hilarious fun that will confirm all your worst fears." [*Daily Telegraph,* 1999]

■ *Interrogations: The Nazi Elite in Allied Hands,* 1945 by Richard Overy:

these conversations with Hitler's chief lieutenants throw an eerie light on the psychology of fanaticism. . . As Overy points out, a high number of the Nazi elite committed suicide. Once the dream had failed and the lights came on, they had nowhere to hide. [*Independent,* 2001]

■ I would recommend *A Fistful of Gitanes,* by Sylvie Simmons, which is a highly entertaining biography of the French singer-songwriter and all-round scallywag Serge Gainsbourg. Also *The Sexual Life of Catherine M,* a "memoir" by Catherine Millet. Is this the most original novel of the year? [*Guardian,* 2002]

■ It isn't often that one reads a book and is convinced that it's an instant classic, but I'm sure that Iain Sinclair's *London Orbital* will be read 50 years from now. This account of his walk around the M25, a stupendous achievement in its own right, is on one level a journey into the heart of darkness, that terrain of golf courses, retail parks and industrial estates which is Blair's Britain, rarely visited by the denizens of heritage London. It's a fascinating snapshot of who we are, lit by Sinclair's vivid prose, and on another level a warning that the mythological England of village greens and cycling aunts has been buried under the rush of a million radial tires. [*Observer,* 2002]

■ Iain Sinclair's *London Orbital* is an instant classic: part social history of the unsung lands that lie beside the M25, and part cultural analysis of this endless terrain of science parks, golf courses, [supermarkets] and speculative housing that makes up the New Britain of 2002. A feast for admirers of Sinclair's rich and quirky style. [*Guardian,* 2002]

■ John Gray's *Straw Dogs* is the most challenging book I have read since Richard Dawkins' *The Selfish Gene* and defies all our assumptions about what it is to be human. Tough-minded and unsentimental, this is the best guide yet to the new millennium. [*Guardian,* 2002]

■ [William Gaddis:] Unreadable. Post-modernism trapped inside an Escher staircase. [*S.F. Eye,* 1991]

■ As Americans work themselves up towards the second Bush war, the rest of us might usefully take a hard look at who we really are. John Gray's *Straw Dogs: thoughts on humans and other animals*, is a clear-eyed assessment of human nature and our almost unlimited gift for self-delusion. A deeply provocative and unsettling book. [*New Statesman,* 2002]

■ Steven Pinker's *The Blank Slate* is another overdue wake-up call, puncturing the modern myth that we are largely creatures of our upbringing. Sadly, as Pinker shows, the savage within us is rarely noble. [*New Statesman,* 2002]

■ Steven Pinker's *The Blank Slate* is another provocative look at our

---

Greatest Writers of the Last 1000 Years: J.G. Ballard's choices

William Shakespeare *The universal writer and poet.*

Miguel Cervantes Don Quixote *is the first great anti-hero.*

Jonathan Swift *The most intelligent writer who ever lived.*

Herman Melville Moby Dick *is the greatest ocean of a novel the human imagination has ever sailed.*

John Keats *The sweetest literary poet of all.*

Franz Kafka *The greatest prophet of the terrifying bureaucracies of the 20th century.*

Fyodor Dostoyevsky *He is the great psychologist of the modern novel.*

Joseph Heller Catch 22 *is the last classic novel written this century.*

George Orwell 1984 *is the prophetic novel of our time.*

Aldous Huxley Brave New World *is a guidebook to the next millennium [2000-on].*

(JGB's top ten writers of the millennium are also listed in the *Guardian* newspaper (March 1, 1999, page 2). [BBC website, 1999]

make-up as social beings. At birth, are we a blank slate on which experience describes our essential nature, or do we arrive in the world with our characters already determined? As always, Pinker is lucid and persuasive. [*Guardian*, 2002]

■ *Right Hand, Left Hand* by Chris McManus is a scientific detective story, a brilliant cross between Edgar Allan Poe and *Gray's Anatomy*. Why are our hearts on the left side? Why do clocks go clockwise? Why are men's testicles unbalanced? An exhilarating read. [*New Statesman*, 2002]

■ [Regarding the rise of "partnership writing," in which a famous writer collaborates with a lesser-known to write a "blockbuster novel," J.G. Ballard writes:] The whole thing is completely mercenary. The only objective appears to be merchandising more copies. People might collaborate on a film script or a play, but writing a novel is an intensely personal activity. [*Independent*, 2003]

■ Joyce's incomprehensible novel [*Finnegans Wake*], which has provided a living for generations of English Literature professors, represents a lamentable tendency in 20th-century fiction: the quest for total obscurity. *Finnegans Wake* is the best example of modernism disappearing up its own fundament. [*Independent*, 2003]

■ *The Loved One* by Evelyn Waugh (Penguin) is by far the funniest and most witty book I can think of for the poolside, a feast of sly humor and a brilliant satire on the American way of death. This is a soufflé with a sting, and the best short novel ever written. [*Sunday Telegraph*, 2003]

■ To keep me company on the sun-lounger I'm taking *Beautiful Shadow: a Life of Patricia Highsmith* by Andrew Wilson. The author of *Strangers on a Train* and *The Talented Mr Ripley* was every bit as deviant and quirky as her mischievous heroes, and didn't seem to mind if everyone knew it. A superb, warts-and-all biography. [*Sunday Telegraph,* 2003]

■ Writers must be among the strangest of people but Patricia Highsmith was one of the most eccentric of all. *Beautiful Shadow* by Andrew Wilson is a superb biography of the creator of *Strangers on a Train* and *The Talented Mr Ripley.* Exile, recluse, sexual predator and bizarre practical joker, she emerges from Wilson's portrait as an authentic monster. How I envy her. [*Observer,* 2003]

■ I just finished *The Moral Animal* by Richard Wright, a study of Neo-Darwinism. That was quite impressive. Actually, the best novel I've read in a while is by the Danish writer Peter Hoeg, *Smilla's Sense of Snow.* I thought it was a wonderful book. My girlfriend is reading his new one (*Borderliners*) now. [intv Marcos Moure, n.d.]

■ Swift's *A Modest Proposal*—always a useful escape hatch. [*Literary Review,* 2001]

■ I have not read [Thomas Pynchon's *Vineland.* Pynchon's work is] over-written in that American idiomatic way. [*S.F. Eye,* 1991]

■ [Umberto Eco:] Unreadable. A marketing triumph, not intelligent and original enough. I much prefer Baudrillard, especially his *America* . . . [Italo Calvino:] Interesting. But I sense more marketing. [*S.F. Eye,* 1991]

■ Back in the early 1950's I was very impressed by [Joseph Campbell's] *Hero With 1,000 Faces.* The TV series was a pale imitation, fatally damaged by the talkshow presenter. [*S.F. Eye,* 1991]

■ I read pretty widely . . . *The Science of Art;* Robert Graves' *White Goddess* (a classic); *Primitive Art in Civilized Places;* and a book on the history of wine! [*Mississippi Review,* 1991]

■ Lautreamont's "Song of Maldoror," almost the basic dream-text of Surrealism, uses *scientific images:* "Beautiful as the fleshy wattle, conical in shape, furrowed by deep transverse lines, which rises up at the base of the turkey's upper beak—beautiful as the chance meeting on an operating table of a sewing machine and an umbrella." Apollinaire's *erotic-scientific* poetry is full of aircraft and the symbols of industrial society, while Jarry, in "The Passion Considered as an Uphill Bicycle Race," unites science, sport, and Christianity in the happiest vein of anti-clerical humor. [*New Worlds #164,* 1966]

■ **The visual arts were able to break free and create the modern movements of the 20th century, but this has yet to happen in fiction.** [intv L. Tarantino, n.d.]

■ What I loathe and detest is the bourgeois novel that totally subsumes itself within reality and accepts the everydayness of life. The poets and writers that I most admire are those who try to remake our world in a more meaningful way. [*Index,* 1997]

■ **Too many novels written today would have been better as short stories.** [*Literary Review,* 2001]

■ The great bulk of people who read fiction are reading, really, for entertainment, but they are also reading for reassurance. They are reading for confirmation of their sense of what the world is about. I'm absolutely opposed to reassuring any potential audience I have. I am trying to, in a sense, unsettle and provoke. [*Index,* 1997]

■ **I've met most of my fellow writers in England, and I always feel completely alienated from them all for the most part ... I am interested in the sciences and medicine. When some idea occurs to me, it's generally in the context of a journal that I have just been reading or something of that kind. That isn't true of most English novelists. They are not interested in the sciences.** [*Index,* 1997]

■ Eccentricity plays a great part in the arts and we [England] have always produced such mavericks. The kind of people who, like Lewis Carroll, Evelyn Waugh, Francis Bacon or Stanley Spencer, are not really concerned about convention. It is an attempt to break away from convention in fact, and perhaps that is why we are particularly good at it. Individual talent is a way of getting away from what you might call the *Habitat culture,* the middle-class version of Woolworths that sets the agenda. [*Observer,* 1999]

■ In literature if you say anything new, people are thrown into a rictus of hostility and fright, like experimental animals being shown too many confusing signs. [*Transatlantic Review,* 1971]

■ Something like 5,000 novels are published every year, and the great majority of them show no advance in vocabulary, technique, style, on Jane Austen's *Pride and Prejudice.* [*Transatlantic Review,* 1971. *Ed. note:* In 2003 175,000 books were published, according to the *N.Y. Times.*]

■ An author can no longer preside like a magistrate over his characters and place their behavior within some sort of moral frame, which is the traditional stance of the author in fiction. Most criticism of the novel sees it as an instrument of moral criticism of life. [*21C,* 1997]

■ [When writing *Crash*] I saw myself in the position of a computer attached to a radar set, tracking an incoming missile. [*21C,* 1997]

■ I regard the subject [of English] itself as a sort of pseudo-subject. The whole attempt to make the study of English a kind of moral discipline, and the sort of elaborate textual analysis that goes on . . . I think some of the scholastic approaches to a novel by Henry James or a play by Samuel Beckett are rather akin to looking at a painting by Leonardo Da Vinci from a distance of three centimeters with a magnifying glass, tracking from left to right across a piece of drapery and analyzing at enormous length the texture of *impasto.* A novel, like a painting, needs to be read within an intelligent and informed set of values, but you can go too far. One's in danger of that sort of guide-book mentality. I've seen friends of mine sitting in the lobby of a hotel in Venice, one reading James Morris's *Venice* and the other reading another guidebook, when what they should be doing is walking around the place! [*Thrust*, 1980]

■ Beckett—I have never really been able to read him. His world is too grey and reductive. I have seen hell—Shanghai 1937–45—and it is nothing like Beckett's. [intv L. Tarantino, n.d.]

■ The difference between British and American writers is that the British writer has always had a much more intelligent critical atmosphere than the American writer. [*Thrust*, 1980]

■ The British are not a very literary people. It's a mistake to think that because we've got this great history of writers and poets, a great literary tradition, that the present-day British read. They're rather like the Italians with respect to their great history of painting. The average Italian isn't interested in Michelangelo—he's more interested in Gucci. The great art is just part of the air they breathe. The average Brit, if he wants to read, reads Jackie Collins. And why not? [*Omni*, n.d.]

■ I don't think there's a genius alive today, in the sense that Shakespeare, Darwin and Einstein were geniuses. All three completely transformed our view of ourselves and the world. Perhaps the sciences are now too specialized to allow for a universal genius. [And] a large part of the arts has been assimilated into the entertainment world. [*Literary Review*, 2001]

■ (J.G. Ballard, whose *Empire of the Sun* is an exam text, mentioned *Gulliver's Travels, Robinson Crusoe, Alice in Wonderland,* the Romantic poets, *Lord of the Flies* by William Golding, *Brave New World* by Aldous Huxley, *1984* by George Orwell [as essential texts]). "We are seeing the last vestiges of a literary culture. It is impossible to impose any kind of old-fashioned literary sensitivity. If you teach the classics at school you are likely to put people off forever. Generations of people have been put off

Shakespeare by being forced to read his plays at school."
[*Independent*, 1992]

■ I never met [William Golding], but I admired him very greatly—for his independence, his unwillingness to play the media game, and for being the only living British writer to have commanded a ship in battle [during the second world war]. And of course the work. *Lord of the Flies* was one of the most important novels since the war. It came out in the mid-1950s, at a time when the English realist novel was dominant and obviously couldn't cope with the kind of society we were. And suddenly here was this novel which addressed the postwar legacy, the evil, the Nazi war camps. It was a parable of the self-destructive human behavior we had all witnessed in the war, and it pointed the way towards a different kind of novel—a *symbolic novel*. I was a novice Science Fiction writer at the time, and took a lot of encouragement from it. We now know that the original of *Lord of the Flies,* before it was edited by Faber, was much closer to an SF novel. The story of the children on the island was framed by a larger story involving a massive air battle. [*Guardian,* 1993]

■ A large part of the modern movement in the 20th century and 19th century literature lies in the area of what I call "imaginative fiction" and underpins the whole of our literature. One can think of *Gulliver's Travels;* Mary Shelley's *Frankenstein;* the *Alice* books; the scientific romances; and then of course, some of the greatest works of 20th century fiction like *Brave New World* and *1984,* not to mention the novels of Kafka, Calvino, Borges and so on. If you took the entire canon of modern literature from, say, the 1890s—the start of the Symbolist movement—and stripped away all the naturalistic fiction, you'd be left with a vast corpus of great works of literature that seem to underpin our consciousness of ourselves. I mean, you scarcely need naturalistic fiction at all. E.M. Forster could vanish into oblivion and not be missed. [*Albedo One,* 1993]

■ The greatest short stories, by Borges, Edgar Allan Poe and Ray Bradbury, are nuggets of pure gold that never lose their lustre. Curiously, there are many perfect short stories but no perfect novels. [*Literary Review,* 2001]

■ [Imaginative fiction is] any fiction that places a premium on the use of the creative imagination—as opposed to realistic fiction. The great river of the human imagination that runs all the way back to the myths and legends of antiquity . . . tales and fairy tales of the Middle Ages, to the first great Romance literature, to the 19th-century novel, books like *Alice in Wonderland.* In our own time, most of the genres—certainly science fiction, the gothic novel, the ghost story, and modern fantasy in its various forms—fit into the category of imaginative fiction. But it also includes a great number of serious works, from *Moby Dick* to *Brave New World* and *1984* and the novels of William Burroughs. [*Omni,* n.d.]

■ I'm very impressed by Gibson and Sterling and the others. What I think they've done is to bring Science Fiction back to its roots in the here and now; to its roots in the real, which was its great strength in the Fifties. A remarkable percentage of Science Fiction stories and novels in those days were concerned with the here and now. Gradually through the Seventies, Science Fiction more and more became an escapist fiction altogether, losing all interest in scientific change, losing all interest in commenting on the present day. It lost interest in its predictive and cautionary roles and turned into nothing but entertainment. Futurist sagas and planetary histories with infusions from the Occult and horror fiction and God knows— a real unholy concoction that lacked all moral authority, something that the Science-Fiction pioneers of the Fifties certainly had. And I think the Cyberpunks have attempted to bring Science Fiction back to the present day. [*Albedo One,* 1993]

■ *Gray's Anatomy* is a far greater novel than *Ulysses.* [*Kindness of*

Women, 1991]

■ The sales of *Mein Kampf* made a fortune for its author, curious though it is to think of the Fuhrer scanning his royalty statements. ["Book of the Century," 1998]

■ The constant striving of the writer over the last few years has been to lower the threshold of fiction in what he writes, to *reduce* the amount of fiction. [intv David Pringle, 1975]

■ De Sade is an enormously important influence on us, and has been for a long while. He creates a highly convincing anti-society, which defies bourgeois society and liberalism by constructing a community based on torturers and their willing victims. Now that's a prospect that the liberal conscience just cannot cope with. I'd like to think that *Crash* is a movie De Sade would have adored. [*21C,* 1997]

■ Sade was rediscovered in the 1930s after the publication of his lost masterpiece, *The 120 Days of Sodom.* The Surrealists embraced him eagerly, hailing him as a precursor of Freud who revealed the infinite perversity of the human mind. Others saw him as a political revolutionary, the ultimate rebel against the bourgeois order, constructing a self-sufficient anti-society from his elaborate hierarchies of torturers and willing victims. [*Daily Telegraph,* 1993]

■ *Empire of the Sun* is based on my experiences as a boy in China. The hero of the book is a teenager so there should be a lot of identification between the young readers and the hero. I think a novel like Alex Garland's *The Beach* would be a good read to have on the list. I think teenagers would love it. It's about young people and is being made into a film with Leonardo Di Caprio. *Empire of the Sun* was filmed by Steven Spielberg. When it ties in with a film, it completes the full circle. People like being able to see the film if they have the book and vice versa." [*Independent,* 1999]

■ [Kerouac's *On the Road*:] This powerful and obsessive book, an elegy for the concrete freeway, is one of the most important novels written since World War II. Kerouac's lonely and isolated characters, endlessly driving their cars from coast to coast across the trans-American highways, a nightmare linear continent, are the first *dispossessed* of the technological landscape. No other book I have read sums up so well the melancholy of the automobile. [*JGB News*, 1993]

■ *The Story of O* is a deeply moral homily. Here all kinds of terrors await us, but like a baby taking its mother's milk, all pains are assuaged. Touched by the magic of love, everything is transformed. [*JGB News*, 1993]

■ Underground publications often show far more vitality and originality than mainstream publications. The original *Search and Destroy* one could spend hours reading. It was full of new and exciting material. Of course, other underground publications are self-indulgent and can be flicked through in a moment. [*S.F. Eye*, 1991]

■ The most fascinating science book of the year [1999] was *The Darwin Wars* by Andrew Brown, an account of the vicious struggle between evolutionary theory's most ferocious rivals, the supporters of Richard Dawkins and Stephen Jay Gould. [*Observer*, 1999]

■ *The Enigma of Giorgio de Chirico* by Margaret Crosland was the best biography I read this year [1999], an entertaining account of the first and greatest of the Surrealists, who turned his back on the movement he helped to create. Chirico denounced his early paintings but secretly continued to make copies of them, and then in due course denounced his own fakes. Margaret Crosland draws a memorable portrait of this quirky, aristocratic and paradoxical man. [*Guardian*, 1999]

■ Not only does the Devil have all the best tunes, but many of the best lines as well. What makes fiction so enjoyable is not the parade of upright and worthy characters, but its abundance of thoroughly unreconstructed rogues. [*Telegraph Weekend*, 1992]

■ The most enjoyable film book I have recently read is *Sergio Leone* by Christopher Frayling. The great Italian director, who cooked up the Spaghetti Western and made a star of Clint Eastwood, was part mountebank and part cinematic genius, but always the liveliest company. [*Daily Telegraph,* 2000]

■ *The Faber Book of Utopias*, edited by John Carey, is the perfect beach read, an anthology of paradise visions from Plato to Aldous Huxley and George Orwell. As you rub in the [sunscreen], marvel at the latest news from nowhere. [*Daily Telegraph,* 2000]

■ Postmodernism represents a dead end, a desperate admission that the author has nothing to say and can only think of ever more devious ways of disguising the fact. [*S.F. Eye,* 1991]

■ I suspect that the great writers of the future will be out-and-out mavericks, like Genet and Burroughs, genuinely people of the fringe. Our perception of serious fiction may have to change. I think that the serious novel in the future will be serious in the sense that Hitchcock's films are serious, and not in the way that *Mrs Dalloway* or *Middlemarch* are serious. The psychological drama will migrate from inside the characters' heads to the settings that surround them. Hitchcock's films demonstrate this well. It's also truer to real life, where we usually have very little idea of what is going on inside people's heads, but are extremely sensitive to the atmosphere around them. [*Literary Review,* 2001]

■ [The Surrealists] certainly [influenced me]. Genet certainly, Jarry. Their language was a big influence; there's no question about it. But not many English writers . . . I certainly admire Graham Greene a great deal . . . He can have a solitary figure standing by a jetty in the Far East, looking at some sampans, and he brings in a few things like the local police chief scratching his neck and so on, and within a paragraph one has a marvelous evocation of the psychology of the hero, and of what the hero and the book are about. Yes, I probably was influenced by Greene, but I never consciously imitated him. [intv David Pringle, 1975]

■ Despite its long application to a legion of neurotic victims, especially in America, psychoanalysis has had only a modest therapeutic success, and some psychiatrists see it as a complete failure. Yet the power of Sigmund Freud's presence and imagination endures. Perhaps he should be seen primarily as a novelist, with a great imaginative writer's ability to explore the human heart through the unfolding drama of a strong confrontational narrative. Freud was a born storyteller, not only in the hundreds of case histories he deployed, but in the master narratives that he devised to underpin all human behavior—the Oedipus complex, the struggle against the tyrannical father and the quest for the lost union with the mother. It may be that Freud is the great novelist of the 20th Century. [1998]

■ Meaningless violence may be the true poetry of the new millennium. Perhaps only gratuitous madness can define who we are. [*Super-Cannes,* 2000]

■ Success often destroys American writers, or at least derails them—Hemingway, Kerouac and Truman Capote never lived up to the popular images of themselves. [*Sunday Times,* 1991]

■ Nathanael West's *The Day of the Locust,* first published in 1939, remains the best of the Hollywood novels, a nightmare vision of humanity destroyed by its obsession with film . . . Hollywood's power over our imaginations is undiminished . . . Sadly, West and his wife died in a car crash in 1940. One wonders what he would have made of Hollywood Boulevard today—tacky and faded, the haunt of hookers, drug dealers and edgy tourists. [*Sunday Times,* 1993]

■ The greatest and most influential French writers of the past fifty years: Sartre, Celine, Camus and Genet. [*Magazine Littéraire*, 1978]

■ Kafka may be the most important writer of the twentieth century, far more important than James Joyce. He describes the fate of the isolated man who is surrounded by a vast and impenetrable bureaucracy, and begins to accept himself on the terms the bureaucracy imposes. Human beings today are in a very similar position. We are surrounded by huge institutions we can never penetrate: the City, the banking system, political and advertising conglomerates, vast entertainment empires . . . They define the tastes to which we conform. They're rather subtle, subservient tyrannies, but no less sinister for that. [*Sunday Times*, 1993]

■ Within the realm of the dream, Kafka is a contemporary author, and quite sufficiently up-to-the-minute . . . Old-fashioned storytelling, in other words, with its ageless appeal and direct access to the great myths and legends that pave the floor of the individual psyche. [*Guardian*, 1986]

■ I dozed on the balcony with Humphrey Carpenter's *Geniuses Together*, an enjoyable memoir of the 1920s Paris of Gertrude Stein, Joyce and Hemingway. [*Guardian*, 1989]

■ Fashions in biography change, as they do in the novel. Ruthless documentation of frailty is now the vogue, a fashion set off in the 1970s by American academic biographers who funded teams of PhD students eager to scan ancient hotel receipts and discover exactly how many whiskey sours Zelda and Scott Fitzgerald drank on a dull afternoon in Atlanta in 1928. [*Guardian*, 1991]

■ What may be a new mode [of biography]: portraits composed by biographers who actively *dislike* their subjects. [*Guardian*, 1991]

■ Einstein the philanderer? The notion seems as odd as Picasso the pickpocket or Jean-Paul Sartre the arm-wrestler . . . But Einstein's philandering had become a career in its own right. Rich and beautiful women flocked around him. [review of Roger Highfield & Paul Carter's *The Private Lives of Albert Einstein,* and Michael White & John Gribbin's *Einstein: A Life in Science, Daily Telegraph,* 1993]

■ Henry Miller bursts into the twentieth-century novel like a reprobate uncle gate-crashing an over-sedate party, scandalizing the company with a string of off-color stories before slipping away with the two prettiest wives. [*Sunday Independent,* 1991]

■ I can still remember reading *Tropic of Cancer* when I first went to Paris after the war, and being stunned by the no-nonsense frankness of Miller's language, and by the novel's sheer zest and attack. The ozone of sex rushed through Miller's pages, and his prose had a life-hungry energy that made Molly Bloom's soliloquy at the close of *Ulysses* seem contrived and mannered. [*Independent,* 1991]

■ The sexual imagination needs every encouragement to remain in the daylight where we can see it, rather than plunge again into the subterranean world of repression and taboo from which Miller helped to free us. [*Independent,* 1991]

■ Smarting from his wife's lesbian friendships, [Henry] Miller was still unable to write until June gave him a volume of Proust and the idea struck him that he could become a working-class Proust, a notion that formed the basis of his entire career. [*Independent,* 1991]

■ Many people already regard Joyce and Proust as the closest thing to a Valium. [*Daily Telegraph,* 1993]

■ I liked [Richard] Matheson's short stories tremendously. I thought they were awfully good. They were probably a bit of an influence on me, because they showed that you could write a Science Fiction set exclusively in the present day—which many of his short stories were, they were psychological stories set in the landscape of '50s America, owing nothing to time travel, interplanetary voyages and so forth. He was one of the SF writers I read when I was in Canada.

[It] was a collection of short stories, which would have been published in paperback in the States in '54. I can't remember the title; I lost it a long time ago. [*JGB News,* 1987]

■ [Richard Matheson] wrote that vampire story . . . *I Am Legend.* Several films were made of it. [*The Incredible Shrinking Man*]—marvelous film, that. I read the novel years after seeing the film . . . The film was a masterpiece in its way. He's presumably still working; he's probably not much older than I am. It's interesting that Spielberg should have turned towards him. [*JGB News,* 1987]

■ Is Alex Garland the new Graham Greene? After *The Tesseract,* the question needs to be asked. There is a powerful narrative drive, exotic locations that unfold like a corrupt and mysterious flower, and a moody intelligence that holds everything together. [J.G. Ballard quoted in ad for *The Beach,* 1999]

■ Cautionary tales take many forms. One of the most famous of all, [Jonathan] Swift's "Modest Proposal," employs the deadpan approach . . . I'd like to think that *Crash* lies in the tradition of that type of cautionary tale. [*Artforum,* 1997]

■ In the past people have criticized my [work] for the absence of warmth and personal relationships, as if these things are bubbling out of Kafka, Hemingway, Sartre and Genet! [*Sunday Times,* 9/22/1991]

■ In the old days a poet had to sacrifice himself in order to master his medium. Now that technical mastery is simply a question of pushing a button, selecting meter, rhyme, assonance on a dial, there's no need for sacrifice, no ideal to invent to make the sacrifice worthwhile . . . ["Studio 5, The Stars," 1961]

■ I love [James Hamilton-Paterson's] elegant and intensely evocative style: strangeness lifts off his pages like a rare perfume. He's one of the very few writers alive today who retains his mystery. [*Guardian,* 2004]

■ Hemingway, Gaudi, Bunuel . . . they're more your world. [*Kindness of Women,* 1991]

■ Terminal documents: the complete works of Freud, Beethoven's blind quartets, transcripts of the Nuremberg trials, and so on. ["The Voices of Time," 1960]

■ Whereas . . . painters and sculptors are expected to find something new to say, writers are expected to find something old and to go on saying it. Nothing will strike terror into the ear of a publisher so much as the word "experimental," and the next most alarming word is "new" . . . Most writers see themselves in the same role as Homer—they're telling the story of how it happened. [*Studio International,* 1971]

■ [On Madonna's book *Sex:*] A commonplace book for our day, by the Daisy Ashford of the 1990s, as filled with homilies and naive dreams as the diary of any Victorian young lady. [*Sunday Times,* 11/29/1992]

■ Reading Hitler's paranoid ravings against the Jews, one is constantly struck by the biological rather than political basis of his entire thought and personality . . . By dispensing with any need to rationalize his prejudices, he was able to tap an area of far deeper unease and uncertainty, and one moreover which his followers would never care to expose too fully to the light of day. In the unanswerable logic of psychopathology, the Jews became the scapegoats for all the terrors of toilet-training and weaning. The constant repetition of the words "filth," "vileness," "abscess," "hostile," "shudder," endlessly reinforce these long-repressed feelings of guilt and desire. [*New Worlds,* 1969]

■ Hitler . . . the epitome of the half-educated man . . . [A child] of the reference library and the self-improvement manual, of mass newspapers creating a new vocabulary of violence and sensation, Hitler was the half-educated psychopath inheriting the lavish communications systems of the twentieth century. Forty years after his first abortive seizure of power he was followed by another unhappy misfit, Lee Harvey Oswald, in whose historic *Diary* we see the same attempt by the half-educated to grapple with the information over-flow that threatened to drown him. [*New Worlds,* 1969]

■ The last book I read was a biography of the American writer Terry Southern, who wrote the script of *Dr Strangelove.* [BBC live chat, 2/2002]

■ I'm very suspicious of literary biographies. I don't believe a word of most biographies that I read. Take yourself, be honest: could you imagine somebody living, say, 30 years after your death creating even the beginnings of an accurate report about what it is like to be inside your head, live your life. They couldn't do it, could they? [*Métaphores,* 1983, quoted in *RE/Search #8/9*]

■ Yes, I start [to read] many books without finishing them. [BBC

My Favorite Books: J.G. Ballard's choices

Nathanael West: *The Day of the Locust*
Ernest Hemingway: *Collected Short Stories*
Samuel Taylor Coleridge: *The Rime of the Ancient Mariner*
ed. Martin Gardner: *The Annotated Alice*
Patrick Trevor-Roper: *The World Through Blunted Sight*
William Burroughs: *Naked Lunch*
Malcolm MacPherson [ed.]: *The Black Box*
Los Angeles Yellow Pages
Jean Baudrillard: *America*
Salvador Dali: *The Secret Life of Salvador Dali*
["The Pleasures of Reading," 1992]

live chat, 2/2002]

■ The essence of the traditional novel is in the formula "that's what happened . . . It was like that." [paraphrase, *Magazine Littéraire #87*, 4/1974]

■ A leader of the avant-garde before the first World War and founder of the review *Blast,* [Wyndham] Lewis's aggressiveness and talent for polemics served him well enough in the last round of the attack on the already routed bourgeoisie. Painter, writer and propagandist, after the war he launched Vorticism, a more cerebral version of cubism, and then turned his withering eye on the prominent writers of the twenties. . . [His] reputation began to slide, particularly as his rightwing views seemed to reveal a more than sneaking sympathy for Hitler and the Nazis . . . He died in 1961, blind and ignored. ["Visions of Hell," 1972]

■ The Goncourt brothers' journal resembles the last years of the Warhol diaries. [*Atrocity Exhibition,* 1990]

■ The novels of Stephen King are much closer to what you would call "general fiction" than the novels of someone like Virginia Woolf. Literary fiction tends to hark back to a golden age when the great modernist writers dominated the first half of the 20th century, but those days have passed. I assume that King thinks he is a completely serious writer. It may be that the future of the novel lies in more popular areas, and that the so-called "serious" novel will shrink into something like the role poetry has today. [*Observer,* 9/17/2000]

■ The courage of professional flight-crews under extreme pressure is clearly shown in *The Black Box,* edited by Malcolm MacPherson, which contains cockpit voice-recorder transcripts in the last moments before airliner crashes. [*Atrocity Exhibition,* 1990]

■ American publishers are aiming their products at the mental equivalent of the armpit . . . Perhaps these publishers secretly admire their ruthless philistinism, their mastery of the ugliest sales conference jargon, the lack of the faintest glimmer of literate sensibility. Sales are what counts, and the big seven-figure advance is the idol that really knocks the knees of the New York publishing executive. [*Patchin Review,* March-May 1983]

■ It seems to me that a significant moral and psychological distance now separates us from Kafka's heroes, who succumbed in the end to their own unconscious feelings of guilt and inferiority. We, by contrast, in an age of optimism and promise, may fall equal victims to our notions of freedom, sanity, and self-sufficiency. [*Backdrop of Stars,* 1968]

■ The writer's role, his authority and license to act, have changed radically . . . His role is that of the scientist . . . faced with an unknown terrain or subject. All he can do is to devise various hypotheses and test them against the facts. [introduction to *Crash,* 1995]

■ One day in the near future, when the last corporate headquarters has been torn down and we all earn our living at the domestic [computer] terminal, anthologies of twentieth-century inter-office memos may be as treasured as the correspondence of Virginia Woolf and T. S. Eliot. [*A User's Guide to the Millennium* dust jacket, 1996]

■ I have always been a voracious reader of what I term "invisible literature"—market research reports, pharmaceutical company house magazines, the promotional copy for a new high-energy breakfast food, journals such as *Psychological Abstracts* and the Italian automobile magazine *Style Auto,* the internal memoranda of TV company planning departments, sex manuals, U.S. government reports, medical textbooks such as the extraordinary *Crash Injuries.* [*Books and Bookmen,* 7/1970]

SCIENCE FICTION

■ Sooner or later all Science Fiction comes true. [*Interzone*, 1987]

■ Future social historians looking back from the middle of the next century, may well regard the totality of 20th-century Science Fiction in all its forms—not only literary, but the iconography of film and television and comic book Sci-Fi, and the *secondary iconography* of Sci-Fi imagery in advertising, not to mention its spin-off in record-sleeve design, fashion, architecture and the like—as being far more expressive of the key imaginative response to the 20th century than the so-called "mainstream" novel. [*C21*, 1991]

■ Vitality marks Science Fiction, even though it's a popular form. It does have enormous energy and its images have had an immense—I don't mean exactly reproductive power, but they've had an immense fertility. [*C21*, 1991]

■ What Sci-Fi does is to put the emotion in so that we can get an idea of what it may *feel* like to live in some future context. [*C21*, 1991]

■ Science Fiction puts the *emotions* into the future—something science tends to leave out. [*Rolling Stone*, 1987]

■ Modern American Science Fiction of the 1940s and 1950s is a popular literature of technology. It came out of the American mass magazines like *Popular Mechanics* that were published in the thirties, and all that optimism about science and technology that you found in those days . . . The Science Fiction written in those days came out of all this optimism that science was going to remake the world. Then came Hiroshima and Auschwitz, and the image of science completely changed. People became very suspicious of science, but SF didn't change. You still found

this optimistic literature, the Heinlein-Asimov-Clarke type of attitude towards the possibilities of science, which was completely false. In the 1950s during the testing of the H-bomb you could see that science was getting to be something much closer to magic. [*Speculation,* 1969]

■ There's more to Science Fiction than *Star Trek* and *Star Wars.* A large number of the most serious writers of this century have written what is without any doubt Science Fiction. Aldous Huxley's *Brave New World,* George Orwell's *1984*—these are Science-Fiction novels. Many serious writers of the present day have also written out-and-out Science Fiction novels: Doris Lessing, Anthony Burgess, Kingsley Amis, and many writers in the States. [*Twilight Zone,* 1988]

■ Published in 1932, [*Brave New World*] is an uncannily accurate prediction of the world we are entering. With its psychedelic drugs, test-tube babies and genetic engineering, its "feelies" that eerily resemble virtual reality cinema, Huxley's benign authoritarian state reminds us that the totalitarian systems of the future may be ingratiating and subservient. ["Book of the Century," 1998]

■ *Brave New World,* a masterpiece of a novel, takes the process one step further and is uncannily accurate in its prediction of the society we are now becoming: soma, feelies, test-tube babies. ["Book of the Century," 1998]

■ I don't consider what Isaac Asimov writes to be Science Fiction; [rather] a sort of technological folktale. [*Spin,* 1989]

■ I don't read either fantasy or Science Fiction anymore. Tolkien has had a disastrous influence. [*S.F. Eye,* 1991]

■ [Barry Malzberg:] Highly intelligent and always interesting . . . [Philip K. Dick:] One of the most original American Science Fiction writers. [*S.F. Eye,* 1991]

■ In a sense Asimov, Heinlein, and the masters of American Science Fiction are not really writing of science at all . . . They're writing a kind of fantasy fiction about the future, closer to the Western and the Thriller, but it has nothing really to do with science . . . Freud pointed out that you have to distinguish between analytic activity, which by and large is what the sciences are, and synthetic activities which are what the arts are. The trouble with the Heinlein-Asimov type of Science Fiction is that it's completely synthetic. Freud also said that synthetic activities are a sign of immaturity, and I think that's where classical Science Fiction falls down. [*Speculation*, 1969]

■ Science Fiction represents a body of popular mythology inspired by science, and it isn't necessary for strict scientific accuracy to play a dominant role. For example, the idea—long since exploded, that the Martian canals were constructed by some ancient race—does have a certain poetic force. It says something to us about our very small place in the great scheme of things. And it inspired at least one great work of literature—Ray Bradbury's *Martian Chronicles*. [*Rolling Stone*, 1987]

■ American Science Fiction is so much a product of commercial magazine fiction in the 1930s and '40s. Modern American Science Fiction was generated during a very brief period. That isn't the case over here [U.K.]. Here Science Fiction has been a part of the broad stream of imaginative fiction . . . some of it written by the greatest writers like Wells, Huxley, Orwell, some by lesser writers. I remember I read a long Science Fiction story by Kipling once. And also there are so many exceptions, writers who have no counterparts in America as far as I know, like David Lindsay, author of *A Voyage to Arcturus,* or C.S. Lewis. So the English writer comes to Science Fiction with a completely different background to what he's going to write than his American counterparts. The young American writer comes to Science Fiction against a background of people like Asimov, Heinlein, Bradbury and the commercial magazines that produced them . . . [*Thrust,* 1980]

■ A lot of American writers were very good—[Ray] Bradbury above all. I thought he was head and shoulders above everybody else . . . I liked [Robert] Sheckley very much—very droll and witty. [Frederick] Pohl, too, I liked. I liked [Richard] Matheson's short stories—the sort of standard story where the character can't remember who he is . . . Fritz Leiber I rather liked . . . [Henry] Kuttner and all those people: they're all good. I think the best American SF novel I've ever read is Bernard Wolfe's *Limbo 90* [aka *Limbo*]. I never liked Asimov, I never liked Heinlein, I never liked Van Vogt . . . I thought John Campbell was a baleful influence. [intv David Pringle, 1975]

■ [Ray] Bradbury in his way was the genius of Science Fiction, but he was kind of naive. [Intv Charles Platt, 1979]

■ Above all, Science Fiction is likely to be the only form of literature which will cross the gap between the dying narrative fiction of the present and the cassette and videotape fictions of the near future. [*Books and Bookmen*, 1971, quoted in *RE/Search #8/9*, 1984]

■ Science Fiction is the literature of "What will happen?" Not necessarily in the sense of prophecy, but in its complete acceptance of the materials of the immediate present, and in its eagerness to explore and analyze them in the context of the future. One is dealing not with a formal sequence of events and relationships, but with a series of shifting networks of possibilities that resemble the anticipated moves of a chess game. [*JGB News*, 1993]

■ What is it that distinguishes Science Fiction from general fiction? In the first place, the idea is king. SF is about change . . . All members of the human race are affected by such change, and therefore the traditional novelistic nuances of character aren't really relevant. We are all in the lifeboat together. A good SF story features, above all, a strong idea. [*Sunday Times*, 1985]

■ It became extremely difficult by the end of the '60s for any kind of specialist magazine to survive in the marketplace, simply because the major distributors like Smith's wouldn't handle a periodical unless it had a guaranteed circulation well above anything that any of the Science Fiction magazines ever had ...And obviously a taste for imaginative fiction of any kind is rather a limited one. [*Thrust*, 1980]

■ In many respects, we're living inside a Science-Fiction novel, and it's not the S-F of *Star Trek*. But, of course, most mainstream writers are working with a set of conventions that haven't really changed since the nineteenth century and early twentieth century, and as a result are rather out of touch with reality. [*Twilight Zone*, 1988]

■ The imagination that expresses itself through Science Fiction does try to place some sort of philosophical frame around man's place in the universe . . . It's a fiction of paradox. It's thought of as escapist entertainment, but in fact in its naive way it's concerned in all its different varieties with a metaphysical understanding of the nature of human existence, especially at a time of change. [*Twilight Zone,* 1988]

■ Science Fiction as a whole is, of course, time-sensitive; its predictive role means that it can be overtaken by events. It's impossible now, except as a spoof, to write a realistic story or novel about the first landing on the moon, as if it had never taken place. The moment Armstrong put his foot on the turf, that was one piece of possibility deleted from the repertory of SF. And the same will happen as we move into an ever more technological landscape. [*Rolling Stone*, 1987]

■ *Crash* is not really Science Fiction. In fact ... I haven't written much Science Fiction since something like 1966. But even though I'm probably more identified with a book like *Crash* than with *The Drowned World,* people still think of me as an S-F writer. The reason is, of course, that I take a hard, cruel look at the everyday reality around me in Western Europe and the United States, and I see science and technology playing an enormous part in creating the landscape of our lives and imaginations. [*Twilight Zone*, 1988]

■ Science Fiction is the literature that responds to change. It's a dynamic form of fiction, whereas most mainstream fiction (which is very retrospective) . . . visualizes a static world, as if society were a large still photograph in which everybody is set in position and the writer's job is to determine where the moral perspectives lie, and that link all these figures in the landscape. Science Fiction assumes a sort of dynamic flux. Nothing is certain, nothing is sure, everything is relative. [*Twilight Zone*, 1988]

■ It's very difficult to grasp how much things have changed just during the past thirty years: TV, computers, heart transplants, extra-uterine fetuses, AIDS—which is like a Science-Fiction disease. It almost seems like a deliberately designed plague by a vengeful deity who has read too much Science Fiction. So a lot of SF of the 1940s and 1950s looks like discarded snakeskins. They may glisten a little bit in the deep grass, but the stuff is perishable. [*Rolling Stone*, 1987]

■ In *The Incredible Shrinking Man* a man and wife are on a power cruiser, just quietly meandering in the Pacific Ocean. The boat drifts through a cloud of radioactive crop chemicals, and this sets up processes in the man's body that begin to make him shrink. And the movie just accelerates away, with the audience thinking, "*Migod*, is this what the future is going to be like? Are we all going to be shrunk down to the size of microdots?" In a film like this, one gets the sense of a speeding replica of the twentieth century caught upon a spinning carousel. [*Rolling Stone*, 1987]

■ In *Star Wars* there are supertechnologies brilliantly described and realized, but there's no sense of time. The action could be in the very far future or the very far past. There's no direct connection with our own world or any other world. The characters inhabit a timeless continuum, such that one senses that any action performed by any one of the characters will have no long-term effect on anything. They're just dealing with events, like speeding dots on a video game. [*Rolling Stone,* 1987]

■ I think there are two movements which have really dominated the imagination of the 20th century. One is Science Fiction. The other is Surrealism. Curiously, both have been produced by a fairly small number of practitioners. Very few in the case of Surrealism, but not many more in the case of Science Fiction. I think that what critics find rather off-putting about Science Fiction is a certain sort of briskness in its effects and a lack of sophistication. But it won't be considered a handicap in the future, any more than we would consider the crudities of Pre-Raphaelite painters to necessarily be a handicap. [*C21,* 1991]

■ Science Fiction is the apocalyptic literature of the twentieth century, the authentic language of Auschwitz, Eniwetok, and Aldermaston. [*Drowned World* dust jacket, Gollancz, 1962]

■ The Science-Fiction movies [in the '40s and '50s] were low-budget films, and the directors had to make them out in the streets, so to speak—they couldn't afford to build fancy sets the way people like George Lucas can today. And in that way they maintained their contact with reality, as did *film noir.* It forces a certain relevance on you. Even . . . *Blue Velvet* was shot against a very stylized American suburb—but it's a *real* suburb, and that lends a lot of power to that film. I think the lifeline to reality is all-important—like the umbilical cord between the fetus and the mother. [*Rolling Stone,* 1987]

■ In Science Fiction at its greatest, archaic myth and scientific apocalypse met and fused. I still think of it as the true literature of the twentieth century and the world we live in now—the Internet, heart transplants, genetic manipulation, the politics of psychopathy—makes sense if seen through a Science Fiction lens. In fact, Science Fiction is so all-pervasive that most of us fail to realize we are living inside a Science-Fiction novel. Sadly, commercial Hollywood Science Fiction now predominates, and it may be that the genre's day is over, and that it was a uniquely twentieth-century form, along with the Detroit gas-guzzler, the tabloid monarchy and the Manhattan psychoanalyst. [*Literary Review,* 2001]

■ Once it gets off the ground into space all Science Fiction is fantasy, and the more serious it tries to be, the more naturalistic, the greater its failure, since it completely lacks the moral authority and conviction of a literature won from experience. [*New Worlds #152,* 1965]

■ People within the Science Fiction world never regarded me as one of them in the first place. They saw me as the enemy. I was the one who wanted to subvert everything they believed. I wanted to kill Outer Space stone dead. I wanted to kill the "far future" and focus on inner space and the next five minutes. I'm some sort of virus who got aboard and penetrated the virtue of Science Fiction and began to pervert its DNA. [*Spike,* 1995]

■ However naively, [Science Fiction] has tried to respond to the most significant events of our time—the threat of nuclear war, over-population, the computer revolution, the possibilities and abuses of medical science, the ecological dangers to our planet, the consumer society as benign tyranny—topics that haunt our minds but are scarcely considered by the mainstream novel. [*Daily Telegraph,* 1993]

■ I believe that if it were possible to scrap the whole of existing literature [and] be forced to begin again, all writers would find themselves inevitably producing something very close to Science Fiction. No other form of fiction has the vocabulary of ideas and images to deal with the present, let alone the future. ["Extreme Metaphor," n.d.]

■ Vast theories and pseudo-theories are elaborated by people with not an idea in their bones. Needless to say, I totally exclude Baudrillard (whose essay on *Crash* I have not really wanted to understand)—I read it for the first time some years ago. Of course, his *Amerique* is an absolutely brilliant piece of writing—probably the most sharply clever piece of writing since Swift; brilliancies and jewels of insight in every paragraph—an intellectual Aladdin's Cave. But your whole "postmodern" view of SF strikes me as doubly sinister. SF was always modern, but now it is "postmodern"—bourgeoisification in the form of an over-professionalized academia with nowhere to take its girlfriend for a bottle of wine and a dance is now rolling its jaws over an innocent and naive fiction that desperately needs to be left alone. You are killing us! Stay your hand! Leave us be! Turn your "intelligence" to the iconography of filling stations, cash machines, or whatever nonsense your entertainment culture deems to be the flavor of the day. [unknown]

FILM

■ Has a festival of *Atrocity Films* ever been held? [*Atrocity Exhibition*, 1990]

■ There's no way to precisely translate the interior—the interiorized—world of the novel to the kind of public world of film. It's like the dream of a neurosurgeon who has taken a shot of heroin. [*Fineline Features Online*, 2002]

■ I'm not sure how big an influence film has had on me. Those films that I most admire—Cocteau's *Orphee, Alphaville, Marienbad, Point Blank, Blue Velvet*—are much closer to dreams than they are movies. Insofar as film resembles the dream it is a uniquely powerful means of exploring the inner world. [intv L. Tarantino]

■ Think of the thousands of silent films of the '20s that have vanished into oblivion. [*Sight and Sound,* 1996]

■ The film of Kennedy's assassination is the Sistine Chapel of our era. [*Art Newspaper,* 1999]

■ Television is awake; film dreams. The 20th century imagination is film in the way that the novel was in the 19th century. A dream has a visionary role; it's an internal eye that sees something invisible to the optical eye. [*The Face,* 1987]

■ [In Hollywood film] Special effects became the real stars. The actors, even Tom Cruise and Nicole Kidman, are little more than glorified extras. Once again, Hollywood has resumed its historic task of making adolescents of us all. [*New Statesman,* 2002]

■ The problem with the new special effects developed by Hollywood is that they aren't convincing, and they turn the film into an animated comic strip. [letter, 2003]

■ The greatest special effect is a woman walking into a room and taking her clothes off. [letter, 2003]

■ I've got a feeling that the first film I saw was *Snow White.* A pretty shocking film, actually. Frightened me out of my wits. I've never forgotten it. All that "Mirror, mirror, on the wall." Pure evil vibrating across the cinema. [Iain Sinclair's *Crash,* 1999]

■ The first film I saw, when it came out in 1937, was *Snow White and the Seven Dwarfs*—it scared the wits out of me. That vicious queen, with her "Mirror, mirror on the wall . . ." took up residence inside my six-year-old brain for months afterwards. If that's an early example of what interactive cinema will be like, I'm glad I won't be around to press the plug into my forehead. [*Sight & Sound,* June 1996]

■ Behind the living-room door was a poster of *The Third Man,* a still showing Alida Valli, a haunted European beauty who expressed all the melancholy of post-war Europe. But the poster reminded me of another Carol Reed film, about a wounded gun-man on the run, manipulated and betrayed by the strangers with whom he sought refuge. [*Millennium People,* 2003]

■ "Kurosawa, Klimov, Bresson . . . ?" "The last gasp. After that came entertainment." [*Millennium People,* 2003]

■ "Burt Lancaster, Bogart, Lauren Bacall . . . they're just movie actors." "*Just?* They poisoned a whole century. They rotted your mind." [*Millennium People,* 2003]

■ Like those Andy Warhol films of eight hours of the Empire State Building or of somebody sleeping, ordinary life viewed obsessively enough becomes interesting in its own right by some sort of neuro-logical process that I don't hope to understand. [*Spike,* 2000]

■ The long-established conventions of the entertainment film guard us from having to look too closely into the sources of our own pleasures. [review of *Lynch on Lynch,* 1996]

■ I thought *2001:A Space Odyssey* was a Pan Am instructional film for weightlessness. The whole psychology of *2001* was very old-fash-ioned, unlike the masterpiece *Dr. Strangelove* a few years earlier. [*Seconds,* 1996]

■ *Star Wars* isn't Science Fiction, it's pure space fantasy, which has nothing to do with SF. The great authority which SF had in the 1940s and 50s and even before that was that it opened a win-dow onto the immediate future. [*NME,* 10/22/1983]

■ Will film survive into the 21st century, at least in the forms we have known? Can the literate and sophisticated cinema created by Alfred Hitchcock have any place in a vast entertainment industry aimed primarily at bored teenagers? I, for one, seriously doubt it, and suspect that the cinema of Hitchcock and Hawks, Ford and Fellini, Wilder and Lean will be seen as an intelligent accident that flourished between the invention of sound and the arrival of television and the arcade video game. [review of *Hitchcock's Secret Notebooks*, n.d.]

■ The illusion that everything in [Hitchcock's] brilliant films was done with the lightest touch is one of the greatest achievements of this sly genius. ["Behind Steely Ambition," *n.d.*]

■ Modesty and self-deprecation often hide a steely ambition.[*Ibid*]

■ Heightened by all the skills of future Roegs and Scorseses, film will be more visceral, more poetic, more emotionally rich than anything in real life. And perhaps as exhilarating but as empty as a roller-coaster ride. [*Sight & Sound*, 1996]

■ Is the main role of Hollywood to save Americans from the need to grow up? The rest of the world has angst, despair, genius and genocide. They have the Hollywood film, a benign dictatorship of optimism, sentimentality and happy endings in which we all secretly believe, until the lights come on and we see the frayed carpet under our feet. Hollywood's influence pervades almost every aspect of our lives, and its amiable yarns mark out our own fault lines. [*New Statesman*, 2002]

■ The sharpest comments on 1950s Hollywood were made by a corpse, that of the failed screenwriter Joe Gillis in *Sunset Boulevard*, lying face down in the swimming pool of the deranged actress Norma Desmond. He had realized too late that the Hollywood dream was a nightmare that devoured the dreamer. [*New Statesman*, 2002]

■ The best war film (apart from the Japanese *Fires on the Plain* and *The Burmese Harp*) is Klimov's *Come and See*, about Russian partisans. One of the twenty best films ever made. [*S.F. Eye*, 1991]

■ Part mountebank and part magician, Fellini was an insecure provincial whose only subject was himself. Yet his visionary eye, like the cinema of the 1950s, was large enough to embrace the world in all its humor, passion and chaos—something that could be said about few filmmakers today. ["All the World in Its Humor and Chaos," n.d.]

■ Throughout his films Spielberg is using the global entertainment culture to explore those constants of our everyday lives that we all take for granted: the wonder of existence, the magic of space-time, and the miracle of consciousness and childhood. ["Peddling Comic Strips: Steven Spielberg," 1997]

■ The constants of our lives, which most of us ignore: the wonder of existence. The magic of space and time. The mystery of consciousness and childhood. Spielberg is using the entertainment culture to explore these rather ignored subjects. I have often thought that Spielberg is the Puccini of cinema . . . You can say that Spielberg, like Puccini, is a little sweet to some people's taste, but what melodies, what orchestrations, what cathedrals of emotion unmatched by anyone else. [*Index,* 1997]

■ In *Duel,* one of the best-ever made-for-TV films [based on a book

CRASH: Rosanna Arquette, Holly Hunter, James Spader.

by Richard Matheson], [Spielberg] displayed most of the qualities present in his subsequent blockbusters: the absence of stars or glamorous roles, the suburban characters and locations, the downplaying of dialogue and dramatic complexity in favor of a relentless, through-the-windscreen view of the road ahead. ["Peddling Comic Strips: Steven Spielberg," 1997]

■ I think [Spielberg] produced a very fine film [*Empire of the Sun*] within the constraints of the Hollywood movie. Of course, the real experience was closer to Rossellini's *Open City* or *Paisan.* [intv L. Tarantino, n.d.]

■ *Citizen Kane*, almost everyone's favorite film, is as good a choice as any, with the added advantage that it is about a media-dominated world our Internet-soaring descendants will never have experienced—the idea of one man's grotesque self-obsession actually reshaping the public's perception of reality—will seem as strange and challenging to them as we find the world of Tyrannosaurus Rex. [*Sight & Sound,* 1996]

■ For all their advanced technology, I very much doubt if future filmmakers, playing their dreams straight into our brains, will ever match the incomparable talent that twentieth-century filmmakers have shown for sheer storytelling. [*Sight & Sound,* 1996]

■ I don't think the Hollywood film has ever come to terms with war, because war runs counter to the whole ethos—the optimistic, positive ethos; every camera angle, every zoom, the language. The grammar of the Hollywood film is diametrically opposed to the rhythm and grammar of the experience of war: most of the time nothing happens . . . then something happens that makes everything even worse. [Iain Sinclair's *Crash,* 1999]

■ For some reason, which neuro-scientists may one day explain, the Hollywood film seems to endow with magic almost anything it touches, and easily ensnares even the most astute minds. [*Observer,* 1998]

■ One problem I have noticed [with Hollywood films] is that producers, who rarely read the books they purchase, now no longer bother to read the screenplays they commission. [*Observer,* 1998]

■ The Hollywood film now rules the entertainment culture of our planet, and seems well on the way to becoming a universal secular religion, the first to offer its devotees anything they want and ask for nothing in return . . . [review of *Working Class Hollywood,* 1997]

■ Whatever its shortcomings, the Hollywood film has managed to plug itself directly into the limbic system of the planetary brain, the power-center of our most visceral emotions, bypassing the frontal lobes altogether. Any concerns about the complexities of human loyalties and relationships it has dismissed to the genre fringe of films like *The Last Seduction.* [review of *Working Class Hollywood,* 1997]

■ Most Hollywood blockbusters are animated comic strips, driven by the relentless demand for action, the equivalent of a climax every four frames, and with the same crane shots and zooms that energize the static panels in the *Batman* and *Superman* strips. The briefest flicker of an adult relationship seems to come with a built-in fast forward button. [*Observer,* 1998]

■ Psychopathology is fun. Or so one assumes after a visit to the neighborhood family cineplex. Night after night, our movie theaters are stalked by rapists, sadists and serial killers. Unending gunfire and exploding bombs assault the soundproofing, as Buicks and Chevrolets cartwheel through the air in slow motion before nesting themselves in the roofs of buses and fire engines. All the while, the rising body count stacks the corpses halfway up the screen. As the lights come on, one almost expects to see pools of blood soaking the carpet of the orchestra pit. But they call it *entertainment.* [*Observer,* 1996]

■ Why does the most powerful and advanced society the world has ever known, which has landed men on the moon and unlocked the secrets of the sun, amuse itself with an entertainment culture devised for bored and violent teenagers? ["American Dreams," 1997]

■ Film seems to be reverting to its earlier days of sheer spectacle. [*Index*, 1997]

■ For me, [David Thomson] is the greatest of today's film writers, author of the rightly acclaimed *A Biographical Dictionary of Film,* one of the best film books ever written and full of quirky and unexpected judgments that linger annoyingly in the mind, like his belief that Cary Grant is the supreme film actor. [*Observer,* 1998]

■ Woe betide any filmmaker, like David Lynch or Cronenberg, who decides to take as read the cinema-goer's relish for the deviant and psychopathic, and then sets out to construct a picture of who we really are. Novelists, poets and painters have openly explored the connections between love, eroticism and death for at least 200 years, but the pornographic violence of some Hollywood films is carefully sealed within a set of entertainment conventions, and shielded by the lack of awareness from the powers-that-be of exactly what the mass audiences are enjoying . . . [*Observer,* 1996]

■ *Blue Velvet was,* for me, the best film of the Eighties—a surreal, voyeuristic and subversive masterpiece of cinema that has lost none of its power to startle, and still ensnares the audience into complicity with its masochistic weirdness. As one of its technicians commented during the shooting, *Blue Velvet* is where Norman Rockwell meets Hieronymus Bosch. The film holds up despite Lynch's uneven career before and since, and is all the more impressive for being made within the restraints of the Hollywood system. [*Observer,* 1996]

■ *Eraserhead* is a classic of underground cinema, a compendium of unrelated events and characters that makes no sense on the surface but is clearly held together by a powerful set of phobias. Lynch's great strength is that he makes no attempt to explain or rationalize them. [*Observer,* 1996]

■ "Are you a detective or a pervert?" Laura Dern's character asks her boyfriend . . . The question lies at the heart of Lynch's films. No moral frameworks enclose his characters, and their psychopathy and deviance are accepted for what they are, like character quirks in an old friend. But on this base, Lynch builds the haunted house of his imagination, part autopsy room into the human soul and part horror museum of the banal. Together they resemble everyday reality with the sound turned down and a sinister, barely audible dialogue that appears in some oblique way to refer to ourselves. [*Observer,* 1996]

■ Somewhere inside [David Lynch's] head, one senses, Francis Bacon is repainting the Bates Motel. [*Observer,* 1996]

■ I think of *Crash* as the first film of the [21st] century. I think that the very influential role of *Psycho* since 1962 will apply to *Crash.* Paul Schrader [scriptwriter of *Taxi Driver*] said, "Wonderful film—if only I'd been so honest." [unknown]

■ *Crash* is Cronenberg's best and most original film, in many ways the first psychopathic film, the first to dispense completely with moral frameworks and assume the complicity of the audience in its Sadeian universe. [*Disturb,* n.d.]

■ I consider [*Crash*] the first film of the 21st century, the prototype of the psychopathic cinema which will liberate the film from its reliance on redemptive story-lines. The French, being more intelligent and sophisticated than the British, saw this immediately. [*Disturb,* n.d.]

■ *Crash* removes the moral framework that reassures the specta-tor that these horrific scenes are, in fact, constrained within some system of moral values. And I think that unsettles people, because they ask questions—I mean, "Do the filmmaker and the writer real-ly believe that auto wrecks are erotically stimulating?" [*Artforum*, 1997]

■ Cronenberg has a sort of visceral, organic style of image-mak-ing that suits the subject matter of *Crash,* particularly if he can fuse that visceral imagery with the hard technology of the auto-mobile. [*Albedo One*, 1993]

■ I never said that I think car crashes are sexually exciting. What I'd said is that the *idea* of a car crash is sexually exciting. We know they're almost the worst thing that can happen to us on the average day, and yet, at the same time, we find the idea of crashing cars very, very exciting . . . This is what I was exploring—the fact that there's something about the car crash that triggers a powerful imaginative response. [*Artforum*, 1997]

■ Most of Cronenberg's heroes are rebelling against whatever mutational process is underway. Only towards the end do they yield. Whereas my characters, right from my early natural-dis-aster novels, accept the transformation taking place, because it's an externalization of some deep, unconscious—or semicon-scious—need of their own. They embrace the catastrophe because they're keen to remythologize themselves, and redis-cover the different world that lies beyond the transformation. [*Artforum*, 1997]

■ In a movie like *Goodfellas*, people get brutally beaten to death, but one can say, "Well, these are the bad guys." But that moral frame-work is completely absent from *Crash*, which provokes the audience, because the implication is that this film is about you, not just these fictional characters. [*21C*, 1997]

■ Jeremy Thomas, the British producer who produced

Bertolucci's *The Last Emperor,* also produced *The Sheltering Sky,* the Paul Bowles adaptation. And he was the producer, of course, of *Naked Lunch.* He's had a very good track record of producing difficult novels. He took an option on *Crash.* It was he who found David Cronenberg. [intv James Call, 1997]

■ *Crash* has been under option, more or less continuously, since it was published . . . In money terms the options were very modest. Nonetheless it did have people in the film world interested—Nick Roeg at one point. He was very close to raising the finance. Back in the Seventies when people were trying to set up *Crash* to film, I can well understand them getting absolutely nowhere. [intv James Call, 1997]

■ Halfway through *Crash's* press conference at Cannes, the

Splendor in the CRASH:
Deborah Kara Unger
and James Spader.

Evening Standard's film critic suddenly got up with a flourish and walked straight out. And when he got back to London, he wrote a piece calling *Crash* the most depraved film ever made. To me, this represents Total Artistic Success! [*Sub Dee*, 1997]

■ *Alphaville* was a brilliant film, a masterpiece . . . The interior space of *Alphaville* is so wonderful . . . I love all those chrome hotels—and the great Akim Tamiroff, in his overcoat, sitting sadly on his bed. Eddie Constantine, the glamorous super-hunk. I think originally Godard was going to call it *Tarzan vs. IBM*. I loved that film. [intv Ian Sinclair, 1997]

■ I remember going to see *T-Men,* which only *cinéastes* have heard of. Hard-edged, really tough gangster film. [Iain Sinclair's *Crash,* 1999]

■ A majority of violent films comes from Hollywood, and this may reflect something I have always suspected, that, for all its glamour and energy, American life is *boring*, and that Americans in their daily lives feel as [the British] do when we spent too long in even the most lavishly equipped funfair or theme park. If only we could press a button and blow the place sky-high. [*Sunday Times,* 1996]

■ John Waters comes clean with "thinking about violence seems to relax me and give me comfort," an admission that is close to the longstanding violence-as-catharsis defense. [*Sunday Times,* 1996]

■ Should there be less, or more, violence on our film and television screens? More, I think, but of the real kind. If films contained scenes of violence (and sex) as close to reality as simulation can bring them, I suspect that a profound hush would fall on the cinemas of the world, and that the stunned audiences would drive home safely and be a lot kinder to their spouses. Having seen what really happens in a bad car accident, or when a machine-gun bullet strikes a face, they would never want to return to their seats in the stalls. But, of course, the Hollywood myth-makers know this, too. [*Sunday Times,* 1996]

■ Nobody has proved convincingly that filmic violence is contagious—in my own case, it's the *Die Hard* series that leaves me yawning, while anything from Merchant Ivory has me trying to break the furniture. [*Sunday Times,* 1996]

■ With its glossy color and tableau-like settings, [the home video] depicts the parents sitting in their drawing rooms, having dinner, parking their cars ... But Jasper and Amanda had added some 25 seconds of footage, culled from TV news documentaries, of car crashes, electric chairs and concentration-camp mass graves. Scattered at random among the scenes of their parents, this atrocity footage transformed the film into a work of eerie and threatening prophecy. [*Running Wild,* 1988]

■ Two glorious film books about the baddest of the Hollywood bad boys. *Sam Spiegel,* by Natasha Fraser-Cavassoni, describes a genuine mountebank, a congenital liar and fraudster who produced *The African Queen, The Bridge on the River Kwai* and *Lawrence of Arabia* ("Dunes, baby, I want dunes"). *The Kid Stays in the Picture* is the autobiography of Robert Evans, another larger-than-life rogue who saved Paramount and produced *Rosemary's Baby, The Godfather* and *Chinatown.* In the worst possible taste and completely fascinating. As Evans comments: "There are three sides to every story: yours, mine, and the truth." [*Guardian,* 2003]

■ *Tough Acts*, by Steven Berkoff is the best film book of the year, an insider's sharp-eyed but affectionate view of the dream factory and its billion-dollar workforce. Berkoff is as good a writer as he is an actor, and his portraits of Sylvester Stallone, Stanley Kubrick, Roman Polanski and Al Pacino are etched with a dry wit that cuts deep but is never malicious. [*Observer,* 2003]

■ . . . the nearest that the consumer society comes to cultural nirvana: the video-rental *classics* shelf. [*Guardian,* 1991]

■ The most interesting films of today—*Blue Velvet, The Hitcher* and the 30-second ads for call-girls on New York's *Channel J* (some of the most poignant mini-dramas ever made, filmed in a weird and glaucous blue, featuring a woman, a bed and an invitation to lust)— are a rush of pure sensation. *Blue Velvet,* like *Psycho,* follows the trajectory of the drug trip. Paranoia rules, and motiveless crimes and behavior ring true in a way that leaves a traditionally constructed movie with its well-crafted plot, characters and story looking not merely old-fashioned but untrue. [*Independent,* 1990]

■ Billy Wilder may have quarreled with Raymond Chandler (over *Double Indemnity*), but they were really on the same side, both lovers of the word. Wilder's films, dominated by their bitter-sweet dialogue and filled with theatrical characters who always seem aware of their audience, are untypical of anything in today's cinema. [*Independent,* 1990]

■ Nostalgia may not be all it used to be, but films really *were* better in the 1940s and 1950s. [*Daily Telegraph,* 1993]

■ Ingrid Bergman said of [Humphrey] Bogart, "I kissed him, but I never knew him," a line worthy of a movie all its own. [*Daily Telegraph,* 1993]

■ Gutsy to the end, [Mae West] reinvented herself as a camp icon, presiding over a Hollywood apartment decorated like a boudoir-scale Versailles . . . Over the years she drifted into eccentricity, urging enema kits on to her friends, obsessed with spiritualism, and surrounding herself with retinues of muscle-builders. The concept of an octogenarian nymphomaniac which she patented and so brilliantly sustained (amazingly, there had long been rumors that she was a man) showed that she had never lost her touch, and makes her a continuing inspiration to the rest of us. [*Guardian,* 1991]

■ [Jean-Luc Godard] blends utopian satire, pop art and comic-book imagery to create the alienated landscape of the distant planet *Alphaville,* whose cowed population is tyrannized by an evil computer . . . For the first time in the Science-Fiction film, Godard makes the point that the media landscape of the present day fantasies of Science Fiction are as "real" as an office block, an airport or a Presidential campaign . . . The film transcends its pop imagery to create a disturbing world that resembles a chromium-plated 1984. [*American Film,* 1987]

■ As a medical student, I was always skipping lectures to see the movies. I knew it was more important to see *T-Men* than hear F.R. Leavis talk about the novel. [ICA interview, 1998]

■ On one level the ultimate road movie *Mad Max 2* is a compellingly reductive vision of post-industrial collapse. Here the end of the world is seen as a non-stop demolition derby, as gangs of motorized savages rove their desert wastes, bereft of speech, thought, hopes or dreams, dedicated only to the brutal realities of speed and violence . . . A host of images wrench the retina—garish vehicles, fearful road armor and weird Punk hairstyles, the sense of a world discarded after Judgment Day. In its raw power and vast scenic effects, *Mad Max 2* is Punk's *Sistine Chapel.* [*American Film,* 1987]

■ I remember seeing *Mad Max 2* in the cinema. I thought, "God, this is so original. It can't be American—migod, it's an Aussie film; something's happening Down Under." That needed the big screen. People who've only seen it on the small screen think, "What's this?" [ICA conversation, 1998]

■ *Dark Star* is the *Catch-22* of outer space. Reportedly made for $60,000, *Dark Star* was originally filmed in 16mm by a group of students . . . Watching this brilliant extravaganza, one is forced yet again to accept that talent alone is always enough. [*American*

Film, 1987]

■ Roger Vadim, who in *And God Created Woman* created Brigitte Bardot, here [in *Barbarella*] turns his affectionate and ironic eye on another of his wives, Jane Fonda, who achieves immortality as she cavorts naked in a fur-lined spaceship. [*American Film,* 1987]

■ . . . the *producer's* creative contribution, always underestimated. The Hollywood of fifty years ago, its greatest era, was a producer's Hollywood where most directors were less important than the cameraman. [*Daily Telegraph,* 1993]

■ [RE *Forbidden Planet*] This remarkably stylish color film is a quantum leap forward in visual confidence and in the richness of its theme—an update of Shakespeare's *The Tempest.* The special effects were unequalled until *2001: A Space Odyssey.* [*American Film,* 1987]

■ Spielberg's mastery of the Science-Fiction medium was already evident in *Duel,* his 1971 classic of highway paranoia. From autogeddon he moved on to two major themes of Science Fiction, monsters (*Jaws*) and interplanetary travel (*Close Encounters* and *ET the Extra-Terrestrial*). That these have become three of the most successful films in the history of the cinema underlines my long-held belief that Science Fiction defines the popular imagination of the twentieth century. [*American Film,* 1987]

■ In 1950 [Akira Kurosawa] produced *Rashomon,* a masterpiece of subjectivity in which the murder of a warrior and the rape of his wife are seen from four conflicting viewpoints . . . what is so tantalizing about *Rashomon* is its refusal to validate any of the witnesses' stories as the true account. These same ambiguities prevail in Kurosawa's films with contemporary settings—*Drunken Angel* and *Stray Dog,* among others—bleak visions of post-war criminality that draw on the same sources as the Italian neo-realist cinema. [*Guardian,* 1991]

■ *The Last Seduction* I thought was quite a subversive film in its way—she got away with it. [ICA conversation, 1998]

■ Filmmakers as a whole: those hustlers, poets, bullies and mountebanks, every one a Cortez glimpsing an imaginary Pacific. [*Guardian,* 1996]

■ [On *La Jetée*] This strange and poetic film, directed by Chris Marker, is a fusion of Science Fiction, psychological fable and photomontage, and creates in its unique way a series of potent images of the inner landscapes of time . . . in my experience, the only convincing act of time travel in the whole of Science Fiction. [*New Worlds,* 1966]

■ *If* [is] a masterpiece of 1960s cinema. Two further remarkable films, *O Lucky Man* and *Britannia Hospital.* [*Sunday Times,* 1996]

■ The technological medium of cinema creates the communication level by which something like the De Niro character in *Taxi Driver* becomes a hero. [*NME,* 1985]

■ With the [VCR] you can build up quite a large library of images. You might get some obsessive, say, who finds himself collecting footage of women's shoes whenever they're shown (it doesn't matter if it's Esther Williams walking around a swimming pool with Forties sound, or Princess Di)—he presses his button and records all this footage of women's shoes . . . After accumulating two hundred hours of shoes, you might have a bizarre obsessive movie that's absolutely riveting. [*RE/Search #8/9,* 1984]

■ [*Crash*] is the most powerful and original film I've seen for years. In many ways it takes off where my novel ends, and is even more erotic and mysterious. The actors are superb. Holly Hunter as the avenging angel, James Spader and Deborah Unger as the husband and wife drawn into this violent and sensual world, Rosanna Arquette as the voluptuous cripple and Elias

Koteas as the hoodlum scientist together help to create a masterpiece of cinema that will be the film sensation of the 1990s. [letter to David Cronenberg, 1996]

■ The paradigm movie of the next ten years will be something like *Con Air. Twister* is a very good example: no character development, no real story. It would be sad to see complex stories fading out. I'm a great believer in strong stories. [ICA interview, 1998]

■ Thirty years ago, after first bruising myself against the silver screen, it occurred to me that the experience of bringing up young children was the best possible training for dealing with people in the film world. Those passionate enthusiasms which could evaporate like the mist on a margarita, the life-long friendships virtually signed in blood that never outlasted a lunch, the sudden treacheries and wounded innocence, reminded me that I was dealing with a tribe of likeable but unreliable four-year-olds. [*Sunday Times,* 1996]

■ The *story* (which the literary novel has neglected, to its cost) is everything. [*Sight & Sound,* 1996]

■ Novelists on the whole don't have a very good record as screen-writers. They have a fundamental misapprehension about what film narrative is. I don't believe that a novelist could have written *Sunset Boulevard.* [ICA interview, 1998]

■ Film is often described as the true art of the 20th century, a conjuring trick played with the human eye, that has created the most potent dreams of our age. ["Behind Steely Ambition," *Sunday Times,* n.d.]

■ We had moved from the earnestness of Bergman and the more facile mannerisms of Fellini and Hitchcock to the classical serenity and wit of Rene Clair and Max Ophuls, though the children, with their love of the hand-held camera, still resembled so many budding Godards. ["The Intensive Care Unit," 1977]

■ [On refusing to write the novelization of the film *Alien*] They offered me $20,000 but it was surprisingly easy to turn down. I wouldn't mind doing the novelization of *Alphaville,* or even Huston's *Moby Dick* or Hawks's *Big Slee*p (Welles's *Macbeth* would pose some problems). [*JGB News #11,* 4/1984]

■ Steven Spielberg poses a huge problem for film critics and cineastes. . . While traditional Hollywood moguls rolled around in stretch limos and dined at *Ma Maison* and *Spago,* Spielberg lived frugally, drove a rented car and dressed in jeans and trainers. . . Were it not for Spielberg's high-concept cinema and the huge audiences and revenues he attracted, the Hollywood of the 1980s would have been stranded among the disappointments of late Kubrick, Coppola and Cimino, sustained by little more than the empty *Star Wars* spectacles of George Lucas. ["Peddling Comic Strips: Steven Spielberg," 1997]

■ I've never really cared for Elizabeth Taylor, although she was undoubtedly the last of the great Hollywood Stars—but the personality always seemed uninteresting, and her magic was entirely due to her imposed celebrity, which I suppose is why I chose her. [letter, 1/23/1997]

■ [Elizabeth Taylor] isn't my type. A pity. But she is the last of the old-style Hollywood stars. I prefer Cher, or the young Ingrid Thulin [in Mai Zetterling's *Night Games*). [*S.F. Eye,* 1991]

■ The [Quentin] Tarantino genre: where quirky stylization disguises the dramatic and moral vacuum at its core, an evasion with which the audience colludes as it takes its nerve endings for a deranged roller-coaster ride. [*Sunday Times,* 1996]

■ I went to see Herzog's *Fitzcarraldo,* and I thought it was terribly disappointing. Magnificent photography—who could miss, given the Amazon sunsets, the lush vegetation. . . But I thought it was overblown, and deficient in story. No Hollywood studio would have allowed that movie out of the factory in 1950, because its story was weak. It wasn't nearly so obsessive as his previous movies, like Aguirre. That was a stunning film—he thought out his plot and storyline, probably. [*RE/Search #8/9*, p. 29, 1984]

■ Jacopetti's *Mondo Cane* series of documentary films enjoyed a huge vogue in the 1960s. They cunningly mixed genuine film of atrocities, religious cults and "Believe-it-or-not" examples of human oddity with carefully faked footage. [*Atrocity Exhibition,* 1990]

■ The Hollywood films that kept hope alive—*Citizen Kane, Sunset Boulevard, The Big Sleep and White Heat*—seemed to form a continuum with the novels of Hemingway and Nathanael West, Kafka and Camus. At about the same time I found my way to psychoanalysis and Surrealism, and this hot mix together fueled the short stories that I was already writing and strongly influenced my decision to read medicine. ["The Pleasures of Reading," 1992]

■ Some of the best American thrillers have been set in the desert— *The Getaway, The Hitcher, Charley Varrick, Blood Simple.* Given that there is no time past and no future, the idea of death and retribution has a doubly threatening force. [*Atrocity Exhibition,* 1990]

■ I'm a keen renter of videos. I love U.S. thrillers—*Cop, The Hitcher, Cohen and Tate,* etc. Also tough French gangster movies. [*S.F. Eye,* 1991]

■ The adult film channel, hours of explicit hardcore. People watched, but in a nostalgic way, as if they were seeing a documentary about Morris dancing or roof thatching. [*Super-Cannes,* 2000]

■ The porn movie is the true future of film. [*Super-Cannes,* 2000]

■ I'd like to organize a Festival of Home Movies! It could be wonderful—thousands of the things—all those babies tottering across lawns . . . You might find an odd genius, a Fellini or Godard of the Home Movie, living in some suburb . . . I'm sure it's coming. [*RE/Search #8/9,* 1984]

ART

■ I think that art is the principal way in which the human mind has tried to remake the world in a way that makes sense. [*Disturb*, n.d.]

■ The mass media have turned the world into a *World of Pop Art*. From JFK's assassination to the war in Iraq, *everything is perceived as Pop Art*. Nothing is true. Nothing is untrue. [intv Hans Obrist, 2003]

■ I'm interested in almost every period of painting, from Lascaux through the Renaissance onwards. [Intv Goddard, 1975]

■ I agree entirely with Warhol, and with Baudrillard. [intv. L. Tarantino, n.d.]

■ It's not their own ambition that corrupts today's artists, but the subject matter facing them. [*Tate Spring*, 2001]

■ "All these CEOs think art is good for their souls." "Not so?" "It rots their brains. Tate Modern, the Royal Academy, the Hayward . . . they're Walt Disney for the middle classes." [*Super-Cannes*, 2000]

■ Art exists because reality is neither real nor significant. [*Disturb*, n.d.]

■ The arts and criminality have always flourished side by side. [*Cocaine Nights*, 1996]

■ London [is] dominated by . . . the Young British Art, force-fed into fleeting notoriety by Charles Saatchi, who unfailingly transforms his adman's gold into the dross of third-rate Conceptual art. [*Bookforum*, 1999]

■ I take a keen interest in what today's painters and sculptors are doing. On the whole my views coincide with those of the great Brian Sewell, but I see the young British artists of the past ten years or so from a different perspective. They find themselves in a world totally dominated by advertising, by a corrupt politics carried out as a branch of advertising, and by a reality that is a total fiction controlled by manufacturers, PR firms, and vast entertainment and media corporations. Nothing is real, everything is fake. Bizarrely, most people like it that way. So in their installations and concept works the young artists are rebelling against this all-dominant adman's media-landscape. They are trying to establish a new truth about what an unmade bed is, what a dead animal is, and so on. Our mistake is to judge them by aesthetic criteria. By contrast, the novel resists innovation, and is much closer to the TV domestic serial. [intv Hans Obrist, 2003]

■ A few, very few, of the New Brit artists are making a genuine point when they assemble their dirty linen and everyday detritus, making a stand against the suffocating orthodoxies of the consumer culture. [*Literary Review*, 2001]

■ Not one of the works of art in the gallery remotely matched the limitless potency of a terrorist bomb. [*Millennium People*, 2003]

■ Abstract Expressionism is about the only kind of painting I haven't responded to. [Intv Goddard, 1975]

■ [According to Robert Hughes,] Abstract Expressionism "encouraged a phony grandiloquence, a confusion of pretentious size with scale, that has plagued American painting ever since." He cautiously approves of the Pop painters, admiring the energy and sheer zest of artists such as Lichtenstein and Rauschenberg, but is scathing about Julian Schnabel and Jeff Koons, darlings of the over-promoted art scene of the 1980s. American art, Hughes believes, has drowned itself in money, in the cult of celebrity and the embrace of the so-called avant-garde by ambitious museums, with their eyes on attendance figures. ["American Dreams," 1997]

■ When the Mona Lisa was exhibited in New York in 1962 she was seen by more than 1 million visitors, who each spent an average 0.79 seconds before the sacred smile. ["American Dreams," 1997]

■ Toulouse-Lautrec's paintings, his music-hall posters and vivid portraits of prostitutes and cabaret artists, were always as up-to-the-minute as a newspaper headline . . . In the few years before his death at the age of 37 he produced a huge volume of work. Kept going by small doses of strychnine, as he drank himself towards oblivion in a local bar and shared his bed with two prostitutes, Lautrec was still trying half-heartedly to work . . . His final letters, written only seven weeks before his death, show him moving into the same hallucinating realm shared by Rimbaud in his last delirium. [*Guardian*, 1991]

■ I was in Florence, in the Uffizi Gallery, looking at, or rather, trying to look at an Annunciation by Leonardo da Vinci. The problem was that between me and the painting were about 200 Japanese tourists . . . I thought, "What on earth do they see in these Renaissance paintings? What do they make of all these winged men kneeling before these rather sly young women? What do they make of this extraordinary universe, with its bizarre loaves of bread and peacocks? What did they make of it all?" If you have no Christian belief and know nothing about the Christian faith, what is going on in this painting is Surreal. [*Art Newspaper*, 1999]

■ He spoke in the kind of fluent, uninflected English of the international executive, with the kind of arts connoisseurship picked up in the antique shops that lined the lobbies of luxury hotels. [*Super-Cannes*, 2000]

■ "A company chairman had discovered Jung's theory of archetypes and was convinced that it outlined the future of kitchenware design." [unknown]

■ There is the revolutionary idea that a domestic appliance could be part of the aesthetic design of the ideal home. Our appliances actually constitute a sophisticated and imaginative mirror of what is important in our lives. [*Art Newspaper,* 1999]

■ " . . . loved Clovis Trouille and all those nuns being buggered." [*Super-Cannes,* 2000]

■ The "Destroy the Museums" cry of Marinettti's futurists had a surprising resonance. [*Millennium People,* 2003]

■ [Robert Hughes's] writing is always witty and fearless—he has never hesitated to castigate the preposterous banalities of the Manhattan art scene, whose patrons are those bankers and corporate chiefs who sit on *Time's* board and surely wince when they read Hughes's trashing of the paintings that hang on their walls. ["American Dreams," 1997]

■ *American Visions* is a banquet of a book, written with all of [Robert] Hughes's entertaining pungency, and with an encyclopedic grasp of hundreds of artists and artists. [*Ibid*]

■ Perhaps America has transcended the arts, in the sense that the fuselage of a 747 is its own aesthetic statement upon itself. No painter could improve upon the Chrysler building or, for that matter, the average showroom Chrysler. America's greatest imaginative achievements are to be found in its skyscrapers and cars, in the electrographic nightscapes of Manhattan and Las Vegas, in its comic strips and Hollywood films. [*Ibid*]

■ The real contrast at the heart of *Vermilion Sands* is that between the artists living in this eventless paradise, and the genuinely radical imagination with which they are unable to cope and which tragically overwhelms them, represented by the primeval forces embodied in the various enchantress figures. It is they who represent archaic reality and its vast creative and destructive energies. The artists sculpting their clouds, etc., are really dilettantes. The same situation applies today, as you see if you go to any art school, where the students are desperately exploring new mediums and concepts (one room filled with sand, the next with chromium-plated sand, etc.) but have no contact with reality. [intv L. Tarantino, n.d.]

■ *Vermilion Sands* is a kind of cross between Palm Springs and Juan-les-Pins, a vision of the leisure society that we were about to enter, though for some reason we stopped and turned away at the door. Music by Brian Eno, metal foil architecture by Frank Gehry, dreams by Sigmund Freud, decor by Paul Delvaux. [*Literary Review,* 2001]

■ Today's Institute of Contemporary Arts (ICA) seems to be successfully repositioning itself as a post-2000 ideas lab. [intv Hans Obrist, 2003]

■ I didn't see exhibitions of Francis Bacon, Max Ernst, Magritte and Dali as displays of paintings. I saw them as among the most radical statements of the human imagination ever made, on a par with radical discoveries in neuroscience or nuclear physics. [*Ibid.*]

■ There's a huge amount of humor in Magritte . . . an enormous apple fills a room. It's threatening and mysterious, but also extremely funny in an unnerving way. That's the kind of humor I aspire to. [*Literary Review,* 2001]

■ Sadly, Warhol's creative imagination failed to join him on the return journey, and the gun shots in the Factory sounded the effective end of his remarkable career. Was Warhol the last important artist to emerge since the Second World War? The works of his fellow pop artists, the comic-strip blow-ups of Roy Lichtenstein and the billboard murals of James Rosenquist, seem as dated as half-forgotten advertisements. [*Guardian,* 1989]

■ What sets Warhol apart is his effortlessly assumed naivety, a wide-eyed innocence that recalls an earlier filmmaker. In many ways Warhol is the Walt Disney of the amphetamine age. [*Guardian,* 1989]

■ One saw blowups of the Kennedy [assassination] motorcade used as backdrops in fashion magazines. Images that should have elicited pity and concern were drained of any kind of human response, in the way that Warhol demonstrated. His art really was *dedicated* to just that. [*Artforum*, 1997]

■ Warhol, of course, was forever his own greatest creation, a Valium-numbed Mickey Mouse in a white fright-wig. His deadpan comments on his own work show a teasing astuteness. "If you want to know about Andy Warhol, just look at the surface of my paintings. There's nothing behind it . . . I want to be a machine . . . Everybody's plastic. I want to be plastic." [*Guardian*, 1989]

■ Endless parties . . . and not a single interesting conversation. [*Guardian*, 1989]

■ Warhol, with his endless round of parties, found a substitute for the Paris cafe. [*Guardian*, 1991]

■ I've always thought Malcolm McLaren was brilliantly clever. He's the English Andy Warhol, isn't he? [*I-D*, 1987]

■ Edward Hopper paintings: another uniquely special world, that silent country of marooned American cities under a toneless, Depression-era sky, of entropic hotel rooms and offices where all clocks have stopped, where isolated men and women stare out of one nothingness into the larger nothingness beyond . . . Hopper depicts that hidden and harder world glimpsed in the original *Postman Always Rings Twice*, and many of his paintings could be stills from some dark-edged James M. Cain thriller. [*Guardian*, 1989]

■ Hopper's passion for all things French extended far beyond painting to take in poetry and the novel, theater and cinema... Hopper's paintings depict an archetypal America of small cities and provincial towns, late-night bars embalmed in the empty night, airless offices and filling stations left behind by the new highway, but seen through an unfailingly European eye. [*Guardian,* 1989]

■ The true poet of metropolitan America, the melancholy observer of provincial offices, empty movie theaters and anonymous bars, was Edward Hopper, for me the greatest of all American painters. ["American Dreams," 1997]

■ A new generation of curators: many of them showmen and theme-parkers. [*Guardian,* 1991]

■ New York, the most vibrant and violent of American cities, became and remains the capital of its visual arts. Newspaper advertising, the billboard and the neon sign created a new language and a new set of icons, as we see in Charles Demuth's "The Figure Five in Gold," perhaps the first Pop Art painting. ["American Dreams," 1997]

■ I think we screen out large areas of possible subject matter for the visual arts when we will not consider the rubble and refuse in a car [wrecker's] yard, or a machine or derelict machinery as the raw material for creating a poetically charged sculpture. [*Art Newspaper,* 1999]

■ In the years leading up to the abolition of censorship in the late Sixties, filmmakers and writers and artists were all pushing against those barriers. But since then we have been fighting back against something different—against the all-pervasive entertainment culture and the sentimentalized values of TV blandness. People are searching for truth through trying to shock, although it may sometimes be an artificial truth that they find. Mainstream entertainment is so manufactured now, and this is what extreme artists are kicking against. As a result of, many younger writers and filmmakers are now simply expressing their own obsessions; that is all that is left that they feel they can say something truthful about. They don't want to accept the values imposed on them by adverts and entertainment corporations—and on the whole that is a good thing. [*Observer,* 8/20/2000]

■ "If someone burgles my house, shoots the dog and rapes the maid, my reaction isn't to open an art gallery." "Not your first reaction, perhaps. But later, as you question events and the world around you . . . the arts and criminality have always flourished side by side." [*Cocaine Nights,* 1996]

■ Graffiti covered every inch of the steel panels, an aerosoled display of fluorescent whorls and loops, swastikas and threatening slogans that continued across the window shutters and front door. Repeated cleanings had blurred the pigments, and the triptych of garage, windows and door resembled the self-accusing effort of a deranged Expressionist painter. [*Cocaine Nights,* 1996]

■ Leonardo's "Virgin of the Rocks" [is] one of the most forbidding and most enigmatic of his paintings. The madonna sitting on a bare ledge by the water beneath the dark overhang of the cavern's mouth was like the presiding spirit of some enchanted marine realm, waiting for those cast on to the rocky shores of this world's end. As in so many of Leonardo's paintings, all its unique longings and terrors were to be found in the landscape in the *background.* ["The Gioconda of the Twilight Noon," 1964]

■ Over the mantelpiece was a huge painting by the early 20th-century Surrealist, Delvaux, in which ashen-faced women danced naked to the waist with dandified skeletons in tuxedos against a spectral bone-like landscape. On another wall one of Max Ernst's self-devouring phantasmagoric jungles screamed silently to itself, like the sump of some insane unconscious. [*Drowned World,* 1962]

■ In Vasari's *Lives* one reads of Michelangelo sleeping for only four or five hours, painting all day at the age of eighty and then working through the night over his anatomy table with a candle strapped to his forehead. Now he's regarded as a prodigy, but it was unremarkable then. ["The Voices of Time," 1960]

■ She was full of anecdotes about Dali, whose entourage at Port Lligat she had penetrated, and his voyeuristic delight in watching young couples have sex. [*Kindness of Women,* 1991]

■ Modernism is the gothic of the information age. Dreams sharp enough to bleed, and no doubts about man's lowly place in the scheme of things. [*Kindness of Women,* 1991]

■ It's probably true that the most maligned species on Earth is the wealthy patron of modern art. Laughed at by the public, exploited by dealers, even the artists regard them simply as meal tickets. ["The Singing Statues," 1962]

■ Pop artists deal with the lowly trivia of possessions and equipment that the present generation is lugging along with it on its safari into the future. [*Books and Bookmen,* 4/1971]

■ What was so exciting about Pop Art was the response it elicited from the public—people were amazed by it. Here for the first time was an art actually about what it was like to buy a new refrigerator, what it was like to be in a modern kitchen, what modern fabrics and clothes and mass advertising were about. The Pop Artists (and "Pop" is an unfortunate term to describe them) were taking the world they lived in seriously, at its own terms. ["From Shanghai to Shepperton," 1982, in *RE/Search #8/9,* 1984]

■ The stylization of televised violence into an anthology of design statements . . . [*Kindness of Women,* 1991]

■ All over the world major museums have bowed to the influence of Disney and become theme parks in their own right. [*Atrocity Exhibition,* 1990]

■ Celebrity and the media presence of the artists [today] are inextricably linked with their work. [*Pretext,* 2004]

■ Fifty thousand years from now our descendants will be mystified by the empty swimming-pools of an abandoned southern California and *Cote d'Azur,* lying in the dust like primitive time machines or the altars of some geometry-obsessed religion. I see [Robert] Smithson's monuments belonging in the same category, artifacts intended to serve as machines that will suddenly switch themselves on and begin to generate a more complex time and space. All his structures seem to be analogues of advanced neurological processes that have yet to articulate themselves. ["Robert Smithson as Cargo Cultist," n.d.]

■ The show "Outsider Art" in London . . . impressed me enormously, because of the way in which these deeply isolated and disturbed people, many of them life-long inmates of mental institutions—cut off from the world entirely, were still struggling, through their drawings and paintings, to make sense of the world they inhabited . . . These deeply isolated people were trying to make contact with the universe as a whole, and were, in fact, driven by the grandest imaginative dreams. I see myself in the same role, actually. [*RE/Search #8/9,* 1984]

■ On the whole, visionary painters like [William] Blake, Samuel Palmer, Stanley Spencer have not been well received—they're too unsettling. [*RE/Search #8/9,* 1984]

■ Margot turned away, feeling her swimsuit slide pleasantly across her smooth tanned skin. The suit was made of one of the newer bioplastic materials, and its living tissues were still growing, softly adapting themselves to the contours of her body, repairing themselves as the fibers became worn or grimy. Upstairs in her wardrobes the gowns and dresses purred on their hangers like the drowsing inmates of some exquisite arboreal zoo. ["Passport to Eternity," 1962]

■ She sat forward happily, turning up her fluorescent violet dress until she glowed like an Algolian rayfish. ["Passport to Eternity," 1962]

■ I'm tremendously responsive to painting of every school from Lascaux onwards. There's hardly a painter in the whole of the

Renaissance I don't find some merit in, and almost every painter since Manet plays a vital role in my life, with the exception of abstract expressionism because that is painting really about itself. [*The Imagination on Trial,* 1981]

■ Too much is made of Conceptual Art—putting it crudely, someone has been shitting in Duchamp's urinal, and there is an urgent need for a strong dose of critical Parazone. [*Pretext,* 2004]

■ Art schools are in a desperate situation . . . They're all hooked on ironic statements . . . Someone fills a room with mud, so now we've got to fill a room with mud that's been chromium-plated. [*Studio International,* 1971]

■ Abstract Expressionism struck me as being about yesterday—it was profoundly retrospective, profoundly passive, and it wasn't serious. [It] didn't share the overlapping, jostling vocabularies of science, technology, advertising, [and] the new realms of communication. [*Studio International,* 1971]

■ [Artists] are trying to redefine the basic elements of reality, to recapture them from the ad men who have hijacked our world. [*Pretext,* 2004]

ON FRANCIS BACON

■ Death sits facing us, his legs straddling a garden chair, a machine-gun resting on a nearby table. His head and left shoulder have vanished, sinking into a psychological abyss that leaves a black hole in the center of the painting. But his gaze is unmistakable, and reminds us of those quiet and patient killers who waited beside the execution pits of the 20th Century. Francis Bacon painted this fearful vision in 1945, the year of Hiroshima and Nagasaki, when the full nightmare of the Nazi death-camps became known. But Bacon scarcely needed the second World War to supply him with a feast of horror. Being human was enough, and together his paintings constitute a vast bestiary in which mankind (and it is mostly men; very few women appear in his paintings) is stripped to its core of pain and despair. After the screaming popes and trapped executives, Bacon set out the private space that dominated his later paintings, an airless interior like a television hospitality room where the guests have been left alone too long. One senses that they are frightened to leave, aware that the headless man with a machine-gun is waiting for them in a quiet park not too far away. Francis Bacon is, for me, the greatest British painter of the last century, unflinching in the way he returned the Gorgon's stare. [*Tate Gallery,* 2000]

■ [Francis] Bacon is almost the only painter who's painted the office world. He likes men in blue suits. Edward Hopper, the American painter, painted people in offices in the 1930s, the Depression era of small American cities and grey skies, but he saw them from the outside. He was always looking at his shirt-sleeved office workers through half-open doors, just as he saw naked women or lonely women through half-open hotel room doors. [*Art Newspaper,* 1999]

ON HELMUT NEWTON

■ Helmut Newton's photographs are stills from an elegant and erotic movie . . . The magic of his art is its complete elusiveness, its cunning refusal to admit the true nature of its subject matter: the failure of reality, and the triumph of desire. ["Lucid Dreamer," 1999]

■ This normalizing of the psychopathic has defused huge areas of the sexually perverse—of the human imagination, generally. Surprisingly, I'm told people are still shocked by Helmut Newton's photography . . . but not by the sexually explicit material that would have shocked them, say, thirty years ago. They're shocked by his voyeuristic, masculinist eye. They're shocked by their sense that this is a man who is degrading women—which is a different matter altogether—you can degrade women just as fiercely when they're fully clothed. I see his photographs as stills in some very elegant movie that might be playing in your local cineplex. In fact, he loved the film of *Crash.* I met him about a month ago, and he said, "You know, that's the sort of film I like." [*Artforum,* 1997]

■ [Newton's] photographs are like stills from a very elegant erotic film. They're charged with narrative possibilities . . . The very mysterious world that he creates: it's elegant, it's curiously sort of asexual . . . I think what Newton does . . . is to desexualize [women] . . . The women are in charge; the men look as if they've got a headache. It is a reversal of conventional roles. [*Art Newspaper,* 1999]

■ By now Newton's world is as recognizable as that of Delvaux or Magritte . . . a company of beautiful women moves through the palatial corridors or gazes into the opaque depths of ornate mirrors, waiting for a last act that will never unfold. Even those women who are naked seem scarcely aware of themselves, as if their sexuality is defused by the strange bedrooms where they wait for the rich and powerful men stepping from their limousines in the courtyards below. The realm that Newton creates for us has the calm light of a lucid dream, glimpsed through a connecting door that links it to the interior space of the Surrealists, to *Last Year at Marienbad* (1961), and the films of Luis Bunuel. [*Bookforum,* 1999]

■ Newton desexualizes his subject matter. His photographs drain the libido from the once charged spaces of the late twentieth century, from hotel bedrooms and luxury bathrooms, and from those penthouse apartments where unwatched porn films play behind the heads of people with more pressing concerns than pleasure or pain. [*Bookforum,* 1999]

■ Since the death of Francis Bacon, the most consistently imaginative—and, in many ways the greatest—visual artist working today is Helmut Newton. [*Artforum*, 1997]

■ Newton has always been very much more than a fashion photographer. I think of him as a figurative artist who uses the medium of photography—and his access to gorgeous women, expensive gowns, and exotic locations—to create a unique imaginative world. [*Bookforum*, 1999]

■ [Helmut Newton's] imaginative universe is extremely sophisticated and highly ambiguous. He has a poetic imagination of a very advanced kind—it's on a par with [Paul] Delvaux. You get a sense of how genuinely provocative his work is when you see others trying to imitate him—David Bailey went through a Newton phase and it was utterly pathetic. [*Frieze*, 1996]

■ I can't think of anyone better [than Helmut Newton]. Certainly not all these installation artists who are pouring out of British art schools. You know, all those sharks in formaldehyde and so on. [*Artforum*, 1997]

■ [Helmut Newton] loved Cronenberg's *Crash* (1996), but one thing bothered him. "The dresses," he whispered. "They were so awful." [*Bookforum*, 1999]

■ Who was there better as a photographer? His influence was just huge. I had only spoken to him very recently on the phone. He and June had gone out to California as they usually did for January. He was a fulfilled man who had drunk from the well of life. No, he wasn't a pornographer and never regarded himself as such. He was a great artist who created amazing dream worlds which touched our deepest fantasies. [*Sunday Times*, 2004]

■ I was a passionate admirer of Helmut. I admired, above all, the power of his imagination. He created a unique dream world using little more than a few beautiful women and a selection of beautiful clothes, and yet that dream world is one of the richest in 20th-century imagination. He was the greatest figurative artist working in his day. Many photographers, including David Bailey, have tried to imitate his uniqueness but not as successfully. [*Sunday Telegraph,* 2004]

■ I talked to Helmut only a few weeks ago when he was in Monte Carlo and just about to leave for Los Angeles. His death is a great loss but at least he lived to a great age and went with some style. He was a delightful companion, mischievous and forever young. I envied him enormously: he spent his life in the company of beautiful women and his own extraordinary dreams. Far from debasing his models, which Newton was sometimes accused of, he placed them at the heart of a deep and complex drama where they rule like errant queens, blissfully indifferent to the few men who dare to approach them. Newton's photography has endured for decades, as poetic and mysterious as when it first appeared in the 1960s. [*Sunday Telegraph,* 2004]

THOUGHTS ON ART

■ One wonders if photography is the Cyclops eye of the late 20th century, recording everything but seeing nothing. [*Daily Telegraph,* 1992]

■ The planet drowns in an ocean of photographic emulsion. [*Daily Telegraph,* 1992]

■ The more civilized we are, the fewer moral choices we have to make. But part of the mind atrophies. A moral calculus that took thousands of years to develop starts to wither from neglect. Once you dispense with morality, the important decisions become a matter of *aesthetics.* [*Super-Cannes,* 2000]

■ I commissioned [copies] of two paintings by Paul Delvaux which were destroyed in the Blitz. I thought it would be rather nice . . . to bring them back to life. A similar sort of principle is at work in a lot of my fiction. It's the whole principle of biographical fiction, isn't it: reconstructing a lost original? [*Sunday Times*, 1990]

■ I hate the phrase "Pop Art" because it has the wrong connotations. The British and American Pop Artists, or people close to them, like [Richard] Hamilton and [Eduardo] Paolozzi over here, and [Tom] Wesselmann, [James] Rosenquist and [Andy] Warhol above all, [were] a tremendous influence on me. [intv David Pringle, 1975]

■ [Paolozzi] used to wander around car wreckyards and yards full of old shipping machinery in Scotland and the like, finding old gear wheels and bits of machine detritus and he'd assemble them into these extraordinary figures. These are powerful, twentieth-century archetypes. When you see them actually standing as they stood in the outdoors on the grass . . . you feel you are arriving at some place where these ancient figures, these Easter Island totems made of machine parts, are waiting for you. [*Art Newspaper*, 1999]

■ Paolozzi's work is somewhere between circuitry and organics, a hybrid. [*Art Newspaper*, 1999]

■ I like traditional museums, the less frequented the better . . . I remember the Louvre in 1949 when it was completely deserted, whereas today it is a theme-park where you can enjoy "the Mona Lisa experience." This isn't only a matter of funding. Museum directors enjoy being impresarios, guru-figures manipulating the imaginations of the public. [intv Hans Obrist, 2003.]

■ Museums shouldn't be *too* popular. The experience within the Louvre or the National Gallery should be challenging and unsettling, and take years to absorb. The Italians had the right idea. Most of their paintings were in dimly lit churches, uncleaned and difficult to see. As a result, the Renaissance endured for centuries. [*Ibid,* 2003]

■ One could argue that today's Turner prize and the exhibitions of work by Damien Hirst, Tracey Emin and the Chapman brothers perform exactly the same role, that they are elaborate attempts to test the psychology of today's public. [*Ibid,* 2003]

■ We have to set people free from all this culture and education . . . they're just ways of trapping the middle class and making them docile. [*Millennium People,* 2003]

■ In the years leading up to the abolition of censorship in the late Sixties, filmmakers and writers and artists were all pushing against those barriers. But since then we have been fighting back against something different—against the all-pervasive entertainment culture and the sentimentalized values of TV blandness. People are searching for truth through trying to shock, although it may sometimes be an *artificial truth* that they find. [*Observer,* 2000]

■ I'm tempted to say that the psychological test is the only function of today's art shows, and that the aesthetic elements have been reduced to almost zero. It no longer seems possible to shock people by aesthetic means, as did the Impressionists, Picasso and Matisse, among many others. In fact, it no longer seems possible to touch people's imaginations by aesthetic means. [intv Hans Obrist, 2003]

■ I admire the British installation artist Tracey Emin for her beautiful breasts and the traces of her bodily fluids smeared across her sheets . . . I also admire the British Pop artist Richard Hamilton and his great Homage to the Chrysler Corporation (painted 40 years ago). [letter, 2003]

■ Mainstream entertainment is so manufactured now and this is what extreme artists are kicking against. As a result of, many younger writers and filmmakers are now simply expressing

their own obsessions; that is all that is left that they feel they can say something truthful about. They don't want to accept the values imposed on them by adverts and entertainment corporations—and on the whole that is a good thing. (However, it is all too easy to exploit shock tactics:) After all, any drunk on an airplane can lean over and vomit on you, and there is nothing original in that. [*Observer,* 2000]

■ **Try bad taste.** [*Millennium People,* 2003]

MUSIC

■ I think I'm the only person I know who doesn't own a record player or a single record. I've never understood why, because my maternal grandparents were lifelong teachers of music, and my father as a choir boy once sang solo in Manchester Cathedral. But that gene seems to have skipped me. [*Paris Review,* 1984]

■ **I've a tin ear, I'm afraid. I've never bought a single record, cassette, CD or whatever. I don't own a record player of any kind . . . It's a big defect, I admit. If my girlfriend's playing Mozart or Serge Gainsbourg's lovely songs, I enjoy them tremendously. But on my own I've never felt the need—I don't know why. It's just some gene that skipped me.** [*NME,* 1996]

■ [At] an outdoor festival somewhere near Brighton, I was doing a reading, and so was William Burroughs. When I arrived, the Hell's Angels security guards said to me, "Dad, you're in the wrong place." [*Q magazine,* 1995]

■ **Obviously, through the '60s I listened to the Beatles and the Stones. I never met any of them, but I saw them around. One or two of the Stones would go to the ICA. There was a nice scene then— pop stars would go to publishers' parties because publishing became a branch of the fashion industry in the '60s.** [*New Musical Express,* 1996]

■ I often listen to classical music on the radio, though never as background. I can't stand people who switch on the record player as soon as you arrive. Either we listen to Mozart or Vivaldi, or we talk. It seems daft to try to do them together, any more than one would hold a conversation during a screening of *Casablanca*. In fact, without thinking I usually stop talking altogether, waiting for the music to finish, to the host's puzzlement. [*Paris Review*, 1984]

■ Popular icons monitor the changes in the cultural landscape and the changes in popular culture far more effectively than any politician. Music is the carrier wave and on it is modulated all this fascinating stuff—what I call the *real news*. [*New Musical Express*, 1985]

■ Punk was so interesting—I still haven't recovered from it. [*New Musical Express*, 1985]

■ Punk: the radical will meets driving ambition. [*Face*, 1987]

■ Not knowing anything about [Punk] music, I saw it as a purely political movement—the powerful political and social resentment of an under-caste who reacted to the values of bourgeois society with pure destructiveness and hate. Bourgeois society offered them the mortgage, they offered back psychosis. [*New Musical Express*, 1985]

■ For me the intentions of background music are openly political, and an example of how political power is constantly shifting from the ballot box into areas where the voter has nowhere to mark his ballot paper. The most important political choices in the future will probably never be consciously exercised. I'm intrigued by the way some background music is surprisingly aggressive, especially that played on consumer complaint phone lines and banks, airplanes and phone companies themselves, with strident non-rhythmic and arms-length sequences that are definitely not user-friendly. [*Elevator Music*, 1993]

■ There's no music in my work. The most beautiful music in the world is the sound of machine guns. [*Face*, 1987]

■ Kurt Weill's "Surabaya Johnny" boomed from the CD player propped against the pillows. Jane swayed around the bedroom, a lurid figure in a spangled crimson minidress and stiletto heels. A frizz of lacquered black hair rose in a retro-punk blaze from her forehead, above kohled eyes and a lipsticked mouth like a wound. [*Super-Cannes,* 2000]

■ I love the songs of Serge Gainsbourg. [letter, 2003]

■ Amplified 100,000 times animal cell division sounds like a lot of girders and steel sheets being ripped apart—how did you put it?—a car smash in slow motion. On the other hand, plant cell division is an electronic poem, all soft chords and bubbling tones. Now there you have a perfect illustration of how microsonics can reveal the distinction between the animal and plant kingdoms. ["Track 12," 1967]

■ He played with a battery-powered tape-recorder which had been mixed up with the child's toys. He recorded his grunts and belches, playing them back to himself. Wilder was amused by the deft way in which he edited the tape, overlaying one set of belches with a second and third. [*High Rise,* 1975]

■ Laing returned to the kitchen and listened to the water-pipes [of the high rise], part of a huge acoustic system operated by thousands of stops, this dying musical instrument they had once all played together. [*High Rise,* 1975]

■ The tall aloof physician, eyes forever hidden behind the dark glasses that seemed to emphasize his closed inner life, spent most of his time sitting in the white-domed auditorium of the School of Fine Arts, playing through the Bartok and Webern quartets. ["The Day of Forever," 1966]

■ An adolescent girl in a white bikini crossed the street at the traffic lights, a violin case in one hand, a hamburger in the other. [*Cocaine Nights,* 1996]

■ Lorraine Drexel: This elegant and autocratic creature in a cartwheel hat, with her eyes like black orchids, was a sometime model and intimate of Giacometti and John Cage . . . Most of her sculpture to date had been scored for various Tantric and Hindu hymns, and I remembered her brief affair with a world-famous pop singer, later killed in a car crash, who had been an enthusiastic devotee of the sitar. ["Venus Smiles," 1957]

■ She told me her name was Jane Ciracylides and that she was a specialty singer . . . Jane created a sensation. After her performance 300 people swore they'd seen everything from a choir of angels taking the vocal in the music of the spheres to Alexander's Ragtime Band. ["Prima Belladonna," 1956]

■ Sonic sculpture was now nearing the apogee of its abstract phase; twelve-tone blips and zooms were all that most statues emitted. No purely representational sound . . . with a Mozart rondo or (better) a Webern quartet, had been built for ten years. ["The Singing Statues, 1962]

Desert Island Discs: J.G. Ballard's choices

The Teddy Bears' Picnic (Bratton/Kennedy)

Don't Fence Me In (Cole Porter) performed by Bing Crosby & The Andrews Sisters

Put the Blame on Mame (Fisher/Roberts) performed by Rita Hayworth

Falling In Love Again (Hollander/Connelly) performed by Marlene Dietrich

The Marriage of Figaro (extract from) (Mozart)

The Girl from Ipanema (Antonio Carlos Jobim)

The Barber of Seville (extract from) (Rossini)

Let's Do It (Cole Porter/Peter Matz) performed by Noel Coward

—BBC Radio 4, 2/2/1992

■ The final triumph of ultrasonic music had come with a second development—the short-playing record, spinning at 900 rpm, which condensed the 45 minutes of a Beethoven symphony to 20 seconds of playing time, the three hours of a Wagner opera to little more than two minutes . . . One 30-second SP record delivered as much neurophonic pleasure as a natural length recording, but with deeper penetration, greater total impact. ["The Sound-Sweep," 1960]

■ Since the introduction a few years earlier of ultrasonic music, the human voice—indeed, audible music of any type—had gone completely out of fashion. Ultrasonic music, employing a vastly greater range of octaves, chords and chromatic scales than are audible by the human ear, provided a direct neural link between the sound stream and the auditory loves, generating an apparently sourceless sensation of harmony, rhythm, cadence and melody uncontaminated by the noise and vibration of audible music. ["The Sound-Sweep," 1960]

■ The re-scoring of the classical repertoire allowed the ultrasonic audience the best of both worlds. The majestic rhythms of Beethoven, the popular melodies of Tchaikovsky, the complex fugal elaborations of Bach, the abstract images of Schoenberg—all these were raised in frequency above the threshold of conscious audibility. Not only did they become inaudible, but the original works were re-scored for the much wider range of the ultrasonic orchestra, became richer in texture, more profound in theme, more sensitive, tender or lyrical as the ultrasonic arranger chose. ["The Sound-Sweep," 1960]

■ In the age of noise, the tranquilizing balms of silence began to be rediscovered. ["The Sound-Sweep," 1960]

■ I'm an old man now and I prefer silence. [letter, 2003]

■ Technology defines the conventions by which we recognize the world. [*Sight and Sound,* 1996]

■ I'm very interested in technology, and the way that cars, highways, skyscrapers, TV, the Internet, mobile phones all act as facilitators, making possible the emergence of new kinds of psychological traffic, revealing to us the latent possibilities within our minds. [letter, 2003]

■ In the case of the helicopter, with its unstable, insect-like obsessiveness, we can see clearly the deep hostility of the mineral world. [*Atrocity Exhibition,* 1990]

■ Many of the transformations made in our lives by science and technology are not visible ones—people aren't aware of the changes that have taken place. Not just the physical landscape has changed, nor its hidden dangers of the kind I've written about in *Crash, Concrete Island,* and *High-Rise,* but a whole new sensibility is being created that people aren't aware of. [*Thrust,* 1980]

■ Real change is largely invisible, as befits this age of invisible technology, and people have embraced VCRs, fax machines, word processors without a thought, along with the new social habits that have sprung up around them. [*Atrocity Exhibition,* 1990]

■ We live in a world which is now entirely artificial, almost as though we were living inside an enormous novel. You have dozens of little machines in your kitchen, in your living room. The range of machinery that surrounds us is quite incredible. [*Fineline Features Online,* 2002]

■ The processes of 20th century technology are continually laying down their own simultaneous fossils, that form ciphers in our minds like the invisible stars of radio galaxies. Computer punchtape, old telephone manuals, printed circuitry whose alphabets have died, the luminescent bodies of dead spacemen—all these form part of the astronomy of dreams that fill our heads. [unknown]

■ Science now, in fact, is the largest producer of fiction. A hundred years ago, or even fifty years ago even, science took its raw material from nature. A scientist worked out the boiling point of a gas or the distance a star is away from the Earth, whereas nowadays, particularly in the social, psychological sciences, the raw material of science is a fiction invented by the scientists. You know, they work out why people chew gum or something of this kind . . . so the psychological and social sciences are spewing out an enormous amount of fiction. They're the major producers of fiction. It's not the writers anymore. [*Speculation*, 1969]

■ I'm not hostile to science itself. I think that scientific activity is about the only mature activity there is. What I'm hostile to is the image of science that people have. It becomes a magic wand in people's minds, that will conjure up marvels, a kind of Aladdin's lantern. It oversimplifies things much too conveniently. [*Speculation*, 1969]

■ [Science] assumes that we are largely rational creatures, driven by calculated self-interest at the group or personal level. But this isn't true, as a million novels, case histories and court transcripts illustrate. [*London Daily Telegraph*, n.d.]

■ Science and reason have had their day; their place is the museum. [*Rushing to Paradise*, 1994]

■ Science is now more and more taking its subject matter not from nature as in the traditional physical sciences, but from the obsessions of its own practitioners. [*Mississippi Review*, 1991]

■ Bizarre experiments are now a commonplace of scientific research. [*Atrocity Exhibition*, 1990]

■ Pangbourne belonged to the new generation of gynecologists who never actually touched their patients, let alone delivered a child. His specialty was the computerized analysis of recorded birth-cries, from which he could diagnose an infinity of complaints to come. He played with these tapes like an earlier generation of sorcerers examining the patterns of entrails. [*High Rise,* 1975]

■ Every morning when [they] get up people will dial the clinic and log in their health data ... Professor Kalman is very keen on faecal smears, but I suspect that's one test too far. He hates the idea of all that used toilet paper going to waste. The greatest diagnostic tool in the world is literally being flushed down the lavatory. [*Super-Cannes,* 2002]

■ Some of the scientific research that is done in specialized laboratories on topics like the psychology of air-crash victims is—first—horrific beyond parody. But it's almost a kind of nightmare fiction in its own right. It's a kind of pornography of science, issuing from these specialized laboratories which I've parodied in some of my stories. [*Twilight Zone,* 1988]

■ Science and pornography will eventually meet and fuse. [*Atrocity Exhibition,* 1990]

■ Conceivably, the day will come when science is itself the greatest producer of pornography. The weird perversions of human behavior triggered by psychologists testing the effects of pain, isolation, anger, etc., will play the same role that the bare breasts of Polynesian islanders performed in 1940s wildlife documentary films. [*Atrocity Exhibition,* 1990]

■ Most of the machines that surround our lives—airliners, refrigerators, cars and [computers]—have streamlined their way into our affections. [*Atrocity Exhibition,* 1990]

■ A fair-skinned man in a turquoise Club Nautico tracksuit was playing against the machine as it fired balls across the net, barrel set to swing at random. . . He was urging on the machine, willing it to beat him, beaming with pleasure when an ace knocked the racket from his hand. Yet I felt that the real duel taking place was not between man and machine, but between rival factions within his own head. [*Cocaine Nights,* 1996]

■ I chose the South of France [as a setting for *Super-Cannes*] because it is probably the nearest Europe has to Silicon Valley. The South of France is a hi-tech zone of advanced science parks and industrial estates. And it is very interesting to see the old pleasure-ground of fifty years ago become a great advanced work-ground. [BBC Online Live Chat, 2002]

■ The new technology of computers and word processors does create a new set of values which you can perceive actually when you go to a big international airport or a [supermarket]. It's this new landscape of values that needs to be tracked. Do we owe more allegiance to multinational companies or to royalty? Do I owe more to Avis Rent-a-Car or to Queen Elizabeth II?—after all, it's now the multinationals who provide the empire on which the sun never sets. [*New Musical Express,* 1985]

■ Maybe future historians will look back on the 20th century and dismiss the entire artistic fields of fiction, poetry or the visual arts as completely irrelevant and as having no value whatsoever; where the greatest achievements of the human imagination in the 20th century took place in the sciences. And they'd probably be right. [ZG, n.d.]

■ [The future is] going to be commercial and nasty at the same time, like the "Rite of Spring" in Disney's *Fantasia.* One's going to need educated feet to get out of the way. In the past, one could invoke "sympathy for the devil" with fancy footwork, but in future times, our internal devils and angels may simultaneously destroy and renew us through the technological overload we have invoked. [*Heavy Metal,* 1982]

■ One has to immerse oneself in the threatening possibilities offered by modern science and technology, and try to swim to the other end of the pool. [*Paris Review,* 1984]

■ Clocks and watches are now far more accurate than we need them to be in our daily lives. Many atomic clocks keep virtually perfect time, and minute inaccuracies are probably the fault of the solar system. Perhaps this need to be in possession of the exact time reflects some fault in our perception of the world, and a defect in our grasp of space-time. [*Impressions of Speed,* 1998]

■ A lot of people misread Kafka in that they assume that in describing his particularly nightmarish world he saw it in an exclusively unfavorable light. I think it had invaded him, and this vast bureaucracy which is so impenetrable, whose value system is so totally elusive, had enfolded him, and the whole power of his fiction rises from this ambivalent response. I'd like to think that I've done the same for technology in novels like *Crash, High-Rise* and *The Atrocity Exhibition*—I hope I've managed to communicate the same ambivalence, in that one has to embrace the possibilities offered by technology, however threatening they may be. We must immerse ourselves in the threatening possibilities in which we're suspended to have a hope of swimming through to the other end. [*New Musical Express,* 1985]

■ A typewriter types us, encoding its own linear bias across the free space of the imagination. ["Project for a Glossary of the 20th Century," *Zone,* 1992]

■ [For Science-Fiction Writers] Science serves much the same role as did psychoanalysis for the Surrealists—a *standpoint* rather than a subject matter. [*Guardian,* n.d.]

■ The age of sophistication is over . . . the benevolent technologies that govern our lives are happy to welcome the era of the naive. ["Peddling Comic Strips: Steven Spielberg," 1997]

■ Modern technology was empowering people's worst impulses. ["Prophet with Honour," n.d.]

■ Science and technology multiply around us. To an increasing extent they dictate the languages in which we speak and think. Either we use those languages, or we remain mute. [Introduction to *Crash*, 1974, reprinted in *RE/Search #8/9*.]

THE SPACE AGE

■ [Rockets] belong to the age of the 19th century, along with the huge steam engines. It's brute-force ballistic technology that has nothing to do with what people recognize as the characteristic technology of this century: microprocessors, microwave data links—everything that goes in the world at the speed of an electron. [*Seconds*, 1996]

■ The Space Age lasted about ten years. [intv David Pringle, 1975]

■ The suspicion dawned that Outer Space might be—dare one say it—boring. Having expended all these billions of dollars on getting to the Moon, we found on our arrival that there wasn't very much to do there. ["One Dull Step For Man," 1997]

■ I always prophesied that the Space Age was over. They should build spaceships of rice-paper and bamboo, decorated with poems. [*Science Fiction Eye*, 1991]

■ It may be possible that the human central nervous system doesn't have a designed capacity to explore Outer Space. Zero gravity perhaps recapitulates on the unconscious level various archaic fears in the human mind—falling off the branch into the jaws of the predator below. There's all sorts of psychological reasons why we may not be suited as a species for space travel. [*Seconds*, 1996]

■ It may be that extreme fear is a built-in extra that can never be erased from space flight. Perhaps the prolonged periods of zero-gravity recapitulate states of infantile dependency, or stir frightening memories of our earlier arboreal existence when the weightlessness of free fall generally ended in a waiting predator's jaws. ["One Dull Step for Man," 1997]

■ Will NASA one day evolve into a religious organization? [*"The Object of the Attack,"* 1984]

■ The latent conundrums at the heart of the space program— those psychological dimensions that had been ignored from its start and subsequently revealed, too late, in the crack-ups of the early astronauts, their slides into mysticism and melancholia. [*War Fever*, 1990]

■ What happened to the Space Age? Its once heroic vision of our planetary future now seems little more than a mirage, fading across the sandbars and concrete of Cape Kennedy like the ghost of a forgotten advertising campaign for last year's science-fiction blockbuster. ["One Dull Step for Man," 1997]

■ Far from lasting for hundreds of years, as seemed likely in 1957, [the Space Age] may have lasted for barely 15, from Gargarin's flight in 1961 to the Skylab splashdown in 1974 that was the first *not* to be shown live on TV, because the American networks realized that the public was bored. [*Ibid*]

■ A curious feature of the Space Age was its lack of any real spin-off, its failure to excite the public imagination, to influence fashion, consumer design or architecture. How different from the Thirties, when the great record-breaking attempts, the ever faster trains, planes and racing cars, exerted an enormous influence on consumer design, streamlining everything from department stores to teapots. [*Ibid*]

■ *Barbarella* treated the dream of space travel as a camp joke. It had nothing to do with reality. There is something faintly comic about the real space program. It does look vaguely adolescent, which the pioneering aviation flights never did. There was nothing adolescent about [Charles] Lindbergh [1902–1974] flying the Atlantic with just a package of sandwiches and his own determination. [*Seconds,* 1996]

■ **The best astronauts never dream.** ["Memories of the Space Age," 1990]

■ The highly controlled, limited environment; the time distortion; the intense subjectivity—it's an asexual and antisocial environment—all these together may make Space Travel not a dream of the future, but a half-remembered nightmare from the past. [*Seconds,* 1996]

■ **To get beyond the solar system means a commitment to a one-way trip. Not many people are prepared to spend their lives in a spaceship that will never return.** [*Seconds,* 1996]

■ The satellite information relays that transmitted the images of Armstrong landing on the moon themselves made the whole exercise redundant and out-of-date. [*I-D,* 1987]

■ **One of the reasons why the public has shown a lack of interest in the space program (which necessitated this poor school teacher going to her death as part of a public-relations exercise) is that the nuts-and-bolts of these ballistic missiles belong to the world of Jules Verne and of the 19th-century engineering pioneers, not to the really advanced technologies. The space program is simply old-fashioned.** [*Interzone,* 1987]

■ The reason why the space program as a whole failed to touch the popular imagination was that people perceived it as belonging to a kind of nineteenth-century heavy engineering technology—a technology of giant engines and vast outputs of physical power belonging really to that age which threw railroads across the world and liners across the oceans. The Apollo program's Saturn rockets represented not the start of a new era but the end of an old one. People already knew that the future of technology lay in invisible streams of data . . . to produce an invisible loom of world commerce and information. They knew at the time of the Apollo landings that this was already a nostalgic enterprise. [*I-D*, 1987]

■ **NASA should be closed down. They've served their purpose. They're just going to go on killing astronauts.** [*Times*, 2003]

■ I'm afraid that since the first man landed on the moon in 1969 it has been downhill all the way. It was quite obvious that these monsters could never launch enough men and equipment into space to maintain large space stations, either in orbit or on the moon's surface. They thought in terms of jut-jawed heroes out of Science-Fiction comics. If you think of the navigators of the 14th and 15th centuries, they were a collection of fanatics, eccentrics and dreamers. But there were no madmen on the early spacecraft. NASA's astronauts were completely unpoetic. [*Times*, 2003]

■ **Space is a totally alien environment. It's probably a waste of time going. People now realize that the moon is about as interesting as an old gravel quarry. There's nothing there.** [*Times*, 2003]

■ (American taxpayers spend $14.5 billion a year on NASA, which Ballard terms:) the most expensive bus route in history. [*Times*, 2003]

■ **"Columbus," Andre Breton once wrote, "had to sail with madmen to discover America."** ["One Dull Step For Man," 1997]

■ *Life* magazine happily appeared on the scene with a $500,000 offer for the astronauts' exclusive stories—their annual pay at the time averaged $8000 . . . As for the wives, looking at the group photograph on the *Life* cover with its heading "Seven Brave Women behind the Astronauts": "They hardly recognized each other. *Life* had retouched the faces of all of them practically down to the bone. Every suggestion of an electrolysis line, a furze of moustache, a crack in the lipstick, a rogue cilia of hair, an uneven set of the lips had disappeared in the magic of photo-retouching." [review of Tom Wolfe's *The Right Stuff, Guardian,* 1979]

■ Is pondering upon the universe really thinking on the largest possible scale? It may be a disguised way of thinking small—for all that superabundance of light years, an infinitude of nothingness is still nothing. [review of Robert Zubrin's *The Case for Mars*]

■ **Has a sex act, of any kind, ever taken place in space?** [*Ibid.*]

■ "Being on the moon?" [The astronaut's] tired gaze inspected the narrow street of cheap jewelry stores, with its office messengers and lottery touts, the off-duty taxi drivers leaning against their cars. "It was just like being here." ["The Man Who Walked on the Moon," 1985]

■ **Our fellow pedestrians had become remote and fleeting figures, little more than tricks of the sun. Sometimes, I could no longer see their faces. It was then that I . . . knew what it was to be an astronaut.** ["The Man Who Walked on the Moon," 1990]

■ "Clearly the police don't bother to come to Cape Canaveral anymore." "I don't blame them. It's an evil place." ["Memories of the Space Age," 1982]

■ **Think of the universe as a simultaneous structure. Everything that's ever happened, all the events that will ever happen, are taking place together . . . Our sense of our own identity, the stream of things going on around us, are a kind of optical illusion.** ["Myths of the Near Future," 1994]

■ Perhaps, for the central nervous system, space was not a linear structure at all, but a model for an advanced condition of time, a metaphor for eternity which they were wrong to try to grasp. ["Myths of the Near Future," 1982]

■ ... you remember the reports of the Russian cosmonaut Ilyushin going insane. ["Journey Across a Crater," 1971]

■ The Russian astronaut Col. Komarov was the first man to die in space, though earlier fatalities had been rumored. Komarov was reported to have panicked when his space-craft began to tumble uncontrollably. [*Atrocity Exhibition,* 1990]

■ We had to get out of time—that's what the Space Program was all about. ["Memories of the Space Age," 1982]

■ Flight and time . . . they're bound together. The birds have always known that. To get out of time we first need to learn to fly. ["Memories of the Space Age," 1982]

■ The successful landing on the Moon, after some half-dozen fatal attempts—at least three of the luckless pilots were still orbiting the Moon in their dead ships—was the culmination of an age-old ambition with profound psychological implications for mankind . . . ["A Question of Re-Entry," 1963]

■ The space-craft and satellites had been launched because their flights satisfied certain buried compulsions and desires, [but] there was no need for these insane projections. [*Ibid.*]

■ All those *I Love Lucys* have reached Alpha Centauri and they're moving on. Maybe we're going to colonize the universe with our sit-coms and our late-night chat shows. [*Seconds,* 1996]

■ Perhaps the collective dream of mankind is the electromagnetic sphere of the planet's television signals expanding confidently across the universe . . . even now bringing to the natives of Proxima Centauri their first episodes of *Dallas* and the Reagan inauguration—dreams of the new Babylon that would take a Daniel to unravel. [*Guardian,* 1986]

■ You could say that the human race is at this very moment colonizing space in terms of that huge expanding sphere, now about eighty light years in diameter, composed of its television and radio signals. In the future we human beings won't need to travel, we'll just send our TV programs! [*Interzone,* 1987]

DISEASES, MEDICINE

■ [AIDS] does seem like a designer disease. It's as though our hour has come. The disease has provided a kind of underpinning to the whole processes of alienation that have been taking place in our culture in the last ten years, to my mind. AIDS seems to put a cap on it. Whenever the population density increases, in order to hang on to their mental space, people do tend to retreat into their own inward mental worlds or spaces. It seems inevitable. [*ZG,* n.d.]

■ He remembered the mongol and autistic children he had left behind in the clinic in Vancouver, and his firm belief—strongly contested by his fellow physicians and the worn-out parents—that these were diseases of time, malfunctions of the temporal sense that marooned these children on small islands of awareness, a few minutes in the case of the mongols, a span of micro-seconds for the autistics. ["Memories of the Space Age, 1982]

■ The institutions of marriage and the family, ideals of parenthood, and the social contract between the sexes, even the physical relationship between man and woman had been corrupted by this cruel disease [AIDS]. ["Love in a Colder Climate," 1989]

■ Terrified of infection, people learned to abstain from every kind of physical or sexual contact. From puberty onward, an almost

invisible cordon divided the sexes. In offices, factories, schools and universities the young men and women kept their distance . . . too often, courtship and marriage would be followed by a series of mysterious ailments, anxious visits to a test clinic, a positive diagnosis and the terminal hospice. ["Love in a Colder Climate," 1989]

■ In a TV interview a few years ago, the wife of a famous Beverly Hills plastic surgeon revealed that throughout their marriage her husband had continually re-styled her face and body, pointing a breast here, tucking in a nostril there. She seemed supremely confident of her attractions. But as she said: "He will never leave me, because he can always change me." [*Atrocity Exhibition,* 1990]

■ The smallpox virus is constantly mutating. We have to make sure that our supplies of vaccine are up-to-date. So the W.H.O. was careful never to completely abolish the disease. It deliberately allowed smallpox to flourish in a remote corner of a Third World country, so that it could keep an eye on how the virus was evolving. Sadly, a few people went on dying, and are still dying to this day. But it's worth it for the rest of the world. ["War Fever," 1989]

OUTDATED TECHNOLOGY

■ The rail-train, like the wind-powered yacht and pedal-driven glider, should have been abandoned years ago, when advances in technology made possible their evolution into the helicopter, the speedboat and the supersonic airliner. In technological terms they represent an artificially perpetuated childhood. [*Speed-Visions of an Accelerated Age,* 1998]

■ Enthusiastically carrying out what they do best and we do worst—high-speed mathematical computation [computers] may have overshot the mark and will soon find that they are little more than indentured clerks, endlessly adding up figures in their electronic ledgers.

Thirty years from now they will probably regroup, slow themselves down and mount a more subtle takeover bid. [*Speed-Visions,* 1998]

■ We live in a world of manufactured goods that have no individual identity until something forlorn or tragic happens, because every one is like every other one. One is constantly struck by the fact that some old refrigerator glimpsed in a back alley has much more identity than the identical model sitting in our kitchen. Nothing is more poignant than a field full of wrecked cars, because they've taken on a unique identity that they never had in life. [*21C,* 1997]

■ There is a deep melancholy about fields full of old machinery or wrecked cars because they seem to challenge the assumptions of a civilization based on an all-potent technology. These machine graveyards warn us that nothing endures. [*21C,* 1997]

■ [About the strange paradoxes implicit in a field of cars, washing machines, or whatever has been junked there:] The rules which govern the birth and life and decay of living systems don't apply in the realm of technology. A washing machine does not grow old gracefully. It still retains its youth, as it were, its bright chrome trim, when it's been junked . . . All these inversions touch a response to the movements of time and our place in the universe. [intv David Pringle, 1975]

■ I'm always struck by the enormous sort of magic and poetry one feels when looking at a junkyard filled with old washing machines, or wrecked cars, or old ships rotting in some disused harbor. An enormous mystery and magic surrounds these objects . . . This very touching poetry is completely absent, say, from a brand-new plane or a brand-new washing machine in a showroom, or a brand-new motorcar in a local garage window. [*RE/Search #8/9,* 1984]

BIOTECHNOLOGY, CLONING

■ When people have complete mastery of their own biologies, genetic selection will allow parents to choose all the mental and physical qualities of their offspring. Maybe parents will reject most of the children they conceive because the children will not match the ideals of their child profile. So people may go through their whole lifetime wanting but not having a child. [*Blitz*, 1984]

■ He stated that synthetic DNA introduced into the human germ plasm would arrest the process of ageing and extend human life almost indefinitely. ["Answers to a Questionnaire," 1985]

■ Suppose that many of us were replicas of each other, sharing the same tricks of character, the same taste for Hitchcock films, Morgan sports cars and holidays in the Maldives . . . such speculations are no longer idle mind-games, or the fantasies of Science Fiction. [*Sunday Times Bookshop,* 1997]

■ When the most famous lamb in history emerged into the world in 1996, she brought with her a host of ethical and scientific dilemmas. The modest shed where she was born, near the Roslin Institute in Scotland, may prove to be one of the most significant sites of the scientific imagination, along with the Cavendish Laboratory in Cambridge where Watson and Crick deciphered the codes of life, or the Pacific atoll where the first hydrogen bomb successfully mimicked the sun, or even Freud's consulting rooms in Vienna, where a vast detonation of a different kind destroyed the notion that our conscious minds *alone* define who we are. [*Sunday Times Bookshop,* 1997]

■ I don't object to cloning, even of human beings—who, after all, are almost identical anyway! [*Disturb,* n.d.]

AMERICA

■ Americans themselves are not in the least awe-struck by their own super-abundance, and in fact take it completely for granted. They expect a refrigerator to have an automatic ice-cube maker, just as they expect a car to have a powerful heater and a four-speaker sound system. The richest society is one where everyone is a millionaire but unaware of the fact; a state like that already exists on the Upper East Side of New York. [intv Zinovy Zinik, 1998]

■ Americans are highly moralistic, and any kind of moral ambiguity irritates them. As a result they completely fail to understand themselves, which is one of their strengths. [*Literary Review*, 2001]

■ [America] can't face anything. It couldn't face Vietnam, it couldn't face Watergate, it cannot face the fact that America is a largely corrupt society. That is why Americans have turned to fantasy. [*NME*, 10/22/1983]

■ There's a tremendous strain of idealism in Americans—one of their greatest strengths, actually—that demands that there is always an acceptable explanation for behavior. I can imagine Oprah Winfrey interviewing Hitler or Goebbels, and saying, "Let's bring this anti-semitism thing into perspective." As if in some way, by analyzing their childhoods or getting them to be frank, one could somehow defuse the threat posed by unreconstructed anti-semitism. [*Frieze*, 1996]

■ Ultimately, I think this idealism is a refusal to look evil in the face and admit that apparently normal people are capable of appalling acts of cruelty [which psychoanalysis cannot shed any light on]. [*Frieze*, 1996]

■ The American dream is of an enormous nipple pressing to our lips its over-sweet milk. We suck contentedly, unafraid of the comic-book demons who howl through our sleeping brains. [letter, 2003]

■ The American Dream has run out of gas. The car has stopped. It no longer supplies the world with its images, its dreams, its fantasies. No more. It's over. It supplies the world with its nightmares now: the Kennedy assassination, Watergate, Vietnam. [*Métaphores #7*, 1983]

■ [The middle class] has no job security, just as the old proletariat did not. They have an education that doesn't equip them for anything much, like the old proletariat getting a craft skill that's no longer needed ... All the privileges that came the way of the middle-class salarist have been lost. More and more, they can't afford private education .. . private medical treatment. So [*Millennium People*] envisages middle-class dissatisfaction reaching crisis point—when they reach that moment where you start overturning cars. [*Independent on Sunday*, 2003]

■ Everything's designed to be bland, homogenized, user-friendly. It's all part of the con, isn't it? Part of the whole project of turning us into docile, uncomplaining wage-slaves. [*Independent on Sunday*, 2003]

■ The United States had based itself on the proposition that everyone should be able to live out his furthest fantasies, wherever they might lead; explore every opportunity, however bizarre. [*Hello America*, 1981]

LOS ANGELES

■ [Los Angeles is] an infinitely mysterious city, right on the edge of the Third World. Driving around there I felt that the Mexican/American border, roughly speaking, ran along Wilshire Boulevard. [*Mississippi Review*, 1991]

■ American writers, painters and filmmakers set off for Los Angeles 50 years ago, abandoning Chicago and New York, because they guessed that Southern California's amorphous sprawl contained the key to America's future. [*Tate,* 2001]

■ My copy of the *Los Angeles Yellow Pages,* which I stole some years ago from the Beverly Hilton Hotel, lists more psychiatrists than plumbers, and more marriage counselors than electricians. ["Book of the Century," 1998]

■ When the devil takes you up to a high place at the end of the century, and offers you all the kingdoms of the earth, you may well find yourself on Mulholland Drive. [*Observer,* 1998]

■ The San Fernando Valley, the dead lands of Burbank and Sherman Oaks [are] hell on earth to social historians but a powerful magnet for most of the people on this planet, who long to be part of its suburban dream. [*Observer,* 1998]

■ Dreams die hard. Forty years after seeing *Sunset Boulevard,* I at last swam in a Hollywood pool. The water was colder than I expected, but I was sure that the pool pump recirculated only the finest perfumes and aftershaves that Rodeo Drive could provide. Later, I stood on my hotel balcony with a Warners publicist, who almost had a heart attack when I confessed that on my unchaperoned Sunday I had driven to Watts. I pointed to the luxury houses on the slopes of Beverly Hills. "Who lives there?" I asked. "Today? Mostly industrialists." "What do they make?" I pressed, "Films?" He thought for a moment, "No. Airplane parts." [*Observer,* 1998]

■ "What would it cost to die here?" I asked the receptionist. She wasn't fazed for a second. "It depends—what sort of death do you have in mind?" [*New Statesman,* 1999]

TRAVEL & TOURISM

■ Travel: Is it a kind of confidence trick? The same hotels, the same marinas, car-rental firms. You might as well stay home and watch it on television. [*Millennium People,* 2003]

■ It may be that the era of cheap travel will come to an end, and that travel will become extremely expensive again—as it was, say, in the Middle Ages, when for an artisan or a parish priest to journey from Edinburgh to London, or from Frankfurt to Paris, a journey of a few hundred miles, he probably consumed a year's income. That may happen again. [*Thrust,* 1980]

■ Today's tourist goes nowhere . . . All the upgrades in existence lead to the same airports and resort hotels, the same *pina colada* bullshit . . . Travel is the last fantasy the 20th Century left us, the delusion that going somewhere helps you reinvent yourself . . . There's nowhere to go. The planet is full. [*Millennium People,* 2003]

■ Jetliners, the color-coordinated nature trail and the Holiday Inn mean that travel has almost died out and been replaced by tourism. [*Literary Review,* 2001]

■ Tourists are a very odd phenomenon. Millions of people crossing the world to wander around unfamiliar cities. Tourism must be the last surviving relic of the great Bronze Age migrations. [*Super-Cannes,* 2000]

■ I wouldn't want to live perpetually in Spain or the south of France because one's sealed off from so much. It's a timeless zone in a way, as you notice when you meet people who've lived out there for a few years—they seem to be curiously stranded, literally marooned on the beach. They may make passing references to Chernobyl or Margaret Thatcher or what have you, but they sound as if they're reading a script that somebody else has written for them. [*Interzone,* 1987]

■ People think you're alone on long-distance swims. But after five miles you're not alone anymore. The sea runs right into your mind and starts dreaming inside your head. [*Rushing to Paradise,* 1994]

■ They have sex on the beach, drink water from the stream, smoke their pot and beg for food. It sounds like sheer heaven. [*Rushing to Paradise,* 1994]

■ Wherever you go in the world, the road from the airport is always the same. [*Mississippi Review,* 1991]

■ A mini-J.G. Ballard Travel Guide: Barcelona—all the Gaudi creations. Above the Var plain, France: science parks and auto routes, including Marina Baie des Anges, Pierre Cardin Foundation at Miramar, Port-la-Galère, Antibes-les-Pins at Golfe-Juan, Sophia-Antipolis north of Antibes. Nostalgic Aviation Museum at Cannes-Mandelieu Airport. [introduction to *Super-Cannes,* 2000]

■ La Grande Motte, the futuristic resort complex on the coast [of the South of France]: the hard, affectless architecture with its stylized concrete surfaces, the ziggurat hotels and apartment houses, and the vast, empty parking lots laid down by the planners years before any tourist would arrive to park their cars, like a city abandoned in advance of itself. [*Concrete Island,* 1973]

■ The Bairro Alto district of Lisbon, a maze of steeply climbing streets . . . The fleet of ancient vehicles with their wooden panelling and cast-iron frames had been installed by British engineers almost a century earlier. But charm and industrial archaeology both came at a price. The tram's brakes failed for a few seconds. [*Millennium People,* 2003]

■ I admire a great many travel writers—Graham Greene and Evelyn Waugh in their day, then Lawrence Durrell, for me the greatest of them all. Gavin Young (especially *In Search of Conrad*), Ian Thompson (for his book on Haiti, *Bonjour Blanc*). Lucy Irvine's *Castaway* is a fine piece of nature writing. [*Literary Review*, 2001]

■ Following the long, cicada miles, the drive became a mobile autobiography that unwound my earlier life along with the kilometers of dust, insects and sun. [*Super-Cannes,* 1996]

■ As the customs officials rummage through my suitcases I sense them trying to unpack my mind and reveal a contraband of forbidden dreams and memories. [*Cocaine Nights,* 1996]

■ I've been to Egypt . . . I've never been to Cape Kennedy. In certain kinds of fiction it would matter enormously, but in imaginative fiction it doesn't matter. Le Douanier Rousseau, who painted those jungles that have implanted themselves indelibly on the 20th-century consciousness, had never been to Africa either. He's supposed to have taken his inspiration from the botanical gardens in Paris. In imaginative fiction, as in imaginative painting, I don't think it matters. [*JGB News,* 1987]

■ I go to Europe every summer—Greece for the beach, Italy for the museums. I know Europe pretty well. [*RE/Search #8/9,* 1984]

■ [J.G. Ballard] would quite like to live in Roquebrune, in the South of France, where he goes every summer for his holidays, and will do so one day when his girlfriend retires. But meanwhile Shepperton is as good as anywhere . . . He finds Shepperton "American" and there is no higher compliment in his book. [Lynn Barber, *Sunday Independent,* 1991]

ARCHITECTURE

■ People are actually beginning to decorate their homes in that international hotel manner . . . I could take you to places around [Shepperton] that are indistinguishable from the lobbies of the

International Hilton. [*New Musical Express,* 1985]

■ I have just read *Dead Cities,* and am a great admirer of Mike Davis, especially for *City of Quartz.* Perhaps he is a little too nostalgic for an idealized America dominated by clean rivers and civic responsibility. I feel that he hasn't come to terms with the form that late 20th and early 21st Century cities have taken—unrestricted urban sprawl, the decentered metropolis, a transient airport culture, gated communities and an absence of traditional civic pride. The problem facing planners and architects is how to accept and make the most of this. [intv Hans Obrist, 2003]

■ The Heathrow Hilton designed by Michael Manser is my favorite building in London. It's part space-age hangar and part high-tech medical center. It's clearly a machine, and the spirit of Le Corbusier lives on in its minimal functionalism. . . Sitting in its atrium one becomes, briefly, a more advanced kind of human being. Within this remarkable building one feels no emotions and could never fall in love, or need to. The National Gallery or the Louvre are the complete opposite, and people there are always falling in love. [intv Hans Obrist, 2003]

■ Vernon Gardens was the nearest town to the Observatory and most of it had been built within the last few years, evidently with an eye on the tourist trade. Along the main thoroughfare the shops and stores were painted in bright jazzy colors, the vivid awnings and neon signs like street scenery in an experimental musical. Around the square were a dozen gift-shops filled with cheap souvenirs: silverplate telescopes and models of the great Vernon dome masquerading as ink-stands and cigarboxes, plus a juvenile *omnium gatherum* of miniature planetaria, space helmets and plastic 3-D star atlases. ["The Venus Hunters," 1963]

■ He would find himself physically repelled by the contours of an award-winning coffee pot, by the well-modulated color schemes, by the good taste and intelligence that, Midas-like, had transformed everything in these apartments into an ideal marriage of function and design ... These people were the vanguard of a well-to-do and well-educated proletariat of the future, boxed up in these expensive apartments with their elegant furniture and intelligent sensibilities, and no possibility of escape. Royal would have given anything for one vulgar mantelpiece ornament, one less than snow-white lavatory bowl, one hint of hope. [*High Rise*, 1975]

■ I had expected a chamber of horrors, but the ordinariness of the disused space had been more disturbing than any blood-stained execution pit . . . [*Super-Cannes*, 2000]

■ Mental asylums, like the prisons they resemble, are so often burdened with the least appropriate names. As I drove through the gates of Summerfield Hospital I wondered who had christened this somber Victorian pile ... These impassive buildings possessed a moral authority far more intimidating than the tired psychiatrists who worked within their wards. [*Kindness of Women*, 1991]

■ The nose and cockpit section of a 1970s jet bomber was mounted on blocks beside the entrance, the equivalent of a cigar-store Indian or a rusting cigarette machine. [*Super-Cannes*, 2000]

■ My favorite building is the Heathrow Hilton by Michael Manser: a brilliant white classic building, like a Space Age hangar. I'd like everything to be like that. I'd like England to look as if everybody was getting ready to leave for Mars. [*Modern Review #20*, 1995]

■ The Millennium Wheel is a delight. Claire and I watched it being raised, and were stunned by its elegance and mystery, and by the special magic shared by all Ferris wheels. There should be more of them, at least one in every borough, and London would become a surrealist and poetic city. [*New Statesman,* 1999]

■ I could see the streamlined balconies and scalloped roof of a large art-deco villa, its powder-blue awnings like reefed sails. The ocean-liner windows and porthole skylights seemed to open onto the 1930s, a vanished world of Cole Porter and beach pajamas, morphine lesbians and the swagger portraits of Tamara de Lempicka. [*Super-Cannes,* 2000]

■ I detest postmodern architecture in any form whatsoever. We're driven by this terrible disease of nostalgia, and postmodernism is a gift to nostalgia and reaffirms that we don't have a future . . . [letter to David Pringle, 1995]

■ I was relieved to see the old Shanghai of the 1930s was alive and well, if a little crumbling in the sunlight. There were the Provençal villas of the French Concession, and the International Settlement's handsome Art Deco mansions with port-hole windows and ocean-liner balconies. ["Unlocking the Past," *Daily Telegraph,* 1991]

■ I have learned to like the intricate network of perimeter roads, the car rental offices, air freight depots and travel clinics, the light industrial and motel architecture that unvaryingly surrounds every major airport in the world. [*Blueprint,* 1997]

■ The dream palace of the Facteur Cheval, a magical edifice conjured out of pebbles the old postman collected on his rounds. Working tirelessly for thirty years, he created an heroic doll's house that expressed his simple but dignified dreams of the earthly paradise. My mother tipsily climbed the miniature stairs, listening to my father declaim the postman's naive verses in his resonant baritone. [*Super-Cannes,* 2000]

Photo: S.M. Gray

AIRPORTS, FLYING

■ Airports and airfields have always held a special magic, gateways to the infinite possibilities that only the sky can offer. [*Blueprint*, 1997]

■ I've always felt strongly that there's a profound magic in airports—and even more so in runways. Deserted runways have a tremendous magnetic pull for me. I can stare forever at aerial photographs of those islands in the Pacific which have abandoned runways—although some of them are still in use by the U.S. army and navy. But they are so powerful as images. The concrete strip just beckons one into new realms. Indeed, any major airport in the world charges me with a powerful sense of inspiration: they offer new points of departure for the imagination. [*ZG*, n.d.]

■ Airports have become a new kind of discontinuous city, whose vast populations are entirely transient, purposeful and, for the most part, happy. . . I suspect that the airport will be the true city of the 21st century. [*Blueprint,* 1997]

■ People like going to airports . . . They like the long-term car parks, the check-ins, the duty-frees, showing their passports. They can pretend they're someone else. [*Millennium People,* 2003]

■ They're living in the suburb of an airport . . . They like the alienation. There's no past and no future. If they can, they opt for zones without meaning—airports, shopping malls, motorways, car parks. They're in flight from the real. [*Millennium People,* 2003]

■ For the past 35 years I have lived in the Thames Valley town of Shepperton, a suburb not of London but of London Airport. The catchment area of Heathrow extends for at least ten miles to its south and west, a zone of motorway intersections, dual carriage-ways, science parks, marinas and industrial estates, watched by police CCTV speed-check cameras, a landscape which most people affect to loathe but which I regard as the most advanced and admirable in the British Isles, and a paradigm of the best that the future offers us. I welcome its transience, alienation and discontinuities, and its unashamed response to the pressure of speed, disposability and the instant impulse. Here, under the flight paths of Heathrow, everything is designed for the next five minutes. [*Blueprint,* 1997]

■ By comparison with London Airport, London itself seems hopelessly antiquated. Its hundreds of miles of gentrified stucco are an aching hangover from the 19th century that should have been bulldozed decades ago. London may well be the only world capital—with the possible exception of Moscow—that has gone from the 19th century to the 21st without experiencing all the possibilities and excitements of the 20th in any meaningful way. [*Blueprint,* 1997]

■ I've long suspected that people are only truly happy and aware of a real purpose to their lives when they hand over their tickets at the check-in. [*Blueprint,* 1997]

■ Those international hotels where they have conferences—two hundred yards away there may be a festering slum of people living in appalling poverty, but the delegates fly to the international airport and are limo'd to the hotel and never stray from those air-conditioned interiors and paging systems. [*New Musical Express,* 1985]

■ It seems to me that the pioneer years of flight at the turn of the century, let's say from the 1850s onwards—ballooning and all this sort of thing to the Wright Brothers and then on until the 1930s—was when aviation was still built around the dimensions of the man. It touched people's imaginations in consequence, in the most powerful sense. It provided some of the most potent metaphors that human beings have ever responded to. I suppose World War II was the last fling, but since then aviation is just Skytrain, which lacks any sort of imaginative dimension whatever. [*Thrust,* 1980]

■ Flying is something that the passenger is scarcely aware of: you step into what is, in effect, a small movie theater, with the latest movies projected on a very low-definition screen while people push strange assortments of food into your lap. Then suddenly the lights come on and you step out into what appears to be an identical airport. That's all part of the curious anonymity of modern living, where everything blurs around the edges into an overall continuum of imperceptible change. Unlike the period when I did my first traveling, back in the '30s and '40s—crossing a frontier, taking a steamer, you were made to recognize the cultural shift very dramatically, even in European countries that had been neighbors for a thousand years. The transformation, say, from France to Italy, France to Spain, across their common borders, was a bigger journey than nowadays coming from England to the States. Then, the national boundaries were real and one had to make huge mental adjustments to cope. Today, of course, the changes are imperceptible, so that you're scarcely aware of them. Now you have these big international hotels and airports all planned in the same style by multinational companies providing the decor of life. [*Omni,* n.d.]

■ Air travel may well be the most important civic duty that we discharge today, erasing class and national distinctions and subsuming them within the unitary global culture of the departure lounge. [*Blueprint,* 1997]

■ Airports and air-fields have always held a special magic. At school in Cambridge . . . I would ride a borrowed motorcycle to the American airbases at Mildenhall and Lakenheath, happy to stare through the wire at the lines of silver bombers and transport planes. Airports then were places where America arrived to greet us, where the world of tomorrow touched down in Europe. [*Blueprint,* 1997]

■ Only thirty years separated the hand grenades dropped over the sides of early biplanes in 1915 from the atom bombs that vaporized Hiroshima and Nagasaki. [review of *Tumult in the Clouds,* n.d.]

■ The open coffins lay empty, ready to catch the American pilots who would soon fall from the air. [*Empire of the Sun,* 1984]

■ Jim stepped under the tailplane of a Zero fighter. Wild sugarcane grew through its wings. Cannon fire had burned the metal skin from the fuselage spars, but the rusting shell still retained all the magic... An immense pathos surrounded the throttle and undercarriage levers, the rivets stamped into the metal fabric by some unknown Japanese woman on the Mitsubishi assembly line. [*Ibid.*]

■ The B-29s awed Jim. The huge, streamlined bombers summed up all the power and grace of America. Usually the B-29s flew above the Japanese anti-aircraft fire, but two days earlier

Jim had seen a single Superfortress cross the paddy fields to the west of the camp, only five hundred feet above the ground. Two of its engines were on fire, but the sight of this immense bomber with its high, curving tail convinced Jim that the Japanese had lost the war. [*Empire of the Sun,* 1984]

■ Flight for me has always been a powerful symbol of transcendence. I live close to London Airport, and I always get a special thrill from watching planes land and take off. [BBC Online Live Chat, 2002]

■ "I like pilots—Beryl Markham is my hero." . . . "A great flyer . . . Totally promiscuous." [*Super-Cannes,* 2000]

■ I remembered my erection after my first solo landing at the RAF flying school, as all the tension of the unaccompanied take-off released itself. [*Super-Cannes,* 2000]

■ Her moods flared and darkened in a few seconds, a shirt of internal weather almost tropical in its sudden turns. She reminded me of the women pilots at the flying club, with their wind-blown glamour and vulnerable promiscuities. [*Super-Cannes,* 2000]

■ Flying is a very strange experience—it's very close to dreaming. The normal yardsticks, the parameters of our movements through space, are suspended. You're traveling at 150mph, but if you're 1,000 feet up you're not moving at all. [*Spike,* 2000]

■ Stepping on a plane is an opportunity to invent oneself afresh. [*Independent,* 9/14/2000]

■ An empty runway moves me enormously (which obviously says something about my need to escape). [*Spike,* 2000]

■ Flying had been interesting and given me another set of myths to live by . . . The fighter attacks by Mustangs that flew so low over Lunghua Camp—I remember looking *down* at them from the second and third floor of the buildings during the air raids. They were flying within ten feet of the paddy fields. I accept the idea that flight is a sort of symbol of escape, but I think more than escape, of *transcendence*, and it played a very large role in my fiction. ["Shanghai Jim," 1991]

■ There's a sort of airport culture—with its transience, its access to anywhere in the world. [Iain Sinclair's *Crash,* 1999]

■ I always wanted to manage a small airport ... You get to be a kind of harbor-master. There are tides in the sky. [*Rushing to Paradise,* 1994]

■ For too many people in the twentieth century the sky was the place from which death came. ["Speed-Visions of an Accelerated Age," 1998]

CITIES

■ A high-rise city like New York, exhilarating though it was, I found very oppressive. The physical mass of the buildings and the discontinuity between street life that existed—the two dimensions of the plane on the city floor and the hidden, concealed life going halfway up to the sky is very constraining. [*Mississippi Review,* 1991]

■ I consider the city to be an outdated structure, incapable of expressing the deep dreams of our time. Cities seem very old-fashioned to me; London in particular. They have had their time—they belong to the 19th-century, when people needed to be physically in (close) proximity in order to carry out trade, commerce, the exchange of goods and ideas. Now, we communicate by electronic means. The Internet is, above all, the dream of suburbia. I see the future as a kind of planetary suburbia, an infinity of boredom interrupted by unpredictable acts of violence. [fax, 1999]

■ Visiting London, I always have the sense of a city devised as an instrument of political control, like the class system that preserves England from revolution. The labyrinth of districts and boroughs, the endless columned porticos that once guarded the modest terraced cottages of Victorian clerks, together make clear that London is a place where everyone knows his place. [*Blueprint,* 1997]

■ Cities are the scar tissue of history, still itchy and festering after centuries of deep pathology that erupted, in my own lifetime, into fascism and totalitarian communism. [*Tate,* 2001]

■ The cities that tourists most enjoy are those in long-term decline—Venice, Florence, Paris, London, New York. The last two are gigantic money-mills, churned by a Centurion-car elite who are retreating into gated communities in Surrey and the Upper East Side. Already their immense spending power has distorted social life in London and New York, freezing out the old blue-collar and middle classes, and validating the notion that the dreams that money can buy are a perfectly fit topic for the young painter, novelist and filmmaker. It's not their own ambition that corrupts today's artists, but the subject matter facing them. [*Tate,* 2001]

■ The ragged skyline of the city resembled the disturbed encephalograph of an unresolved mental crisis . . . [*High Rise,* 1975]

■ I regard the city as a semi-extinct form. [Iain Sinclair's *Crash,* 1999]

■ London is basically a nineteenth-century city. And the habits of mind appropriate to the nineteenth century, which survive into the novels set in the London of the twentieth century, aren't really appropriate to understanding what is really going on in life today. [Iain Sinclair's *Crash,* 1999

■ New York City is a total write-off. Manhattan's under hundred-foot waves, most of the big skyscrapers and office blocks are down. Empire State Building toppled like a falling chimney stack. Same story everywhere else. Casualty lists in the millions. Paris, Berlin, Rome—nothing but rubble, people hanging on in cellars. [*Wind from Nowhere,* 1962]

■ This triangular patch of waste ground had survived by the exercise of a unique guile and persistence, and would continue to survive, unknown and disregarded, long after the motorways had collapsed into dust. [*Concrete Island,* 1973]

■ The cafe was decorated in the same futuristic motifs. The chairs and tables were painted a drab aluminum grey, their limbs and panels cut in random geometric shapes. A silver rocket ship, ten feet long, its paint peeling off in rusty strips, reared up from a pedestal among the tables. ["Venus Hunters," 1967]

■ We walk into the toilets in a public building and look in those unkind, revealing mirrors and see ourselves, "God, help!"—it is this that these early [Francis] Bacons capture. [*Art Newspaper,* 1999]

■ [Flats and houses are] service stations, where people sleep and ablute. The human body as an obedient coolie, to be fed and hosed down, and given just enough sexual freedom to sedate itself. We've concentrated on the office as the key psychological zone. [*Super-Cannes,* 2000]

■ The administrative headquarters: late modernist in the most minimal and self-effacing way, a machine above all for thinking in. [*Super-Cannes,* 2000]

■ Fluted columns carried the pitched roofs, an attempt at a vernacular architecture that failed to disguise this executive-class prison. [*Super-Cannes,* 2000]

■ Ornamental pathways led to the electricity substations feeding power into the business park's grid. Surrounded by chain-link fences, they stood in the forest clearings like mysterious and impassive presences . . . [*Super-Cannes,* 2000]

■ I circled the artificial lakes, with their eerily calm surfaces, or roamed around the vast car parks. The lines of silent vehicles might have belonged to a race who had migrated to the stars. [*Super-Cannes,* 2000]

■ People worry about security in their office buildings. That's always a key indicator of internal stress: the obsession with the invisible intruder in the fortress—the other self, the silent brother who clones himself off from the unconscious. [unknown]

■ We're all looking for some sort of vertical route out of the particular concrete jungle that we live in. [*Thrust,* Winter 1980]

■ The first "intelligent city" of the Riviera . . . The 10,000 inhabitants in their high-tech apartments and offices will serve as an "ideas laboratory"' for the cities of the future, where "technology will be placed at the service of conviviality." Fiber-optic cables and telemetric networks will transmit databanks and information services to each apartment, along with the most advanced fire, safety and security measures. . . In case the physical and mental strain of actually living in this electronic paradise proves too much, there will be individual medical tele-surveillance in direct contact with the nearest hospital. ["Under the Voyeur's Gaze," 1989]

■ Pinned to the walls around him were a series of huge whiteprints and architectural drawings, depicting various elevations of a fantastic Martian city he had once designed, its glass spires and curtain walls rising like heliotropic jewels from the vermilion desert. In fact, the whole city was a vast piece of jewelry, each elevation brilliantly visualized but as symmetrical, and ultimately as lifeless, as a crown. ["The Cage of Sand," 1962]

■ Townscapes are changing. The open-plan city belongs to the past— no more Ramblas, no more pedestrian precincts, no more Left Banks and Latin Quarters. We're moving into the age of security grills and defensible space. As for living, our surveillance cameras can do that for us. People are locking their doors and switching off their nervous systems. [*Cocaine Nights,* 1996]

SUBURBS

■ I think the suburbs are more interesting than people will let on. In the suburbs you find uncentered lives. The normal civic structures are not there. People have more freedom to explore their own imaginations, their own obsessions—and the discretionary spending power to do so. [Iain Sinclair's *Crash,* 1999]

■ Social trends of various kinds tend to reveal themselves first in the suburbs. The transformation of British life by television in the Sixties took place, most of all, in the suburbs. In the suburbs you have nothing to do except watch TV. [Iain Sinclair's *Crash,* 1999]

© ANA BARRADO

■ I feel that suburbia, which is generally regarded as a place where not that much happens, is in fact more crucial in terms of social change than people realize. Changing lifestyles, changes in social consciousness—they are much more apparent in a place like this. [*Publishers Weekly,* 1998]

■ I consider suburbia to be enormously undervalued. I consider it to be really the center of life in England—in the western world—the most creative zone and the only urban area with its eye fixed firmly on the future. All the most important innovative trends that have emerged since the Second World War, such as car ownership, television, the leisure society, wife-swapping and alienation, first flourished in suburbia. It's no coincidence that the Rolling Stones and the Beatles both emerged from the suburbs. James Bond is a suburban dream. [fax, 1999]

■ I've always felt that out in the suburbs one finds the real England—out here with takeaways and video rental culture people are better off as their imaginations can follow their money. [BBC News Online, 2002]

■ I think suburbs are also great places of anxiety and uncertainty. People find living in suburbia stimulating. The uncertainty gives an edge of excitement and danger to the most humdrum activities, like pouring a gin and tonic, or putting the Range Rover through a car wash. Whenever I go to London, I feel I am stepping back into the novels of Kafka: people are burdened by shabbiness and guilt. In the suburbs, we are free. There are no moral decisions to be made in suburbia: we leave moral decisions to the CCTV (closed circuit television) cameras. [fax, 1999]

■ If I have to make a guess, I'd say the future was going to be like a suburb of Dusseldorf. The whole of Germany is like an enormous well-heeled housing estate. There are all these immaculate, brand-new suburban houses in nicely wooded suburbs; every house has a boat and a BMW in the driveway. The schools are built according to the most advanced thinking about what a school should be like; there are recreation aids and sports facilities. Even a drifting leaf looks like it's got too much freedom! And this all adds up to the death of the soul in the whole place. There's a desperation just waiting to be born there. If you live in a totally civilized society, madness is the only way you can express your own freedom. [*Heavy Metal*, 1982]

■ We trundled through endless immaculate suburbs of executive housing . . . There was a Mercedes or a BMW in every driveway, motorboats on their trailers, identical children identically dressed. We might have been looking at a population of brilliantly designed robots placed there merely to establish a contextual landscape! And this went on and on. I suddenly realized that the future of this planet was not going to be like New York City or Tokyo or London or Moscow but rather like a suburb of Dusseldorf. And you know, most of the Baader-Meinhof gang in fact grew up in these suburbs, and I realized why that kind of terrorism erupted from this kind of landscape. Because in that world, madness is the only freedom. [*Rolling Stone*, 1987]

■ Once you move to the suburbs, time stops. People measure their lives by consumer goods, the dreams that money can buy. I think that's more dangerous. [*The Face*, 1987]

GATED COMMUNITES

■ I'm not trying to say that the majority of people, thirty years from now, will be living in ultra high-tech enclaves with no contact with the rest of the human race, turning the inner city centers into a kind of urban guerilla battleground. However, you can see in the U.S. and Europe extraordinary urban developments based absolutely on the need for total security. [*Sub Dee*, 1997]

■ Over the last 20 or 30 years in Europe—longer in the U.S.—a minority of middle-class professionals retain the greatest energizing and creative input into life. And they've decided for reasons of security to remove themselves from the hurly-burly of city life. American cities were the first to show this; it's now happening here, Nairobi, Singapore. They're subtracting themselves from the whole of these civic interactions that depend on them, virtually conducting an internal immigration—and that's dangerous. It's the middle classes who are now abandoning hope and that's not a good sign, particularly as they're moving into these sterile communities where, by the nature of security systems, they're isolated and their only form of contact is via a TV screen. [*Sub Dee,* 1997]

■ If you think of what society invests in the training of its leading professionals, its doctors, architects, lawyers and so on, for them then to opt out and move into a gated community where they exist behind huge arrays of electronic padlocks, and have no interaction with the rest of society in their social hours, is a deplorable state of affairs. I think the way in which the gated community is springing up all over the world now is an *ominous* sign. It's a sign that something is deeply wrong with the societies that have evolved at the end of the 20th Century . . . People aren't moving into gated communities simply to avoid muggers and housebreakers, they're moving into gated communities to get away from other people. Even people like themselves, that's the curious thing. [Because] inside most gated communities there's very little social life; people are happy to enter their executive houses and stay there. [BBC Radio 3, 1998]

■ There were no parking problems, no fears of burglars or purse-snatchers, no rapes or muggings. Civility and polity were designed into [the gated community], in the same way that mathematics, aesthetics and an entire geopolitical world-view were designed into the Parthenon and the Boeing 747. [*Super-Cannes,* 2000]

■ [In *Cocaine Nights*] I'm writing about a quite clear tendency which is the professional middle class retreating into fortified enclaves [gated communities] . . . It's a very dangerous shift; people are tearing up the social contract they have with their fellow human beings . . . It's a preview of what I see coming in the future. [*NME*, 1996]

■ Halder pointed to a nearby surveillance camera. "Think of it as a new kind of *togetherness*." [*Super-Cannes*, 2000]

■ What I fear for my grandchildren is a benign dystopia of ever present surveillance cameras watching us *for our own good*, a situation in which we will acquiesce, all too well aware of our attraction to danger. [intv Hans Obrist, 2003]

■ Everywhere you look—Britain, the States, western Europe—people are sealing themselves off into crime-free enclaves. That's a mistake—a certain level of crime is part of the necessary roughage of life. Total security is a disease of deprivation. [*Cocaine Nights*, 1996]

■ The children were being watched every hour of the day and night. This was a warm, friendly junior Alcatraz. Swimming at eight, breakfast eight-thirty, archery classes, origami, *do this, do that.* [*Running Wild*, 1988]

■ The residents had eliminated both past and future, and for all their activity they existed in a civilized and eventless world. [*Running Wild*, 1988]

■ People are obsessed with the phenomenon of total security now without realizing that it's bought at such a huge price. The home is now an electronic fortress: you switch on your triple security locks and your hidden cameras and you're virtually switching off the world. But, in a sense, you're also switching off the central nervous system that evolution provides us with. [*Sub Dee*, 1997]

■ The ultimate gated community is a human being with a closed mind. [*Super-Cannes*, 2000]

Photo: Mike Ryan

FREEWAYS

■ The highway system is now a huge reticular prison, granting the illusion of speed, direction and self-chosen destiny to millions of men confined within their mobile cells. But for women the car was an immense force for liberation, freeing them from the home and sending them out to enjoy the unique social pleasures of the traffic jam and the [supermarket] car-park. ["Speed-Visions of an Accelerated Age," 1998]

■ The beauty of these vast motion sculptures, and their intimate involvement with our daily lives and dreams, may be one reason why the visual arts have faltered in the second half of the twentieth century. No painter or sculptor could hope to match the heroic significance of freeway interchanges. In many ways they also threaten the novel, their linear codes inscribing a graphic narrative across the landscapes of our lives that no fiction could rival. [*Ibid*]

■ World War II accelerated everything—the speed of warfare, the growth of aviation and weapons technology, shifts in mass psychology and the emancipation of women, and the evolution of the road. Built in the 1930s, Hitler's autobahns were both high-speed panzer arteries and ancient runic megaliths laid down like stone dreams that pointed towards the east. ["Speed-Visions of an Accelerated Age," 1998]

HIGH RISE

■ The ultimate goal of the high-rise: a realm where their most deviant impulses were free to exercise themselves in any way they wished. At this point, physical violence would cease at last. [*High Rise*, 1975]

■ The high-rise was a huge machine designed to serve, not the

Photo: S.M. Gray

collective body of tenants, but the individual resident in isolation. [*High Rise,* 1975]

■ Without knowing it he had constructed a gigantic vertical zoo, its hundreds of cages stacked above each other. [*High Rise,* 1975]

■ The new order had emerged, in which all life within the high-rise revolved around three obsessions—security, food and sex. [*High Rise,* 1975]

■ The internal time of the high-rise, like an artificial psychological climate, operated to its own rhythms, generated by a combination of alcohol and insomnia . . . [*High Rise,* 1975]

■ In the early hours of the morning, the two thousand tenants subsided below a silent tide of seconal. [*High Rise,* 1975]

■ All the evidence accumulated over several decades cast a critical light on the high-rise as a viable social structure, but cost-effectiveness and high profitability kept pushing these vertical townships into the sky against the real needs of their occupants. [*High Rise,* 1975]

■ Graffiti: a fifty-million-dollar office building and a few francs' worth of paint turn it into something from the Third World. [*Super-Cannes,* 2000]

■ In a sense, life in the high-rise had begun to resemble the world outside—there were the same ruthlessness and aggression concealed within a set of polite conventions. [*High Rise,* 1975]

■ Living in high-rises required a special type of behavior: one that was acquiescent, restrained . . . A psychotic would have a ball here. [*High Rise,* 1975]

■ Deep-rooted antagonisms were breaking through the surface of life within the high rise . . . Many of the factors involved had long been obvious—complaints about noise, abuse of the building's facilities, rivalries over the better-sited apartments (those away from elevator lobbies and service shafts, with their eternal rumbling). In here was even a certain petty envy of the more attractive women who were supposed to inhabit the upper floors. [*High Rise*, 1975]

■ [The high rise had many "vagrants"]—bored apartment-bound housewives and stay-at-home adult daughters who spent a large part of their time riding the elevators and wandering the long corridors of the vast building, migrating endlessly in search of change or excitement. [*High Rise*, 1975]

■ A new social type was being created by the apartment building: a cool, unemotional personality impervious to the psychological pressures of high-rise life, with minimal needs for privacy, who thrived like an advanced species of machine in the neutral atmosphere ...the sort of resident content to do nothing but sit in his over-priced apartment, watch television with the sound turned down, and wait for his neighbors to make a mistake ... [*High Rise*, 1975]

■ The residents moving along the corridors were the cells in a network of arteries, the lights in their apartments the neurons of a brain. [*High Rise*, 1975]

■ He would often awake from an uneasy dream into the suffocating bedroom, conscious of each of the 999 other apartments pressing on him through the walls and ceiling, forcing the air from his chest. [*High Rise*, 1975]

■ The presence of the fifty or so dogs in the high rise had long been a source of irritation . . . The dogs barked when they were walked in the evening, fouling the pathways. On more than one occasion elevator doors were sprayed with urine. *High Rise*, 1975]

■ Dog excrement had been deliberately dropped into the air-conditioning flues by the upper-level tenants ... [*High Rise*, 1975]

■ An electrical failure temporarily blacked out the 9th, 10th and

11th floors . . . During the blackout two of the twenty elevators were put out of action. The air-conditioning had been switched off. [*High Rise,* 1975]

■ Not one of the twenty elevators in the apartment building now functioned, and the shafts were piled deep with kitchen refuse and dead dogs. [*High Rise,* 1975]

■ Vandalism had plagued these slab-and-tower blocks since their inception. Every torn-out piece of telephone equipment, every kicked-in electricity meter represented a stand against decerebration. [*High Rise,* 1975]

■ Far below him, a car drove along the access road to the nearby high rise, its three occupants looking up at the hundreds of crowded balconies. Anyone seeing this ship of lights would take for granted that the two thousand people on board lived together in a state of corporate euphoria . . . [*High Rise,* 1975]

■ He gazed up at the derelict washing-machine and refrigerator, now only used as garbage bins . . . Sometimes he found it difficult not to believe that they were living in a future that had already taken place, and was now exhausted. [*High Rise,* 1975]

■ Before starting *High-Rise,* I was staying one summer in a beach high-rise at Rosas on the Costa Brava, not far from Dali's home at Port Lligat, and I noticed that one of the French ground-floor tenants, driven to a fury by cigarette butts thrown down from the upper floors, began to patrol the beach and photograph the offenders with a zoom lens. He then pinned the photos to a notice board in the foyer of the block. A very curious exhibition, which I took to be another green light to my imagination. [*Paris Review,* 1984]

■ I'm planning to do a television documentary about high rises—a really hard look at the physical and psychological pressures of living

in a huge condominium. [*High Rise,* 1975]

SWIMMING POOLS

■ During the night the swimming-pool had drained itself. The once mysterious world of wavering blue lines, glimpsed through a cascade of bubbles, now lay exposed to the morning light. The tiles were slippery with leaves and dirt, and the chromium ladder at the deep end, which had once vanished into a watery abyss, ended abruptly beside a pair of scummy rubber slippers. [*Empire of the Sun,* 1984]

■ There was something sinister about a drained swimming-pool, and he tried to imagine what purpose it could have it if were not filled with water. It reminded him of the concrete bunkers in Tsingtao, and the bloody handprints of the maddened German gunners on the caisson walls. Perhaps murder was about to be committed in all the swimming-pools of Shanghai, and their walls were tiled so that the blood could be washed away? [*Empire of the Sun,* 1984]

■ Over the swimming pools and manicured lawns seemed to hover a dream of violence ... [*Super-Cannes,* 2000]

■ Nakedness, as any skinny-dipper knows, deliciously increases the sensuality of swimming . . . Dawn Fraser maintained that she could have broken every record if she had been allowed to swim naked, and why not, I eagerly agree . . . Virginia Woolf swam naked with Rupert Brooke, and one can scarcely imagine anything more chaste or, in its eerie way, so intriguing . . . Edgar Allan Poe [was] himself a devotee of long and mysterious river-swims. [*Daily Telegraph,* 1992]

■ I'm never happier than when around drained swimming pools, for reasons I don't understand. At the time, in 1941, they represented the many dangers posed by the Japanese waiting to seize the International Settlement in Shanghai, a sure sign that the game was up. I think that for me now the drained pool and abandoned hotel stand for psychological zero. In Marbella a few years ago I found an abandoned hotel with a drained swimming pool. Time seemed to stand still forever, and I was tempted to move in. [*Literary Review,* 2001]

■ I enjoy the notion of drained swimming pools and abandoned hotels, which I don't really see as places of decadence, but rather like the desert in that I see them merely as psychic zero stations, or as "Go" in Monopoly terms. [*Paris Review,* 1984]

■ I'm never happier than when I can write about drained swimming pools and abandoned hotels. But I'm not sure if that's decadence or simply an attempt to invert and reverse the commonplace, to turn the sock inside out. I've always been intrigued by inversions of that kind, or any kind. I think that's what drew me to an interest in anatomy. [*Paris Review,* 1984]

■ I began to count the [swimming] pools. Ten thousand years in the future, long after the Cote d'Azur had been abandoned, the first explorers would puzzle over these empty pits, with their eroded frescoes of tritons and stylized fish, inexplicably hauled up the mountainsides like aquatic sundials or the altars of a bizarre religion devised by a race of visionary geometers. [*Super-Cannes,* 2000]

■ From an observation post high above Grasse [France], there is the astounding sight of scores of blue rectangles cut into the mountain sides—swimming pools. 100,000 years from now, when the human race has vanished, visitors from the stars will observe these drained concrete pits, many decorated with tritons and solar emblems. What were they—submerged marine altars? All that is left of the time-machines which these people used to escape from their planet? Three-dimensional symbols in a ritual geometry, models of a state of mind, votive offerings to the distant sea? One has the same

impression flying over Beverly Hills. [*Atrocity Exhibition,* 1990]

■ Give me an abandoned hotel or a drained swimming pool any day . . . [*Independent on Sunday,* 2003]

NATURE

■ **By any degree to which you devalue the external world, so you devalue yourself.** ["The Overloaded Man," 1967]

■ In a way those wildlife programs . . . are falsifications of reality. They're children's encyclopedia versions of Nature which . . . present Nature as a large placid beast that can easily be domesticated. Nature isn't like that. [*Interzone,* 1987]

■ **Is there such a thing as authentic "Nature" these days? Or is it now merely an adjunct to the electronic media, almost a TV gimmick? Is it rapidly turning into a theme park?** [*Time Out,* 1987]

■ There's a positive plague of white ants in the garden, like something out of a Science-Fiction nightmare. I've tried to convince Edna that their real source is psychological. Remember the story "Leiningen vs the Ants"? A classic example of the forces of the Id rebelling against the Super-Ego. ["The Venus Hunters," 1963]

■ **Invisible encyclopedias lay in every hedge and ditch.** [*Empire of the Sun,* 1984]

THE BEACH

■ The beach is where the sun goes to doze and dream. ["Sands of Time," *Sunday Times,* n.d.]

■ *The Beach: The History of Paradise on Earth* . . . **is a witty and entertaining account of the remarkable role this strip of sand and shingle** has played in human history, and in the evolution of lifestyle, fashion and sexuality. The authors describe the beach as Nature's most potent anti-depressant, an aphrodisiac cocktail of sun and water. ["Sands of Time," *Sunday Times,* n.d.]

■ If land-based life began on the beach, there were times in the recent past when it seemed that everything might also end there. Bikini Atoll, where the early atomic bombs were tested, and Eniwetok Atoll, over which the hydrogen bomb was detonated, are among the most sinister sites of the 20th-century imagination. There the human race mastered the secrets of the sun and threatened itself with a new kind of mass death. Yet Bikini gave its name to a swimsuit: the three small triangles, a minimalist geometry of eye-catching modesty, appeared with all the startling charm of Ursula Andress on *Dr. No*'s beach, and signaled a newly confident female sexuality. [*Atrocity Exhibition,* 1990]

■ If you're interested in painting, Bonnard's house is here in Le Cannet. Picasso worked at Antibes, Matisse further down the coast at Nice. In many ways modern art was a culture of the beach. [*Super-Cannes,* 2000]

■ If the sun is the ultimate TV station, then the beach is its most popular program, and life at a holiday resort resembles a chaotic rehearsal for the last great sitcom, a fusion of *Baywatch* and Armageddon. ["Sands of Time," *Sunday Times, n.d.*]

■ Despite the occasional squabble over a desirable poolside seat, the beach is where the human race at last manages to *detribalize* itself. The greatest city of the 20th century, and the largest the world has ever known, is the linear city that stretches along the northern shores of the Mediterranean from Gibraltar to Glyfada beach outside Athens: 4,000 miles long and 400 feet deep, and with a transient summer population that numbers more than 150 million. Its endless balconies look down on a strip of hot silica that may well be the last remnant of our memory of Eden before the fall. The hotels and apartment houses stand shoulder to shoulder, and under the force of population pressures may one day coalesce. I can hear the proud boast of the Mediterranean Super-Hilton: "Travel from Gibraltar to Athens in the air-conditioned comfort of our corridors." ["Sands of Time," *Sunday Times,* n.d.]

■ A linear city, some 3000 miles long, from Gibraltar to Glyfada beach north of Athens, and 300 yards deep. For three summer months the largest city in the world, population at least

Photo: S.M. Gray

50 million, or perhaps twice that. The usual hierarchies and conventions are absent; in many ways it couldn't be less European, but it works. [*Atrocity Exhibition,* 1990]

■ At Estrella de Mar the residential complexes stood shoulder to shoulder along the beach. The future had come ashore here, lying down to rest among the pines. The whitewalled pueblos reminded me of my visit to Arcosanti, Paolo Soleri's outpost of the day after tomorrow in the Arizona desert. The cubist apartments and terraced houses resembled Arcosanti's, their architecture dedicated to the abolition of time, as befitted the aging population of the retirement havens and an even wider world waiting to be old. [*Cocaine Nights,* 1996]

■ People think you're alone on long-distance swims. But after five miles you're not alone anymore. The sea runs right into your mind and starts dreaming inside your head. [*Rushing to Paradise,* 1994]

■ The retirement pueblos lay by the motorway, embalmed in a dream of the sun from which they would never awake. . . The white facades of the villas and apartment houses were like blocks of time that had crystallized beside the road. Here on the Costa del Sol nothing would ever happen again, and the people of the pueblos were already the ghosts of themselves. [*Cocaine Nights,* 1996]

■ The beaches beside the coastal road were littered with forgotten film magazines and empty bottles of suntan cream, the debris of a dream washed ashore among the driftwood. [*Super-Cannes,* 2000]

■ Her wide hips rolled snugly in the water, and she might have been lying in the lap of a trusted lover. When she passed me I noticed a crescent-shaped bruise that ran from her left cheekbone to the bridge of her strong nose, and the apparently swollen gums of her upper jaw. Seeing me, she swiftly turned into a fast crawl, hands ransacking the waves, a pigtail of long black hair following her like a faithful water-snake. [*Cocaine Nights*, 1996]

■ I think beaches are my spiritual home. There are very few I dislike. [*Observer*, 2002]

■ If the sea was a symbol of the unconscious, was space perhaps an image of unfettered time, and the inability to penetrate it a tragic exile to one of the limbos of eternity, a symbolic death in life? ["A Question of Re-Entry," 1963]

■ During beach holidays I devour foreign-language news magazines, though I can't speak a word of French, Italian or Spanish, and always rent a TV set. In England I watch most TV with the sound turned down, but in France or Spain I boost the volume, particularly of news bulletins. [*Atrocity Exhibition*, 1990]

■ *In Search of a Beginning: My Life With Graham Greene* by Yvonne Cloetta and Marie-Francoise Allain, is the perfect beach read, especially if the beach is anywhere near Antibes, Greene's home in the south of France. In the 1980s, I watched Yvonne Cloetta at Chez Felix warning off with her laser stare any tourists tempted to approach Greene. He seemed to tower three feet above her. In these conversations with Allain, she comes over as a larger and warmer figure, utterly devoted to Greene and clearly the light of his life. [*Observer*, July 4, 2004]

■ He watched a succession of wavelets lapping at the sloping roof, wishing that he could walk straight down into the water, dissolve himself and the ever-present phantoms which attended him like sentinel birds in the cool bower of its magical calm, in the luminous, dragon-green, serpent-haunted sea. [*Drowned World*, 1962]

■ I noted the features of this silent world: the memory-erasing white architecture; the enforced leisure that fossilized the nervous system; the almost Africanized aspect, but a North Africa invented by someone who had never visited the Maghreb; the apparent absence of any social structure; the timelessness of a world beyond boredom, with no past, no future and a diminishing present. Perhaps this was what a leisure-dominated future would resemble? Nothing could ever happen in this affectless realm, where entropic drift calmed the surfaces of a thousand swimming pools. [*Cocaine Nights,* 1996]

■ The cult of physical perfection had gripped everyone's imagination. Bodies deformed by years bent over the word-processor and fast-food counter were now slim and upright, as ideally proportioned as the figures on the Parthenon frieze. The new evangelism concealed behind the exercise and fitness fads of the 1980s now reappeared. A devotion to physical perfection ruled their lives more strictly than any industrial taskmaster. ["The Largest Theme Park in the World," 1989]

■ Athletic prowess was admired above all, a cult of bodily perfection mediated through group gymnastic displays on the beaches, quasi-fascistic rallies, in which thousands of well-drilled participants slashed the dawn air with their karate chops and chanted in a single voice at the sun. These bronzed and handsome figures with their thoughtless sexuality looked down on their tourist compatriots with a sense of almost racial superiority. ["The Largest Theme Park in the World," 1989]

■ All the most interesting things in the world take place where the sea meets the land and you're between those two states of mind. On that border zone, you're neither one nor the other, you're both. And people take their clothes off, which is always a plus. [*Observer,* 2002]

■ Homo sapiens *en masse* presented a more unsavory spectacle than almost any other species of animal. A corral of horses or steers conveyed an impression of powerful nervous grace, but this mass of articulated albino flesh sprawled on the beach resembled the diseased anatomical fantasy of a Surrealist painter.

["The Reptile Enclosure," 1963]

■ **I think the psychological role of the beach is much more interesting ... If you accept the sea as an image of the unconscious, then this beachward urge might be seen as an attempt to escape from the existential role of ordinary life and return to the universal time-sea ...** ["The Reptile Enclosure," 1963]

■ My perfect beach is in the south of France at a place called Roque-brune, which lies between Menton and Monte Carlo. It's small, secluded and has a spectacular view with Cape Martin on the left and Monaco on the right. It's a shingle beach, which I usually hate, but this one has a wooden shack bar and it's close to Paradise. I like to go down there and swim in the salt water, and at my present age of 71, I'm still able to reach the diving platform, which is at least half a mile out to sea (although, actually, it's more like 75 yards).

It has other charms for me because the great architect Corbusier had a cabin about 50 yards from the beach, and he had a heart attack and died while having his morning swim here. I'm always conscious of his presence here. Only a small group of people use the beach, but there are all sorts of other comings and goings. Hang-gliders launch themselves from the mountain behind the beach, sail over the water and then land on the shingle. It's an exhilarating spectacle. Another kind of flying machine uses this stretch of water. The forest firefighters fly down low to scoop up water and then fly off to bomb whatever areas of the French Riviera are catching fire. One unusual visitor a few years ago was a swan, a bird you don't often find on salt water, which became quite celebrated in a local paper... It really is a place of character. It's probably a mistake to tell anyone about it, but it is very difficult to find, so there's no point looking for it. [*Observer,* 2002]

OTHER TERRAINS

■ Deserts possess a particular magic, since they have exhausted their own futures, and are thus free of time. Anything erected there—a city, a pyramid, a motel—stands outside time. [*Atrocity Exhibition*, 1990]

■ By the time I came to England at the age of sixteen I'd seen a great variety of landscapes. England seemed to be very dull, because I'd been brought up at a much lower latitude—the same latitude as the places which are my real spiritual home as I sometimes think: Los Angeles and Casablanca. I'm always much happier in the south—Spain, Greece—than I am anywhere else. The rural landscape of meadow didn't mean anything to me. . . [intv Goddard, 1975]

■ Everywhere a deranged horticulture was running riot. Vivid new shoots pushed past the metal debris of old ammunition boxes, filing cabinets and truck tires. Strange grasping vines clambered over the scarlet caps of giant fungi, their white stems as thick as sailors' bones. ["Dream Cargoes," 1991]

■ The jungle wall of cycads, giant tamarinds and tropical creepers crowded the beach to the waterline, and the reflected colors drowned in swathes of phosphorescence that made the lagoon resemble a cauldron of electric dyes. ["Dream Cargoes," 1991]

■ They seemed to be strange hybrids of pomegranate and pawpaw, cantaloupe and pineapple. There were giant tomato-like berries and clusters of purple grapes each the size of a baseball. Together they glowed through the overheated light like jewels set in the face of the sun. ["Dream Cargoes," 1991]

■ Graceful, feather-tipped wraiths like gaudy angels, their crimson plumage leaked its ravishing hues onto the air. When he fixed his eyes onto them they seemed suspended against the sky, wings fanning slowly as if shaking the time from themselves. ["Dream Cargoes," 1991]

■ There were a dozen towers around the perimeter of the lagoon, built in the 1960s to house the remote-controlled cameras... [They] had been swallowed by the advancing forest—ancient megaliths left behind by a race of warrior scientists obsessed with geometry and death. [*Rushing to Paradise*, 1994]

■ After Freud's exploration within the psyche, it is now the outer world of reality which must be quantified and eroticized. [*Ambit #36*, 1968]

■ Weapons ranges have a special magic: all that destructive technology concentrated on the production of nothing, the closest we can get to certain obsessional states of mind. Even more strange are the bunkers of the Nazi Atlantic Wall, most of which are still standing, and are far larger than one expects. Space-age cathedrals, they threaten the surrounding landscape like lines of Teutonic knights, and are examples of *cryptic architecture*, where form no longer reveals function. They seem to contain the codes of some mysterious mental process. At Utah Beach, the most deserted stretch of the Normandy coast, they stare out over the washed sand, older than the planet. On visits with my agent and his wife, I used to photograph them compulsively. [*Atrocity Exhibition*, 1990]

Photo: Charles Gatewood

PSYCHOPATHOLOGY

■ We are violent and dangerous creatures. We needed to be to survive all those hundreds of thousands of years when we were living in small tribal groups, faced with an incredibly hostile world. And we still carry those genes. [*Frieze,* 1996]

■ We like spin, contrary to what most journalists tell us. We like PR campaigns and having our emotions manipulated. We like mood music, and we like promises that will never be kept … We spend our happiest moments in [supermarkets] and shopping malls, where everything is designed to make us feel better, while often making us feel worse. [*New Statesman,* 2001]

■ As a species, human beings need to be approached with caution. I would say that we are at heart a half-civilized race, and probably have more in common with our nearest relatives, the chimpanzees, than we like to think. We are brilliant, violent, romantic, cruel—superb parents and dangerous neighbors. [BBC Online Live Chat, 2002]

■ "Most people don't have any individuality anyway." A curious remark for a novelist [Joyce Carol Oates] to make, one has to say. In fact, our belief in our unique selves is all we have. [*Sunday Times Bookshop,* 1997]

■ Human beings aren't meant to be comfortable. We need tension, stress, uncertainty . . . The kind of challenge that comes from flying a Tiger Moth through zero visibility, or talking a suicide bomber out of a school bus. [*Super-Cannes,* 2000]

■ Only one thing is left which can rouse people, threaten them directly and force them to act together: *crime and transgressive behavior.* By which I mean all activities which aren't necessarily illegal, but provoke us and tap our need for strong emotion, quicken the nervous system and jump the synapses, deadened by leisure and inaction. [*GQ,* 1996]

■ Maybe Americans are not satisfied with the world they've created, and they need to destroy it. [*Seconds,* 1996]

■ We're tired of being taken for granted. We're tired of being used. We don't like the kind of people we've become. [*Millennium People,* 2003]

■ People will kill to get on television. [*Super-Cannes,* 2000]

■ The Vietnam war enormously increased the availability of psychopathology; large areas of pop music do. One gets the notion nowadays of the psychopath as saint. The technological medium of cinema creates the communication level by which something like the De Niro character in *Taxi Driver* becomes a hero. Our moral values are neutralized by the whole technological boom; by movies, rock music, videos. Our notion of the world as a whole is neutralized. Sooner or later we are going to have to face the fact that a whole section of what has become our consciousness is not very far removed from criminal psychology. [*New Musical Express,* 1985]

■ A landscape of sensation, dominated by the mass media, who are selling everything on the strength of eroticism, violence, and, in terms of advertising, [offers] huge claims to a mythic wonderland of possibility that buying the latest refrigerator or electric toothbrush will usher you into. My grandparents would have thought this place absolutely mad, and they might well think that someone as disturbed as some of the characters in my fiction were rather sensible in the way they behaved. [BBC Radio 3, 1998]

■ The psychopath may not be well adjusted to a society such as existed, say, 30 or 40 years ago, but there are periods of history (and we've passed through quite a number of them, and are still doing so) where the psychopath is highly adjusted to whatever is going on around him. Look at the Second World War; look at the former

Yugoslavia today. Psychopaths roved both these sort of nightmare terrains and were probably the best adapted of all ... The sane and cautious and "well adjusted" were the people who sadly were unable to cope. [BBC Radio 3, 1998]

■ On the other hand, being quite serious, the future may be boring. It's possible that my children and yours will live in an eventless world, and that the faculty of imagination will die, or express itself solely in the realm of psychopathology. In *The Atrocity Exhibition* I make the point that perhaps psychopathology should be kept alive as a repository—probably the last repository—of the imagination. [*Paris Review,* 1984]

■ We are vastly more tolerant of aberrant strains in the human character than we were 30 years ago ... Now modern technology tames these aberrant desires and makes them part of the furniture of everyday life. [*I-D,* 1987]

■ It's just a fact that we're getting what I describe in [*The Atrocity Exhibition*] as the "death of affect"; the death of emotion, of any sort of emotional response, is taking place. Let's hope that it gives birth in the future to a new kind of affect; but I think it will be one that will be in partnership with the machine. [*Evergreen Review,* 1973]

■ It's a curious thing that some of my earlier work predicted global warming and desertification and pollution; whether we'll see the psychological effects that I also predicted, we'll have to wait to find out—if people will embrace the catastrophes for their own psychological needs. But given we're entering the millennial dream, it may well be the case: embracing the end of the world might extend to an embracing of global warming, coastal flooding, pollution. [*The Sunday Times,* 1990]

■ Outwardly, some behavior in *The Atrocity Exhibition* might seem very bizarre, but in fact it's all logically constructed.

They're constructing their own logical alternative universe to what they see as a sort of poisoned realm, which is a fair description of the world today, still. [BBC Radio 3, 1998]

■ You see people, these days, who give the impression that their minds are a complete vacuum—no dreams or hopes of any importance, even to themselves, emanate through the sutures of their skulls ... But that doesn't matter, in a sense, because the environment itself is doing the dreaming for them. [*21C*, 1997]

■ Look closely in the mirror ... What do you see? Someone you don't like very much ... By now you're a stage set—one push and the whole thing could collapse at your feet. At times you feel you're living someone else's life in a strange house you've rented by accident. The "you" you've become isn't your real self. [*Millennium People*, 2003]

■ Visitors traveling across the US soon become aware of a missing dimension, a gap in the psychological space around them. The strains of pessimism and wariness that everywhere else seem innately human have been erased from the American psyche, presumably by the Hollywood ethos absorbed since childhood. The people one meets, even the beggars who haunt the airport exit roads, are likable, cheerful and friendly, as if the entire nation had been recruited into a remake of a 1950s Rock Hudson movie. But no one should be *that* likable or friendly. [*New Statesman*, 2002]

■ There are many things that people don't like to be reminded of. People are always surprised to discover in themselves that they covet their neighbor's wife, or that they harbor small racist feelings; they automatically think, "Ohmigod, I'm not worthy of myself." And they immediately turn away from it. ["Prophet with Honour," n.d.]

■ What do you know about the psychology of chauffeurs? [*Cocaine Nights*, 1996]

■ Our latent psychopathy is the last nature reserve, a place of refuge for the *endangered mind*. [*Super-Cannes, 2000*]

■ Psychopathy is the only engine powerful enough to light our imaginations, to drive the arts, sciences and industries of the world. [*Super-Cannes, 2000*]

■ I must be careful, and hide behind those facades of conventional behavior that I intend to subvert. ["The Enormous Space," 1989]

■ They were terrified that I was brewing up an even more advanced psychosis—they couldn't grasp that I was opening the door to a

Photo: Charles Gatewood

new world. ["Memories of the Space Age," 1982]

■ If you said to me, "Do you think we should all go out and crash our cars?" I would say, "Of course not!" This is a very important distinction. I've never said that car crashes are sexually exciting; I've been in a car crash, and I can tell you it did nothing for my libido! What I have said is that the idea of car crashes is sexually exciting, which is very different and, in a way, much more disturbing. Why is it that our imaginations seem so fixated on this particular kind of accident? [*21C,* 1997]

■ Already he seemed to have decided that she was leaving him only in the sense that she was dying of pancreatic cancer, and that he might save her by constructing a unique flying machine. ["Notes Towards a Mental Breakdown," 1976]

■ The grass rustled excitedly, parting in circular waves, beckoning him into its spirals . . . Fascinated, Maitland followed the swirling motions, reading in these patterns the reassuring voice of this immense green creature eager to protect and guide him. The spiral curves swerved through the inflamed air, the visual signature of epilepsy. [*Concrete Island,* 1985]

■ "All psychiatrists secretly dream of killing themselves." "And surgeons?" "They dream of killing their patients." [*Super-Cannes,* 2000]

■ Hungerford? A young misfit named Michael Ryan had shot his mother dead, then strolled through the town shooting at passersby. He had killed sixteen people, picking them off at random, set fire to the family home and shot himself. The murders were motiveless . . . [*Running Wild,* 1989]

■ A young man in a small English town started walking around shooting people. He killed about fourteen people. It's extraordinary to me to see a complete drawing down of the mental shutters over this. People who ought to know better are absolutely refusing to acknowledge the immense hold that violence exerts over people. It seems to me that it's unhealthy. One should face up to the realities of human nature. That way one can do something about *improving* it, steering it into safer channels. [*Twilight Zone,* 1988]

■ The rich know how to cope with the psychopathic. The squirearchy have always enjoyed freedoms denied to the tenant farmers and peasantry. De Sade's behavior was typical of his class. Aristocracies keep alive those endangered pleasures that repel the bourgeoisie. They may seem perverse, but they add to the possibilities of life. [*Super-Cannes,* 2000]

■ I needed to think of other assassins, those deranged men who stared through the telescopic sights of their sniper's rifles, ready to grace with their own madness the last moments of a President or a passing pedestrian. Above all, I needed to dream the psychotic's dream. [*Super-Cannes,* 2000]

■ Madness—that's all they have, after working sixteen hours a day, seven days a week. Going mad is their only way of staying sane. [*Super-Cannes,* 2000]

■ Despair was screaming through the bars of the corporate cage, the hunger of men and women exiled from their *deeper selves*. [*Super-Cannes,* 2000]

■ Porn, drugs, fascist ideas . . . not exactly serious crimes these days. [*Super-Cannes,* 2000]

■ The most potent drug of all: pure imagination. [*Literary Review,* 2001]

■ If you don't keep busy, it's easy to find yourself in a state close to sensory deprivation. All kinds of chimeras float free; reality becomes a Rorschach test where butterflies turn into elephants. [*Super-Cannes,* 2000]

■ *Homo sapiens* is a reformed hunter-killer of depraved appetites, which once helped him to survive. He was partly rehabilitated in an open prison called the first agricultural societies, and now finds himself on parole in the polite suburbs of the city state. The deviant impulses coded into his central nervous system have been switched off. He can no longer harm himself or anyone else. But nature sensibly endowed him with a taste for cruelty and an intense curiosity about pain and death. Without them, he's trapped in the afternoon shopping malls of a limitless mediocrity. We need to revive him, give him back the killing eye and the dreams of death. Together they helped him to dominate this planet. [*Super-Cannes*, 2000]

■ Sadism, cruelty and the dream of pain belong to our primate ancestors. When they surface in a damaged adolescent with a taste for strangling cats, we lock him away. [*Super-Cannes*, 2000]

■ I'm talking about a carefully metered violence, micro-doses of madness like the minute traces of strychnine in a nerve tonic. In effect, a voluntary and elective psychopathy, as you can see in any boxing ring or ice-hockey rink; the armed forces. [*Super-Cannes*, 2000]

■ Psychosis is the most dramatic remaking of the mind that one can embark upon. [*KGB*, 1995]

■ Our own century has romanticized madness . . . The entire realm of the psychopathic has been elevated into the ultimate alternative lifestyle, particularly if combined with alcohol or suicide to make the headiest cocktail of them all. [*Independent*, 1991]

■ It's a grim prospect, though I suspect that we may be saved by our own obstinacy and perversity, qualities that science scarcely notices. It assumes that we are largely rational creatures, driven by calculated self-interest at the group or personal level. But this isn't true, as a million novels, case histories and court transcripts illustrate. The danger is that we may unconsciously grasp that our only hope of freedom, and our only chance of teasing the genie of science back into its bottle, lies within our own psychopathology. ["Our Odds Are 50-50," n.d.]

■ Our responses have become numb, to an enormous extent. Attention spans are shorter and shorter; we crave greater and greater stimulation. [21C, 1997]

■ [On the O.J. Simpson trial:] It's like one of these plays that [the Marquis de] Sade put on in his lunatic asylum using the patients. You'd think that [Judge] Ito was some brain-damaged Japanese-American whose car crashed, asked to play the part of the judge. He's the one that doesn't have a script; he fumbles and stumbles. It's completely obvious to me that Simpson is going to walk out of that court and be paid 100 million dollars to star in the film of his life, which will of course include the murder of that poor couple. [KGB, 1995]

■ In the 1890s the French psychologist Pierre Janet elaborated the concept of the unconscious act, describing a submerged mental world that operated independently of normal consciousness and could give rise to inexplicable actions and emotions. [Daily Telegraph, 1994]

■ Hitler is completely up-to-date . . . The whole apparatus of the Nazi superstate, its nightmare uniforms and propaganda . . . Certainly, Nazi society seems strangely prophetic of our own— the same maximizing of violence and sensation, the same alphabets of unreason and the fictionalizing of experience. [New Worlds, 1969]

■ Dr Charles Fisher of the Mount Sinai Medical Center:"Dreaming permits each and every one of us to be quietly and safely insane every night of our lives." [Guardian, 1986]

■ In Orwell's 1984, disobedience to Big Brother starts in a dream. [Guardian, 1986]

■ We've seen the effects of cults themselves since the Manson gang—what happens when a charismatic leader goes too far—Reverend Jim Jones in Guyana; Waco, Texas; all these weird militias that are springing up all over the States, culminating in this Oklahoma bombing . . . we see extremist fringes popping up all over the place. One could imagine a nightmare scenario of all these extremist cults coalescing. [*KGB*, 1995]

■ I'm not advocating an insane free-for-all. A voluntary and sensible psychopathy is the only way we can impose a shared moral order . . . A controlled psychopathy is a way of resocializing people and tribalizing them into mutually supportive groups. [*Super-Cannes*, 2000]

■ Fascism was a virtual psychopathology that served deep unconscious needs. Years of bourgeois conditioning had produced a Europe suffocating in work, commerce and conformity. Its people needed to break out, to invent the hatred that could liberate them, and they found an Austrian misfit only too happy to do the job. [*Super-Cannes*, 2000]

■ Think . . . Think like a psychopath. [*Super-Cannes*, 2000]

■ All games infantilize, especially when you're playing with your own psychopathy. [*Super-Cannes*, 2000]

■ In the case of women, the system of imposed psychopathy is already in place. It's called men. [*Super-Cannes*, 2000]

■ Women don't dislike men. We bring them into this world and spend the rest of our lives helping them to understand themselves. If anything, we've been too kind to them, letting them play their dangerous games. [*Super-Cannes*, 2000]

■ I'm interested in the freedoms that the feminist movements have won over the past 40 years. But there is an extremist fringe represented by people like Andrea Dworkin, who are female separatists wanting to break the social contract between men and women and put nothing in its place. [*REVelation*, 1994]

■ Female separatists want to destroy the social contract between men and women and replace it with nothing; they seem to believe that all penetrative sex is rape, if a wife loves her husband she's exhibiting a slave mentality. How do you cope with that sort of fanaticism? Satire seems one way. [*KGB*, 1995]

■ He wanted to kill the people who'd corrupted him. At least five or six had to die, to make the kind of splash that would reach the evening news and stay there. [*Super-Cannes*, 2000]

■ We may need to play on deep-rooted masochistic needs built into the human sense of hierarchy. [*Super-Cannes*, 2000]

■ Nazi Germany and the old Soviet Union were Sadeian societies of torturers and willing victims. People no longer need enemies—in this millennium, their great dream is to become victims. Only their psychopathies can set them free.[*Super-Cannes*, 2000]

■ My real vocation was to be a psychiatrist. I spend so long analyzing my motives I've no time left to act. [*Super-Cannes*, 2000]

■ Some people used to maintain that consciousness is nothing more than a special category of the cytoplasmic coma, that the capacities of the central nervous system are as fully developed and extended by the dream life as they are during what we call the waking state . . . [*Drowned World*, 1962]

■ Sexual pathology is such an energizing force. People know that, and will stoop to any depravity that excites them. [*Super-Cannes*, 2000]

■ We don't give in to every passing whim or impulse. But it's a mistake to ignore them. [*Super-Cannes*, 2000]

■ However selective the conscious mind may be, most biological memories are unpleasant ones, echoes of danger and terror. Nothing endures for so long as fear . . . How else can you explain the universal but completely groundless loathing of the spider, only one species of which has ever been known to sting? Or the equally surprising—in view of their comparative rarity—hatred of snakes and reptiles? Simply because we all carry within us a submerged memory of the time when the giant spiders were lethal, and when the reptiles were the planet's dominant life form. [*Drowned World,* 1962]

■ A more important task than mapping the harbors and lagoons of the external landscape was to chart the ghostly deltas and luminous beaches of the submerged neuronic continents. [*Drowned World,* 1962]

Photo: Charles Gatewood

■ There's nothing more satisfying than confessing to a crime you haven't committed. [*Cocaine Nights*, 1996]

■ I imagine my mental patients conflating Freud and Liz Taylor in their Warhol-like efforts, unerringly homing in on the first signs of their doctor's nervous breakdown. *The Atrocity Exhibition's* original dedication should have been "To the insane." I owe them everything. [*Atrocity Exhibition*, 1990]

■ I watched an elderly woman patient helping the orderly to serve the afternoon tea ... She began to stare at the bobbing liquid, then stepped forward and carefully inverted the brimming cup in her hand. The hot liquid dripped everywhere in a terrible mess, and the orderly screamed: "Doreen, why did you do that?," to which Doreen matter-of-factly replied: "Jesus told me to." ... I like to think that what really impelled her was a sense of the intolerable contrast between the infinitely plastic liquid in her hand and the infinitely hard geometry of the table, followed by the revelation that she could resolve these opposites in a very simple and original way. [*Atrocity Exhibition*, 1990]

■ He wants to see a nuclear war—one sun is not enough. [*Rushing to Paradise*, 1994]

■ I feel we should immerse ourselves in the most destructive element, *ourselves,* and swim. [*Atrocity Exhibition*, 1990]

■ Obsessive attention to microscopic detail is usually a symptom of underlying neurosis. ["Impressions of Speed," 1998]

■ The mysterious mushroom clouds, rising above the Pacific atolls from which the B-29s had brought to Nagasaki the second day of apocalypse, were a powerful incitement to the psychotic imagination, sanctioning everything. [*Kindness of Women*, 2003]

■ What is a lunatic? ... Merely a man with more understanding than he can contain. ["Venus Hunters," 1963]

■ In a completely sane world, madness is the only freedom! [*Super-Cannes,* 2001]

■ The psychotic never escapes from anything. He's much more sensible. He merely readjusts reality to suit himself. ["Manhole 69," 1957]

■ Only in the darkness could one become sufficiently obsessive; deliberately play on all one's repressed instincts. He welcomed this forced conscription of the deviant strains in his character. [*High Rise,* 1975]

■ An inexplicable act of violence had a fierce authority that no reasoned behavior could match. [*Millennium People,* 2003]

■ The mentally ill were on their own, spared pity and consideration, made to pay to the hilt for their failings. The sacred cow of the community was the psychotic, free to wander where he wanted, drooling on the doorsteps, sleeping on sidewalks, and woe betide anyone who tried to help him. ["The Insane Ones," 1962]

■ Hitler tapped into all kinds of psychopathic traits in the German people—the race hatred in particular: Jews, Gypsies, non-Germans, all "biological inferiors." These were very potent ideas that are probably carried in all of us from our distant past when it made sense to fear strangers because they were probably trying to steal your cattle, kill you, or rape your wife. Hitler tapped those buried layers of psychopathy. [*Spike,* 2000]

■ [In Richard Overy's *Interrogations: The Nazi Elite in Allied Hands*] transcripts of prison conversations with Goering, Hess, Keitel and others, prior to the Nuremberg Trials, show them moving in a realm beyond morality, pity or even self-knowledge. [*Guardian,* 12-20-01]

■ To my eyes, the single thing that widens the landscape of the 20th century is psychopathology. Psychopathology has become the motor of a great part of our daily life. [paraphrase, *Cahiers du cinema #504,* 1996]

■ I believe in the fundamental freedom that consists in playing with our psychopathology. In the realm of poetry and the imagination, we can explore the territories that remain forbidden to us. [paraphrase, *Cahiers du Cinema #504*, 1996]

■ We live like figures embalmed in moral Lucite. We're totally suffocated in moral systems of one kind or another . . . How we care for and educate our children, our behavior with our spouses, is closely regulated by law . . . You can happily and responsibly live your life today without ever making a moral decision at all. [*Independent*, 9/14/2000]

■ [It's] the death of feeling . . . One's more and more alienated from any kind of direct response to experience. [*Studio-International*, 1971]

■ Everyone is a victim these days—of parents, doctors, pharmaceutical companies, even love itself. And how much we enjoy it! Our happiest moments are spent trying to think up new varieties of victimhood. [*Pretext*, 2004]

■ Normal? Careers have foundered trying to define what that means. Be careful, we've moved into a world where it's dangerous to be normal. Extreme problems call for extreme solutions. [*Super-Cannes*, 2000]

■ The brain does settle down after the age of forty, physiologically. Nobody becomes psychopathic, I gather, after the age of forty. The brain quietens. A lot of people with long-standing mental problems do emerge into some sort of calm plateau after the age of forty. [*Thrust #14*, 1980]

■ We all mythologize ourselves to try and make sense of our lives. [*REVelation*, 1994]

CAR CRASH

■ [A car crash] is the most dramatic experience that anyone will ever go through in their whole lives, apart from their own deaths, simply because one is insulated in late Twentieth Century life from real and direct experience. Even sexual experience is muffled by a whole overlay of conceptualization—fashion, chitchat and everything else. The car crash is *real*; it is a violent experience that you are not likely to get in any other area. It is a massive collision of the central nervous system . . . a total explosion of the senses. [*Friends,* 10/30/1970]

Photo: S.M. Gray

■ The car crash is the most dramatic experience in most people's lives, apart from their own deaths, and in many cases the two coincide. I think there's something about the automobile crash that taps all kinds of barely recognized impulses in people's minds and imaginations. It's a mistake to adopt a purely rational attitude towards events like the car crash; one can't simply say that this is a meaningless and horrific tragedy. It is that, but it's other things as well, and in *Crash* I've tried to find out what exactly that it is. [*Evergreen Review,* 1973]

■ The car is that part of modern technology which we're most involved with and which offers us the greatest number of possibilities for aggression, death and self-mutilation. *Crash* is about the unconscious marriage which takes place between the human imagination and technology, the way in which modern technology offers us a back-door pass into the realm of psychopathology. [*I-D,* 1987]

■ The car is, in fact, a powerful force for good in its perverse way. And even the car crash can be conceived of—in *imaginative* terms—as a powerful link in the nexus of sex, love, eroticism and death, that lies at the basis of our own sexual imagination, with its heart wired into the central nervous system of all human beings. [Iain Sinclair's *Crash,* 1999]

■ As we drive a motor car, we literally have our own deaths at our fingertips. [*Frieze,* 1996]

■ About [44,000] people a year are killed on the roads in America. Of course, every death is deplored, but collectively it's manslaughter on a gigantic scale . . . tolerated as part of the price to be paid [for] the sort of lives we've opted for. [*Mississippi Review,* 1991]

■ In *Crash,* I'm taking certain tendencies that I see inscribed in the world we live in and I'm following them to their point of contact. Putting it crudely, I'm saying, "So you think violence is sexy? Well, this is where it leads." [*21C*, 1997]

■ *Crash* is a warning about the desperate need people have to make contact with each other, and how they'll find the most deviant means of doing so. It's a love story in many ways, about the love between a wife and husband. [*Sub Dee, 1997*]

■ In respect to *Crash,* I'm the forensic pathologist looking at this decaying corpse, a corpse that's emitting some wonderfully colorful gases and giving some enticing twitches, and saying, "Well, this is where I see things going." *Crash* is an extreme-case scenario. [*21C,* 1997]

■ When a young man driving his car is overtaken by an attractive young woman who deliberately sprays her exhaust on his windshield, and he slams his foot down on the gas pedal to catch up to her, we can assume there's a partial sexual component there. [*Seconds,* 1996]

■ Every woman knows there are lots of men around who can't bear to be overtaken by a woman driver. A lot of men find driving extremely competitive. Obviously, the experience of driving taps all sorts of aggressive strains in our make-up and it's necessary; after all, you have to be decisive if you're going to overtake on a narrow road at sixty miles an hour. You've got to call on a certain amount of aggression. My novel and the film face up to it fairly and squarely. [Fineline Features Online, 2002]

■ The excitements of *Crash* are the excitements of danger. The characters are exploring a wholly new sexuality. If the audience is excited, good. But neither the book nor the film is meant to be erotic—both are about a far more serious subject, sex, and how the many diverse forms of sexuality today are competing with themselves, in a straightforwardly Darwinian sense, to ensure their survival into an age of advanced and very strange technologies. [*21C,* 1997]

■ I think we've gotten much more honest about human nature

and we're more open about the truth of our own identities. At the time I wrote [Crash] (I started it in 1970) the idea that people could get any kind of excitement from the idea of car crashes—well, people just couldn't cope with it, they thought it was totally insane. Now people are much more honest about the psychology of the late twentieth century and people can see, moreover, the way in which the car crash is built into the entertainment culture. No respectable Hollywood thriller has anything less than six car crashes. And people realize the extent to which aggression and libido are built into the experience of driving a car. [Fineline Features, 2002]

■ If you look at the entertainment culture that people amuse themselves with, it's obvious that the car crash has a very powerful role to play in people's imaginations . . . something is happening in the imagination that tends to entangle the elements of violence and sexuality, and it's fed by this relentless flow of appealingly-violent imagery that we get in our movies. Crash is an attempt to follow these trends off the edge of the graph paper to the point where they meet. Basically the message is, "So you think violence is sexy? OK, this is where you're going." I see the ultimate effect of Crash as cautionary, as a warning against the role of violence and sex in our entertainment culture and the way the two can become intertwined. ["Prophet with Honour," n.d.]

■ Crash attempts to look at the psychology of violence. [Fineline Features Online, 2002]

■ How has technology changed our lives? We're loaded with technological systems, all converging in the automobile. I'm interested in the psychology arising from these systems and how they modify our imaginations . . . [Sub Dee, 1997]

■ [Crash] is written in the first person—these are my own speculations and obsessions, whatever you like to call them. This is my psychopathology; the book is a psychopathological hymn and I'm singing it. Attaching my name to the protagonist's reminds the reader where these ideas are coming from: a real human being, a "real" reality. [1997]

■ It would have been easy to write a conventional book about car crashes in which it was quite clear that the author was on the side of sanity, justice and against injuring small children, deaths on the road, bad driving, etc. I chose to provoke the reader by saying that these car crashes are good for you, you thoroughly enjoy them, they make your sex life richer, they represent part of the marriage between sex, the human organism, and technology. I say all these things in order to provoke the reader and also to test him. [intv David Pringle, 1975]

■ [In a car] people are aware of a whole range of emotions they can't express when they're in their office, dealing with other people, that they can express alone in a car. You can't swear at your secretary for making a spelling mistake, but you can swear at another driver behind your windshield and you're—generally—safe. [*Fineline Features,* 2002]

■ In writing books like *Crash* or *The Atrocity Exhibition* or *High Rise,* I was exploring myself, using myself as the laboratory animal, as it were, probing around. I had to take the top off my skull when I was writing *Crash* and start touching pain and pleasure centers to see what happened. Now I can distance myself from the book and see it as a cautionary tale. [*Heavy Metal,* 1982]

■ I've had some extraordinary mail, particularly from Los Angeles. Things like sadomasochistic erotic fantasies. Letters that start straightforward, which soon get into a zone of "as I ride my bike," which I assume means a motorbike with enough power to go into orbit, "I think of *Crash.*" All these letters adopt a sort of "lyrical death" tone and they all culminate in some horrendous accident image: "As I read your book I stroke my wounds" kind of stuff. I thought,

"*Gawdalmighty!* I hope this is confined to a very small number of people." I wouldn't want to cause any accidents on your beautiful highways! "Why don't we do it in the road?" [*Heavy Metal*, 1982]

■ I think we're living at a time when we need, for some reason, an enormous amount of perverse behavior and violence in our psychological diet. They seem to provide some sort of grit which helps us to digest the business of being alive. But they're also stepping stones; they're part of some sort of evolving formula for reaching a better world. [*Evergreen Review*, 1973]

■ At the turn of the century [1900] the first European limousines featured fully equipped kitchens, silk brocade armchairs that could be converted into beds, and, designed for a wealthy American, a built-in flush toilet. [*Guardian*, 1984]

■ The automobile culture that Americans have had since the 1920s really arrived in Europe in the 1960s: mass ownership of the motorcar; motorways were being built for the first time. The whole car culture had come into being with everything that went with it; dating and sex in cars suddenly became a part of the global way of life. [*Kulture Deluxe*, 1997]

■ The editors [Julian Pettifer and Nigel Turner] of *Automania* estimate that 15–20 million people have been killed by the car in its first century. [*Guardian*, 1984]

■ One Texan lady infatuated with her Ferrari was buried in it. [*Guardian*, 1984]

■ Famous people who died in car crashes like [James] Dean and Jayne Mansfield and Albert Camus and of course, the greatest of them all, Kennedy . . . their deaths had a resonance that wasn't present in the case of famous people who died in, say, plane crashes or hotel fires or whatever . . . The car crash had a special significance. [*Kulture Deluxe*, 1997]

■ For me the heroic period of the Rolls-Royce lies well in its past, in a pre-war epoch of archdukes and maharajahs, the latter being emperors of eccentricity—one fitted a throne, another made his steering wheel from elephants' tusks, a third crowned his Rolls with a thatched roof. [*Guardian*, 1984]

■ Think of the twentieth century—what key image most sums it up? . . . A man in a motor car, driving along a concrete highway to some unknown destination. Almost every aspect of modern life is there, both for good and for ill—our sense of speed, drama and aggression, the worlds of advertising and consumer goods, engineering and mass manufacture, and the shared experience of moving together through an elaborately signalled landscape . . . Here we see, all too clearly, the speed and violence of our age, its strange love affair with the machine, and, conceivably, with its own death and destruction. [*Drive*, 1971]

■ If my novel or Cronenberg's film [*Crash*] had been about a small group of people who got their kicks from crashing aircraft, you would be getting close to the absurdity of *Catch-22*. Yet all sorts of connections between cars and sexuality have been evident for years. [*LA Weekly*, 1997]

■ A crashed automobile has a reality, and a poignancy, and a unique identity that no showroom car ever has. [*Intv Charles Platt*, 1979]

■ I see this profane Mass [the car crash] as the greatest mystery of the 20th century, aside from the assassination of President Kennedy. And a large part of that mystery resides in the fact that the motorcade assassination was a peculiar kind of car accident. Had Kennedy been shot down as he was walking across the tarmac at the airport, it wouldn't have had the same emblematic significance. [*LA Weekly*, 1997]

■ The French are the most dangerous drivers in the world unless you go to somewhere like Thailand . . . *Crash* did well in France. They'll say, "Of course!" The book caught on there in a big way. [*Kulture Deluxe,* 1997]

■ It wasn't altogether a coincidence that [*Crash*] did well in France. Unlike the United States and Great Britain, the French have this long tradition of serious works of fiction using explicitly sexual elements, particularly sexual fantasy. You go back all the way to the Marquis de Sade and on into the 19th century and into the 20th century with people like Georges Bataille and Genet and *The Story of O,* etc. And Surrealist writing, too—we've never had that. [*Kulture Deluxe,* 1997]

■ It's quite clear from the closing moments [of David Cronenberg's movie *Crash*], when the Ballards embrace in the most tender way, that a car crash has elicited the love they still feel for each other. This may sound silly or perverse, but seeing the film was a life-enhancing experience for me. You could say that it made me feel young again. [*Time Out,* 1997]

■ My guess is that the car will remain much in its present form for the next thirty years. [*Drive,* 1971]

■ The sight of the Renault burning in the night had excited me. Roused by flames that seemed to leap across the bedroom ceiling, I ran to the balcony and saw the passenger cabin lit like a lantern, smoke swirling in the headlamps of the members' cars as they backed away to safety. One of the modern world's Pagan rites was taking place, the torching of the automobile, witnessed by the young women from the disco, their sequined dresses trembling in the flames. [*Cocaine Nights,* 1996]

■ Car crashes mean for him what bull-fights mean for everyone else—sex and death. [*Kindness of Women,* 1991]

■ Needless to say, the ultimate role of *Crash* is cautionary, a warning against that brutal, erotic and overlit realm that beckons more and more persuasively to us from the margins of the technological landscape. [unknown]

■ A car crash harnesses elements of eroticism, aggression, desire, speed, drama, kinesthetic factors, the stylizing of motion, consumer goods, status—all these in one event. I myself see the car crash as a tremendous sexual event really: a liberation of human and machine libido—if there is such a thing. [*Penthouse*, 1970]

■ In particular the automobile crash contains a crucial image of the machine as conceptualized psychopathology. Tests on a wide range of subjects indicate that the automobile, and in particular the automobile crash, provides a focus for the conceptualizing of a wide range of impulses involving the elements of psychopathology, sexuality and self-sacrifice. [*Atrocity Exhibition,* 1990]

■ The car crash differs from other disasters in that it involves the most powerfully advertised commercial product of this century, an iconic entity that combines the elements of speed, power, dream and freedom within a highly stylized format that defuses any fears we may have of the inherent dangers of these violent and unstable machines. [*Atrocity Exhibition,* 1990]

■ Writing a novel like Crash was to some extent a psychopathic act: the deliberate immersion of one's imagination in all sorts of destructive impulses. [paraphrase, *RE/Search #8/9,* p. 47, 1984]

■ Some tabloid journalists seemed to think I'd orchestrated [Princess] Diana's accident and planned the whole thing. I felt like saying, "Everything went nearly perfectly, but it should have been a Buick." [*Spectator,* 2000]

■ Violence took the place of sex, I think, as the most exciting subject available to writers and filmmakers, and became sort of the key engine of the entertainment culture. The car crash came into its own. ["Prophet with Honour," n.d.]

■ I think [*Crash*] will be one of those films that will grow in time, because it says so much about the way of the world we're living in. It's a pitiless searchlight playing over the secret, nasty spaces of the late 20th century. It's a remarkable film. You'll be profoundly unsettled by it. [*Salon*, 1996]

■ The latest figures published by the World Health Organization on automobile fatalities show that probably 250,000 people are killed [yearly], and that's probably an underestimate. Millions are injured, and seriously too. What logic is at work that allows this to happen? [*The Imagination on Trial*, 1981]

■ I'm not interested in street crime. I'm interested in the communications landscape, where your responses to violence are on a much more conceptual level. The danger lies in ambiguous responses, where one doesn't know one's own moral direction. How should you, as a responsible and moral human being, react at a Grand Prix when there's a big pileup and cars start exploding all over the track? Should you enjoy it? Should you give in to the thrills and excitement? . . . Then, if it's okay to enjoy that sort of stylized violence, what happens when on the TV after the commercial break, you're getting newsreels from the latest war? Are you allowed to enjoy those? There's a whole new moral system to contend with. [*Heavy Metal*, 1982]

VIOLENCE

■ He had killed seven senior executives at Eden-Olympia, executed his three hostages and then turned his rifle on himself . . . The murders were part political manifesto, so the newspaper believed, and part existential scream. [*Super-Cannes*, 2000]

■ I see that people's lives these days are saturated with images of violence of every conceivable kind. The strange thing is that although in the past we perceived violence at our nerve endings, in terms of pain and pumping adrenalin, now we perceive violence purely intellectually—purely as an imaginative pastime. [*Evergreen Review,* 1973]

■ Tens of millions of years of evolution trained humans to react to violence with their nerve endings. But that training is now largely

Photo: Charles Gatewood

gone to waste. We see violence now purely through film, television, and the news media. We experience it almost as part of the entertainment landscape of our lives. But we've got this huge inherited apparatus for coping with violence—flight or fight, whatever—yet it's being officially denied now that it exists. Violence is being treated here in the same way that sex was treated in the pre-Kinsey era. [*Twilight Zone*, 1988]

■ The refusal to acknowledge human nature is a mistake because it will find some other, possibly more lethal, way out. Just as repressive attitudes toward sex generated ignorance and superstition, so the repression of violence will generate an equally unfortunate set of fantasies and delusions. Not only do some of our politicians want to ban violence entirely on TV (sometimes I think these people have an extra channel inside their heads that I don't get to watch), they even want to ban images of violence from the news. They say the news should not be too explicit. You know, reports of an air disaster or car crashes or film from a war zone like Beirut, anything like that. Well, this is a very dangerous kind of censorship. [*Twilight Zone*, 1988]

■ Perhaps violence, like pornography, is some kind of an evolutionary standby system, a last-resort device for throwing a wild joker into the game? [*RE/Search #8/9*, 1984]

■ Madness lies within us. It shows itself in countless ways, from road rage to the behavior of football hooligans. [*Spectator*, 2000]

■ People are violent. Yet most have not seen a dead body or handled a firearm ... [*Sunday Times*, 9/22/1991]

■ Camille Paglia's view of women I would endorse 100 %: that they are dangerous, passionate, potentially quite cruel and more than a match for any man. I think there is a common female fantasy about cutting the throats of all the men in the world. [*Spectator*, 2000]

■ Our whole inherited expertise for dealing with violence, our central nervous systems, our musculature, our senses, our ability to run fast or to react quickly, our reflexes, all that inherited expertise, is never used. We sit passively in cinemas watching movies like *The Wild Bunch* where violence is just a *style*. [*Studio International*, 1971]

■ Most of us would take the view that violence is wholly bad in all its forms—I would myself—but it may be that certain kinds of violence, particularly those transmitted through the communications media, through television and the news magazines, and so on, have a *beneficial* role. This is the terrifying irony of an appalling experience like Vietnam—that it may have certain beneficial roles to play. What they are I don't know. I try to offer certain suggestions in [*The Atrocity Exhibition*]. [*Evergreen Review*, 1973]

■ Human beings today display a deep and restless violence, which no longer channels itself into wars but has to emerge in road rage, Internet porn, contact sports like hyperviolent professional rugby and US football, reality TV, and so on. [intv Hans Obrist, 2003]

WAR

■ World War III began on the installment plan around 1945. [*Newsweek*, 1985]

■ There is a good case to be made for the proposition that no one should fight in a war, or put on a uniform, until the age of 40. [*New Statesman*, 2002]

■ Men carry a weakness they've borne with them from the past. Their genes have been poisoned by all that aggression and competition, so they're like soldiers who have seen too much of battle. [*Rushing to Paradise*, 1994]

■ If there were a nuclear war in Western Europe, you'd probably have a situation not dissimilar to Shanghai at the end of the

Second World War, with rival roving gangs, drifting allegiances, and complete confusion. In the camp, we weren't certain that the war had ended. Nor were the Japanese. [*City Limits,* 1984]

■ [In] Jean Baudrillard's polemic *The Gulf War Did Not Take Place,* the impish philosopher argued that the heavily censored news reports, the absence of casualties and the video-game footage of smart bombs dropping down chimneys did not constitute a true war in our minds. [*New Statesman,* 2001]

■ How could Japan and Germany, two of the most advanced nations on our planet, have unleashed wars of ferocious barbarity against their neighbors, murdering millions of civilians in the most cruel and savage way? How could these same peoples, only a few years later, sharing the same airliners with us and strolling around the same museums, seem virtually indistinguishable from ourselves, as kindly and generous to strangers? ["Licence to Kill," *Sunday Times,* 1999]

■ During the Sino-Japanese war, from 1937 to 1945, the Japanese army killed at least *ten million Chinese civilians.* [*Sunday Times,* 1999]

■ The real horror of this [20th] century's war crimes is that they were carried out by ordinary human beings, farmers and factory workers and office clerks, who returned to their jobs and brought up their children. Faced with a threat to themselves, human beings become cruel and dangerous, and the murder and torture of enemy civilians is an unhappy part of their natural behavior, only restrained by the prevailing moral codes, the political leadership and the officers in charge. When rulers and generals urge on racial war, ordinary soldiers become their core selves, as vicious as the chimpanzee raiding parties who work themselves up with bloodcurdling screams and tear the enemy limb from limb. [*Sunday Times,* 1999]

■ The Falklands and Vietnam newsreels gave us a convincing idea of what it was like to be a soldier, but the TV reports from the Gulf incite our imaginations in a wholly new way, urging us to become a cruise missile . . . Already one can visualize the combatants in a future war returning from their sorties and fire-fights to scan the evening rushes, and perhaps planning the next day's tactical strike in terms of its viewer potential. ["The Artist at War," 1991]

■ Adults persist in this naive notion of the war coming to an end. The war never comes to an end—it just changes form. [NME, 1985]

■ Peace . . . another kind of war. [NY Times, 1991]

■ I think you're right—[Empire of the Sun] is about World War III, despite the fact that it is also partly autobiographical. [NME, 1985]

■ Curtis LeMay, fresh from the Korean War, where his conventional bombing raids had killed *two million Koreans*, urged a preventive nuclear first strike against the Soviets [that would have killed 100 million], though fortunately he was reined in by President Eisenhower. ["Dark Sun," 1997]

■ The seeds of the next global conflict were laid down in the Far East in the '20s and '30s. [City Limits, 1984]

■ If there is a Third World War, I don't think it will start in western Europe. [City Limits, 1984]

■ Particularly from the civilian point of view, war isn't a matter of continuous gunfire and dive bombers. Anybody who's been in the armed forces will tell you that most of the time you're doing nothing. Even if you're a frontline infantryman or driving a tank, you're doing nothing. There are brief moments of violence, but you'll probably never see the enemy. [Omni, n.d.]

■ For a long period during the occupation, running from 1937 when the Japanese invaded China and seized most of Shanghai, all the way through to '45, there was a mysterious sense of a lull before a storm, or a very mysterious lull after a storm. Everything seemed pregnant with hidden danger and possibility—in a sense, like the world we live in now. [*Omni*, n.d.]

■ Was there a Gulf War? . . . The devastated Basra escape highway looked like a traffic jam left out to rust, or a discarded *Mad Max* film set, the ultimate autogeddon. [*Guardian*, 1991]

■ The virus of war. Or, if you like, the martial spirit. Not a physical virus, but a psychological one even more dangerous than smallpox. ["War Fever," 1989]

■ The rats in the war laboratory had been happy pulling a familiar set of levers—the triggers of their rifles and mortars—and being fed their daily pellets of hate. ["War Fever," 1989]

■ What's really frightening is all the possible consequences of a war . . . the hatred of the entire Arab world focused on the U.S. and Britain . . . The possibility of a terrorist attack in London or elsewhere in Britain is frightening. [*Observer*, 1/19/2003]

■ ARCO PRODUCTIONS INC.: Hunting and shooting. Your own war to order. Raiding parties, revolutions, religious crusades. In anything from a small commando squad to a 3,000-ship armada. ARCO provide publicity, mock War Crimes Tribunal, etc. ["Passport to Eternity," 1962]

■ A futile war dragged on, so pointless that the world's news media had long since lost interest. ["War Fever," 1989]

■ [The UN observers] photographed the latest atrocity victims, or debriefed the survivors of a cruel revenge attack, like prurient priests at confession. How could they put an end to the hate that was corrupting them all? ["War Fever," 1989]

■ "What was he fighting for?" "Are you serious? We're fighting for what we believe." "But nobody believes anything!...We're fighting and dying for nothing." ["War Fever," 1989]

■ All this talk of peace. The oldest trap in the world, and we walked straight into it . . . ["War Fever," 1989]

■ The real map of the city was endlessly redrawn by opportunist deals struck among the local commanders—a jeep bartered for a truckload of tomatoes, six rocket launchers for a video recorder. What ransom could buy a cease-fire? ["War Fever," 1989]

■ The American Army? One of the world's greatest environmental threats. [*Rushing to Paradise*, 1994]

DEATH

■ During my childhood I saw an enormous number of dead bodies. ["Raising the Dead," n.d.]

■ I haven't really had any private fantasies about an alternative life, even in the daydream sense. I rather like the idea of ending my days drinking myself to death on a mountainside in Mexico. [*Paris Review*, 1984]

■ It may be that the thought of death—any mention of it—probably will be banished in the future. [*Index*, 1997]

■ There are so few *real* events any more. A plane crashes in a London airport but we don't see a photograph of a single body, so we don't feel the impact of death. People don't die at home, they die in hospitals. In this country the coffin lid is not open; death is factored out of our lives. People are subtracted from life like contestants in *Big Brother*. People leave like guests in a holiday hotel who booked a week before you did and then suddenly are not there any more. [*The Spectator*, 2000]

■ We accept deaths when we feel they're justified—wars, climbing Everest, putting up a skyscraper, building a bridge.

[*Millennium People*, 2003]

■ The old don't face death with any more courage or dignity than the young. Nor are there any moments of great catharsis or increased wisdom as one gets older. [*The Spectator*, 2000]

■ Death was a secret door through which the threatened and the weary could slip to safety. [*Rushing to Paradise*, 1994]

■ He remembered his father's funeral and the eerie non-denominational service in the north London crematorium, with its sliding coffin and remote-controlled curtains, and his mother gasping as the teak doors briefly re-opened before closing for the last time. [*Rushing to Paradise*, 1994]

■ Contrary to general belief, no one's death diminishes us. [Rushing to Paradise, 1994]

■ People realize that their lives are largely meaningless. They look at their designer kitchens and then realize, *those polyps in my colon may have other plans for me.* And it's impossible to attribute any real meaning to the consumer-driven society in which we live. So the simplest way out is to just shut one's eyes. [*Index*, 1997]

■ I think you can look at outbreaks of lunatic violence as a reaction to the blandness of everything. It's very curious that these killings take place in locations that don't seem to possess any kind of obvious trigger, like university campuses, children's schools, McDonalds. It may be that these killers see the whole of society as endlessly and unsettlingly bland and that they're desperate to restore reality of some kind. They may even see themselves as playing a necessary social role. [*Frieze*, 1996]

■ Raymond Roussel (1877–1933), author of *Impressions of Africa* and *Locus Solus*, traveled with a coffin in which he would lie for a short time each day, preparing himself for death. [*Atrocity Exhibition*, 1990]

■ He merely smiled at me, the reassuring smile of professional sympathy reserved for the bereaved at funeral chapels. [*Cocaine Nights*, 1996]

■ Graveyards and cemeteries have the same calming effect, the more ornate the better. A visit to Pere Lachaise in Paris adds a year to one's life, and the pyramids of Egypt stare down time itself. [*Atrocity Exhibition*, 1990]

■ It would be intriguing to construct a mausoleum that was an exact replica, in the most funereal stone, of one's own home, even including the interior furniture (reminiscent of Magritte's strange stone paintings, with their stone men and women, stone trees and stone birds). One could weekend in this alternate home, and probably soon find oneself stepping out of time. [*Atrocity Exhibition*, 1990]

■ There's something about the theatrical way that cadavers lie on their glass-top tables under the cool light of the dissection room. It's like a strange cross between a Conceptual Art installation and a nightclub. And the cadavers, of course, are naked, and reveal all their personal histories in scars and blotches, in facial lines, in skin color. One's looking at the entire life of a human being, not just at a dead version of the person. [*Artforum*, 1997]

■ Funerals celebrate another frontier crossing, in many ways the most formal and protracted of all. As the mourners waited in the Protestant cemetery, dressed in their darkest clothes, it struck me that they resembled a party of well-to-do emigrants, standing patiently at a hostile customs post and aware that however long they waited only one of them would be admitted that day. [*Cocaine Nights*, 1996]

■ The experience of war is deeply corrupting. Anybody who witnesses years of brutality can't help but lose a sense of the tragedy and mystery of death. I'm sure that happened to me. The 16-year-old who came to England after the war carried this freight of "matter-of-factness about death." So spending two years dissecting cadavers was a way of reminding me of the reality of death itself, and gave me back a respect for life. ["Raising the Dead," n.d.]

■ Nature in its wisdom created death to give each of us our unique sense of life. Each of us is an island, and death is the price we pay to keep ourselves from drowning in the larger sea. [*Rushing to Paradise,* 1994]

■ Each breath you take is a celebration, with a special ceremony for the last breath. Not just our last breath, but the last breath of every bird and flower. [*Rushing to Paradise,* 1994]

■ I was watching the last episode of Robert Hughes' New Theory for American Vision . . . and it showed a wonderful piece of film—the burial of Ed Kienholz . . . Kienholz's corpse was seated in the front seat of a 1940 Packard . . . with a bottle of wine, a deck of cards, the cremated remains of his dog Smash, and a dollar bill . . . then his wife drove the car down a ramp about twenty feet below the ground. Once she got out, he was entombed . . . He was buried like a pharaoh. It was profoundly moving, actually—partly, of course, because of the car. Without the car there it would have been just another burial. [*Artforum,* 1997]

■ He often watched the eyes of the patients as they died, trying to detect a flash of light when the soul left. [*Empire of the Sun,* 1984]

■ In the trenches between the burial mounds hundreds of dead soldiers sat side by side with their heads against the torn earth, as if they had fallen asleep together in a deep dream of war. [*Empire of the Sun,* 1984]

■ The dead were buried above ground, the loose soil heaped around them. The heavy rains of the monsoon months softened the mounds, so that they formed outlines of the bodies within them, as if this small cemetery beside the military airfield was doing its best to resurrect a few of the millions who had died in the war. Here and there an arm or a foot protruded from the graves, the limbs of restless sleepers struggling beneath their brown quilts. [*Empire of the Sun,* 1984]

■ Once he had helped Dr Ransome as he massaged the naked chest of a young Belgian woman wasted by dysentery. Dr Bowen had said that she was dead, but Dr Ransome squeezed her heart under her ribs and suddenly her eyes swivelled and looked at Jim. At first Jim thought that her soul had returned to her, but she was still dead. Dr Ransome explained that for a few seconds he had pumped the blood back into her brain. [*Ibid.*]

■ The creeks and lagoons were filled with saffron water, the conduits of a perfume factory blocked by dead mules and buffaloes drowned in its scents. [*Empire of the Sun,* 1984]

■ The verges were littered with the debris of the air attacks. Burnt-out trucks and supply wagons lay in the ditches, surrounded by the bodies of dead puppet soldiers, the carcasses of horses and water buffalo. A glimmer of golden light rose from the thousands of spent cartridge cases, as if these dead soldiers had been looting a treasury in the moments before their death. [*Empire of the Sun,* 1984]

■ [The dead soldier's] head had been bludgeoned to a pulp that resembled a crushed watermelon, filled with the black seeds of hundreds of flies. [*Empire of the Sun,* 1984]

■ The nuclear testing-ground had a stronger claim on his imagination. No bomb had ever exploded on Saint-Esprit, but the atoll, like Eniwetok, Muroroa and Bikini, was a demonstration model of Armageddon, a dream of war and death that lay beyond the reach of any moratorium. [*Rushing to Paradise,* 1994]

■ Suicide is a highly suggestive act. ["The Insane Ones," 1962]

■ Human beings have an extraordinary instinct for self-destruction, and this ought to be out in the open where we can see it. [*Pretext,* 2004]

■ Chromium cyanate. Inhibits the coenzyme system controlling the body's fluid balances, floods hydroxyl ions into the bloodstream. In brief, you drown. Really drown, that is, not merely suffocate as you would if you were immersed in an external bath. ["Track 12," 1958]

■ On one of the empty coffin shelves was a collection of metal objects stripped from his car, a wing mirror and manufacturer's medallion, strips of chromium trim, laid out like an elaborate altarpiece on which would one day repose the bones of a revered saint. [*Concrete Island,* 1973]

■ Why do the dying think they're floating through tunnels? Under extreme pressure, the various centers in the brain which organize a coherent view of the world begin to break down. The brain scans its collapsing field of vision, and constructs out of the last few rings of cells what it desperately hopes is an escape tunnel. Right to the end the brain is trying at all costs to rationalize reality—whether it's starved of input or flooded with sensory data it builds artificial structures that try to make sense of the world. Out of this come not only near-death experiences but our visions of heaven and hell. [*Kindness of Women,* 1991]

■ Ultimately, a videotape playback will allow you to watch your own death live. ["Journey Across a Crater," 1971]

■ [On being asked "What would you leave to whom and why?," Ballard replied:] I would leave Andrea Dworkin my testicles. She could have testicles flambés. [*Observer,* Sept 10, 1995]

■ If somebody came round and said, "Mr. Ballard . . . would you like to bequeath your body to the dissecting room?" I would happily sign on the dotted line. ["Raising the Dead," n.d.]

■ At a certain intensity, the will to suicide becomes a deranged affirmation of life. One has to assume that there will be other suicide attacks on the US mainland, and that the American response will be ever more decisive, and, sadly, ever more provocative. [*New Statesman*, 2002]

NUCLEAR BOMBS

■ I was always interested in the Pacific test islands as a result of my wartime experiences as a civilian internee, being keenly aware that my life was saved by the atomic bombs dropped on Hiroshima and Nagasaki. Unlike so many people I'm a supporter of nuclear defense. I've watched the Campaign for Nuclear Disarmament [CND] movement, which although it's well-meaning, seems to me that the people in it are living in a dream world in the post-nuclear world. [*Disinfo.com,* 2000]

■ No weapon ever placed in our hands has confronted us more ambiguously than the hydrogen bomb, offering unlimited destructive power as it mimics the life-giving engine of the sun. The vast fireballs above the vaporizing sand-bars of Eniwetok Atoll, one of the sacred sites of the modern imagination, prompt both delusions of omnipotence and the deepest dreams of world annihilation. In a now planetary arena, archaic myth and the fantasies of twentieth-century super-science collide and fuse. [review of *Dark Sun,* 1997]

■ With [the] obliteration [of Hiroshima and Nagasaki] by two primitive atomic bombs, Little Boy and Fat Man, one a uranium gun and the other a plutonium implosion device, the age of nuclear war began and ended at the same moment. During the next decades the skies above our heads were crossed by immense bombers armed with pieces of the sun. A vast nuclear arms race was under way, as weapons technology created the huge arsenals that exist to this day and a new vocabulary (ground zero, fallout, mega-death and MAD) stepped out of science fiction and into our nightmares. [review of *Dark Sun,* 1997]

■ The growth of technology and science, in particular, rapidly transformed the world for the better, a process that everyone assumed would stretch forever into the future . . . Our faith in science was shaken by the nuclear bombs that destroyed Hiroshima and Nagasaki, by the Chernobyl disaster, and by our fears that scientists may have their own secret agendas as they pursue their research into genetic engineering and the deep structures of the brain. ["Anything Could Happen," 1996]

■ Whatever mythology I constructed for myself would have to be made from the commonplaces of my life, from the smallest affections and kindnesses, not from the nuclear bombers of the world and their dreams of planetary death. [*Kindness of Women,* 1991]

■ The power of the atomic test explosions, portents of a now forgotten apocalypse . . . the vast detonations over the Eniwetok and Bikini lagoons, sacred sites of the twentieth-century imagination. [*Rushing to Paradise,* 1994]

■ It may be that the specter of nuclear destruction burns so brightly in our minds that it somehow uncouples our will to destroy ourselves, a technological miracle like the apparition of the Mons angel that stilled the Great War battlefields. But will the spell be broken when the first nuclear weapon is detonated in anger, as I assume it will, by some future Saddam or Pol Pot? Then at last the sky will be full of suns. [review of *Dark Sun,* 1997]

■ Eniwetok and Muroroa: I've never met anyone who dreamed of nuclear islands. [*Rushing to Paradise,* 1994]

■ You have a disco mentality. Hiroshima was not a light show. [*Rushing to Paradise,* 1994]

Photo: S.M. Gray

SEX

■ One thing we can say for certain about the future of sex—there's going to be a lot more of it. Already we can see that new forms of social structure will emerge to cope with the sexual imagination. What you and everyone else think of as the pornographic mind may well allow us to transcend ourselves and, in a sense, the limits of sex itself. [*Kindness of Women,* 1991]

■ Sex isn't about anatomy anymore. It's where it always belonged—inside the head. [*Super-Cannes,* 2000]

■ Sex is such a quick route to the psychopathic, the shortest of short cuts to the perverse. [*Super-Cannes,* 2000]

■ Rhapsodizing over the thousand scents of her body, I exclaimed: "I'll grow orchids from your hands, roses from your breasts. You can have magnolias in your hair . . . In your womb I'll set a fly-trap!" [*Unlimited Dream Company,* 1979]

■ I visualized a series of imaginary pictures I might take of her: in various sexual acts, her legs supported by sections of complex machine tools, pulleys and trestles; with her physical education instructor, coaxing this conventional young man into the new parameters of her body, developing a sexual expertise that would be an exact analogue of the other skills created by the multiplying technologies of the twentieth century. [*Crash,* 1973]

■ The deformed body of the crippled young woman, like the deformed bodies of the crashed automobiles, revealed the possibilities of an entirely new sexuality. [*Crash,* 1973]

■ I looked through the color photographs in the magazines; in all of them the motor car in one style or another figured as the centerpiece—pleasant images of young couples in group intercourse around an American convertible parked in a placid meadow; a middle-aged businessman naked with his secretary in the rear seat of his Mercedes; homosexuals undressing each other at a roadside picnic; teenagers in an orgy of motorized sex on a two-tier vehicle transporter, moving in and out of the lashed-down cars; and throughout these pages the gleam of instrument panels and window louvers, the sheen on over-polished vinyl reflecting the soft belly of a stomach or a thigh, the forests of pubic hair that grew from every corner of these motor car compartments. [*Crash,* 1973]

■ Through the darkness I smelled the changing odors of her body— the vivid spice of her sweat. [*Unlimited Dream Company,* 1979]

■ I dreamed of other accidents that might enlarge this repertory of orifices, relating them to more elements of the automobile's engineering, to the ever-more complex technologies of the future . . . the extraordinary sexual acts celebrating the possibilities of unimagined technologies. [*Crash,* 1973]

■ *Crash* [is concerned] with a pandemic cataclysm that kills hundreds of thousands of people each year and injures millions. Do we see, in the car crash, a sinister portent of a nightmare marriage between sex and technology? Will modern technology provide us with hitherto undreamed-of means for tapping our own psychopathologies? . . . Throughout *Crash* I have used the car not only as a sexual image, but as a total metaphor for man's life in today's society. As such, the novel has a political role quite apart from its sexual content. . . [Introduction to *Crash,* 1995 edition]

■ I spent many excited weekends dialing deserted offices all over London and dictating extraordinary sexual fantasies into their answering machines, to be typed out for amazed executives by the unsuspecting secretaries . . . [*Unlimited Dream Company,* 1979]

■ I had been able to spot Catherine's affairs within almost a few hours of her first sex act simply by glancing over any new physical or mental furniture—a sudden interest in some third-rate wine or filmmaker. . . [*Crash*, 1973]

■ Young mothers steered small children in and out of the launderette and supermarket, refueled their cars at the filling station...I was moving among these young women with my loins at more than half cock, ready to mount them among the pyramids of detergent packs and free cosmetic offers. [*Unlimited Dream Company*, 1979]

■ I knew then that I would stay in this small town until I had mated with everyone there—the women, men and children, their dogs and cats, the cage-birds in their front parlors, the cattle in the water-meadow, the deer in the park, the flies in this bedroom—and fused us together into a new being. [*Unlimited Dream Company*, 1979]

■ Nothing about sex ever shocks women. At least, men's kind of sex. We clean up after you, like those charladies with brooms who follow the coronation coach. [*Super-Cannes*, 2000]

■ I dreamed of repopulating Shepperton, seeding in the wombs of its unsuspecting housewives a retinue of extravagant beings, winged infants and chimerized sons and daughters, plumed with the red and yellow feathers of macaws. Antlered like the deer, and scaled with the silver skins of rainbow trout, their mysterious bodies would ripple in the windows of the supermarket and appliance stores. [*Unlimited Dream Company*, 1979]

■ I wanted to mate with Miriam St Cloud on the wing, sail with her along the cool corridors of the sky, swim with her down this small river to the open sea, drown the currents of our love in the ebb and flow of oceanic tides . . . [*Unlimited Dream Company*, 1979]

■ Leaving the door unlocked, she undressed like a conjuror, revealing the body of a breasted child, and immediately set to work. Her white face hovered over him, hiding a world closed to the emotions.

She stared at Neil as if he were a rare creature snared in the depths of the lagoon and now to be relieved of his vital spawn, as precious as the roe harvested from a royal sturgeon . . . The briskness of the sexual act between them had startled Neil. Still breathless, he touched the bruises on his shoulders where Mrs Saito had gripped him with her strong hands . . . "Lazy boy . . . lazy . . ." she had murmured. . . [*Rushing to Paradise,* 1994]

■ Two of the girls kept elaborate secret journals . . . with a startling frankness about their sexual activities. Together they convey the impression of *Pride and Prejudice* with its missing pornographic passages restored. [*Running Wild,* 1998]

■ Now we reach our climax, returning to that primitive fount from which all the rivers of the earth have sprung, the moment when consciousness moved into the daylight, from the reptile to the mammalian brain. . . [*Day of Creation,* 1987]

■ Sexual pathology is such an energizing force. People know that, and will stoop to any depravity that excites them. [*Super-Cannes,* 2000]

■ The stuttering light transformed us into players in a clandestine film. The silver streamers of jetting water seemed to caress the young woman's naked body. . . Her hands were trapped against my chest, but I felt her palms embrace me as our shared fevers came together in the trembling night. [*The Day of Creation,* 1987]

■ You always have to find the extreme position. [*The Day of Creation,* 1987]

■ Frances had smiled the microsecond smile of an escort agency whore. She smoothed the damp hair from my forehead, already working out the next move in the game she was playing with me, like an older sister with a docile small brother who would end up trussed and gagged in the toy cupboard. [*Super-Cannes,* 2000]

■ By watching our wives have sex with strangers, we dismantled the mystery of exclusive love, and dispelled the last illusion that each of us was anything but alone. [*Super-Cannes*, 2000]

■ It occurred to me that three of us would sleep together in this large and comfortable bed ... [*Super-Cannes*, 2000]

■ They say flying and sex go together. [*Super-Cannes*, 2000]

■ I stopped by a glass cabinet that displayed two life-size mannequins in full orthopaedic rig. Replicas of a man and a woman, they each wore a cuirass of pink plastic around the torso, and their jaws were supported by molded collars that encased them from the lower lip to the nape of the neck. Elaborately sculptured corsets and cuisses, like the fantasies of an obsessive armorer, surrounded their hips and thighs, discreet apertures provided for whatever natural functions were still left to these hybrid creatures. [*Super-Cannes*, 2000]

■ Sadomasochism, excretory sex-play, body-piercing and wife-pandering can easily veer off into something nasty. [*Super-Cannes*, 2000]

■ A perverse sexual act can liberate the visionary self in even the dullest soul. [*Super-Cannes*, 2000]

■ Remembering the familiar sexual symbolism of the foot, I knew that the glass slipper was nothing more than a transparent and therefore guilt-free vagina. And as for the foot to be placed within it, of course this would not be her own but that of her true lover, the erect male sexual organ from which she fled. ["A Host of Furious Fancies," 1980]

■ During that week, Anne Godwin did her best to help Sheppard construct his "machine." All day she submitted to the Polaroid camera, to the films of her body which Sheppard projected on to the wall above the bed, to the endless pornographic positions in which she arranged her thighs and pubis. Sheppard gazed for hours through his stop-frame focus, as if he would find among these images an anatomical door, one of the keys in a combination whose other tumblers were the Marey chronograms, the Surrealist paintings and the drained swimming pool in the ever-brighter sunlight outside. In the evenings Sheppard would take her out into the dusk and pose her beside the empty pool, naked from the waist, a dream-woman in a Delvaux landscape. ["Myths of the Near Future," 1994]

■ [They] approached the freeports of sex like sophisticated tourists in a strange souk, exploring any alleyway that might offer an intriguing cuisine. To these educated travelers, even human flesh would prompt no more than a mild query about the recipe. [*Super-Cannes*, 2000]

■ Both sex and violence are hugely sentimentalized, and a clear look at what really happens between a husband and wife, or when a bus crashes on a motorway, would do wonders for our sense of the world. [*Literary Review*, 2001]

■ There should be far more eroticism in our lives. [*S.F. Eye*, 1991]

■ You're like all men—violence is your real turn-on, not sex. [*Super-Cannes*, 2000]

■ Selfish men make the best lovers. They're prepared to invest in the woman's pleasure so that they can collect an even bigger dividend for themselves. [*Cocaine Nights*, 1996]

■ Sex is a branch of gastronomy—the best cooks make the best lovers. Every woman soon discovers that. [Kindness of Women, 1991]

■ He could smell her vulva on his hands. ["Zodiac 2000," 1978]

■ When she was pleasantly drunk, she liked to make love in the bathroom, taking up her positions against the mirrors and white enamel like a perverse gymnast. She watched me without expression, as if we were having sex in a space capsule hundreds of miles above the earth, conceiving the first of a new race of astronauts. [*Kindness of Women,* 1991]

■ This was a language outside time, whose grammar was shaped by the contours of Ursula's breasts in his hands, by the geometry of the apartment. The angle between two walls became an Homeric myth. He and Ursula lisped at each other, lovers talking between the transits of the moon, in the language of birds, wolves and whales. From their start, their sex together had taken away all Franklin's fears. Ursula's ample figure at last proved itself in the fugues. ["News from the Sun," 1981]

■ Each of her deformities became a potent metaphor for the excitements of a new violence. Her body, with its angular contours, its unexpected junctions of mucous membrane and hair, detrusor muscle and erectile tissue, was a ripening anthology of perverse possibilities . . . Our sexual acts were exploratory ordeals. [*Crash,* 1973]

■ He was staring at her body with an almost clinical detachment, as if measuring her abdomen and buttocks for yet another new perversion. All week, as they lay on the bed in this rented apartment, their acts of intercourse had become more and more abstracted. These strange perversions had at first disgusted her, but she now realized their real identity—bridges across which he hoped to make his escape. ["Journey Across a Crater," 1971]

■ The eyes of the insane watched them in intercourse. ["Journey Across a Crater," 1971]

■ The landscape we live in is absolutely saturated with sexual imagery of every conceivable kind. There's a sense in which we are all taking part in sexual activity, whether we want to or not, and whether we are aware of it or not . . . Elements of sexual imagery are constantly being jolted into the psychological space we inhabit. One has to be aware of these things and the unconscious role they play. [*Mississippi Review,* 1991]

■ When I was 20 (in the late 1940s), there were much greater restraints—going to bed with a girl was a pretty rare occurrence. But because the experience was rarer, it certainly had a powerful charge added to it that casual sex can't have. [*RE/Search #8/9,* 1984]

■ Jane was well aware that she had stolen the magazine. But she shrugged and smiled cheerfully, accepting that a benign lightning strike had illuminated our excessively ordered world. The emotion had been draining from our lives, leaving a numbness that paled the sun. The stolen magazine quickened our lovemaking. [*Super-Cannes,* 2000]

Photo: S.M. Gray

■ During his studied courtship of injured women, Vaughan was obsessed with the buboes of gas bacillus infections, by facial injuries and genital wounds. [*Crash,* 1973]

■ . . . that overlit amusement park called commercial sex: If anything is more threatening than the union of sex and the imagination, it is the union of sex, the imagination and money. [*Pornucopia,* 1998]

■ The sexual imagination is unlimited in scope and metaphoric power, and can never be successfully repressed. [*Atrocity Exhibition,* 1990]

RELATIONSHIPS

■ Who wants relationships? You bore me right now. You never had any love and affection as a child. Don't commit any acts of violence tonight. [*Concrete Island,* 1985]

■ The rider, in full biker's gear, switched off the engine and sat back to savor the last tang of the exhaust. Behind him on the pillion was a small Chinese woman . . . They sat together, black astronauts of the road, in no hurry to dismount, preparing themselves for re-entry into the non-biker world. [*Millennium People,* 2003]

■ I was wearing the standard-issue Prince Valiant suit, which a careful survey of the TV programs of the 1960s had confirmed to be the most sexually attractive costume for the predatory male. In a suit like this Elvis Presley had roused Las Vegas matrons to an ecstasy of abandon, though I found its tassels, gold braid and tight crotch as comfortable as the decorations on a Christmas tree. ["Love in a Colder Climate," 1989]

■ The morose and dowdy peahen is sexually excited by the flamboyant tail, so males with the largest tails attract the most mates and pass on to the next generation a tendency towards larger tails. [*Daily Telegraph,* 1992]

■ After a moment's reflection she leaned forward and kissed me, lightly enough not to disturb her lipstick, and long enough to leave me thinking of her for an hour after the elevator doors closed behind her. [*Cocaine Nights,* 1996]

■ It may be that we thrive when certain of our relationships are drained of emotion—that we may then be able to explore our lives more fully, because emotions tend to act as a brake. They reinforce the status quo. They set up a kind of tyranny rather like the psychology of a very small child, which may be entirely governed by passionate emotions that are in fact very limiting. [*Frieze,* 1996]

■ Only when I learned to admire this flawed and dangerous man was I able to think of killing him. [*Super-Cannes,* 2000]

■ [Chatting with a medical nurse] I had a strong sense that we were friends who had known each other for years. Yet I had forgotten her face within seconds of leaving her. [*Super-Cannes,* 2000]

■ The contents of a [wife's] dressing table were as close as a husband could ever get to her unconscious mind. [*Super-Cannes,* 2000]

■ Elements of sexual imagery are constantly being jolted into the psychological space we inhabit. One has to be aware of these things and the unconscious role they play. [*Mississippi Review,* 1991]

■ Only the pornographic images of ourselves could really bring us together and draw out the affection we felt for each other. [*Cocaine Nights,* 1996]

■ The early decades of the next century may well be a time when we need to explore a whole new set of possibilities in our own lives, and emotions may cramp our style. I'm not saying we should abandon them altogether, but that we should wait to see where they fit into the new scheme of things. [*Frieze,* 1996]

■ We conducted an animated dialogue, neither speaking a word of the other's language, but apparently understanding everything. ["Unlocking the Past," *Daily Telegraph*, 1991]

■ Sex has never been merely a genital matter, and the input of the imagination can transform—especially if that imagination contains strong elements of fantasy, passion, fear, jealousy, love and obsession. [*Disturb*, n.d.]

■ By the time of their marriage there had been a general revulsion against perverse sex of every kind. Chastity and romantic love, pre-marital celibacy and all the restraints of monogamy came back in force. ["Low-Flying Aircraft," 1975]

■ "Said hello to lots of people, who said hello to me" . . . This entry in November 1976 virtually sums up the entire contents of the diaries which Warhol kept for the last ten years of his life. [*Guardian*, 1989]

■ Whoring is something a good few women have tried, more probably than you realize. That's one education most men never get. [*Cocaine Nights*, 1996]

■ Commercial sex demanded special skills from the client as much as from the provider. Self-styled mother-and-daughter teams always made me uneasy, especially in Taipei or Seoul, where too many were *real* mothers and daughters. However pleasant, with "mother" pacing the over-eager "daughter," I often felt that I was the intermediary in an act of incest. [*Cocaine Nights*, 1996]

■ *Crash* illustrates what I call the normalizing of the psychopathic—the way in which formerly aberrant or psychopathic behavior is annexed into the area of the acceptable. The normalizing of the psychopathic is most advanced, of course, in the area of sexuality. Sexual behavior that my parents would have deemed a one-way ticket to a criminal insane asylum is now accepted in the privacy of the bedroom, tolerable if both parties are in agreement. [*21C,* 1997]

■ I wanted to provoke you, to test you to destruction. I wanted to find your dirtiest little secret, and then work on it until you became disgusted with yourself and needed to explode. [*Super-Cannes,* 2000]

■ There's nothing too weird to switch a man on sexually. [*Super-Cannes,* 2000]

■ You were a great fan of threesomes. [*Super-Cannes,* 2000]

■ Sex has become a sort of communal activity. It's an explicit element in all sorts of other activities—advertising, publicity, sales promotion as well as in film and TV—every conceivable thing you can think of. [*Mississippi Review,* 1991]

■ I was like one of those affectionate wives who look the other way when their husbands stand a little too close to an attractive young man . . . [*Super-Cannes,* 2000]

■ [She] swayed around the bedroom, a lurid figure in a spangled crimson mini-dress and stiletto heels. A frizz of lacquered black hair rose in a retro-punk blaze from her forehead, above kohled eyes and a lipsticked mouth like a wound—Miss Weimar, 1927. [*Super-Cannes,* 2000]

■ She embraced me fiercely before she left. When I winced, uneasy with this bogus affection, she looked at me with sudden concern. [*Super-Cannes,* 2000]

■ The test of a language is how well it can be translated into other tongues, and sex is the most negotiable language of all. [*Atrocity Exhibition,* 1990]

■ Have a few [drinks] too many after a football match and give some Arab a good kicking—it fires you up. Your wife finds you more of a man, and you work better the next day. [*Super-Cannes,* 2000]

■ Cars cruised the curb, drivers staring ahead but communicating by some sixth sense with the pimps who stood with their backs to the road. Everyone trafficked in time, sex displaced into blocks of darkness, thirty-minute cages of the night where pleasure flared and was gone like a shooting star. [*Super-Cannes,* 2000]

■ **In marriage it's women who do the work and the men who take it easy—it's called going to the office.** [*Rushing to Paradise,* 1992]

■ For me the most interesting aspect of the work of Masters and Johnson, collected in *Human Sexual Response,* was its effect on themselves. How were *their* sex lives influenced, what changes occurred in *their* sexual freedoms and fantasies? In conversation they seemed almost neutered by the experiments. I suspect that the copulating volunteers were really training the good doctors to lose all interest in sex, just as computerized diagnostic machines, where patients press buttons in reply to stock questions, are inadvertently training them to develop duodenal ulcers or varicose veins. [*Atrocity Exhibition,* 1990]

■ **Experiments often test the experimenter more than the subject. One remembers the old joke about the laboratory rat who said: "I have that scientist trained—every time I press this lever he gives me pellets of food."** [*Atrocity Exhibition,* 1990]

■ He was surprised that it pleased him, even slightly, to humiliate the young woman, playing on her muddled feelings of guilt and deriding her in a way that he had never thought himself capable of doing. By contrast, his humiliation of Proctor had been entirely calculated; he had degraded the old tramp in the crudest way he could . . . He was well aware that both of them, by some paradoxical logic, were satisfied being abused. [*Concrete Island,* 1985]

■ The number of exhilarating, important experiences is limited.

There's that school of anthropologists who have come up with the "village theory." They found that everybody had basically the same pattern . . . you had, say, two powerful sexual partners who transcended all the others. You fell in love once, there was one member of your family you really loved, etc. In your life you're going to meet two adult friends whom you're going to be really close to—if you've had them, you've had them—the slots are filled in the brain, because the brain has a certain finite capacity for friendship . . . And if you have too much experience, you exhaust your capacity for further experiences. [*RE/Search #8/9,* 1984]

■ All of them possessed some special skill with which they paid for their places. [*The Drought,* 1965]

■ Her kiss was quick and functional, like the automatic peck of some huge bottle-topping machine. ["The Overloaded Man," 1961]

■ As she poked among the half-eaten fruit, Ransom looked down at the dirty cuffs and collar of the beachrobe, and at the soiled top of the slip she wore loosely around her breasts. She noticed him gazing down at her and gave him an evil smirk, pushing back her hair with one wrist in an almost comically arch gesture. "What's the matter, doctor? Do you want to examine me or something?" [*The Drought,* 1965]

■ First she would try to kill him, but failing this give him food and her body, breast-feed him back to a state of childishness and even, perhaps, feel affection for him. Then, the moment he was asleep, cut his throat. The synopsis of the ideal marriage. [*High Rise,* 1975]

■ Together, women formed a conspiracy of glances entirely exchanged behind the backs of their menfolk. [*Kindness of Women,* 1991]

SEX x TECHNOLOGY = THE FUTURE

■ Sex times technology equals the future. [*Corridor #5*, 1974]

■ I think the future of this planet can be summed up in one word: sex. I think sex times the computer equals tomorrow. I think the future of sex is limitless. [*Evergreen Review*, 1973]

■ Sex times technology equals the future—that's one of the most powerful equations there is going. You can't shut it off, you can't smother it. [*Spin*, 1989]

■ There are certain processes in train which I describe as "a sinister marriage between sex and technology." These processes will lead to a *new kind of value system* . . . One can already see strains of that new value system in . . . the *Mad Max* movies and other films which celebrate violence as consumer spectator sport. [*C21*, 1991]

■ I think the whole of history over the last two or three hundred years has been the harnessing of machines, and of technological systems, to various human activities: to transport, to agriculture, to industry, and so forth. We are getting around to the harnessing of the machine, of computer systems and recording devices, to the sexual impulse. And I think this is absolutely going to transform sex in the way that, say, the jet engine has transformed travel. [*Evergreen Review*, 1973]

■ The notion of there being any kind of normal sex, that is, heterosexual sex of a genital character oriented around the reproductive principle—I think that is over and done with now. It might be a phase through which people pass in their early twenties, say, when they get married and have children. But I think it will just be a transient phase in their lives, and they will then move on to their real puberty, a sort of secondary puberty. [*Evergreen Review,* 1973]

■ The old fantasies—drinking someone's urine, being beaten by a beautiful woman in black leather—are dead. A new Krafft-Ebing is being written by car crashes, televised violence, modern architecture and design. What we see through the window of the TV set is just as important, sexually, as what the old-fashioned voyeur could see through the window of a bedroom. [*Evergreen Review,* 1973]

■ In the future of sex, men and women may not be necessary to one another. Sex might take place between you and an idea, or you and a machine. An incredible range of new unions, new perversions if you will, could be realized by using computer data banks, videotape cassettes, or instant-playback closed-circuit TV. I can see a sexual experience of extraordinary complexity, beauty, tenderness, and love. I can see the magic of sex on a planetary scale, revivifying everything it touches. [*Evergreen Review #96,* 1973]

■ Car crashes, traveling in jet aircraft, the whole overlay of new technologies, architecture, interior design, communications, transport, merchandising—these things change the interior design of our sexual fantasies. [paraphrase, *Penthouse,* 1970]

■ Her hips pressed against the BMW, and the curvature of its door deflected the lines of her thigh, as if the car was a huge orthopaedic device that expressed a voluptuous mix of geometry and desire. [*Super-Cannes,* 2000]

PORNOGRAPHY

■ A widespread taste for pornography means that nature is alerting us to some threat of extinction. [*News From the Sun,* 1982]

■ [*Crash* was] the first pornographic novel based on technology. [*I-D,* 1987]

■ In a sense, pornography is the most political form of fiction, dealing with how we use and exploit each other in the most urgent and ruthless way. [*Seconds,* 1996]

■ In many ways pornography is the most literary form of fiction—a verbal text with the smallest attachment to external reality, and with only its own resources to create a complex and exhilarating narrative. [*Atrocity Exhibition,* 1990]

■ Pornography is a powerful catalyst for social change, and its periods of greatest availability have frequently coincided with times of greatest economic and scientific advance. [*Atrocity Exhibition,* 1990]

■ Morality covers our conduct—not what goes on inside our heads. [*Spectator,* 2000]

■ ...only the pornographic image of ourselves could really bring us together and draw out the affection we felt for each other. [*Cocaine Nights,* 1996]

■ Everybody's going to be starring in their own porno films as an extension of the Polaroid camera. Electronic aids, particularly domestic computers, will help the inner migration, the opting out of reality. Reality is no longer going to be the stuff out there, but the stuff inside your head. [*Heavy Metal,* 1982]

■ *Guns and Ammo, Commando Small Arms, The Rifleman,* and *Combat Weapons of the Waffen SS* ...The real porn? I agree. [*Running Wild,* 1988]

Photo: V. Vale

WILLIAM S. BURROUGHS

■ I admire [William Burroughs] as a writer who in his way has created the landscape of the twentieth century completely as new. He's produced a kind of apocalyptical landscape, he's close to Hieronymus Bosch and Brueghel. He's not a pastoral writer by any means. He's a writer of the nightmare. [*Speculation*, 1969]

■ True genius and first mythographer of the mid-20th century, William Burroughs is the lineal successor to James Joyce, to whom he bears more than a passing resemblance—exile, publication in Paris, undeserved notoriety as a pornographer, and an absolute dedication to The Word—the last characteristic alone sufficient to guarantee the hostility and incomprehension of the English reviewers. [*New Worlds #142*, 1964]

■ I think Burroughs was very much aware of the way in which language could be manipulated to mean absolutely the opposite of what it seems to mean. But that's something he shared with George Orwell. He was always trying to go through the screen of language to find some sort of truth that lay on the other side. I think his whole cut-up approach was an attempt to cut through the apparent *manifest* content of language to what he hoped might be some sort of more truthful world—a world of meaning that lay beyond. In books like *The Ticket that Exploded* and *The Soft Machine,* you see this attempt to go through language to something beyond. [*Salon*, 1997]

■ I admire [William Burroughs] above all for his radical imagination, which he uses like a weapon against his readers. Everything he writes is a challenge, just as his life was a challenge against bourgeois America, which offered suburban values, the family, and a passive acceptance of the capitalist ethos with all its corruption and power-hunger. Burroughs was the ultimate non-conformist, the model for all writers who believe in their own obsessions. [intv Hans Obrist, 2003]

■ The bourgeois novel is the greatest enemy of truth and honesty that was ever invented. It's a vast, sentimentalizing structure that reassures the reader, and at every point, offers the comfort of secure moral frameworks and recognizable characters. This whole notion was advanced by Mary McCarthy and many others years ago, that the main function of the novel was to carry out a kind of moral criticism of life. But the writer has no business making moral judgments or trying to set himself up as a one-man or one-woman magistrate's court. I think it's far better, as Burroughs did and I've tried to do in my small way, to tell the truth. [*Salon,* 1997]

■ Imaginative fiction requires an effort on the part of the reader, but I think it's an effort that is repaid, because one gets to the psychological truth behind the world of appearances. The novels of William Burroughs are much closer to the reality of life today than the novels of John Updike, let's say. Though it's fair to say that most readers are more comfortable with John Updike than they are with William Burroughs, I've no doubt in my mind which is reaching the truth more accurately. [*Publishers Weekly,* 1998]

■ I have met Burroughs quite a few times over the last fifteen years, and he always strikes me as an upper-class Midwesterner, with an inherent superior attitude towards policemen, doctors, and small town politicians—the same superior attitude that Swift had to their equivalents in his own day, the same scatological obsessions and brooding contempt for middle-class values, thrift, hard work, parenthood, etc, which are just excuses for petit-bourgeois greed and exploitation. But I admire Burroughs more than any other living writer, and most of those who are dead. It's nothing to do with his homosexual bent, by the way. I'm not a member of the "homintern," but a lifelong straight who prefers the company of women to most men. The few homosexual elements in *Crash* and *Atrocity Exhibition* are there for reasons other than the sexual—in fact, to show a world beyond sexuality, or at least beyond *clear* sexual gender. [*Paris Review*, 1984]

■ Burroughs said somewhere that the paranoid is the person who really does know what's going on, and quite a lot of the time the paranoid view of things is actually proved right. People will gravitate towards something that does appear to explain what's happening. [*New Musical Express*, 1985]

■ *Naked Lunch* may be the *Alice in Wonderland* of the amphetamine age, but its bizarre sexual fantasies and disconnected narrative soon unsettle readers of conventional realistic fiction. They open its pages and are instantly accosted by a cross between Lenny Bruce at his most scatological, a demented neurosurgeon entangled inside his patient's nightmares, and the Ancient Mariner on an acid trip. [*Guardian*, 1985]

■ "Life is very dangerous and few survive it," Burroughs writes in *The Western Lands,* and like its predecessors this novel sidles up with the sinister charm of a garrulous but spaced-out pimp in a strange red-light district who plucks at the reader's sleeve, picks his pocket of his five-and-dime delusions, and entices him into a bizarre round of brothels and freak shows. But there, of course, the names over the doors are those of the CIA and the world's media conglomerates, its politicians, bankers, lawyers and doctors. [*Washington Post*, 1985]

■ [Burroughs's] novels are among the terminal documents of the late 20th-century, scabrous and scarifying, a progress report from an inmate in the cosmic madhouse. [*Washington Post,* 1985]

■ The great successor to [H.G. Wells, Huxley's *Brave New World* and Orwell's *1984*] is Burroughs. [*Blitz,* 1987]

■ Burroughs, the professional outsider, sometime petty criminal and drug addict, has produced an unmatched critique of the nature of modern society and the control and communication systems that shape our view of the world . . . the most original and important body of fiction to appear since the Second World War. [*Independent,* 1991]

■ Genet, living out his last days in the tiny hotel rooms that reminded him of his prison cells, consciously turned his back on the world and returned himself to the realm of his own pages, while Burroughs has never left them . . . More than in the case of almost any other writer, Burroughs's life merges seamlessly into his work. [*Independent,* 1991]

■ [Burroughs wrote to Allen Ginsberg] "Unless I can reach a point where my writing has the danger and immediate urgency of bullfighting, it is nowhere." How many of today's novelists would dare to agree with him? [*Guardian,* 1993]

■ While his young boyfriend, "love" and "hate" tattooed on his knuckles, carved a roast chicken, Burroughs described the most effective way to stab a man to death . . . His imagination was filled with bizarre lore culled from *Believe It Or Not* features, police pulps and Hollywood spy movies of the cold war years. [*Guardian,* 1997]

■ [Ronald] Reagan rambling into his [teleprompter] seems like one of Burroughs's own creations. [*Guardian,* 1985]

■ Burroughs, of course, I admire to the other side of idolatry, starting with *Naked Lunch,* then *Ticket, Soft Machine,* and *Nova Express.* I'm less keen on his later books. In his way he's a genius. It's a pity that his association with drugs and homosexuality has made him a counterculture figure, but I suppose his real links are with Jack Kerouac, Allen Ginsberg, and the Beats. Still, I think he's much more of an establishment figure, like Dean Swift, with a despairing disgust for the political and professional establishments of which he is a part. [*Paris Review,* 1984]

■ I read William Burroughs's *Naked Lunch* in 1959, in the green Olympia edition smuggled from Paris. At the time, my confidence in the novel as a still-fertile form had begun to fade. The writers I admired, Lawrence Durrell and Graham Greene, had escaped abroad, and the home scene was dominated by C.P. Snow, Angus Wilson and Kingsley Amis, all deeply parochial. *Naked Lunch* was a grenade tossed into the sherry party of English fiction, a terrorist novel that was visionary and deranged, and written in a language of its own. Forty years on, the bourgeois novel has triumphed again and we desperately need another Burroughs. [*Guardian,* 1998]

■ In a radical view of the world, and assuming that the role of the imagination is to reorder reality in a way that makes a little more sense and tells the truth about ourselves and shows us some kind of possibilities of what our lives could be . . . if that's the job of the writer, and it always has been, then the whole modern school of American fiction has produced nothing that remotely compares with Burroughs. His work seems as fresh and exciting and as absolutely radical as it ever was. It takes its place alongside Swift, Lewis Carroll, Rimbaud, Kafka—the radical reshapers of the imagination, of all the possibilities of our lives. There seems no point in writing unless you're going to do that. That's a kind of unpopular viewpoint in these safe, dull, conservative times, but it's one that I've attempted to cling to. We're in an era where the role of the writer—or the poet, the painter, the musician, the filmmaker—is to offer reassurance, which is a great shame. [*NME,* 10/22/1983]

■ The poets and writers that I most admire are those who try to remake our world in a more meaningful way. The Surrealists, of course, are first and foremost—these are the remakers of reality in an attempt to reveal the *reality within.* I would include Jonathan Swift, go on to Edgar Allan Poe and Rimbaud, all the way up to William Burroughs. [*Index,* 1997]

■ That William Burroughs lived to such an immense age [he was born Feb 5, 1914, and died Aug 2, 1997] is a tribute to the rejuvenating powers of a misspent life. More than half a century of heavy drug use failed to dim either his remarkably sharp mind or his dryly cackling humor. [*Guardian,* 1997]

Photo: Mindaugis Bagdon

■ [Burroughs had a] magnificently paranoid imagination. He changed little over the next decades, and hardly needed to—his weird genius was the perfect mirror of his times, and made him the most important and original writer since the Second World War. Now we are left with the *career novelists.* [*Guardian,* 1997]

SURREALISM

■ Surrealism celebrated the imagination, and the dark side of the dream that underpins so much of who we are. The deepest myths and the strangest chimeras of the twentieth century, which culminated in world war and Nazi barbarism, were fully anticipated by the great Surrealist painters. Surrealism was a warning screamed at the top of its voice, but no one listened. [*Literary Review,* 2001]

■ The critical establishment absolutely disdained Surrealists, and World War II seemed to confirm their hostility. [*Art Newspaper,* 1999]

■ The Surrealists have been a tremendous influence on me, though, strictly speaking, *corroboration* is the right word. The Surrealists show how the world can be remade by the mind. In Odilon Redon's phrase, they place the logic of the visible at the service of the invisible. They've certainly played a very large part in my life, far more so than any other writer I know. [*Paris Review,* 1984]

■ Surrealism is in fact the first movement, in the words of Odilon Redon, to place "the logic of the visible at the service of the invisible." This calculated submission of the impulses and fantasies of our inner lives to the rigors of time and space, to the formal inquisition of the sciences, psychoanalysis preeminent among them, produces a heightened or alternate reality beyond and above those familiar to either our sight or our senses. What uniquely characterizes this fusion of the outer world of reality and the inner world of the psyche (which I have termed "inner space") is its redemptive and therapeutic power. To move through these landscapes is a journey of return to one's innermost being . . . At the same time we should not forget the elements of magic and surprise that wait for us in this realm. In the words of Andre Breton, "The confidences of madmen: I would spend my life in provoking them. They are people of scrupulous honesty, whose innocence is only equaled by mine. Columbus had to sail with madmen to discover America." [*New Worlds #164*, 1966]

■ The uneasy marriage of reason and nightmare which has dominated the 20th century has given birth to an increasingly Surreal world. More and more, we see that the events of our own times make sense in terms of Surrealism rather than in any other view—whether the grim facts of the death-camps, Hiroshima and Vietnam, or our far more ambiguous unease at organ transplant surgery and the extra-uterine foetus, the confusions of the media landscape with its emphasis on the glossy, lurid and bizarre, its hunger for the irrational and sensational. [*Dali,* 1974]

■ I think there is a certain anarchic part in all of us that, given a bit of luck, will burst out of whatever conventional framework. There is something to be said for living in a total bourgeois society and that is that it gives maximum opportunity for the Surrealist spirit. At least one's got something to flex the imagination *against.* [*New Musical Express,* 1985]

■ The reality of life in the late 20th century demands analytic tools that can come to grips with it, and I don't think realism can any more. One route is the postmodernist novel, which gets around the problem of being realistic by playing a lot of ironic games with reality—I'm not interested in that. I follow the more classic, imaginative/Surrealist route. You can write in a Surrealist mode and achieve a psychological realism, which is what I'm after—an *imaginative* realism, not a literal realism. [*Spin*, 1989]

■ The Surrealists deal in an external world that has been remade by the mind. They also start from the premise that there's no firm basis of reality anywhere. [*Transatlantic Review*, 1971]

■ The Surrealists were, in fact, intensely interested in science, in optics, physiology, and, above all, psychoanalysis. This was their key to understanding the human mind and the way the world worked. [*Art Newspaper*, 1999]

■ I've always been very interested in the Surrealists, I think primarily because they're one of the few schools of painting that embrace the imagination without any restraints whatever, but also embrace the imagination within the terms of the scientific language. The Surrealists were interested in optics and all sorts of scientific advances. This climaxed, of course, in psychoanalysis, which was the perfect scientific mythology, if you like, for the investigation of the imagination. And this *marriage of science and imagination* seemed very close to what I wanted to do as a writer. [*Evergreen Review*, 1973]

■ Inexplicable and senseless protests were the only way to hold the public's attention. During the past month . . . action groups had attacked a number of "absurd" targets—the Penguin pool at London Zoo, Liberty's, the Soane Museum and the Karl Marx tomb at Highgate Cemetery . . . The public was unsettled, aware of a deranged fifth column in its midst, motiveless and impenetrable, Dada come to town. [*Millennium People*, 2003]

■ Where Ernst and Burroughs transmit their reports at midnight from the dark causeways of our spinal columns, Dali has chosen to face all the chimeras of our minds in the full glare of noon. [*Dali*, 1974]

■ Elements from the margins of one's mind—the gestures of minor domestic traffic, movements through doors, a glance across a balcony—become transformed into the materials of a bizarre and over-lit drama. [*Dali*, 1974]

■ It is not only Oedipal and other unconscious symbols that frighten us, but any dislocation of our commonplace notions about reality. The latent significance of curvilinear as opposed to rectilinear forms, of soft as opposed to hard geometries, are topics that disturb us as much as any memory of a paternal ogre. Applying Freud's principle, we can see that reason safely rationalizes reality for us. Dali pulls the fuses out of this comfortable system. [*Dali,* 1974]

■ You could almost reconstruct the inner landscapes of the 20th century from [Salvador Dali's painting, "The Persistence of Memory"] . . . It's a familiar landscape made from everyday things: soft watches, the string, dead embryo, fused sand extending forever, the rocky headland that we'll never reach. There's a strange sort of rectilinear section of the sea, as if the brain had decided to slot it off. This is a world beyond clock time, a world where everything has happened. There's nothing more to be done. This is where the human race beaches itself. [*Art Newspaper,* 1999]

■ If Surrealism is the greatest imaginative venture of the twentieth century, its course has in large part been set by Dali. His luminous beaches with their fused sand, his melting watches, marooned lovers and exploding madonnas have become the popular archetypes of the dream and unconscious, images so familiar from film and stage design, paperback jackets and department store windows that it is easy to forget their source in this single extraordinary mind. [*Guardian,* 1986]

■ I think Surrealism is the greatest imaginative adventure embarked upon during [the 20th] century. It eclipses Cubism, which is of no interest except to art historians. The world of the imagination of poetry thrives within the Surrealist space. I think contemporary art has lost sight of the poetic facility that was there in abundance in Magritte and Delvaux and Max Ernst. [*Art Newspaper*, 1999]

■ [Salvador] Dali . . . created a completely new landscape out of the concepts of Freudian psychology. No other painter that I know of has so well represented the world of the Oedipus complex, of our own childhood anxieties about memory—always done within the context of the Twentieth Century. [*Friends*, 1970]

■ At their best, Dali's paintings reveal in the most powerful form the basic elements of the Surrealist imagination: a series of equations for dealing with the extraordinary transformations of our age. Let us salute this unique genius, who has counted for the first time the multiplication tables of obsession, psychopathology and possibility. [*Dali*, 1974]

■ Surrealism also had its positive side, reassembling the world in a way that made poetic sense. Psychoanalysis was its main critical engine, and I was drawn to Surrealism in my late teens because it seemed clear to me that postwar England, with all its repressions and taboos, needed to be laid out on the couch and analyzed. [*Literary Review*, 2001]

■ The classic landscapes of the Surrealists like Tanguy, Ernst and Dali confirmed my own hazy views—my own interior landscape. They have always been not a tremendous inspiration, because I would have written the same fiction had I never seen a Dali painting, but reminders that these landscapes extended beyond the borders of my own head. [*Friends*, 1970]

■ In Surrealism, the events of the interior world of the psyche are represented in terms of commonplace situations. In fantastic art, Brueghel, and Bosch, you have the nightmare represented extremely well . . . chariots of demons and screaming archangels and all the materials of horror. What you don't have is what Surrealism has: the representation for the first time of the inner world of the mind in terms of *ordinary* objects—tables, chairs, telephones. [*Friends,* 1970]

■ ... the classic Surrealist paintings of Max Ernst, Salvador Dali, Giorgio de Chirico and Paul Delvaux, where the laws of time and space are constantly being suspended, and where reality is decoded in an attempt to discover the *superreality* that lies behind the facade of everyday life. And that means everything from the world of politics and mass merchandising to something as trivial as the fabrics people have in their homes. [*Rolling Stone,* 1987]

■ [Key paintings of Surrealism]: Giorgio de Chirico's "The Disquieting Muses." Max Ernst's "Elephant of Celebes" and "The Eye of Silence." Rene Magritte's "The Annunciation." Dali's "The Persistence of Memory." Oscar Dominguez's "Decalcomania." [*RE/Search #8/9,* 1984]

■ One of the Surrealists—Bréton, I think—said that the ultimate Surrealist act would be to take a revolver and fire at random into a crowd. Now, one can salute the brilliance of that insight, but at the same time, if somebody actually found a revolver and put that insight into practice, one would have to deplore it. This same ambivalence, this ambiguity, is at the heart of something like *Crash,* and this is what people find difficult to cope with—that there's no clear moral compass bearing. [*21C,* 1997]

■ During the dark days of the late 1940s, when I was first discovering Surrealism for myself, the name of Edward James began to appear in catalogues and reference books . . . Who was this mysterious collector, all the more strangely an Englishman, for years the patron of a group of artists regarded as little more than charlatans? A tantalizing clue appeared in Magritte's "Not to be Reproduced," a double portrait of the back of James's head as he stood beside a mirror with Lautréamont's *Song of Maldoror,* the black bible of Surrealism. [review of John Lowe's *Edward James,* and Philip Purser's *Poeted: The Final Quest of Edward*

James, Guardian, 1991]

■ *Little Nemo in Slumberland* [is] a dreamlike masterpiece that transcends the limits of the popular medium, and has rarely been matched since. [*Guardian,* 1991]

■ Just as the distinction between the latent and manifest contents of the dream had ceased to be valid, so had any division between the real and the super-real in the external world. Phantoms slid imperceptibly from nightmare to reality and back again, the terrestrial and psychic landscapes were now indistinguishable, as they had been at Hiroshima and Auschwitz, Golgotha and Gomorrah. [*Drowned World,* 1962]

■ The environment is filled with more fiction and fantasy than any of us can singly isolate. It's no longer necessary for us individually to dream. This completely cuts the ground from under all the tenets of classical Surrealism. [*Studio International,* 1971]

■ I am interested in the Surrealists altogether, because I am a great believer in the need of imagination to transform everything, otherwise we'll have to take the world as we find it, and I don't think we should. We should re-make the world . . . The madman does that . . . the psychopath does that . . . But the real job is to re-make the world in a way that is meaningful. [*Métaphores #7,* 1983]

■ I thought that Surrealism was the most important imaginative enterprise this century has embarked on. And I still do. For me the paintings of the Surrealists have opened windows on the real world . . . I mean that literally. [*RE/Search #8/9,* p. 23, 1984]

■ The [Surrealist] movement is noted for the remarkable beauty of its women—Georgette Magritte, demure sphinx with the eyes of a tamed Mona Lisa; the peerless Meret Oppenheim, designer of the fur-lined cup and saucer; Dorothea Tanning, with her hieratic eyes; the mystic Leonora Carrington, painter of infinitely frail fantasies . . . One could write a book about these extraordinary creatures—

nymphs of another planet, in your orisons be all my dreams remembered. [*New Worlds #164, 7/1966*]

■ I watched her stalk around my sitting-room, shaking her head over the Magritte and Dali reproductions on the mantelpiece, and the novels by Camus and Boris Vian. [*Kindness of Women,* 1991]

■ It's the external world which is now the realm, the paramount realm of fantasy. And it's the internal world of the mind which is the one node of reality that most of us have. [*Studio International,* 1971]

■ Why Surrealism never took root in England: our Protestantism, our intolerance of ideas, and, perhaps most important of all, the absence of café life. [*Guardian,* 1991]

■ Most people are too unsettled to face up to the Surrealist imagination. They want everyday Naturalism. They want to feel that what they are watching moves seamlessly from their own lives. [intv James Call, 1997]

IMAGINATION

■ I think we're living at a transfer point, where we're moving from one economy of the imagination and the body to a future economy of the imagination and the body. And during this unhappy transfer period it's sadly true that, for all kinds of reasons, people seem to be generating more cruelty than love. I deplore this, but as a writer I've got to face it. [*Evergreen Review,* 1973]

■ As I write, I take it for granted that many of my characters wish to escape the time and space of these walls or this ball-point pen, and they try to break out of all of this by some sort of rearrangement of the perceptual apparatus, which they think can be fueled by the imagination. [*Rolling Stone,* 1987]

■ The imagination can make the quantum leaps that are going to be

necessary to ride the rollercoaster of the future. [*C21*, 1991]

■ Most [people] do not even grasp the fact that they need information to keep their imagination up to par. [*Studio International*, 1971]

■ **Part of the job of the imagination is to remind us of the marvelous.** [*RE/Search #8/9*, p. 51, 1984]

■ [As an artist] unless you've got a really powerful imagination (it doesn't matter what the form or medium is), you will have nothing . . . Unless you've got some idea of your own, you'll get nowhere—you can juxtapose all the bizarre images in the world, [but] unless there's some *new myth* emerging . . . nothing is more tiresome than yesterday's experimental movie or experimental fiction. [*RE/Search #8/9*, p.19, 1984]

■ In this overlit realm ruled by images of the space race and the Vietnam war, the Kennedy assassination and the suicide of Marilyn Monroe, a unique alchemy of the imagination was taking place. In many ways the media landscape of the 1960s was a laboratory designed specifically to cure me of all my obsessions. Violence and pornography provided a kit of desperate measures that might give some meaning . . . [*Kindness of Women*, 1991]

■ **The brain colludes in a whole system of repressive mechanisms which it willingly accepts in order to make sense of its own identity and of the universe around it . . . and these mechanisms are limiting.** [*RE/Search #8/9*, 1984]

■ The mystical view is that there is a larger order beyond the one we impose. But I don't think there is something out there for the imagination to find. The human imagination is our only way of getting past that. It should be guarded and encouraged. It is a precious resource. [*The Face #96*, 1988]

■ **Imagination is the shortest route between any two conceivable** points, and more than equal to any physical rearrangement of the brain's functions. [*Paris Review*, 1984]

■ Just as the optical centers of the brain construct a wholly arti-ficial three-dimensional universe through which we can move effectively, so the mind as a whole creates an imaginary world that satisfactorily explains everything, as long as it is constantly updated. [*Paris Review*, 1984]

■ One has to foster one's own imagination to a very intense degree, far more than most people realize. Most people have a huge capacity for imaginative response to the world that is scarcely tapped. [*Mississippi Review*, 1991]

■ Everywhere is infinitely exciting, given the transforming power of the imagination. [*Vector*, 1980]

■ It has always seemed to me that Science Fiction and Surrealism have a great deal in common. They both represent the marriage of reason and unreason. In both Science Fiction and Surrealism the basic source of imagination is one's own mind rather than the external world. Both are the perfect model for dealing with the facts of the Twentieth Century. [*Friends*, 1970]

RELIGION

■ I'm aware that there's a visionary sense in my work, but I don't have any orthodox or conventional religious feelings, and I can't real-ly call myself "mystical." [*Rolling Stone*, 1987]

■ *Science is a new religion waiting to be born.* Infinitely more important than literature, which is an old religion—poetry— waiting to die. [intv Hans Obrist, 2003]

■ [*Rushing to Paradise*] is about the new eco-fanatic of the past 20 years, and attempts to answer the question of how David

Koresh persuaded his Branch Davidian followers to die with him, or how Reverend Jim Jones persuaded 914 followers to commit suicide in Guyana. [*Disinfo.com, 2000*]

■ Looking for God is a dirty business. [*Millennium People, 2003*]

■ States of voluntary madness—I think you put religions into that category. [*Millennium People, 2003*]

■ I think most people realize the gods have died, we've lost our faith in the far future, and that we're living in a commodified world where everything has a price tag; a world filled with dreams that money can buy . . . but dreams that soon pall. [BBC Radio 3, 1998]

■ All these myths of world destruction of which *The Bible* is full—I think they represent an attempt to re-order the universe. [*Seconds, 1996*]

■ Religious belief demands a vast effort of imaginative and emotional commitment, difficult to muster if you're still groggy from last night's sleeping pill. [*Cocaine Nights, 1996*]

■ Catholicism is much better adapted to us: it accepts sin and sex and has its roots in our dark side. Look at all those Christs squirming away in their own blood, pinned to their crosses like characters in a horror comic. The Catholic Church is steeped in blood and death and the awful lives of horribly martyred saints. How can the Church of England compete? [*Spectator, 2000*

■ A Raphaelesque reproduction of the Savior's undernourished face and uplifted eyes—the image of a tubercular sexual fanatic that must have appealed to the girls who lay around gossiping and smoking their cigarettes. [*Super-Cannes, 2000*]

■ Adam comes across as a crashing bore, wandering around Eden in his lobotomized way, obviously the victim of some nutritional deficiency . . . Eve, of course, seems a bit of a pushover. [*Telegraph Weekend, 1992*]

■ Religions emerged too early in human evolution—they set up symbols that people took literally, and they're as dead as a line of totem poles. Religions should have come later, when the human race begins to near its end. Sadly, crime is the only spur that rouses us. We're fascinated by that "other world" where everything is possible. [*Cocaine Nights,* 1996]

■ That's the fearful prospect a little further down the road, that people will accept that their lives are meaningless and that everything else is a fiction designed to assuage the sort of desperate anxiety of a meaningless world. [BBC Radio 3, 1998]

■ Given the hollowness of existence, I think people are beginning to wonder: what *does* life really offer us in terms of its possibilities? Some people reach out to bizarre cults, others move into drudges, but these are all rather desperate remedies and I don't think they touch the truth. [BBC Radio 3, 1998]

■ I saw Kennedy's death as a sort of religious sacrifice: a god-king was slain for inexplicable reasons. What had the Fates decided? We were moving into an area close to that of Aeschylus; we could see the Furies sitting on the cornices above Dealey Plaza, chanting some kind of blood-hate elegy. [*21C*, 1997]

■ Crash victims like Jayne Mansfield, James Dean, Aly Khan, Jim Clark and President Kennedy (the first man to be murdered in a motorcade) act out the Crucifixion for us. Their deaths heighten our vitality in a blinding flash. The death of Kennedy was a sacrificial murder, connived at by the millions of people who watched it endlessly recapitulated on television. If Christ came again, he would be killed in a car crash. [*Sunday Mirror,* 1968]

■ One aspect of *Crash* which I think is even more explicit in David Cronenberg's film is the sacramental aspect of the car crash. I don't want to sound too pretentious, but there's almost an undercurrent of religion to it—religion of a Pagan kind. These crashes are celebrated as a kind of profane mass. Bertolucci, whom I know slightly, called the film "a religious masterpiece," and I know what he meant. The compulsive rehearsal of the same scenario—these endless crashes being planned and executed—is in fact no more than the sort of repetitions you find in religious observance. The same mantras are recited, the same knees are bent before the same bleeding Christ up on his cross. [*Frieze*, 1996]

■ What turns you on? The seven deadly sins, like everyone else. But we need some new vices. [*Literary Review,* 2001]

■ I stepped through ... the doors of the church ... I was irritated by these timid people in their well-pressed suits and flowered dresses, with their polite religion ... I was tempted to pen them there while I performed some kind of obscene act in the aisle ... expose myself, urinate in the font—anything to shake them out of their timidity. [*Unlimited Dream Company*, 1979]

■ I'm waiting for the first new religion on the Internet—one that is unique to the Net and to the modern age. It'll come. [*Spike*, 2000]

■ Jim had always been impressed by strong religious beliefs. His mother and father were agnostics, and he respected devout Christians in the same way that he respected people who were members of the Graf Zeppelin club or who shopped at the Chinese department stores, for their mastery of an exotic foreign ritual. [*Empire of the Sun*, 1984]

■ At times, as I joined a demonstration against animal experiments or Third-World debt, I sensed that a primitive religion was being born, a faith in search of a god to worship. [*Millennium People*, 2003]

■ I can understand how religions always started in the desert—it's like an extension of one's mind. Far from being a wildernesss, every rock and prickly pear, every gopher and grasshopper seems to be part of one's brain, a realm of magic where everything is possible. [*Hello America*, 1981]

■ . . . the idea of God as a huge imaginary void, the largest nothingness the human mind can invent. Not a vast something out there, but a vast *absence*. [*Millennium People*, 2003]

■ Only a psychopath can cope with the notion of zero to a million decimal places. The rest of us flinch from the void and have to fill it with any ballast we can find—tricks of space-time, wise old men with beards, moral universes . . . [*Millennium People*, 2003]

■ Even a meaningless universe has meaning. Accept that and everything makes a new kind of sense. [*Millennium People*, 2003]

■ "It's all part of the great search." "For what?" "This and that. Some kind of tentative explanation. The mystery of space-time, the wisdom of trees, the kindness of light." [*Millen. People,* 2003]

■ Think of yourself in a wider context. Every particle in your body, every grain of sand, every galaxy carries the same signature. ["The Voices of Time," 1960]

■ We wait here, at the threshold of time and space, celebrating the identity and kinship of the particles within our bodies with those of the sun and stars, of our brief private times with the vast periods of the galaxies, with the total unifying time of the cosmos. ["The Day of Forever," 1966]

■ The gods have died, and we distrust our dreams. We emerge from the void, stare back at it for a short while, and then rejoin the void . . . We listen, and the universe has nothing to say. There's only silence, so we have to speak. [*Millennium People,* 2003]

■ The hands of his broken watch contained the one point of finite time left to him, like a fossil cast on to a beach, crystallizing forever a brief sequence of events within a vanished ocean. [*High Rise,* 1975]

■ "Is this how new religions begin?" "There's nothing new here. It's the oldest religion there ever was—sheer magnetic egoism." [*Rushing to Paradise,* 1994]

■ He was much intrigued by the representations of Jesus, Zoroaster and the Gautama Buddha, and commented on the likenesses. [*"Answers to a Questionnaire,"* 1985]

■ Messiahs usually emerge from deserts, and I expect the next Adolf Hitler or Mao to emerge from the wilderness of the vast North American and European shopping malls. The first credit card Buddha, at its best, or at its worst, the first credit card Stalin. [intv Zinovy Zinik, 1998]

■ We may see a new religious leader appearing, who'll unite the Green movement and all these New Age movements. The various ecological movements, anti-progress movements, may be united by such a figure into something very close to a new religion. [*JGB News,* 1993]

■ The French seem to drive much more aggressively than people do over here ... The French are ruthless; they don't stop for anybody. Jesus Christ himself could be crucified by the wayside and nobody would stop. [intv David Pringle, 1975]

■ It was curious that images of heaven or paradise always presented a static world, not the kinetic eternity one would expect, the roller-coaster of a hyperactive fun fair, the screaming Luna Parks of LSD and psilocybin. It was a strange paradox that given eternity, an infinity of time, they chose to eliminate the very element offered in such abundance. [*War Fever,* 1990]

■ What do we see at the end of the 20th Century? We see the churches empty, in the West that is, and people in the most advanced societies, in Western Europe and the United States, moving more and more into gated communities, where security is the dominant concern. And that's in many ways to be deplored. [BBC Radio 3, 1998]

■ The shaman's supposed ability to leave his physical form and fly with his spiritual body, the psychopomp guiding the souls of the deceased and able to achieve a mastery of fire ... we should have welcomed them. ["Memories of the Space Age," 1982]

■ Is pondering upon the universe really thinking on the largest possible scale? It may be a disguised way of thinking small—for all that superabundance of light years, an infinitude of nothingness is still nothing. [review of *The Case for Mars,* 1997]

■ Our greatest evolution may occur when we have long since discarded our biological identity and become computers, which are much more enduring and capable of being endlessly duplicated if anything goes wrong. [*Blitz,* 1984]

Photo: Mike Ryan

■ The royal family are just bad entertainment now. They are our equivalent of Hollywood, and Diana was the leading actress. I sometimes think that the outpouring of grief after her death was a collective mourning for the demise of the whole royal family. Perhaps we were grieving for the loss of our whole country because Diana was, in our eyes, the last perfect and wonderful thing. Here in Shepperton, when she died, there was a memorial tree on the high street surrounded by a great sea of bouquets and notes. One of them read: "Dear Di, were you Jesus?" Touching.

Weird. [*Spectator,* n.d.]

■ The kidney-shaped pool resembled a sunken altar reached by the chromium ladder. Votive offerings of a dead rat, a wine bottle and a sun-bleached property brochure waited for whatever minor deity might claim them. [*Cocaine Nights,* 1996]

■ [After confessing to being an atheist, J.G. Ballard says] That said, I'm extremely interested in religion. I see religion as a key to all sorts of mysteries that surround the human consciousness. [*JGB News,* 1995]

■ [Film] is a secular religion; great stars [are] the presiding priesthood. The gods are the gods of violence, sensation, spectacle. [ICA conversation, 1998]

■ The car wash sequence in *Crash*—which I think is one of the great scenes of cinema—is very ritualistic. The characters are aware that some sort of transcendent experience is taking place. [*Frieze,* 1997]

■ Our belief in our unique selves is all we have, the one reassurance that our lives have some kind of special meaning simply by being unique. Even when we shrink into virtual anonymity, at a football match or political rally, we still sense that our own particular bundle of quirks and reflexes, our private grip on existence, give us our chief reason for being alive at all. [*Sunday Times,* 1997]

■ The next religion might come from the world of fashion rather than from any conventional one. [*Friends #17,* 1970]

■ Reality is often pregnant with utterly unexpected possibilities. A powerful spiritual dimension can be found in one's life through the exercise of the imagination. [*Independent,* 11-10-2001]

■ The whole purpose of imaginative enterprise—Surrealist paintings or the sort of fiction I try to write—is to find one's real nature. [*Métaphores #7,* 1983]

■ Particle physics has unlocked the secrets of the sun, but the mystery of existence still endures. Colossal intellectual leaps have taken us back to within micro-seconds of the big bang, but a conceptual barrier deep inside our brains may be one door we will never open—at least until *homo sapiens* makes a significant evolutionary jump, and the processing capacity of our brains allows us to escape from the constraints of space-time. ["Speed-Visions of an Accelerated Age," 1998]

■ There used to be huge Darwinian advantages to believing in God: you'd fight hard because if you fell in battle, you were going to the happier hunting grounds. But although we still have some semi-dormant needs for religious experience, the Church . . . is ill-equipped to provide them. It has shut its eyes to the inherent flaws in human nature and the unconscious mind, and focuses on man as a rational, reasonable human being. [*Spectator,* 2000]

■ [In *The Third Reich: A New History,* author Michael Burleigh] suggests that Hitler was the leader of a pseudo-religion, and that his followers formed an almost suicidal congregation. [*Guardian,* 12-20-01]

■ Tony Blair strikes me as a dangerous man, a would-be Messiah with a pocketful of nails, searching for a cross to die on. [*Independent,* 12/30/2003]

■ The satellite dishes on the roofs resembled the wimples of an order of computer-literate nuns, committed to the sanctity of the workstation and the pieties of the spreadsheet. [*Super-Cannes,* 2000]

■ The human race takes part in a perpetual genetic lottery in which everyone is a winner, holding the most precious ticket of all: life. [*Sunday Times,* 1997]

■ You find God in a child's shit. [*Millennium People, 2003*]

TIME

■ If time is a primitive mental structure, we're right to reject it. [*War Fever*, 1990]

■ There's no time anymore—everything's too beautiful for time. ["Dream Cargoes," 1991]

■ The concept of anything other than real time had never occurred to anybody until the first slow-motion movies were shown, and this radically changed people's perception of the nature of time. [*RE/Search #8/9*, p. 49, 1984]

■ Time, like a film reel running through a faulty projector, was moving at an erratic pace, at moments backing up and almost coming to a halt. One day it would stop, freeze forever on one frame. ["Memories of the Space Age," 1982]

■ Time is a very strong theme in my fiction. If you look at Renaissance paintings, a Vermeer or Rembrandt, or the Impressionists, Monet or Renoir, it's like real time. It's 3 o'clock in the afternoon and she's having a bath or having tea in the garden. You can set your watch to those paintings. Whereas the Surrealists are quite different; there's a world beyond Time. Time does no longer exist. I think all my fiction is really an attempt to get beyond Time into a different Realm—I don't know what. [*Métaphores*, 1983]

■ In a lot of my stories . . . the characters were searching for a world that was, in a sense, beyond time. [*RE/Search #8/9*, p. 51, 1984]

■ For some reason, I don't know why, we seem to be in a sort of circular time trap, just going round and round. You're not aware of it, and I can't find anyone else who is either. ["Escapement," 1956]

■ There's a sense in which not only the shaman's but *all* mystical and religious beliefs are an attempt to devise a world without time.

["Memories of the Space Age," 1982]

■ Fossils fascinate me—they're like time capsules. If only one could unwind this spiral it would probably play back to us a picture of all the landscapes it's ever seen—the great oceans of the Carboniferous, the warm shallow seas of the Trias. ["Prisoner of the Coral Deep," 1964]

■ The light-filled world had transformed itself into a series of tableaux from a pageant that celebrated the founding days of creation. In the finale every element in the universe, however humble, would take its place on the stage in front of him. ["Memories of the Space Age," 1982]

■ Instead of treating time like a sort of glorified scenic railway, I'd like to see it used for what it is, one of the perspectives of the personality, and the elaboration of concepts such as the time zone, deep time and archaeopsychic time. I'd like to see more psycholiterary ideas, more metabiological and metachemical concepts, private time systems, synthetic psychologies and space times, more of the remote, somber half-worlds one glimpses in the paintings of schizophrenics, all in all a complete speculative poetry and fantasy of science. [*New Worlds #118*, 5/1962]

■ In *The Drought* I was interested in future time, the image being sand. I see the future as being abstract, geometric—the landscape of the moon seems to me to be a good image of the future landscape for earth. The crystal is a symbol of a timeless world. In *The Crystal World* I described a

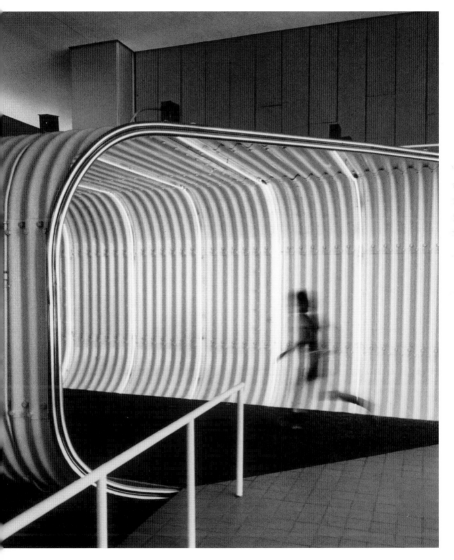

Photo: Charles Gatewood

situation in which time doesn't exist at all. The crystallizing forest, in which the people become crystallized, describes a state beyond death, a kind of non-living existence. [*Transatlantic Review,* Spring 1971]

■ The facts of time and space are a tremendous catastrophe, aren't they? Each day millions of cells die in our bodies, others are born. Every time we open a door, every time we look out across a landscape—I'm deliberately trying to exaggerate this— millions of minute displacements of time and space are occurring. One's living in a continuous cataclysm anyway—our whole existence takes place in the eye of a hurricane. [*Penthouse,* 1970]

■ "It's against the law to have a gun because you might shoot someone. But how can you hurt anybody with a clock?" "Isn't it obvious? You can time him, know exactly how long it takes him to do something." "Well?" "Then you can make him do it faster." ["Chronopolis," 1960]

■ Where would you like to be when the world ends? ["The Waiting Grounds," 1959]

■ The roots of shamanism and levitation, and the erotic cathexis of flight—can one see them as an attempt to escape from time? ["Memories of the Space Age," 1982]

■ He seems to have embraced the destruction of time, as if this whole malaise were an opportunity that we ought to seize, the next evolutionary step forward. ["Memories of the Space Age," 1982]

■ The slower a clock, the nearer it approximated to the infinitely gradual and majestic progression of cosmic time—in fact, by reversing a clock's direction and running it backwards one could devise a time-piece that in a sense was moving even more slowly than the universe, and consequently part of an even greater spatio-temporal system. [*Drowned World,* 1962]

■ Brain waves move slowly, as the potassium pumps at millions of synapses throw their cumbersome electromagnetic switches.

Decisions move through the cortex like population shifts across a continent, and reach our consciousness half a second after the brain has come to its own conclusions. The neurosciences seem to suggest that free will, like consciousness itself, is a virtual artifact created by the interplay of neural networks, as vivid but as illusory as the image of ourselves in the mirror. ["Speed-Visions of an Accelerated Age," 1998]

■ Time is a neuro-psychological structure that we may have inherited from the distant past, along with other no-longer-needed organs like the appendix and the little toe, and the saline concentration of our blood streams, etc. We are to some extent trapped by this archaic structure of our day-to-day sense of time, which limits our perception of a much larger world. [*Omni,* n.d.]

■ We're beginning to think that time itself is a primitive psychological structure that we've inherited from the distant past, along with the appendix and the little toe. Yet we're totally trapped by this archaic structure with its minutes and hours trailing after each other like a procession of the blind. Once we get hold of a more advanced notion of time—let's say, time perceived as simultaneity—we reach the threshold of a far larger mental universe. [*Kindness of Women,* 1991]

■ Look at most people and you will find that they have declared a moratorium on the past—they are just not interested. [*Friends,* 10/30/1970]

■ Once we can get away from our sense of serial time into some more complex notion of time, into time perceived as a simultaneity, we are beginning to reach the threshold of a larger mental consciousness of the kind that's perceived by the mystics and by ordinary people during moments of revelation or at times of great crisis as in, say, near-death experiences. [*Omni,* n.d.]

HOW I WORK

■ I try to provoke, challenge, unsettle, question, and offer the reader the keys to a door he or she has never noticed before in a side corridor of their minds. [letter, 2003]

■ I began as a short-story writer—the best way of learning one's craft as a writer, and something denied to so many young novelists today, when the short story seems, sadly, to be heading for extinction. My first short story was published in 1956, the last high summer of short-story publishing. Many newspapers printed a short story *every day*. Sadly, I think most people have lost the knack of reading them. [*Literary Review*, 2001]

■ My stories were written in snatched minutes, snatched half hours here and there, scribbled on the backs of envelopes . . . it was all done in a kind of spur-of-the-moment, knocked-out-rapidly fashion. ["From Shanghai to Shepperton," 1982, reprinted in *RE/Search #8/9*]

■ [My characters are] experimenting with themselves as if they were dreaming. ["Shanghai Jim," 1991]

■ In my early fiction I was always more interested in psychological roles . . . psychiatric case histories . . . In psychiatric case history, one is getting to the mythic core of what makes up human nature. This is what I was interested in. ["Shanghai Jim," 1991]

■ I always work with a fairly detailed synopsis. I like to know the dramatic shape of the book. I like to have a good idea of the internal atmosphere, how the book will dramatically engage the reader, and it's difficult to do that without writing a synopsis. But that is only the start, because the actual resonances that you find the text gives off are almost impossible to predict. [*Albedo One*, 1993]

■ Two subjects have always fascinated me—women, and the bizarre. ["The Smile," 1976]

■ I [write] from the point of view of the ordinary man in the street. I'm interested in the man watching the TV, not the man making the programs. [*Omni*, n.d.]

■ Writing is the way in which I have validated the world for myself. [intv Jean-Paul Coillard, n.d.]

■ I feel that the fictional elements in experience are now multiplying to such a point that it's almost impossible to distinguish between the real and false: that one has many layers, many levels of experience going on at the same time . . . on one level, the world of public events; on another level, the immediate personal environment; on a third level, the inner world of the psyche. Where these planes intersect, images are born. [*The New Science Fiction*, 1969]

■ My interest in medicine and the sciences is largely because I see them as the best possible tools for dismantling the conventionalized reality that forms our lives. [*Omni*, n.d.]

■ When people are not quite certain about a meaning in my books I don't feel obliged to offer an exact explanation. Once you begin to itemize too much you are effectively doing an autopsy on the corpse of the imagination. You should leave the reader to participate in the creative process. [*Books*, 1987]

■ I quite consciously rely on my obsessions in all my work. I deliberately set up an obsessional frame of mind. In a paradoxical way, this leaves one free of the subject of the obsession. It's like picking up an ashtray and staring so hard at it that one becomes obsessed by its contours, angles, texture, etc, and forgets that it is an ashtray—a glass dish for stubbing out cigarettes. [*Paris Review*, 1984]

■ Presumably all obsessions are extreme metaphors waiting to be born. That whole private mythology, in which I believe totally, is a collaboration between one's conscious mind and those obsessions that, one by one, present themselves as stepping stones. [*Paris Review*, 1984]

■ I hope everything I have written is ambiguous, reflecting the paradoxical facets that make up human nature. [intv Hans Obrist, 2003]

■ I take for granted that for the imaginative writer, the exercise of the imagination is part of the basic process of coping with reality, just as actors need to act all the time to make up for some deficiency in their sense of themselves. [*Paris Review*, 1984]

■ I'm not a *literary* man, I don't work within a literary frame of things at all. [*Thrust,* 1980]

■ I don't see [my] novels as pessimistic, which many people say they are. I see them as stories of psychological fulfillment. In all cases the heroes of these novels find the truth about themselves—often paying a very steep price, but they get to embrace the catastrophes around them. They rush open-armed towards these disasters, because these disasters are very potent machinery for finding the truth about *themselves.* [*Spin,* 1989]

■ Light, time, the attempt to break out of the metaphysical structures that lock us all into our little rooms and mental cubicles and categories—it's a strain that runs through all of my work. [*Rolling Stone,* 1987]

■ My stuff is about the fall of the American empire . . . [I was brought up in] an area dominated by Americans, by American cars, by American styles and consumer goods . . . What I've been writing about in a way, is the end of technology, the end of America. A lot of my fiction is about what America is going to be like in 50 years time. [Intv David Pringle, 1975]

■ If by postmodernism you mean a reflexive, self-conscious fiction that plays games with its own fictional identity, then I don't see myself as a forerunner in any way. I detest this kind of fiction. I am much closer to the Surrealists, in that I employ a traditional narrative space, in whose illusions I completely believe, while at the same time stretching the imaginative demands made on the reader by an extreme subject matter. [Intv L. Tarantino, 1994]

■ External landscapes directly reflect interior states of mind. [unknown]

■ I have a walk every day and a good think about things. I

sometimes think maybe this town [Shepperton] is a complete conspiracy, or maybe it's a very advanced kind of psychological experiment—all these ideas occur to me and every now and again I think: "Hey, that's not bad. That's worth pursuing." [*Observer,* 2002]

■ As for learning to be creative, I think there's a lot of basic-level storytelling skills that you need to be born with. I wrote from a pretty early age, eight or nine, and I've always had a very vivid imagination. If you've got a strong imagination it's there all the time, it's working away. You're kind of remaking the world as you walk down a street, sort of reinventing it. [*Observer,* 2002]

■ For me the hydrogen bomb was a symbol of absolute freedom. I feel it's given me the right—the obligation even—to do anything I want. ["The Terminal Beach," 1964]

■ I'm not a literary man, and I'm not a commercial writer either. I'm really a kind of naive, a perpetual innocent, not far removed from the village bumpkin who still hasn't worked out what a set of traffic lights is. [*Independent,* 1991]

■ My writing is a kind of private, personal mythology . . . We all mythologize ourselves to try and make sense of our lives. That aspect is true of my characters generally—they're driven by personal mythology. [*Disinfo.com,* 2000]

■ There are people who are constantly rediscovering the world on a second-by-second basis, for whom every minute is a new excitement. Whether it's a sort of naiveté or not I don't know, but I've always been one of those. I wake up in the morning and look out at Shepperton and I'm always amazed and think, "What is this?" [*Independent,* 1991]

■ [In *The Kindness of Women*] David Hunter is really another side of me . . . my dark side. Even the character of the TV psychologist represents part of me in a small way. [C21, n.d.]

■ Young doctors simply have no time to exercise their imaginations. So I decided I would become a writer. [Publishers Weekly, 1998]

■ The reason I didn't continue as a doctor was that I wanted to be a writer; I had so much to write about. My time in the dissecting room has given me an enormous fund of images and ideas and metaphors that I've fed into my fiction. Some people have criticized me for being a bit too clinical about the human body. But I think one consequence of spending two years dissecting it is that you have no illusions about it. A book like *Crash,* for example, draws heavily on the years I spent doing anatomy. So did *Empire of the Sun.* ["Raising the Dead," n.d.]

■ Once you've dissected the cadaver—thorax, abdomen, head and neck, etc, you go on to the more exhaustive anatomy of, say, the inner ear, and the metaphors aren't so generously forthcoming. So I'd had enough of it in two years. In some ways I wish I *had* become a doctor. Such a mind-blowing course. The feats of memory required are really absolutely gigantic. [intv David Pringle, 1975]

■ Autobiographies tend to be written from the perspective of maturity with the benefit of hindsight, by people who are able to weigh their lives on some sort of moral scales, and chart the overall direction of their lives in retrospect . . . By writing a work of fiction you can dramatize the immediate present with the maximum emotional force and engage the sympathies of the reader. [*Albedo One,* 1993]

■ People think that it's all imagery; hotels, drained swimming pools, and the sort of architecture that underpins most of my fiction is all carefully blueprinted in advance, like the structure of an aircraft. But that isn't the case. I've simply written about what interested and intrigued me. [*Albedo One,* 1993]

■ I see myself as a neutral observer. I'm not trying to impose some kind of private or personal vision on the world. All I'm doing is looking out and seeing what's going on in the street. ["Prophet with Honour, n.d.]

■ The future will be a struggle between huge competing systems of psychopathology. Stultifying boredom, interrupted by random acts of unpredictable violence. It's only writers of the extreme who will be able to cope in fiction with such events. [*Independent,* 2001]

■ There are the imaginative writers who often tend to be mavericks: Genet, Celine, Burroughs, and so on. And I like to think of myself as a maverick. [intv Marcos Moure, 1995]

■ I've always operated on the fringe—a complete maverick. [Intv Claire MacDonald]

■ My fiction is all about one person—one man coming to terms with various forms of isolation . . . That seems to exclude the possibility of a warm fruitful relationship with anybody, let alone anyone as potentially close as a woman. [intv David Pringle, 1975]

■ I'm interested in science and medicine, the media landscape, and so on. My reflexes are not the reflexes of a literary man. I'm more of a magpie pecking at any bright pieces of foil. I'm interested in the world, not the world of literature. [intv Marcos Moure, 1995]

■ The confusions and sudden transformations of war, which of course were well known to the French during WWII, taught me that reality is little more than a stage set, whose cast and scenery can be swept aside and replaced overnight, and that our belief in the permanence of appearances is an illusion. [*Disturb,* n.d.]

■ My characters are almost all engaged in mythologizing themselves and in then exploring that mythology to the furthest end, whatever the price. [intv L. Tarantino, 1994]

■ [My stories], in the sense of the narrative sequence of events, come last. First comes the central imaginative idea, which is generally the fruit of long obsession. [intv L. Tarantino, 1994]

■ I'm always pushing some moralistic line. There are almost no evil characters in my fiction, and the few there are tend to be evil for the public good (or so they assume). [*Literary Review*, 2001]

■ Through my books, what I'm seeking to discover is whether a new sensibility exists on the far shore. [unknown]

■ My fiction is investigative, exploratory, and comes to no moral conclusions whatever. *Crash* is a clear case of that; so is *Atrocity Exhibition*. [unknown]

■ The environment today is itself so filled with pressures of every conceivable kind—the pressures to conform, the pressures to amuse oneself, the pressures to find oneself—and the constant bombardment of everyday life by advertising, the media landscape, together represent a continuing kind of challenge to one's sanity. And, of course, many of my characters are wilting under the pressure; they don't want to buy any more refrigerators or electric toothbrushes . . . They want to find some truth about themselves. So they embark, generally speaking in my fiction, on some sort of voyage of discovery. [BBC Radio 3, 1998]

■ Sensation rules our world, and a sort of perverse logic is operating which thrives on violence, and to a lesser extent, sex. The media landscape is saturated with images of violence and sexuality, desperately trying to extract a sort of flicker, a galvanic response from the sort of dead frog's leg of the human spirit. And my characters are trying to establish a more meaningful psychological circuitry that at present is completely overwhelmed by our perverse entertainment landscape. [BBC Radio 3, 1998]

■ I christened the new terrain I wished to explore "inner

space," that psychological domain (manifest, for example, in Surrealist painting) where the inner world of the mind and the outer world of reality meet and fuse. [intro, French ed. of *Crash,* 1974]

■ [*The Drowned World*] should be put in its context as the first inner space novel. "Inner Space" was the flag which I nailed to my mast, and *The Drowned World*—written in '62 or whenever it was—is literally the first Inner Space novel. Up until that point, catastrophe stories were being done on a very literal level as adventure stories, but the *psychological* adventure became the subject matter for me. [*NME,* 1983]

■ The hero embraces the catastrophe as a means by which he can express and fulfill his own nature, pursue his own mythology to the end, whatever that may be. He can accept the logic of his own personality and run that logic right down to the end of the road. That's a different approach; that's what *The Drowned World* is about. That's what nearly all my fiction is about. [*NME,* 10/22/1983]

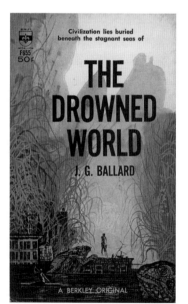

Civilization lies buried beneath the stagnant seas of
THE DROWNED WORLD
J. G. BALLARD
A BERKLEY ORIGINAL

■ I would guess that a large part of the furniture of my fiction was provided ready-made from the landscape of wartime Shanghai: all those barren hotels and deserted beaches, empty apartment blocks . . . the whole reality of a kind of stage set from which the cast has exited, leaving one with very little idea of what the actual play is about. Something like *The Drowned World* comes straight out of that landscape: flooded paddy fields with apartment buildings in the distance rising out of them, which I used to watch from my camp every day ... that sun, that very hot sun. [*NME*, 10/22/1983]

■ *The Drowned World* is about time past, biological memory, the sources of the psyche deep in the buried levels of spinal column, whereas *The Drought* is my image of what the future is going to be. I see the future as very lunar; very arid, very static, sudden tremors and harsh black-and-white shadows, bursts of sensation like signals reaching a cathode ray tube from a crashing airliner or from a distant galaxy. [*NME*, 10/22/1983]

■ Writing a novel is one of those modern rites of passage, I think, that lead us from an innocent world of contentment, drunkenness, and good humor, to a state of chronic edginess and the perpetual scanning of bank statements. By the eighteenth book, one has a sense of having bricked oneself into a niche, a roosting place for other people's pigeons. I wouldn't recommend it. [*Paris Review*, 1984]

■ In the case of an imaginative writer, especially one like myself with strong affinities to the Surrealists, I'm barely aware of what is going on. Recurrent ideas assemble themselves, obsessions solidify themselves, one generates a set of working mythologies, like tales of gold invented to inspire a crew. I assume one is dealing with a process very close to that of dreams—a set of scenarios devised to make sense of apparently irreconcilable ideas. [*Paris Review*, 1984]

■ I like to live where the battle is fought most fiercely, and it's in suburbs like Shepperton. You're at the crux of that great emerging struggle of the consumer landscape. [ICA conversation, 1998]

■ We should immerse ourselves in the destructive element. Far better to do so *consciously* than find ourselves tossed into the pool when we're not looking. [*Paris Review*, 1984]

■ I learned the importance of sheer story-telling, a quality which was about to leave the serious English novel. [*The Pleasure of Reading*, 1992]

■ As in Dali's paintings, there are more elements of collage [in my writing] than might meet the eye at first glance. A large amount of documentary material finds its way into my fiction, certainly [in] *Atrocity Exhibition,* where I adopt a style of pseudoscientific reportage closely based on similar scientific papers. And there's the piece "Theater of War," in *Myths of the Near Future,* where all the dialogue except for the commentator's is taken from Vietnam newsreel transcripts. There is a scene in *Concrete Island* where the girl Jane Shepherd is berating Maitland. That is a transcript of a secret tape recording I made of my then-girlfriend in a rage—well, secret is the wrong word; she was simply too angry to notice that I had switched the machine on. [*Paris Review,* 1984]

■ I've never had any problems stimulating my imagination—rather, the opposite. At times, I need to damp it down. [*Paris Review,* 1984]

■ All my fiction is a fiction of analysis, where I've tried to identify certain ongoing trends that seem to be apparent. I don't think it took a great deal of prophetic skill to guess what was going to happen as the Sixties and Seventies unfolded. I could see all these social trends, with an entertainment culture that thrived on violence and sensation and a rootless urban and suburban population with nothing to do other than play with their own psychopathic fantasies. Modern technology, whether in the form of a motor car or a motorway or a highrise building, was empowering people's worst impulses . . . the technology involved pandered to and facilitated the eruption of people's worst natures. ["Prophet with Honour," n.d.]

■ No writer writes all the time. [*Index,* 1997]

■ I never switch off from the business of writing . . . one is always a writer—my kind of writer, anyway. [*Blitz,* 1987]

■ I am a rather obsessive writer, a very driven writer. So the kind of background noises that would unsettle frailer, more refined souls didn't bother me in the least—I thrived on it. My fiction is not an ivory tower fiction. It is written out of the daily experiences of taking children to school and helping them with their homework and all the rest of it. Fortunately, we have a school system which is really an excuse for babysitting. And when they get home there is that wonderful child-minder called television. [*Index*, 1996]

■ I can't have enough information coming into my life—I want to read everything. I want to eavesdrop on the shop talk of specialists in any field. [*NY Times*, 1989]

■ I've always been interested in writing a fiction about the present day that was strongly influenced by the scientific imagination. [*Blitz*, 1987]

■ The person that is both insider and outsider at the same time brings with him an ambivalence which serves the author very well, because you have mixed emotions about the subject—you love it and hate it. You know it and yet don't know it, so it's constantly surprising in little ways. [*NME*, 1985]

■ [My characters] embrace the catastrophe because they're keen to remythologize themselves, and rediscover the different world that lies beyond the transformation. [*Artforum*, 1997]

■ All my heroes are trying to break through all these layers of enamel which society and social conventions paste over us. [*NME*, 10/22/1983]

■ I don't think I've been given enough credit for the humor I have. [*Salon*, 1997]

■ There is a lot of humor [in my work], but of a very deadpan kind—perhaps too deadpan. There's a huge amount of humor in Magritte, perhaps of a similar kind. An enormous apple fills a room. It's threatening and mysterious, but also extremely funny in an unnerving way. That's the kind of humor I aspire to. [*Literary Review,* 2001]

■ **Most humor comes from the provinces—Arthur Askey, Ken Dodd, etc.** [*Literary Review,* 2001]

■ Jim enjoyed trigonometry. Unlike Latin or algebra, this branch of geometry was directly involved in a subject close to his heart— aerial warfare. [*Empire of the Sun,* 1984]

■ **I've always been a great believer in the strong story. I don't believe in a fiction of nuance.** [intv Charles Platt, 1979]

■ Shanghai was a huge, wide open city full of political gangsters, criminals of every kind . . . gambling, racketeering, prostitution, and everything that comes from the collisions between the very rich—there were thousands of millionaires—and the very poor—no one was ever poorer than the Shanghai proletariat. On top of that, superimpose World War II . . . [Patrick Mulvaney] my best friend lived in an apartment block in the French concession, and I remember going there and suddenly finding that the building was totally empty, and wandering around all those empty flats with the furniture still in place, total silence, just the odd window swinging in the wind . . . I remember going around looking at drained swimming pools by the dozen . . . One day you'd see the familiar scene of freighters and small steamers at their moor-

ings, and the next day the damn things would all be sunk . . . I remember rowing out to these ships, and walking onto the decks, with water swilling through the staterooms. Given the stability of the society we now live in, this is very difficult to convey. I think all that was fed into my psyche. [Intv Charles Platt, 1979]

■ As they stepped from their landing craft the Chinese surged forward, gangs of pickpockets and pedicab drivers, prostitutes and bartouts, vendors hawking bottles of home-brew Johnny Walker, gold dealers and opium traders—the evening citizenry of Shanghai in all its black silk, fox fur and flash. [*Empire of the Sun*, 1984]

■ Dr Barbara in *Rushing to Paradise* is a part-portrait of Margaret Thatcher, and Carline of George Bush—I hope that doesn't spoil the book for you. [letter to David Pringle, 1995]

■ I haven't taken any drugs since one terrifying LSD trip in 1967— a nightmarish mistake. It opened a vent of hell that took years to close and left me wary even of aspirin. Visually it was just like my 1965 novel, *The Crystal World,* which some people think was inspired by my LSD trip. It convinced me that a powerful and obsessive enough imagination can reach, unaided, the very deepest layers of the mind. (I take it that beyond LSD there lies nothing.) [*Paris Review,* 1984]

■ Most of my fiction, whatever its settings may be, is not pessimistic. It's a fiction of psychological fulfillment. Most people think that I write a fiction of unhappy endings, but it's not true . . . All my fiction describes the merging of the self in the ultimate metaphor, the ultimate image, and that's psychologically fulfilling. It seems to me to be the only recipe for happiness we know. [Intv Charles Platt, 1979]

■ [*The Atrocity Exhibition* has] always been for me one of my most important books, where I really tried to analyze what was going on at the point where the media landscape meets our own central nervous systems. What is the real significance of Marilyn Monroe's death or of the Kennedy assassination? What do they do to us on a neural level, on the unconscious levels of the brain? [*Omni,* n.d.]

■ I never consciously shaped my ideas or my style. I simply followed my obsessions, and was confident that they would take me to strange destinations beyond the edge of the map. [intv Hans Obrist, n.d.]

■ After I got married, children began to appear. I needed some kind of much more settled life, so I could write in the evenings and weekends. So I took a job on the Chemistry Society journal called *Chemistry & Industry* which was a weekly scientific journal. The office of any scientific magazine is the most wonderful mail drop, the ultimate sort of information crossroads. I was sort of filtering it, like some sort of sea creature sailing with jaws open through a great sea of delicious plankton. I was filtering all this extraordinary material. I certainly remember reading with great interest the first scientific papers on the chemistry of hallucinogenic drugs. That was *very interesting* to me. ["Shanghai Jim," 1991]

■ I had children before I began to publish short stories professionally. So the children came first—that was creation on the grandest scale. The writing of fiction seemed a pretty trivial enterprise by comparison with bringing up infants and watching them construct the universe. That is all children do. [*Index,* 1997]

■ Soon after [the death of my wife] I started to write *The Atrocity Exhibition,* which led on to *Crash.* I felt that a terrible crime had been committed by nature against this young woman and her children, and much of my subsequent fiction was a desperate attempt to make sense of it, by proving that black is white, that what we think of as evil may actually be good in some deviant way. So the Kennedy assassination was a fructifying event, fertilizing us with the blood of this young prince, and the car crash was a sexualizing and positive event. In the same nightmare logic the twelve-year-old Jim in *Empire of the Sun* could see war as a good thing. Strangely, all these propositions contain more than a germ of truth, distasteful though it is to think about them. [*Literary Review*, 2001]

■ At the time I wrote *Crystal World*, and through the five years of *Atrocity Exhibition*, I used to start the working day once I returned from delivering the children to school, at 9:30 in the morning, with a large scotch. It separated me from the domestic world, like a huge dose of Novocaine injected into reality in the same way that a dentist calms a fractious patient so that he can get on with some fancy bridgework. [*Paris Review*, 1984]

■ I've been writing now for 35 years [age 60], as a published writer. I've only written 11 novels in that time, so I haven't written continuously by any means. I've generally had a fallow period after finishing writing a novel, when I think about where I'm going next. [*C21*, n.d.]

■ I believe that the tongue is just as important as other organs. If you have an appetite for food, you'll have an appetite for sex. [*Observer*, 2003]

■ I'm always suspicious of people who lack an appetite, and I admire people with strong appetites. However, now I'm 72 I don't eat a great deal and, let's say, my tastes have simplified. It is a matter of metabolism, and I'm bored. I've eaten everything. [*Observer*, 2003]

■ There's no secret [to my writing process]. One simply pulls the cork out of the bottle, waits three minutes, and two thousand or more years of Scottish craftsmanship does the rest. [*Paris Review*, 1984]

■ I wake at 8 AM and have a couple of cups of tea. Midmorning

I make a coffee to get my brain in gear—I used to have a large scotch, and that worked even better. Alcohol used to provide a large proportion of my calorie intake and my life enhancement, but I'm too old for that now. I don't drink spirits any more. [*Observer,* 2003]

■ I've always drunk instant coffee at home—ever since I read Elizabeth David, who wrote about its virtues. For lunch I eat odd things—Parma ham with a few drops of truffle oil. Dinner is usually an omelette. [*Observer,* 2003]

■ I'm also very fond of game. I love quail, but I like grouse best of all. I eat a lot of game because the flavor is richer—it's darker. I drink with it a good red wine. I prefer French wines. [*Observer,* 2003]

■ I have always followed my own obsessions, and I have always had a slightly schoolboy urge to shock and scandalize. I might not have been able to do it, say, living in New York. The standard of living in Britain is low, so you don't need to make so much money to keep going. And I, for the most part, lived modestly. [*Index,* 1997]

■ All you can do is cling to your own obsessions—all of them, to the end. Be honest with them; identify them. Construct your own personal mythology out of them and follow that mythology; follow those obsessions like stepping stones in front of a sleepwalker. I think if you compromise with your own obsessions, that way lies disaster. [*Index,* 1997]

■ As a writer you have to be faithful to your own subjective obsessions—if you try to be something else disaster occurs, and you lose your unique vision. [*Disinfo.com,* 2000]

■ I follow my obsessions wherever they take me; I try to remain completely faithful to them. I expect that tests the reader in some way because it is testing me as a writer. It's as if an engine is pulling this old ferry boat up whatever river runs inside my head. [*Publishers Weekly,* 1998]

■ I've always tried to do justice to my obsessions, and never hold anything back in anything I've written. I put everything on the page. I don't pretend that I am something that I am not as the author, because I do have an idealistic belief that human beings are not a gang of raging psychopaths. We're not a sort of huge Manson gang. On the other hand, one mustn't deny the imagination. The alternatives aren't Charles Manson on the one hand and—I don't know, the Puritan fathers on the other. There is a middle way. [*Spin,* 1989]

■ Anatomy and physiology seem to be a wonderful storehouse of images and metaphors of every conceivable kind. [*Artforum,* 1997]

■ I tend to follow my obsessions. I am never happier than when writing about drained swimming pools and abandoned hotels, which of course spring straight from my childhood. The real question about my fiction is: "Is JGB's childhood relevant to anyone living in today's world?" I think it is, and that Shanghai, the first artificial and media city (as much a fiction as Las Vegas) was a paradigm for *all the urban landscapes of the future living on the edge of catastrophe.* [intv L. Tarantino, 1994]

■ I try to maintain a fairly ambiguous pose, while trying to unsettle and provoke the reader, to keep the unconscious elements exerting their baleful force. [*Salon,* 1997]

■ My stories aren't really set in the future, but in a kind of visionary present. [*Salon,* 1997]

■ What happens after a major catastrophe is generally very unexpected, might even be ludicrous . . . The sort of landscapes I describe are not meant to be real in the strict sense of the term. They are landscapes that involve in some way the inner landscape of the minds of the protagonists. What I try to depict in my novels are changes in the external environment that match exactly changes in the internal environment, so there are certain points where these two come together. You can see this happening in ordinary life—in times of war, for example. [*Friends,* 1970]

■ Novelists are not the nicest people. Touchy, unloved, and aware that the novel's greatest days lie back in the age of steam, we occupy a rung on the ladder of likability somewhere between tax inspectors and immigration officials, with whom all too many of us share an unworthy interest in money and social origins. [*London Times,* 1991]

■ The early novels of mine are stories of psychological fulfillment. They're stories of characters mythologizing goals. That's what happiness is, by any definition. [*Seconds,* 1996]

■ Dali said, "The only difference between me and a madman is that I am not mad!" I would say that the only difference between me and a madman is that I am mad. [*S.F. Eye,* 1991]

■ James Joyce's *Ulysses* had an immense influence on me—almost entirely for the bad. [*Guardian,* 1990]

■ There's too much jargon around—"voyeurism and the male gaze," "castration anxieties." Marxist theory-speak swallowing its own tail. [*Millennium People,* 2003]

■ My copy of the *Los Angeles Yellow Pages* I stole from the Beverly Hilton Hotel three years ago. It has been a fund of extraordinary material, as Surrealist in its ways as Dali's autobiography [The Secret Life of Salvador Dali]. ["The Pleasure of Reading," 1992]

■ Part of the problem that some critics have with the apparent lack of depth in my characters arises from the fact that my characters, right from the earliest days when I started writing fiction, were already these disenfranchised human beings living in worlds where the fictional elements constituted a kind of externalized mental activity. They didn't need great psychological depth, because it was all out there, above their heads. [*21C*, 1997]

■ We saw the new world of technological society emerging. I started writing about that, the way all these things overlaid politics, advertising, private fantasies, and the way it was all mixed together so you couldn't look at any single event. I regard the assassination of Kennedy as the catalyst for all this because it was an assassination which virtually took place live on television, as did the Vietnam war. This new landscape [was] a nightmare marriage between reason and fantasy. Out of it came first *The Atrocity Exhibition* and then *High Rise,* where I could see the dark side of the sun—the hidden logics that underpinned technological society were beginning to reveal rather scary aspects of themselves. [*Blitz*, 1987]

■ I never said we should shy away from or retreat from technology. I thought that maybe we should embrace these apparently dangerous ideas and run them down, pursue them to the end. [*Blitz*, 1987]

■ I don't think the [typewriter] affected my writing, but it certainly has happened in respect to the word processor, hasn't it? I do a lot of book reviewing, and although I've never used a PC, I'm absolutely certain that I can tell the difference between books that are written on PCs and those that are not. Books written on the PC have very high definition in the sense of line-by-line editing, grammar, sentence construction and the like. But the overall narrative construction is haywire. There's a tendency to go on and on and on, in a sort of logorrhea, and to lose one's grasp of the overall contents. Imagine, say, James Joyce at a word processor; *Finnegans Wake* would have been incomprehensible! [*21C*, 1997]

■ I took up painting in my youth and found I hadn't any talent for it, but I always regretted that I didn't, because I think I would've been far happier as a painter. I would love to have been a painter in the tradition of the Surrealist painters whom I admire so much. [*Salon*, 1997]

■ Sometimes I think that all my writing is nothing more than the compensatory work of a frustrated painter. [*Paris Review*, 1984]

■ My daughter, about two years ago, bought me a paint set for my birthday. I'm still waiting to use it. When I start painting I shall stop writing! All my fiction consists of paintings. [intv Goddard, 1975]

■ I've always used a kind of scientific vocabulary and a scientific approach to show subject matter in a fresh light. One can describe [a car crash] in a kind of Mickey Spillane language with powerful adverbs and adjectives. But another approach is to be cool and clinical and describe it in the way that a forensic scientist would describe a man

and a woman making love. Instead of using all the cliches that are marshaled wearily once again in most novels, approach it as if it were some sort of forensic experiment that you were describing—an event that is being watched with the calm eye of the anatomist or the physiologist. It often prompts completely new insights into what has actually happened. [*Salon*, 1997]

■ When I was writing *Crash* I thought I was following certain trends that I saw inscribed in the sensation-hungry, rather affectless landscape that was emerging in the Sixties. I was following these trends that I saw inscribed across the graph paper to the point where they seemed likely to intersect way off the page. I saw this new logic, a nightmare logic, emerging, and this was what I was exploring. I was, in a sense, carrying out an autopsy before the cadaver was cold. [*Artforum*, 1997]

■ The first time around [*Crash*] was a complete flop. Although it did have a small intense following—a few psychopaths and amputees—sending me their porno photos. [*I-D*, 1987]

■ [In writing *Crash*] I was trying to achieve *complete honesty*. Of course, the book is a description of an obsession, an extreme metaphor at *a time when only the extreme will do.* [*Cypher*, 1973]

■ I had an accident, about a week after finishing *Crash*. My Ford Zephyr, a big English Ford, had a front blowout at the foot of the Chiswick Bridge. It rolled over, crossed the dual carriageway and ended up on its back. The windscreen was shattered . . . I had the car repaired. [intv Iain Sinclair, 1997]

■ I always saw myself as merely an observer, tracking various trends and tendencies and trying to uncover the hidden logic that was at work behind the Technicolor surface that so enchants most people. This doesn't mean that I endorse a world where we can play with our own psychopathologies as a game. I think that may, in fact, be the greatest threat the human race has ever faced. [*21C*, 1997]

■ Given that external reality is a fiction, the writer's role is almost superfluous. He does not need to invent the fiction because it is already there. So he now has a much more *analytic* role. [*Friends*, 1970]

■ The great thing about Freud is that from the writer's standpoint it is an extremely useful psychology. Freud sees the unconscious as a narrative stage upon which the whole business of human experience is being dramatized. His psychology is one of dramatics; of dramatic re-enactments. Things like the Oedipus complex are dramatic structures. [*Friends*, 1970]

■ I'm a speculative writer. I conceive of certain possibilities and extend them through an act of imagination. The point is, living is one of the most boring things one can do—the most interesting and exciting things are happening inside one's own head. [*GQ*, 1996]

■ If you focus on anything, however blank, in the right way, then you become obsessed by it. It's like those Andy Warhol films of eight hours of the Empire State Building or of somebody sleeping. Ordinary life viewed obsessively enough becomes interesting in its own right by some sort of neurological process that I don't hope to understand. [*Spike*, 2000]

■ The sort of images that have appealed to me over the years: all the drained swimming pools, abandoned hotels, strange business parks, gated communities, and retirement complexes—these are what I want to convey: the peculiar latent psychology waiting to emerge into the daylight. That's what I'm trying to do: look at the world and see its latent content. I treat the external world as if it were a solidified dream. [*Spike*, 2000]

■ I have thought about the subjects of my novels for a long time, often many years, before I decide to write a novel. In a real sense, my novels write me. [BBC Online Live Chat, 2002]

■ As I'm approaching 57, one becomes more relaxed and adopts a rather more gentle view of things. Also one tends to go back to one's sources. [*Blitz*, 1987]

■ I think [the] sense of being an outsider looking in on myself has been a very great advantage to me as a writer. [intv L. Tarantino, 1994]

■ Catastrophe? Yes, I think much of my fiction is an attempt to remake the landscapes of Western Europe and America so that they resemble the landscape of wartime Shanghai, where I presumably glimpsed some truth about myself and the human beings around me. [intv L. Tarantino, 1994]

■ My imagination was hardwired by the time I was fifteen, shaped by my experiences during the war. In all my fiction I've gone on re-using that, in that I perceive everyday reality as if it is some kind of continuation of [World War II] by other means. [*Omni*, n.d.]

■ I never read my own fiction—the mistakes seem to leap off the page, and I avoid mirrors for the same reason! [*Disturb*, n.d.]

■ All my work as a writer has been an attempt to discover reality beyond that of appearances, and I like to think that I follow faithfully in the footsteps of the Surrealist masters. [*Disturb*, n.d.]

■ Having been a reviewer myself, I can always tell when somebody has stopped reading the book he's reviewing. [intv David Pringle, 1975]

■ I'm fascinated by the immediate past—the treasures of the Triassic compare pretty unfavorably with those of the closing years of the Second Millennium. [*Drowned World*, 1962]

■ Back in the Sixties and Seventies, one felt that the novelist was working with an obsolete technology, that the conventions and techniques of the writer seemed completely out-of-date compared to cinema, mass magazines, mass advertising and television. I've changed my view on that completely. Now I feel the novelist has got something unique, that his work is the product of a single imagination which he can share intimately with one other single imagination, the reader. The resurgence in the popularity of the novel in recent years is a reflection of the fact that people know that they are being smothered by all this manufactured fiction that giant media organizations and conglomerates like the BBC are trying to suffocate them with. [*Blitz*, 1987]

■ I remake the familiar world and distort it. This gives the impression I want to destroy it—but I don't, not necessarily. In *The Drowned World* I appear to flood London, but I replace the present London with one that I feel to be far more marvelous, that touches the marvelous in us all. The same with *The Crystal World*. I may appear to fossilize reality in this palace of crystal, but I'm imposing a far more marvelous and perhaps more meaningful reality, not devastating it. Likewise in *Crash* and *High Rise,* I'm implying that beyond what seems to be this technological nightmare lies a richer—maybe more dangerous, but far richer—future. [*Blitz,* 1987]

■ I just follow my obsessions as they arise. I never give any thought to things in a long-term sense. I've never thought of myself as having a career which is unfolding like a great arch spanning a canyon where every piece has to be in place, and where one is anticipating where the other end of the arch will fall. [*Blitz,* 1987]

■ As far as reading for research is concerned, I've always been very fortunate in my friends. For years, Dr. Christopher Evans, a psychologist in the computer branch of the National Physical Laboratory . . . literally sent me the contents of his wastebasket. Once a fortnight, a huge envelope arrived filled with scientific reprints and handouts, specialist magazines and reports, all of which I read carefully. Another close friend, Dr. Martin Bax, sends me a lot of similar material. The sculptor Eduardo Paolozzi is a restless globetrotter who culls Japanese and American magazines for unusual material. Vale, the San Francisco publisher of the RE/Search series—with excellent volumes on Burroughs and Gysin, and the *Industrial Culture Handbook*—is a one-man information satellite beaming out a stream of fascinating things. Readers of mine send in a lot of material, for which I'm grateful. The leader of the rock group SPK told me that he believes there is a group of some two or three thousand people in Europe and the States who circulate information among each other. Sadly, modern technology, which ought to be so liberating, threatens all this. Already, I've received the first videocassettes in the place of the old envelopes crammed with odd magazines and cuttings. As I don't own a video recorder, the cassettes sit unseen on my bookshelves; the first volumes of the invisible library. One of my daughters reported on one tape, "It's rather weird—all about autopsies." [*Paris Review*, 1984]

■ Perhaps what's wrong with being a writer is that one can't even say "Good luck"—luck plays no part in the writing of a novel. No happy accidents as with the paint pot or chisel. I don't think you can say anything, really. I've always wanted to juggle and ride a unicycle, but I dare say if I ever asked the advice of an acrobat he would say, "All you do is get on and start pedaling." [*Paris Review*, 1984]

■ The fiction writer's whole role has changed. The fiction is already there; I feel the writer's job is to put the reality in. [*Evergreen Review*, 1973]

■ If you're bringing up children or looking after the elderly and making something of your own life—whether it's tending a little garden or starting an aircraft company—there are yardsticks that define reality and responsibility. You mustn't lose sight of these. And I hope I've never done so in my work; otherwise, I'd consider myself simply a pure fantasist, and I've never wanted to lose the sense of moral compass bearing. I mean, even in a book like *Crash* which some people consider to be out-and-out pornography, I attempt—I hope—to make some kind of sense of the marriage of reason and nightmare that has dominated the twentieth century. [*Rolling Stone*, 1987]

■ As a writer I've always had complete faith in my own obsessions. [*Twilight Zone*, 1988]

■ I've always been a very disciplined writer, because that's the only way you ever get anything done. Usually when I'm writing a novel I set myself 1,000 words a day, and I stick to it religiously. I sometimes stop in the middle of a sentence, which isn't a bad idea, as the next day it's very easy to get back into it. [*Observer*, 2002]

■ If you look at the novels I wrote in the '70s, they're all about the effects on human psychology of the changes brought about by science and technology, the modern urban landscape, the freeways and motorways, the peculiar psychology of life in vast highrise condominiums. [*Spin*, 1989]

■ Almost everything around us is produced by committees . . . but writers work alone. [*Literary Review*, 2001]

■ As a writer I get intensely involved with something, and then the moment it's finished it's sort of dead for me. [*Thrust*, 1980]

■ I set myself a target, about a thousand words a day—unless I just stare out of the window, which I do a lot of anyway. I generally work from a synopsis, about a page when I'm writing a short story, longer for a novel . . . I spend a tremendous amount of time—I won't say doing research, but just soaking myself in the mental landscapes, particularly of a novel. Most of the time I'm thinking about what I'm writing, or hope to write . . . I just tend to write whatever comes mentally to hand, and what I find interesting at a particular time . . . One can't consciously say, "That's what I'm going to write." It doesn't work out like that! [intv David Pringle, 1975]

■ Q: What ideals do you hold as a writer? A: I suppose to isolate the truth of any situation as I see it and to try and create in my fiction the *moral possibilities* of any situation. [*Friends #17*, 1970]

■ A typical Ballard hero finds himself in some sort of gathering crisis external to himself . . . This external crisis allows him to discover his true self . . . The characters at last find themselves. [*Independent*, 11-10-2001]

■ [*The Atrocity Exhibition* has] always been for me one of my most important books, where I really tried to analyze what was going on at the point where the media landscape meets our own central nervous systems. What is the real significance of Marilyn Monroe's death or of the Kennedy assassination? What do they do to us on a neural level, on the unconscious levels of the brain? Do these media events, like the suicide of Monroe, the assassination of Kennedy, the election of Reagan (who is referred to in *The Atrocity Exhibition* fifteen years before the event), have some deep significance buried within our minds, do they touch our imaginations in unexpected ways? I was trying to analyze the formulas of the world we live in. So that was an important book for me. I keep thinking that I ought to write a follow-up book in the same form: perhaps one of these days I will. [*Omni,* n.d.]

■ All my fiction is driven by—I wouldn't say a social conscience, exactly, but—I'm highly critical of what I see as dangerous trends developing around us. A lot of my fiction consists of warning signs. [BBC, n.d.]

■ I love writing about abandoned hotels, drained swimming pools and deserted runways. I think one should always be faithful to one's obsessions. [paraphrased, *Independent,* 11-10-2001]

■ Reading Freud in *The Interpretation of Dreams,* for example, teaches you to look at yourself in a different way and you begin to see elements of your own make-up that normally you would ignore. [*Métaphores #7,* 1983]

■ The great thing about Freud is that from the writer's standpoint it is an extremely useful psychology. Freud sees the unconscious as a narrative stage upon which the whole business of human experience is being dramatized. His psychology is one of dramatics; of dramatic re-enactments. Things like the

CRASH: Deborah Kara Unger and James Spader

Oedipus complex are dramatic structures. The whole dynamics of Freudian psychology lend themselves very well to a writer who would find other types very much more difficult to handle. One cannot discount everything Freud said . . . As a metaphor it is true even if it may not be completely true in fact. It works as a metaphor the same way the life of Christ works even if you are not a Christian. Make a distinction, therefore, between a literal and a metaphorical truth. [*Friends #17*, 1970]

■ I suppose one could say that my humor is deadpan. [*Telegraph*, 9-23-03]

■ I think I have an almost maniacal sense of humor. The problem is that it's rather deadpan. [*Pretext*, 2004]

■ My fiction is investigative, exploratory, and comes to no moral conclusions whatever. *Crash* is a clear case of that; so is *Atrocity Exhibition*. [unknown]

■ I had wasted my own youth dissecting cadavers and training to be a military pilot, trying to match myself against the realities of the postwar world. But the 1960s had effortlessly turned the tables on reality. The media landscape had sealed a technicolor umbrella around the planet, and then redefined reality as itself. [*Kindness of Women*, 1991]

■ Most of [my] ideas come, if anywhere, from visual sources: Chirico, the expressionist Robert Chand, and the Surrealists, whose dreamscapes, manic fantasies and feedback from the *Id* are as near to the future, and the present, as any intrepid spaceman rocketing round the galactic centrifuge. Writers who interest me are Poe, Wyndham Lewis, and Bernard Wolfe, whose *Limbo 90* I think the most interesting Science-Fiction novel so far published. [*New Worlds #54*, 1956]

■ I generally begin a book with a large sheaf of notes, covering everything from the main themes to the details of the setting, the principal characters, etc, al of which I've daily speculated upon in the months before I begin. I write the complete first draft before returning to the beginning, though of course I'm working from a fairly detailed synopsis, so I'm sure of my overall structure. I then do a fair amount of cutting of superfluous phrases, occasionally of paragraphs of pages. [*Paris Review,* 1984]

■ There were no museums or galleries in Shanghai, but I was very keen on art—I was always sketching and copying, and sometimes I think that my whole career as a writer has been the substitute work of an unfulfilled painter. [*Pretext,* 2004]

■ I'm afraid all the characters are completely made up. . . [But] some of [*The Kindness of Women*] is composed of literal descriptions. The birth of my baby. The LSD trip. The Japanese killing a Chinese on a station platform after the surrender. I watched that. That was a minute-by-minute account of what happened. [*Sunday Times,* 9/22/1991]

■ The written word is under threat, and has been for a long time, but is unique in a vital respect: a relationship of unparalleled closeness between reader and writer. Almost everything else—film, drama, ballet, even painting and sculpture—are produced by committees. [*S.F. Eye,* 1991]

■ I don't think the printed word is dying out; if anything the novel is undergoing a certain mini-renaissance, which curiously enough has coincided with a fall in television viewing figures. I think the reason is that the novel is the only form of fiction where you are reading the product of another human being; it's the only private medium of communication. The writer is in sole control of this imaginative universe. When you read a novel you're as close to another human being as you can be—even closer than if you were in bed with them. [*New Musical Express,* 1985]

■ In *The Drowned World,* I wanted to look at our racial memory, our whole biological inheritance, the fact that we're all several hundred million years old, as old as the biological kingdoms in our spines, in our brains, in our cellular structure; our very identities reflect untold numbers of decisions made to adapt us to changes in our environment, decisions lying behind us in the past like some enormous, largely forgotten journey. I wanted to go back along that road to discover what made us what we are, [and] water was the central image of the past. In *The Drought* I was interested in future time, the image being sand. I see the future as being abstract, geometric—the landscape of the moon seems to me to be a good image of the future landscape for Earth. The crystal is a symbol of a timeless world. In *The Crystal World* I described a situation in which time doesn't exist at all. The crystallizing forest, in which the people become crystallized, describes a state beyond death, a kind of non-living existence. [*Transatlantic Review*, 1971]

■ I wrote a couple of pieces for *New Worlds,* one called "Princess Margaret's Face-Lift." I got a textbook of cosmetic surgery—this was an attempt to lower the fictional threshold right to the floor—and I used the description of a face-lift word for word except I made it all happen to Princess Margaret. [*The Imagination on Trial*, 1981]

■ I've always been conscious since I started writing that the tide was running the wrong way for the writer, whereas the visual artist, the painter or sculptor, was in a seller's market; the direction of the twentieth century was ever more visual. One couldn't anymore rely on the reader, you couldn't expect him to meet you anymore than halfway. One's in the arena on the lion's terms. [*The Imagination on Trial*, 1981]

■ I [write] from the point of view of the ordinary man in the street. I'm interested in the man watching the TV, not the man making the programs. [*Omni*, n.d.]

■ The need to re-mythologize oneself remains as pressing as ever, for reasons I have never understood, unabated by the passage of time and all the fictions we invent to escape it. [Introduction, *J.G. Ballard: The First 20 Years*, 1976]

■ "He's got a sort of desperate imagination"—that sort of sums me up as a human being and as a writer. [BBC Radio, 2002]

SHORT STORIES

■ A close friend of mine, Emma Tennant, began [publishing *Bananas*] in 1975, at which point I wrote a story for almost every one of the issues which she edited. At that point I had not written any short stories at all for something like four years, largely because there was nowhere to publish. This has nothing to do with payment, by the way—I never was paid a penny for any of the stories I wrote for *Bananas,* nor for any that I've ever written for *Ambit.* [*Thrust,* 1980]

Le livre d'or de la science-fiction

Ballard J.G.

■ It is much easier to write a good short story than a good novel. Many hundreds of perfect short stories have been written—perfect in the sense that a good carpenter can construct a perfectly-made table. Hundreds of perfect short stories have been written by the masters of the short story—Maupassant, Chekhov, O. Henry, the Edwardian ghost story writers, Saki . . . and the masters of modern SF. People like Bradbury have probably written 20 perfect short stories. It's much easier to achieve formal perfection in the short story, and this is the sort of yardstick which you just can't apply to the novel. Has anyone written a perfect novel? One doesn't think of the novel in those terms. It's such an open structure, it defies any kind of definition—whereas the short story is actually extremely hostile to innovation. [*Thrust*, 1980]

■ There's a deep need for stories; it seems to be built into the central nervous system. And there are many perfect short stories, but no perfect novels. [*Independent*, 11-10-2001]

■ [The short story:] It's like a snapshot or a cabaret sketch. You've got to get to the point and hold the audience's attention. [*Independent*, 11-10-2001]

■ The cataclysmic story is particularly interesting because it shows how even a minor variation in one of the physical constants of the environment can make life totally untenable—a corollary of the biological rule that the more specialized the organism, the narrower the margin of safety. [*New Worlds #111*, 1961]

DREAMS

■ I did record dreams at one period. I based one or two—not many—short stories of mine on dreams. [Iain Sinclair's *Crash*, 1999]

■ Dreams died different deaths, taking unexpected doors out of our lives. [*Millennium People*, 2003]

■ No theory ever seems likely to account for those strange safaris on which each of us sets out every night across the width of our own heads. Reason rationalizes reality for us, defusing the mysterious, but at the cost of dulling the imagination. [*Guardian*, 1986]

■ I have never seen a dream with a subtitle, or gone into a flash-back, though the constant watching of television, apart from dimming the frontal lobes, must have some effect on the way the optical centers of the brain shape their interior world. [*Guardian,* 1986]

■ Dreaming permits each and every one of us to be quietly and safely insane every night of our lives. [*Guardian,* 7/4/1986]

■ In Orwell's *1984* disobedience to Big Brother starts in a dream. [*Guardian,* 7/4/1986]

■ For Freud the essence of dreams lay in the expression of repressed desires, while for Jung they offered reassuring glimpses of the collective unconscious and the primordial models of social behaviour [*Guardian,* 7/4/1986]

■ We're living in a commodified world where everything has a price tag; a world filled with—you know, dreams that money can buy—but dreams that soon pall. [BBC Radio 3, 1998]

■ The old dreams were dead, Manson and Mickey Mouse and Marilyn Monroe belonged to a past America. It was time for new dreams, worthy of a real tomorrow . . . [*Hello America,* 1981]

JGB'S ART SHOW

■ It occurred to me, when I started thinking about *Crash,* that I ought to put on a show of crashed cars to test my hypothesis, and I mounted the show as a fine-arts collection of sculpture. I had an opening night and invited all the art critics and media people. I laid on a lot of wine. And although it appeared to be a gallery opening, I was really setting up a confrontation. [*Heavy Metal,* 1982]

■ There were just three crashed cars under the neutral gallery lighting. Of course, everyone got immensely overexcited. The exhibition was planned as a psychological experiment, that was its sole purpose. I hired a young woman to interview the guests at the opening on closed-circuit TV, which was a real novelty back in 1969. The intention was to deliberately overload the imagination of the guests by having them see themselves interviewed on closed-circuit television by this naked young woman. When she arrived, oddly enough, earlier in the evening, she walked in, took one look at the cars and then told me that she would interview everyone, but only topless. She would be clothed from the waist down. We'd agreed beforehand that she would interview people fully naked, but when she looked at the cars she said, "I won't appear naked, I'll just appear topless." I thought, "That's interesting." [*Artforum,* 1997]

■ Before starting *Crash,* in 1969, I staged an exhibition of crashed cars at the New Arts Laboratory in London—three crashed cars in a formal gallery ambience. The centerpiece was a crashed Pontiac from the last great tailfin period. The whole exhibition illustrated a scene from my previous book, *Atrocity Exhibition,* where my "Travis" hero stages a similarly despairing exhibition. What I was doing was testing my own hypotheses about the ambiguities that surround the car crash, ambiguities that are at the heart of the book. I hired a topless girl to interview people on closed-circuit TV. The violent and overexcited reaction of the guests at the opening party was a deliberate imaginative overload which I imposed upon them in order to test my own obsession. The subsequent damage inflicted on the cars during the month of the show—people splashed them with paint, tore off the wing mirrors—and at the opening party, where the topless girl was almost raped in the rear seat of the Pontiac (a scene straight from *Crash* itself), convinced me I should write *Crash.* The girl later wrote a damningly hostile review of the show in an underground paper. [*Blitz,* 1984]

■ I've never seen people get so drunk so quickly. Admittedly, I probably went over the top, because I had a closed-circuit television system, and I hired a topless girl to interview people on TV among the cars. It was obviously too much for the girl, because she originally agreed to come nude and when she saw the cars she suddenly said she would only go topless. It was too much for the people who watched themselves being interviewed—the girl was nearly raped in the back of a Pontiac. [*Heavy Metal,* 1982]

■ While the cars remained on show, they were repeatedly attacked. There was an enormous latent hostility released, a whole range of ambiguous emotion that surprised me. [*Heavy Metal,* 1982]

■ The behavior of people who visited the gallery absolutely convinced me that I was onto something. At the opening, people got so drunk, and over the course of the month they were on display the cars were attacked; one of them was overturned. Nobody would have noticed these cars in the street outside, but because they were isolated beneath the white gallery lighting they triggered enormous, confused emotions. So I thought, this is the green light. And so I sat down and began to write *Crash*. [*Spike,* n.d.]

■ I had an opening party to which I invited a large number of art critics and members of the demimonde. We had closed-circuit television and a topless girl who interviewed everybody in front of the crashed cars so they could see themselves on the TV set. It was a genuine opening, and also an experiment to test one or two of the hypotheses in the book. [*Evergreen Review,* 1973]

■ In fact the party was an illustrated episode from the book. What happened was that everybody got extremely drunk incredibly quickly. I've never seen people get drunk so fast. I was certainly within half an hour the only sober person at that gathering. People were breaking the bottles of red wine over the cars, smashing the glasses, grabbing the topless girl and dragging her into the back of one of the cars. Brawls broke out. [*Evergreen Review,* 1973]

■ There was something about those crashed cars that tripped off all kinds of latent hostility. Plus people's crazy sexuality was beginning to come out. In a way, it was exactly what I had anticipated in the book without realizing it. [*Evergreen Review,* 1973]

■ The show was on for a month. During that time, the cars were regularly attacked by people coming to the gallery. Windows that weren't already broken were smashed in, doors were pulled off, one of the cars was overturned, another car was splashed with white paint. When the exhibition was over, the cars were well and truly wrecked, which I thought was an interesting example of people's real responses to the whole subject of crashed cars. [*Evergreen Review,* 1973]

COMMANDER OF THE BRITISH EMPIRE

■ I received a letter from the Cabinet Office using this weird locution that the prime minister was minded to recommend me for a Commander of the British Empire. I had visions that if only I was allowed to call myself "Commander Ballard" I could put on a nautical cap and splice the main-brace. It was a CBE for so-called services to literature, another weird locution, but I declined. It was not for me.

I am opposed to the honors system. The whole thing is a preposterous charade. Thousands of medals are given out in the name of a non-existent empire. It makes us look a laughing-stock and encourages deference to the crown. I think it is exploited by politicians and always has been. Half the honors are given to people in the armed forces and civil service as a way of keeping their loyalty. I can't take it seriously.

I must say I find it sad to see left-wing playwrights who have traded on their socialist credentials throughout their careers accepting knighthoods. People like David Hare who have worn their socialist credentials on both sleeves kneel in front of the

Queen. It's too much. [*Sunday Times,* 2003]

■ It's a pantomime where tinsel takes the place of substance. I might have been tempted had I been entitled to call myself Commander Ballard—it has a certain ring. I could see a yachting cap and a rum ration as perks of the job. If I was French and was awarded the Legion of Honor, I might well accept. But as a republican, I can't accept an honor awarded by the monarch. There's all that bowing and scraping and mummery at the palace. It's the whole climate of deference to the monarch and everything else it represents. They just seem to perpetuate the image of Britain as too much pomp and not enough circumstance. It's a huge pantomime where tinsel takes the place of substance.

A lot of these medals are Orders of the British Empire, which is a bit ludicrous. The dreams of empire were only swept away relatively recently, in the '60s. Suddenly, we seem to have a prime minister who has delusions of a similar kind. It goes with the whole system of hereditary privilege and rank, which should be swept away. It uses snobbery and social self-consciousness to guarantee the loyalty of large numbers of citizens who should feel their loyalty is to fellow citizens and the nation as a whole. We are a deeply class-divided society.

I think it's deplorable when leftwing playwrights like David Hare, who have worn their socialist colors on both sleeves for so many years, should accept a knighthood. *Godalmighty,* this man actually knelt down in front of the Queen. I'm in impressive company [in refusing]. Most of them are thoughtful people and people of spirit and independence. It's good to see quite a few show-business people, like Albert Finney, a great actor. There were Aldous Huxley, Robert Graves—it suggests there's quite a large number of people who reject the whole notion of honors in their present form. And it might do something towards bringing the whole system down. [*Guardian,* 2003]

■ It's a system of antiquated gongs and ribbons that really belong on a Christmas tree. [*Independent,* July 14, 2004]

■ Q: Why did you refuse your honor?

A: As a republican, I can't accept an honor awarded by a monarch—all that bowing and scraping. The whole system of hereditary privilege and rank should be swept away.

Q: How would you change the present system?

A: Demolish it altogether.

Q: Who would you give an honor to?

A: No one. [*Independent,* 2003]

MY PAST

■ I don't think it's possible to escape from one's past. The brain and the imagination are imprinted forever with the images of one's first years. [intv Hans Obrist, 2003]

■ I came from a background where there was no past. Shanghai was a new city. The department stores and the sky-scrapers didn't exist before the year 1900. It was just a lot of mosquito-ridden mud-flats. I was brought up in a world which was new, so the past has never really meant anything to me. [Intv David Pringle, 1975]

■ It is difficult to remember just how formal middle-class life was in the 1930s and '40s. I wore a suit and tie at home from the age of 18. One dressed for breakfast. One lived in a very formal way and emotions were not paraded. And my childhood was not unusual. [*Observer,* 1994]

■ A thousand images of childhood, forgotten for nearly forty years, filled his mind, recalling the paradisal world when everything seemed illuminated by that prismatic light described so exactly by Wordsworth in his recollections of childhood. [*Crystal World,* 1966]

■ I think the experience that I went through as a boy—from 1937 when the Japanese invaded China, through Pearl Harbor, and into the postwar period, when all these rival groups, the Americans and Chiang Kai-shek crowd on the one side and Communists on the other, were acting out a kind of preview of Vietnam—I think those years were for me a kind of preview of the future. [*Spin,* 1989]

■ Shanghai was almost a 21st century city: huge disparities of wealth and poverty, a multilingual media city with dozens of radio stations, dominated by advertising, befouled by disease and pollution, driven by money, populated by twenty different nations … The significant thing for me was that all this was turned upside down by war. Friends suddenly vanished, leaving empty houses like the *Marie Celeste,* and everywhere I saw the strange Surrealist spectacles that war produces. [intv Hans Obrist, 2003]

■ When I refer to my own childhood, and how people behaved in the Far East during the Second World War, it seemed that some people simply enjoy killing and tormenting others. But that doesn't make them sadists. When I joined the Royal Air Force in 1953, most of our instructors were veterans from the Second World War, and they used to tell us, "Killing is such tremendous fun." They'd tell stories about how they'd machine-gunned villages just for the hell of it. [*Frieze,* 1996]

■ Up to the age of 14 or 15, I read everything from *Life* magazine, *Reader's Digest,* to American best-sellers. You read as part and parcel of childhood all the English children's classics: *Treasure Island, Alice in Wonderland,* etc. Nothing out of the ordinary—what everybody else my age was reading. [intv David Pringle, 1975]

■ As a child I was a bit hyperactive. I got into tremendous danger on a lot of occasions. [BBC Radio, 2002]

■ One of the benefits of my camp upbringing was that I was in very close contact, practically 24 hours a day, with a lot of girls my age who had to fight for survival too, so I always saw them as equals.

[*Independent,* 1991]

■ [In *Empire of the Sun*] I think the character Jim is fairly true to the boy that I was. The whole point of the book really is that he's learning to love the war, because the war represents security. That's a sort of nightmare truth about war: however unpleasant things are, people get used to it and they begin to rely on it—even people in prison camps. People are under enormous physical and mental pressure. It's the Stockholm Syndrome in a kind of way: you begin to love your captors because they represent security. [BBC Radio, 2002]

■ There is a strain of sadness in the Japanese. I think the Japanese actually enjoy being sad in a peculiar kind of way, and I think that appealed to me. It gave them a sort of dignity, which many Europeans didn't have. It's one of the main themes of [*Empire of the Sun*]: how to identify yourself with the enemy. This allows you to enter a strange sort of world. [BBC Radio, 2002]

■ There was a big difference between myself and the Jim in [*Empire of the Sun*], and that is my parents were with me in the camp. At the same time they didn't have very much control over me, and I think a certain estrangement sprang up between myself and my parents which I never really recovered from. [BBC Radio, 2002]

■ I saw something in the camp that children very rarely see. I saw my parents under stress and I saw other adults under stress. It was a great education, but it was alienating. I never really was ever close to my parents again. [BBC Radio, 2002]

■ I've often said of my wartime experiences: it took me 20 years to forget and then 20 years to remember . . . [While] Spielberg produced a very fine film, [*Empire of the Sun*] within the constraints of the Hollywood movie . . . the real experience was closer to Rossellini's *Open City* and *Paisan.* [intv L. Tarantino, 1994]

■ In a way *Empire of the Sun* is my first book, except that I waited 40 years to write it. There were plenty of drained swimming pools in the Shanghai of the Japanese occupation, and they've always had a special magic for me, along with abandoned hotels and apartment houses and that whole psychological no-man's land of old battlefields. In all my fiction I think I was just trying to recreate the landscape of Shanghai in Western Europe and the US. [*I-D,* 1987]

■ There was a period when we didn't know if the war had ended, when the Japanese had more or less abandoned the whole zone and the Americans had yet to come in, when all the images I keep using—the abandoned apartment houses and so forth— obviously had a big influence—as did the semi-tropical nature of the place: lush vegetation, a totally waterlogged world, huge rivers, canals, paddles, great sheets of water everywhere. It was a dramatized landscape thanks to the war and to the collapse of all the irrigation systems—a landscape dramatized in a way that is difficult to find in, say, Western Europe. [intv Goddard, 1975]

■ I don't think you can go through the experience of war without one's perceptions of the world being forever changed. The reassuring stage set that everyday reality in the suburban West presents to us is torn down; you see the ragged scaffolding, and then you see the truth beyond that, and it can be a frightening experience. The war came, I spent three years in the camp, and I saw adults under stress, some of them giving way to stress, some recovering and showing steadfast courage. It was a great education; when you see the truth about human beings it's beneficial, but very challenging, and those lessons have stayed with me all my life. ["Prophet with Honour," n.d.]

■ [War] taught me many lessons, above all that the unrestricted imagination was the best guide to reality. [intv Hans Obrist, 2003]

■ During my childhood I saw an enormous number of dead bodies. ["Raising the Dead," n.d.]

■ I remember the procession of chauffeur-driven Packards and Buicks that stopped near a devastated village, and the hundreds of dead Chinese lying by the roadside and in the abandoned paddy fields. Wearing their silk dresses, my mother and the other wives stepped with their husbands among the bright cartridge cases, a sight that even at the age of seven struck me as bizarre. [*London Times,* 1999]

■ I found England a very strange place, but that was to be expected because it differed from the Shanghai I'd known in almost every conceivable way. The England I came to in 1946 was exhausted. The English talked as if they won the war, but acted as if they'd lost it. The middle classes in particular had lost their confidence. I find it very difficult to feel at home here, and I'm not sure that I do to this day. [BBC Radio, 2002]

■ We made a trip to America in '39, just before the outbreak of the war. [intv David Pringle, 1975]

■ When I went into the dissecting room at the anatomy school in Cambridge as a young man of 18, I had seen a lot of corpses, unlike most of my fellow students. I remember the professor of anatomy giving the welcoming lecture and warning that a few of us would be so unsettled by the experience of dissection that we might not be able to face it ... I can understand that some people were shocked, and I was quite. You walked into this huge room, which was a cross between a butcher's shop and a nightclub, with rather eerie overhead lighting, and there were 20 tables, each with a cadaver lying on it. At first it took one's breath away; it was quite unsettling. ["Raising the Dead," n.d.]

■ When I was a student in Cambridge, you could then in England buy amphetamines across the counter in drugstores without a prescription. And we took them regularly without even thinking about it—if you wanted to work all night, or just feel a bit keyed-up . . . I've never taken heroin. [*KGB*, 1995]

■ The kinds of violent confrontations I conducted imaginatively in the Seventies were like hand grenades thrown into a crowded cinema. [*Blitz*, n.d.]

■ The only thing I wasn't thrown out of was advertising. After I'd been in advertising for a while, I suddenly realized that I hadn't been thrown out of it. It told me, "Run, don't walk!" I threw myself out. ["Ballard's Worlds," 1984]

■ Instead of advertising a product I would advertise an idea. I've done three advertisements now, and I hope to carry on. I'm advertising extremely abstract ideas in these advertisements, and this is a very effective way of putting them over. If these ideas were in the middle of a short story people could ignore them. They could just say, "It's Ballard again; let's get on with the story." But if they're presented in the form of an advertisement, like one in *Vogue* magazine, people have to look at them, they have to think about them . . . I hope eventually the magazines will pay me to put advertisements in their pages. [*Speculation*, 1969]

■ In some respects [writing *Empire of the Sun*] was a testing time, going back to that period so many years ago, but it's always been so immensely vivid in my mind that it wasn't difficult to do. Curiously enough, I had very strong visual memories of the camp, but writing about it in detail brought back other memories that I'd completely forgotten: the terrible smell of the place, the heat and terrific humidity in the summer, and the fierce cold in the winter. All those things I'd forgotten; the texture of everyday life in the camp, came back. The particularly awful taste of sweet potatoes—not, I may say, the golden sweet potato that Americans eat, but the gray sweet potato that was a cattle-feed in China: small foul things. All that came back . . . It was grueling to that extent. [*Omni*, n.d.]

■ San Juan, near Alicante in Spain, where I once pushed my tank-like Armstrong-Siddeley to 100 mph on the beach road, and where my wife died in 1964. [*Atrocity Exhibition,* 1990]

■ I think the war did help shape my view of the world. As a child you can't see grown-ups under extreme stress without learning something about human nature. [*Telegraph,* 9-23-03]

■ I went in as a child and emerged as the beginnings of an adult. I was happy there. It was like having a huge slum family. My parents had very little control over me, because they had none of the levers of power . . . And living in close proximity to 2,000 people of all social backgrounds was a unique education in a way . . . It teaches one not to be judgmental because we're all made of the same bruised flesh. [BBC, n.d.]

■ Many people who read *Empire of the Sun* when it first came out said, "Ugh—it's so horrific! It's so gruesome!" In fact, I think I rather *downplayed* the truth of the reality of wartime Shanghai. It was a terribly brutal place. . . You could see bodies lying in the streets, small coffins with a few flowers over them—children that had died in the night, parents too poor to arrange a funeral so they'd just put the coffin by the side of the road. It was a big shock. [BBC, n.d.]

■ Shanghai was a media city. There was no TV, but it was in every other sense a complete sort of media construct . . . It was a city of relentless public relations, advertising [billboards], stunts of every conceivable kind. I describe in the book a scene where my parents took me to the premiere of "The Hunchback of Notre Dame" and the management of the theater had laid on an honor guard of something like 50 or 100 hunchbacks, all dressed up like Charles Laughton . . . The whole media landscape had gone over the top. In many ways Los Angeles reminds me a bit of it—the sort of Third World [feeling], the huge flooding of refugees from the civil war and the famine areas of China into the city and its great slum sections, where people lived in houses built of old tires and tin cans. [*Publishers Weekly*, 1998]

■ Three months earlier, when his parents had taken Jim to the premiere of *The Hunchback of Notre Dame,* there had been 200 hunchbacks, recruited by the management of the theater from every back alley in Shanghai. As always, the spectacle outside the theater far exceeded anything shown on its screen. [*Empire of the Sun,* 1984]

■ Years ago, sitting at the cafe outside the American Express building in Athens, I watched the British actor Michael Redgrave (father of Vanessa) cross the street in the lunchtime crowd, buy *Time* at a magazine kiosk, indulge in brief banter with the owner, sit down, order a drink, then get up and walk away—every moment of which, every gesture, was clearly acted—that is, stressed and exaggerated in a self-conscious way, although he obviously thought that no one was aware who he was, and he didn't think that anyone was watching him. I take it that the same process works for the writer, except that the writer is assigning himself his own roles. [*Paris Review,* 1984]

■ All these French *Crash* freaks used to come out to see me, expecting a miasma of child-molestation and drug-abuse. What they found was a suburban house full of kids and their friends with a big dog, and me writing a short story in the middle of it all. ["Ballard's Worlds," n.d.]

■ People came here expecting a sort of miasma of drugs and child abuse and perversion. Instead they got this bourgeois little setup—golden retriever, cat, pet rat and children's parties. [*Washington Post,* 1992]

■ I loved Los Angeles; I really felt at home there. I regret that I did not make a life for myself in Los Angeles thirty years ago, when I might have done so. [*Mississippi Review,* 1991]

■ I assume that I looked back on Shanghai and the war there as if it were part of some huge nightmare tableau that revealed itself in a violent and gaudy way—that remade world that one finds in Surrealism. Perhaps I've always been trying to return to the Shanghai landscape, to some sort of truth that I glimpsed there. I think that in all my fiction, I've used the techniques of Surrealism to remake the present into something at least consonant with the past. [*Paris Review*, 1984]

■ For a psychiatrist to say, "You're beyond psychiatric help"—in a way, that's the greatest compliment you can be paid! You've achieved freedom then—absolute freedom. [*Rolling Stone*, 1987]

NOTES ON LIFE

■ [On his 70th birthday] I've come down with a nasty virus but I shall have an enormous, wild party as soon as I'm better. In a way, 70 is quite a frightening road sign. I find strange warning lights I've never noticed before glowing red on my personal dashboard. It's the biblical threescore-and-ten—I feel I can no longer pretend I'm not an old person. There are no dramatically new areas I want to explore in my writing. Most of my ideas circle inside my head like old luggage. Perhaps it would be fun to get rid of all the luggage. My remaining ambition is to open a bar in Marbella. [*Daily Telegraph*, 2000]

■ We take too much for granted in everyday life. And much of it is just a stage set—it only needs the slightest pressures to just see reality collapse. [BBC Radio, 2002]

■ At my age nobody loves you for your prose style, just as nobody loves a beautiful woman for her kind nature. [*Omni*, n.d.]

■ I've always vastly preferred the company of women. [*Independent*, 1991]

■ Just as all women are pretty, at heart all wines are good, though some are very much better. [*Weekend Telegraph*, 1991]

■ Oddly enough, as you near the end of life, you begin to treasure the commonplace and ordinary in a way that you don't in your twenties and thirties. I mean, the play of light on a window sill—since it may be the last one that you see, you treasure it. And you treasure the intimacies of ordinary human relationships which you take for granted when you're younger. [*Independent,* 1991]

■ What's so sad about most people's lives, my own included, is that they accept the roles that are given them. We're like people who always go to the same restaurant and always order the same meal. [*Sunday Express,* 1987]

■ It's very difficult to remythologize one's life. You tell yourself these tales of gold to sustain yourself, to inspire this one-man team. You need a new set of dreams, landscapes, forests. And what happens? I just sit with a whisky and soda, watching *The Rockford Files.* ["Ballard's Worlds," n.d.]

■ Cyril Connolly, English man of letters [& author of *The Unquiet Grave*], said you can judge a man by the state of his wife's health. [letter, 1999]

■ Roaming around Greece some years ago, I tracked the [River] Styx down to the northern Peloponnese, where it is reached by a nerve-wrenching rack-and-pinion railway. I was tempted [to swim across it], but my guidebook warned that its waters were "cold and treacherous." To my everlasting regret, I decided to wait for the ferry. [*Daily Telegraph,* 1992]

■ I used to think I'd like to go and live in Spain. Now I think I should be more adventurous and live in Las Vegas. [ICA conversation, 1998]

■ Once you are exposed to a relentless tide of human evil, you no longer make judgments about it. [BBC Radio, 2002]

■ There are some people who place enormous value on their

home and feel that it *defines* them—that a stain on the carpet is a personal defilement. There are others, and I think I am one of them, who are entirely indifferent to where they live. [*Observer*, 1994]

■ This planet is genuinely strange. If we were all flown to the moon or to Mars and walked around on them, they wouldn't seem that strange to us because there would be no yardsticks or anything to measure their strangeness by—they're just vast museums of geology. Whereas the earth is a deranged zoo, and somebody left the doors of the cages open. We have real strangeness because we can measure the degree to which things are or are not what they ought to be. [*Rolling Stone*, 1987]

■ We all have a very conventionalized view of our bodies and minds, and yet we are entirely the creatures of our own central nervous systems: the way in which these function tells us a great deal about who we are and why we behave as we do. [*Omni*, n.d.]

■ I take the standpoint of modern neuro-science, which seems to believe that the world that presents itself to our senses—this room, the streets we drive down and so on—is in fact a kind of *construct* that our brains have devised to allow us to move around more or less successfully in our tasks of maintaining ourselves and reproducing our species. One needs to dismantle this ramshackle construct in order to understand what is actually going on. [*Omni*, n.d.]

■ When I was cutting up cadavers in the anatomy theater at Cambridge University back in the late 1940s, *Gray's Anatomy* sat beside me as I separated nerve from blood-vessel. It struck me that in a curious way there was absolutely no connection between *Gray's* and the human cadaver that I was dissecting—even though *Gray's Anatomy* is a huge atlas of the human body, packed with the most beautiful color illustrations of dissected parts. There was no connection between the two! The reality of the dissected human body and the illustrations and diagrams in *Gray's Anatomy* are completely separate. [*Omni,* n.d.]

■ As I've said, in many ways *Gray's Anatomy* is a great work of fiction, perhaps the greatest. It represents the sort of view we all have of our bodies: we're extremely familiar with them, at least from the outside, but it's a highly conventional view, rather like a very conventionalized marriage where the partners after many years never embrace, never even touch each other. [*Omni,* n.d.]

■ The apparent visual space that we occupy—that garden, the houses in this street—does not actually coincide with the optical reality. The brain warps a large part of the data that strikes the retina. For example, shadows in reality are far deeper than they appear to us; the brain softens out the sharp contrasts that exist between light and dark spaces in order to be able to analyze the physical environment more clearly—otherwise it would be a mass of zebra stripes. It warps the perspective lines a little: these are things that are familiar to anybody who's come back after a holiday and can't understand why the apartment or house is so small. Our consciousness is an elaborate artifact constructed by the central nervous system to make the environment around us negotiable. These are very complex neuro-psychological devices, and one needs to analyze them (insofar as it is possible to do so by the imagination) to try to grasp what is going on. [*Omni,* n.d.]

■ If you're a complete insider it's very difficult to get any perspective lines going. It's like being the member of a closed institution, like a prison or a boarding school. [*New Musical Express,* 1985]

■ Time goes by, one loses contact with one's previous incarnations, one's previous selves. My mind has moved on. [*RE/Search #8/9,* 1984]

■ I wish I'd done many more things than I have done. I wish I'd had more children. I wish I'd had more dogs. I particularly wish I'd had more wives. [*Sunday Express,* 1987]

■ I would hesitate to teach anyone anything. [*S.F. Eye,* 1991]

PARENTING

■ I was present at the birth of my two daughters, who were both born at home ... Not only was I present when the girls were born but I practically elbowed the midwife aside and delivered them myself. I remember Fay's head emerging into daylight; it was an extra-ordinary moment. Most people imagine that a newborn child is very young, as young as a human being can be, but in fact for the first few seconds I had the sense she was immensely old. She had the whole of the human race behind her, she looked like something from Egyptian sculpture, streamlined by time. Within a few seconds she was suddenly very young. [*Sunday Times Magazine,* 1988]

■ I published my first story in 1957, the year my son was born, so my output as a writer has come within the hurly-burly of family life. Not only were there three children, but a golden retriever, a family cat, Bea's pet rat and an assortment of hamsters and gerbils, most of which got free and probably set up little colonies of their own everywhere. Along with all the children's friends it was like Waterloo station at rush hour. [*Sunday Times Magazine,* 1988]

■ I married at a very early age. My first child arrived when I was 24. So I have had children around almost throughout my entire adult life. [*Index,* 1996]

■ In many ways [my children] brought me up, and I realize that now I often did what they suggested. Back in the Sixties we traveled abroad each summer ... Entering Barcelona or Athens, it was always the children who decided where to stay. [*Sunday Times Magazine,* 1988]

■ I loved [raising my three children in Shepperton]. We were all living here and I didn't have much help, but they were the happiest days
of my life. They really were. [*Telegraph*, 9-23-03]

■ With children, you see the human imagination grappling with
the extraordinary possibilities of its intelligence. All mothers
have great material, I always feel. They've witnessed the evolution of an adult human being from nothing. [*Washington Post*, 1988]

■ From our earliest days [my wife] had always pushed me along, giving up holidays so that I could finish a book, taking the children to
London Zoo to allow me a few hours of peace. Her confidence in me
had never wavered, even during the time of endless rejection slips.
She hid bank statements, quietly borrowed money . . . In many ways
she had remade me. I owed her everything, my children, my first published books, my refound confidence in the world. [*Kindness of Women*,
1991]

■ I knew that the children were braver than I was. [*Kindness of
Women*, 1994]

■ My children had set off for their universities, leaving a vacuum in
my life that would never be filled. The house in Shepperton was like
a warehouse discarded by the film studios. The old toys and model
aircraft that crammed the cupboards were the props of a long-running family sitcom which the sponsors, despite its high ratings and
loyal audience, had decided to drop . . . When they came home on
their brief visits—eerily like cast reunions—I knew that I was the last
of us to grow up. [*Kindness of Women*, 1991]

■ I found that a major news story about a child prodigy came up
once every two years . . . Every ingredient was the same: the
press conference, TV cameras, presiding officials, the high school
principal, doting mother—and the young genius himself . . . For
some reason, though, nothing ever came of these precocious tal-
ents. Once the parents, or an unscrupulous commercial sponsor,

had squeezed the last drop of publicity out of the child, his so-called genius seemed to evaporate and he vanished into oblivion. ["The Comsat Angels," 1968]

■ I think our characters, our personalities, are set at an early age. Probably by the time we're 10 our world views are virtually hard-wired into our brains. [*Independent on Sunday*, 2003]

■ Take the case of my own daughters. One works for the BBC and the other worked for many years for the Tate Gallery. Almost all their after-tax salaries went to pay for the nannies and child-care, without whom they couldn't have gone out to work at all. There they are, trapped in this circular bind . . . They're up against a society that has de-privileged the middle classes. [*Independent on Sunday*, 2003]

■ What our children have to fear is not the cars on the highways of tomorrow but our own pleasure in calculating the most elegant parameters of their deaths. [*Atrocity Exhibition*, 1990]

■ Private schools are brainwashing their children into a kind of social docility, turning them into a professional class who will run the show for consumer capitalism. [*Millennium People*, 2003]

■ There was a tremendous vacuum when [my children] all grew up and left home to go to university, a vacuum which has never been filled. Nature hasn't provided a contingency plan for dealing with that vacuum—or rather, nature's contingency plan is death. Whether it's thanks to the miracles of modern medicine or to will power, I've managed to avoid that so far. [*Sunday Times Magazine*, 1988]

■ All three of [my children], I thought, had great potential talent as artists. Each of them could draw in the most vivid and original way. I am an unfulfilled painter myself. It's what I've always wanted to do but have had no talent. When I discovered that they had the talent I lacked, I may have come on too strongly in trying to urge them to become artists. That mistake is my one regret. [*Sunday Times Magazine,* 1988]

■ Today's children, across a large part of the planet, are dressed in trainers and Day-Glo track suits, and they have voices and a body language to match or mimic their television culture heroes. A bored and indulgent adult world has foisted onto its offspring the image of a kind of dandified super-infant, adept at computerspeak by the age of four, tuned in to the latest consumer fads, and canny in its reading of its parents' psychology. [review of Robert Capa's *Children of War, Children of Peace, NY Times,* 1991]

■ I remember well [that strange limbo] from my own childhood during a similar Japanese occupation, when the adults seemed to lose their belief in themselves, like actors in a play whose run is about to be canceled. Hillen describes superbly how a child's watching eye soon expands to take in every detail of adult weakness and uncertainty, a disturbing lesson that lasts a lifetime. [review of Ernest Hillen's *The Way of a Boy: a Memoir of Java, Daily Telegraph,* 1994]

■ As everyone who's had children knows, family life is a matter of constant negotiation. Little bribes are offered; little pressures are brought to bear. Parents offer treats . . . [BBC Radio, 2002]

■ J.G. BALLARD, author. Born 1930, Shanghai. Son of chemist who worked for a British textile company. Attended Leys School in Cambridge. On death of wife Helen [aka Mary], he brought up son, Jim, now 35, and two daughters alone. "Having brought up a son and two daughters myself as a single parent I know how much physical affection is the cement that holds a life together in later years. My own father was a physically affectionate man, but in my adolescence I won't say I had a very close relationship, and in my late teens we actually fell out." [*Daily Mail,* 11/23/1992]

■ If you don't receive a great deal of affection in the very early years you'll feel the loss forever, but you shouldn't feel entitled to turn to drugs or whatever. I'm sure my children turned out to be confident adults because they had been given the security of knowing they were loved. Kissing and cuddling is just a shorthand for physical affection, which is more likely to be an arm around your son's shoulder than a shower of kisses. Whatever form it takes, children need a show of affection to prove you're taking an interest in what really matters in their lives. [*Daily Mail*, 1992]

■ As parents we are delighted when our children resemble us, but do we really want them to be us, with all our dreams, ambitions and fears?" [*Sunday Times Bookshop*, 1997]

■ Parents are worried about the way their kids are no longer literate, no longer reading, and just living for a diet of the transient. They're interested in pop music and fashion, not interested in vocational training. They're living in an endless present of clothes, fashions and pleasant sensations . . . waiting for a rude awakening. [*Mississippi Review*, 1991]

■ For the sake of my children and grandchildren, I hope that the human talent for self-destruction can be successfully controlled, or at least channeled into productive forms—but I doubt it. [*Disturb*, n.d.]

SHEPPERTON

■ [Steven Spielberg] offered me a line of dialogue [in the film *Empire of the Sun*], but I was too shy. My role was to stand there with a glass of whisky in my hand, and that is something I've had a lot of practice at. [*Time Out*, 1987]

■ The film people [working on *Empire of the Sun*] had done their research well. Although this house was just down the road [in Shepperton], it felt exactly like Shanghai and I suddenly realized why. Because most of the people who lived in Shanghai had come from places like Shepperton and built houses just like the one they'd left behind in England. [*Sunday Express,* 1987]

■ So when you—and not only you but all my friends—ask why I live in Shepperton, I now know the answer. I was drawn here because, on a subconscious level, it reminded me of Shanghai. But I had to wait 25 years to understand my reason for doing so. [*Sunday Express,* 1987]

■ I suddenly realized: perhaps my coming to live in Shepperton was a deep-level assignment that my central nervous system gave me 27

years ago. I was waiting for the day when I wrote the novel [*Empire of the Sun*], knowing that the movie would be made and that they would have to use large houses in places like Weybridge and Walton-on-Thames, in the immediate vicinity of Shepperton—the models that the British in Shanghai used to build their own houses. It was rather like a dream to see my neighbors being recruited into this film—just as in dreams one's own neighbors, and familiar houses and buildings, are recruited by the sleeping mind. Dreams are fusions of past and present. It was strange in that respect, playing this small part: the whole business of the filming was very like a dream. [*Interzone*, 1987]

■ I didn't come [to Shepperton] till my early 30s, and I had quite an adventurous life before that. I was a medical student, a pilot, an encyclopedia salesman, a Covent Garden porter. It was really only because of the children that I settled here. And that wasn't boring; that was the biggest experience of my life. [*Sunday Express,* 1987]

■ When I first came here I liked it because it was green and quiet. It was as simple as that, really. [*Telegraph,* 9-23-03]

■ I felt that Shepperton was a magical place, rather in the way that the painter Stanley Spencer thought of Cookham. [BBC live chat, 2/2002]

■ I always thought we were Shepperton's beatniks without realising it. [*Kindness of Women,* 1991]

■ If you're not brought up in a place, you always go on seeing it afresh every day . . . I've been living in Shepperton for 43 years, but I look out of the window every morning and think, "This place is a bit odd—what's going on?" [*Independent on Sunday,* 2003]

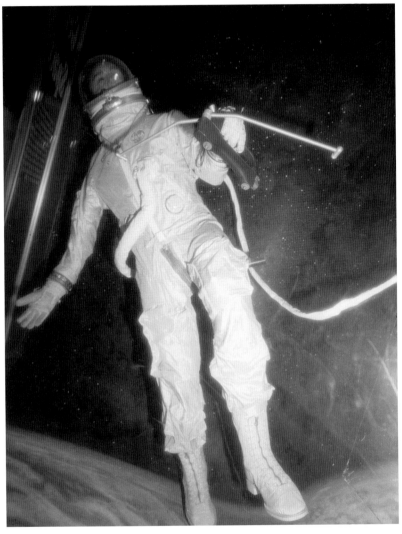

REFLECTIONS

■ The planet is turning into a gigantic Disneyland. A gigantic theme park where Japan equals the future, Europe is the past and Africa is a giant apocalyptic disaster area, a continental disaster movie screened for the West's benefit. [*I-D,* 1987]

■ I think the modern imagination does take the whole universe as its subject. It's concerned with metaphysical questions about the nature of consciousness, of experience, of perception. It takes a very large field of enterprise as its arena. [*Twilight Zone,* 1988]

■ We are swayed powerfully by forces that suddenly erupt in our plans—we may marry someone, end a marriage, embark on an unexpected career—there are deep currents beneath the surface. [*Books #6,* 1987]

■ *Homo sapiens* has won his intelligence from the ordeal of surviving an extremely hostile environment. [*Interzone,* 1987]

■ The human body's capacity for painkillers is almost unlimited. [*Super-Cannes,* 2000]

■ People aren't ennobled by suffering . . . At the same time, it does strip away a lot of illusions. One pays a terrible price for that, but at least one glimpses some kind of truth. [*City Limits,* 1984]

■ Only the artificial can be completely real. [*S.F. Eye,* 1991]

■ Today nothing is real and nothing is unreal. [intv L. Tarantino]

■ [A person's] obsessions are as close to reality as you can get. [*I-D,* 1987]

■ We're trapped by categories, by walls that stop us from seeing around corners. [*Millennium People,* 2003]

■ We tolerate everything, but we know that liberal values are designed to make us passive. [*Millennium People,* 2003]

■ The most prudent and effective method of dealing with the world around us is to assume that it is a complete fiction. [introduction, *Crash*, 1995]

■ Everything is clean and shiny but oddly threatening. [*New Statesman*, 2000]

■ [Joseph] Conrad once said that it's necessary to immerse yourself in the most destructive elements of the times, and then attempt to swim ... [French intv, 1976]

■ Lists are fascinating; one could almost do a list novel. [*Paris Review*, 1984]

■ Learn the rules, and you can get away with anything. [*M.P.*, 2003]

■ Crossing frontiers is my profession. [BBC, 2002]

■ Freud's classic distinction between the latent and manifest content of the dream, between the apparent and the real, now needs to be applied to the external world of so-called reality. [*Crash*, 1995]

■ A general rule: if enough people predict something, it won't happen. [*New Statesman*, 2000]

■ "I always tell the truth ... It's a new way of lying. If you tell the truth people don't know whether to believe you. It helps me in my work." [*Millennium People*, 2003]

■ It's not what you believe—who really knows? Far more important is the map you draw of yourself. [*Millennium People*, 2003]

■ The future has turned its back and lost interest in us. [*New Statesman*, 2000]

■ Freedom: the last great illusion of the twentieth century. [*Hello America*, 1981]

■ My fear is that in a totally sane society, madness is the only freedom. [BBC News Online, 2002]

- Bourgeoisification threatens everything. [*S.F. Eye,* 1991]

- The urge for destruction as a way of redefining oneself is very strong. [BBC Radio, 2002]

- People have no loyalties anymore. [*The Face,* 1987]

- I have great hope for human beings. [BBC Online Live Chat, 2002]

- Doctors are no more to be trusted than lawyers or real estate agents. [*S.F. Eye,* 1991]

- Ambiguity is at the heart of everything. [*Salon,* 1997]

- First wives are a rite of passage into adult life. In many ways it's important that first marriages go wrong. That's how we learn the truth about ourselves. [*Millennium People,* 2003]

- We believe in progress and the power of reason, but are haunted by the darker sides of human nature. We're obsessed with sex, but fear the sexual imagination and have to be protected by huge taboos. We believe in equality but hate the underclass. We fear our bodies and, above all, we fear death. We're a few steps from oblivion, but we hope we're somehow immortal. [*Millennium People,* 2003]

- Breaking the law is a huge challenge for professionals. [*Millennium People,* 2003]

- An almost intangible network of rivalries and intrigues bound them together. [*High Rise,* 1975]

- These people were the first to master a new kind of late twentieth-century life. They thrived on the rapid turnover of acquaintances, the lack of involvement with others, and the total self-sufficiency of lives which, needing nothing, were never disappointed . . . [*High Rise,* 1975]

- The trouble with Marxism is that it is a social philosophy for the poor—what we need is a social philosophy for the rich. [*IT,* 1969]

■ I'm a Libertarian; I'm all for maximum freedom—within the law. [*Seconds,* 1996]

■ The mass media have turned the world into a world of pop art. From JFK's assassination to the war in Iraq, everything is perceived as pop art. [intv Hans Obrist, 2003]

■ Violence is like a brush fire, it destroys a lot of trees but refreshes the forest, clears away the stifling undergrowth, so more trees spring up. [*Millennium People,* 2003]

■ Freedom has no barcode. [*Millennium People,* 2003]

■ There are bridges in the mind. They carry us to a more real world, a richer sense of who we are. Once these bridges are there, it's our duty to cross them. [*Millennium People,* 2003]

■ As he grew older, he found himself becoming more romantic and more callous at the same time. [*High Rise,* 1975]

■ His expression was not so much penetrating as detached and impersonal, as if he were assessing Ward with an utter lack of bias, so complete, in fact, that it left no room for even the smallest illusion. Previously Ward had only seen this expression in the eyes of the very old. ["The Venus Hunters," 1963]

■ Surrender to a logic more powerful than reason. [*High Rise,* 1975]

■ The most exciting spaces of the imagination are where you least expect to find them. [Tate, 2001]

■ It's the inexplicable rebellion from within that's impossible to predict. [*New York Times Magazine,* 1990]

■ Games, for anyone rich from birth, were always the most serious business in life. [*Rushing to Paradise,* 1994]

■ Creative work is its own recreation. [*Super-Cannes,* 2000]

■ One rule in life ... If you can smell garlic, everything is all right. [*High*

Rise, 1975]

- My greatest ambition is to turn into a TV program. [*War Fever,* 1990]

- Life isn't an avant-garde movie! [*War Fever,* 1990]

- The destruction of time: the next evolutionary step forward? [*War Fever,* 1990]

- The roots of shamanism and levitation, and the erotic cathexis of flight—can one see them as an attempt to escape from time? [*War Fever,* 1990]

- "Old" has a special sort of echo or vibration, doesn't it, and it's not a *good* one. Saying "old" means: Junk it, get rid of it, replace it with a new model. [*Independent on Sunday,* 2003]

- Place the logic of the visible at the service of the invisible. [quoted in *Kindness of Women,* 1991]

- To me the aliens are here on earth, right now. [*S.F. Examiner,* 1987]

- Money is the original digital clock. [*Kindness of Women,* 1991]

- I think that art is the principal way in which the human mind has tried to remake the world in a way that makes sense. [unknown]

- Have you noticed how vocabularies fluctuate in order to cope with our need to justify ourselves? [*Millennium People,* 2003]

- Superstitions, I often noticed, had a habit of coming true. [*Kindness of Women,* 1991]

- There are no answers. But maybe that is the answer. [*Independent on Sunday,* 2003]

- Perhaps the world needs a few people ready to burn themselves out. [*Cocaine Nights,* 1996]

- Ernst, Dali, the Facteur Cheval . . . they're your real syllabus. [*Kindness of Women,* 1991]

■ Almost everything we do has a sexual component in it some-where. [*RE/Search #8/9*, p. 48, 1984]

■ We are not moral creatures, except for reasons of mutual advantage, sad to say. [*Pretext,* 2004]

■ Despair erodes everything—courage, hope, self-discipline, all the better qualities. It's so damned difficult to sustain that impersonal atti-tude of passive acceptance implicit in the scientific tradition. I try to think of Galileo before the Inquisition, Freud surmounting the endless pain of his jaw cancer surgery. ["The Voices of Time," 1960]

■ I think the future is about to die on us. I think it may have died a few years ago. [*Index,* 1996]

■ We theme-parked the future just as we theme-park everything. We theme-parked the past. We theme-parked the future, and visit it only when we feel we want some sort of glittery gimmick. [*Index,* 1996]

■ Almost anything you predict will come true. [*Index,* 1996]

■ What you consume modifies your behavior. [paraphrased from *ZG,* 1985]

■ So money is the ultimate adult toy? [*Super-Cannes,* 2000]

■ People create their own mythologies. [*Kindness of Women,* 1991]

■ You can make anything mean anything. [*Kindness of Women,* 1991]

■ I treat the reality I inhabit as if it were a fiction—I treat the whole of existence as if it were a huge invention. [*RE/Search #8/9,* p. 43, 1984]

■ By any degree to which you devalue the external world so you devalue yourself. ["The Overloaded Man," 1961]

■ Two subjects have always fascinated me—women and the bizarre. ["The Smile," 1976]

■ The temper of the times seems to be one of self-love, if of a strange sort—Caliban asleep across a mirror stained with vomit. But perhaps the story also illustrates the paradox that the only real freedom is to be found in a prison. Sometimes it is difficult to tell on which side of the bars we really are—the real gaps between the bars are the sutures of one's own skull. [*Dangerous Visions,* 1967]

■ The phrase that sums up everything: quantifying and eroticizing. [*RE/Search #8/9,* p.49, 1984]

■ Often, behind the most trivial things, lie enormous mysteries. [*RE/Search #8/9,* 1984]

■ When you see the truth about human beings it's beneficial—but very challenging. ["Prophet With Honour," n.d.]

■ Remember, the police are neutral—they hate everybody. Being law-abiding has nothing to do with being a good citizen. It means not bothering the police. [*Millennium People,* 2003]

■ Memories of the people you love are supposed to last forever, but often they're the first to go. [*Kindness of Women,* 1991]

■ These days one needed a full-scale emergency kit built into one's brain, plus a crash course in disaster survival, real and imagined. [*Concrete Island,* 1985]

■ These days we don't notice other people's selfishness until we're on the receiving end ourselves. [*Concrete Island,* 1985]

■ Women work harder and survive on less. [*Rushing to Paradise,* 1994]

■ Who were the first domesticated animals? Women! We domesticated ourselves. But I know women are made of fiercer stuff. We have spirit, passion, fire, or used to. We can be cruel and violent, even more than men. [*Rushing to Paradise,* 1994]

■ Men? We simply don't need so many men today. The biggest

problem the world faces is not that there are too few whales or pandas, but too many men. Their time has passed, they belong with the dugong and the manatee. [*Rushing to Paradise*, 1994]

■ Men exhausted themselves building the world. Like tired children they're always fighting each other, and they can't see how they hurt themselves. It's the women's turn to take over now—we're the only ones with the strength to go on. Think of all-women cities . . . parks and streets filled with women. [*Rushing to Paradise*, 1994]

■ People are never happier than when they're inventing new vices. [*Concrete Island*, 1985]

■ Suicide is a suggestive act; it runs in families. [*Concrete Island*, 1985]

■ The more they hate you, the more they stay on their toes. [*Super-Cannes*, 2000]

■ Chance can work for terrorists. [*Super-Cannes*, 2000]

■ Play is demanding. It requires special qualities and offers special rewards. [*Super-Cannes*, 2000]

■ There should be a ceremony for everything. [*Rushing to Paradise*, 1994]

■ The totalitarian systems of the future would be subservient and ingratiating, but the locks would be just as strong. [*Super-Cannes*, 2000]

■ Representative democracy has been replaced by the surveillance camera and the private police force. [*Super-Cannes*, 2000]

■ Sexual pathology is such an energizing force. People know that, and will stoop to any depravity that excites them. [*Super-Cannes*, 2000]

■ We desperately need new vices. [*Super-Cannes*, 2000]

■ Guilt is so flexible, it's a curency that changes hands, each time losing a little value. [*Cocaine Nights,* 1996]

■ People are so immersed in their work they wouldn't recognize the end of the world. [*Super-Cannes,* 2000]

■ When people say something is important, never do it. [*Rushing to Paradise,* 1994]

■ Idealists can be dangerous. [*Super-Cannes,* 2000]

■ Attention spans are shorter and shorter; we crave greater stimulation. [*21C,* 1997]

■ I think the future is about to die on us. I think it may have died a few years ago. [*Index,* 1997]

■ Human beings have an extraordinary instinct for self-destruction, and this ought to be out in the open where we can see it. [*Pretext #9,* 2004]

■ Nothing is more irksome than the sight of people working all day. [*Rushing to Paradise,* 1994]

■ Our problem is not that too many people are insane, but too few. [*Super-Cannes,* 2000]

■ Psychopathy is freedom, psychopathy is fun? [*Super-Cannes,* 2000]

■ In a totally sane society, madness is the only freedom . . . A controlled and supervised madness. [*Super-Cannes,* 2000]

■ Psychopathy is its own most potent cure, and has been throughout history. At times it grips entire nations in a vast therapeutic spasm. No drug has ever been more potent. [*Super-Cannes,* 2000]

■ Revenge, anger, envy—invent a new sin. We need one. [*Super-Cannes,* 2000]

■ Senior policemen are either philosophers or madmen. [*ibid*]

■ The only real philosophers left are the police. [*Cocaine Nights,*

1996]

■ We all have a conventionalized view of human beings: we see them every day, we see ourselves in the mirror. We don't think of what lies beneath the skin. ["Raising the Dead," n.d.]

■ The dead go on opening doors in our minds. [*Super-Cannes,* 2000]

■ Reality is always a threat. I'm not worried by any rival ideology— there isn't one. [*Super-Cannes*, 2000]

■ I've always thought of the whole of life as a kind of disaster area. [*Burning World,* 1964]

■ The dream of a leisure society was the great 20th century delusion. [*Super-Cannes,* 2000]

■ Great fires have always been the prelude to even greater futures. [*Burning World,* 1964]

■ Remember, it's not enough to make history—you've got to arrange for someone to record it for you. [*Wind from Nowhere,* 1962]

■ All women are beautiful. [*S.F. Eye,* 1991]

■ Adaptability is the only real biological qualification for survival. At the moment a pretty grim form of natural selection is taking place. [*Wind from Nowhere,* 1962]

■ It's astonishing how the weak always judge the strong by their own limited standards. [*Wind from Nowhere,* 1962]

■ Our relationship was based on mutual contempt. ["Now: Zero," 1959]

■ The middle class ... police themselves ... with social codes. The right way to have sex, treat your wife, flirt at tennis parties or start an affair. There are unspoken rules we all have to learn. [*Millennium People,* 2003]

■ A perverse sexual act can liberate the visionary self in even the dullest soul. [*Super-Cannes,* 2000]

■ We're not rational creatures. Madness lies within us; it shows itself in countless ways—from road rage to the behavior of football hooligans. [*Spectator,* n.d.]

■ I care about preserving wildlife on the planet. The concrete is looking after itself; the entire planet is going to be covered in the stuff. [*Observer,* 1994]

■ Politics is over . . . it doesn't touch the public imagination any longer. [*Frieze,* 1996]

■ I do welcome the modern world: high-rise blocks, motorways . . . My ideal building is the Heathrow Hilton by Michael Manser. Stunning: pure white geometry. [*Observer,* 1994]

■ [Attacks on pornography are] attacks on the sexual imagination itself: Morality covers our conduct, not what goes on inside our heads. [*Observer,* 1994]

■ The sexual imagination is unlimited in scope and metaphoric power, and can never be successfully repressed. [*AtExhib,* 1990]

■ Art exists because reality is neither real nor significant. [*Disturb*]

■ Fiction is a branch of neurology. [Iain Sinclair's *Crash,* 1999]

■ Human beings have a terrible temptation to imagine a happier past. [*Seconds,* 1996]

■ Most people lead what on the whole are largely undocumented lives, bar birth, marriage and death certificates . . . [Introduction, *J.G. Ballard: The First 20 Years,* 1976]

■ There's always spare processing capacity in the brain—we see that when we sleep, dream. [Iain Sinclair's *Crash,* 1999]

■ Nothing is real until you put it in the VCR. [*Seconds,* 1996]

■ Everyone who has served in the armed forces knows that there are military bases where the regime of discipline and brutality is far more excessive than it needs to be, and yet doesn't provoke any revolt and may even satisfy some need to be brutalized. [intv Zinovy Zinik, 1998]

■ It's so easy to be more frightened of one's feelings than of the things that prompt them. [*Crystal World*, 1966]

■ Deep assignments run through all our lives; there are no coincidences. [*Atrocity Exhibition*, 1990]

■ The crime wave is already there. It's called consumer capitalism. [*Super-Cannes*, 2000]

■ Invisible technologies rule our lives, transmitting their data-loads at the speed of an electron. Vast cash balances move around the world's banking systems, bounced off satellites we never see, but whose electromagnetic footprints bestride continents and form our real weather. ["Speed-Visions of an Accelerated Age," 1998]

■ In a real war no one knew which side he was on, and there were no flags or commentators or winners. In a real war there were no enemies. [*Empire of the Sun*, 1984]

■ Confidences given to adults often led further than intended. [*Empire of the Sun*, 1984]

■ He stared at the blades of grass, trying to work out the speed at which the leaves grew—an eighth of an inch each day, a millionth of a mile per hour? [*Empire of the Sun*, 1984]

■ Never confuse the map with the territory. [*Empire of the Sun*, 1984]

■ Plant classification was an entire universe of words; every weed in the camp had a name. Names surrounded everything; invisible encyclopedias lay in every hedge and ditch. [*Empire of the Sun*, 1984]

■ Like all scientists, you can't bear anything that challenges your own prejudices. [unknown]

■ The human breeding cycle is so stretched. [*Rushing to Paradise*, 1994]

■ Chapters of my life are still hidden from me. [*War Fever*, 1990]

■ Just as the sleeping mind extemporizes a narrative out of the random memories veering through the cortical night, so our waking imaginations are stitching together a set of narratives to give meaning to the random events that swerve through our conscious lives. [*Mississippi Review*, 1991]

■ I realize that I could change the course of my life by a single action. To shut out the world, and solve all my difficulties at a stroke, I had the simplest of weapons—my own front door. I needed only to close it, and decide never to leave my house again. ["The Enormous Space," 1989]

■ Sooner or later, everything turns into television. [*The Day of Creation*, 1987]

■ My own obsession, which had carried me so far, was all that I had. [*The Day of Creation*, 1987]

■ He was asleep, but seemed to be thinking very hard about something with one half of his head. [*Empire of the Sun, 1984*]

■ Think only of essentials: the physics of the gyroscope, the flux of photons, the architecture of very large structures. [*War Fever*, 1990]

■ I am free at last to think only of the essential elements of existence—the visual continuum around me, and the play of air and light. [*"The Enormous Space," 1989*]

■ I swallowed several of the Drinamyl tablets. Ten minutes later I was soaring around the house like a bird, my mind a window filled with light. I raced into the garden, my feet scarcely touching the ground. Years later, when I took up gliding, I realized what had spurred me on. [*Super-Cannes,* 2000]

■ I thought I could do good, but people resent that—judges and juries above all. Doing good unsettles them . . . Nothing provokes people more than acting from the highest motives. [*Rushing to Paradise,* 1994]

■ His voice had sounded sincere but curiously distant—lines from a previous week's play spoken by a distracted actor. [*Cocaine Nights,* 1996]

■ . . . the belief that impulsive acts alone gave meaning to life. [*Super-Cannes,* 2000]

■ Like all great visionaries, he needs a disciple. [*Super-Cannes,* 2000]

■ Too many of the props in my own life were baggage belonging to someone else that I had offered to carry. [unknown]

■ Every step we've taken in our evolution is a milestone inscribed with organic memories. [*Drowned World,* 1962]

■ Maybe we're going to live in an eventless future. In a hundred years, the world might be very, very boring. [*Face,* 1987]

■ The brief span of an individual life is misleading. Each one of us is as old as the entire biological kingdom, and our bloodstreams are tributaries of the great sea of its total memory. The uterine odyssey of the growing foetus recapitulates the entire evolutionary past, and its central nervous system is a coded time scale, each nexus of neurons and each spinal level marking a symbolic station, a unit of neuronic time. [*Drowned World,* 1962]

■ There may well be some fundamental distinction between light and dark that we inherit from the earliest living creatures. After all, the response to light is a response to all the possibilities of life itself. For all we know this division is the strongest one there is—perhaps even the only one—reinforced every day for hundreds of millions of years. In its simplest sense, time keeps this going. [*Crystal World*, 1966]

■ [Earth] is the only alien planet. [*Spin*, 1989]

■ I marked her down as a professional rebel, who resented the trappings of managerial success, club-class upgrades and company credit cards—the *fool's gold* that could buy an entire life and offer no discount for idealism or integrity. [*Super-Cannes*, 2000]

■ I had begun to shed the hard core of misanthropy, often masked by a professional dedication to good works. [*Day of Creation*, 1987]

■ Refusals opened the door to other possibilities. [*Day of Creation*, 1987]

■ Success, an even more demanding challenge than failure. [*Sunday Times*, 1991]

■ New Means *Worse*. [*Guardian*, 1981]

■ The trouble is, too many people *are* conforming. [*NME*, 1985]

■ Most major institutions are discredited, or under threat. [*NME*, 1996]

■ In a world of absolute relativity, there is no way of knowing who is telling the truth. [*Guardian*, 1991]

■ Ambiguity is very important . . . Ambiguity is part and parcel of the whole thing. [*21C*, 1997]

■ We don't really perceive with our own eyes any longer. We perceive through the artificial eye of the mass media. [*Blitz*, 1987]

■ Only a truly innocent man can know the meaning of guilt. Only a truly guilty man can conceive of the concept of innocence. ["Backdrop of Stars," 1968]

■ Nobody wants to hear the truth. [ICA conversation, 1998]

■ The psychopath never dates. [*New Worlds,* 1969]

■ A significant moral and psychological distance now separates us from Kafka's heroes, who succumbed in the end to their own unconscious feelings of guilt and inferiority. We, by contrast, in an age of optimism and promise, may fall equal victims to our notions of freedom, sanity and self-sufficiency. ["Comment on End-Game," 1968]

■ The oyster, a true hermaphrodite, alternately male and female, can live in the wild for fifty years, but loses its flavor after five. [review of Maguelonne Toussaint-Samat's *A History of Food, Daily Telegraph,* 1993]

■ People are never happier than when inventing new—or rather, exposing—new vices. People are full of Puritan relish. [KGB, 1995]

■ Too many of us would rather be involved in a sex crime than in sex. [*New Worlds,* 1969]

■ We are bombarded by this absolute deluge of fictional material of every conceivable kind, and all this has the effect of preempting our own original response to anything. All these events are presented to us with their prepackaged emotions already in place, so if you are shown an earthquake or airliner crash you are told what you think. [*Mississippi Review,* 1991]

■ If you compromise with your own obsessions—that way lies disaster. [*Index,* 1996]

■ My advice to anyone in any field is to be faithful to your obsessions. Identify them and be faithful to them, let them guide you like a sleepwalker. [I-D, 1987]

■ All our responses are pre-empted before we have even made a direct human response. We are reaching a point in the world today when a direct human response to practically anything is impossible. [*Blitz*, 1987]

■ I detest postmodern architecture in any form whatsoever. [letter, 1995]

■ There's nothing to believe in now. All ideology is gone. The great churches are empty; political ideology is finished; there's just a scramble for power. . . There's a nagging sense of emptiness. So people look for anything; they believe in any extreme— any extremist nonsense is better than nothing. [*KGB*, 1995]

■ I think the enemy of creativity in the world today is that so much thinking is done for you. [*Observer*, 2002]

■ People do the strangest things for the most trivial reasons. [*Cocaine Nights*, 1996]

■ You can do all the housework in five minutes if you don't make a fetish of it. [*Sunday Independent*, 1991]

■ Each of us is little more than the meagre residue of the infinite unrealized possibilities of our lives. ["Terminal Beach," 1964]

■ I was searching for a different kind of magic. [*Day of Creation*, 1987]

■ It was time for a naming of new things, of new hours and new days. [*Day of Creation*, 1987]

■ The only definition of real happiness: to find yourself and be who you are. [*Métaphores*, 1983]

■ I love it when the imagination is genuinely touched. It's a wonderful moment. [*Kulture Deluxe*, 1997]

■ Nothing is true. Nothing is untrue. [intv Hans Obrist, 2003]

THE BALLARD GLOSSARY

The editors of *Zone* invited me to contribute to a special issue on The Body, and suggested a list of possible topics. Rather than tackle one of them at length, I provided short reflections on each of them. —*JGB, 1992*

Abortion Do-it-yourself genocide.

Aerodynamism Streamlining satisfies the dream of flight without the effort of growing wings. Aerodynamics is the modern sculpture of non-Euclidean space-time.

Answering machines They are patiently training us to think in a language they have yet to invent.

Apollo mission The first demonstration, arranged for our benefit by the machine, of the dispensability of man.

Automobile All the millions of cars on this planet are stationary, and their apparent motion constitutes mankind's greatest collective dream.

Body-building Asexual masturbation, in which the entire musculature simulates a piece of erectile tissue. But orgasm seems indefinitely delayed.

Epidemiology Catastrophe theory in slow motion.

Fashion A recognition that Nature has endowed us with one skin too few, and that a fully sentient being should wear its nervous system externally.

Biochemical warfare Nerve gases—the patient and long-awaited revenge of the inorganic world against the organic.

Camouflage The camouflaged battleship or bunker must never efface itself completely, but confuse our recognition systems by one moment being itself, and the next not itself. Many impersonators and politicians exploit this same principle.

Criminal science The anatomizing of illicit desire, more exciting than desire itself.

Cybernetics The totalitarian systems of the future will be docile and subservient, like super-efficient servants, and all the more threatening for that.

Chaplin Chaplin's great achievement was to discredit the body, and to ridicule every notion of the dignity of gesture. Ponderous men move around him like lead-booted divers trying to anchor the central nervous system to the seabed of time and space.

Crowd theory Claustrophobia masquerading as agoraphobia or even, conceivably, Malthusianism.

Disease control A proliferation of imaginary diseases may soon be expected, satisfying our need for a corrupt version of ourselves.

Duncan, Isadora The machine had its own fling with her overdisciplined body, the rear wheel of her car dancing its lethal little jig around the end of her scarf.

Ergonomics The Protestant work ethic disguised as a kinaesthetic language.

Food Our delight in food is rooted in our immense relish at the thought that, prospectively, we are eating ourselves.

Forensics On the autopsy table science and pornography meet and fuse.

Furniture and industrial design Our furniture constitutes an external constellation of our skin areas and body postures. It's curious that the least imaginative of all forms of furniture has been the bed.

Genetics Nature's linguistic system.

Genocide The economics of mass production applied to self-disgust.

Hallucinogenic drugs The kaleidoscope's view of the eye.

Jazz Music's jettisoned short-term memory, and no less poignant for that.

International Standard Time Is time an obsolete mental structure we have inherited from our distant forebears, who invented serial time as a means of dismantling a simultaneity they were unable to grasp as a single whole? Time should be decartelized, and everyone should set his or her own.

Lysenkoism A forlorn attempt not merely to colonize the botanical kingdom, but to instill a proper sense of the Puritan work ethic and the merits of self-improvement.

Miniaturization Dreams of becoming very small pre-date Alice, but now the probability grows that all the machines in the world, like the gold at Fort Knox, might be held in one heavily guarded location, protected as much from themselves as from the rest of us. Computers will continue to miniaturize themselves, though, eventually disappearing into a microverse where their ever-vaster calculations and mathematical models will become one with the quarks and the charms.

Modernism The Gothic of the Information Age.

Money The original digital clock.

Neurobiology Science's Sistine Chapel.

Pasolini Sociopath as saint.

Personal computers Perhaps unwisely, the brain is subcontracting many of its core functions, creating a series of branch economics that may one day amalgamate and mount a management buy-out.

Phenomenology The central nervous system's brave gamble that it exists.

The pill Nature's one step back in order to take two steps forward, presumably into the more potent evolutionary possibilities of wholly conceptualized sex.

Pornography The body's chaste and unerotic dream of itself.

Prosthetics The castration complex raised to the level of an art form.

Retroviruses Pathogens that might have been invented by science fiction. The greater the advances of modern medicine, the more urgent our need for diseases we cannot understand.

Robotics The moral degradation of the machine.

Satellites Ganglions in search of an interplanetary brain.

Schizophrenia To the sane, always the most glamorous of mental diseases, since it seems to represent the insane's idea of the normal. Just as the agnostic world keeps alive its religious festivals in order to satisfy the vacation needs of its workforce, so when medical science has conquered all disease certain mental afflictions, schizophrenia chief among them, will be mimicked for social reasons. By the same token, the great appeal of alcoholism, and the reason why it will never be eliminated, is that it provides an opportunity for the honorable and even heroic failure.

Science fiction The body's dream of becoming a machine.

Skyscraper The eight-hour city, with a tidal population clinging to the foreshore between Earth and the yet-to-be navigated oceans of space.

Suburbs Do suburbs represent the city's convalescent zone or a genuine step forward into a new psychological realm, at once more passive but of far greater imaginative potential, like that of a sleeper before the onset of REM sleep? Unlike its unruly city counterpart, the suburban body has been wholly domesticated, and one can say that the suburbs constitute a huge petting zoo, with the residents' bodies providing the stock of furry mammals.

Telephone A shrine to the desperate hope that one day the world will listen to us.

Time and motion studies I am both myself and the shape that the universe makes around me. Time and motion studies represent our attempt to occupy the smallest, most modest niche in the surrounding universe.

Transistor If the wheel is 1 on the binary scale, the transistor is 0—but what will be 1000001?

© ANA BARRADO

Trench warfare The body as sewer, the gutter of its own abattoir, flushing away its fears and aggressions.

Typewriter It types *us*, encoding its own linear bias across the free space of the imagination.

The Vietnam War Two wholly incompatible martial systems collided, with desperate result. Could the Vietcong, given a little more TV savvy, have triumphed sooner by launching an all-women guerrilla army against the *Playboy*-reading GIs? "First Air Cavalry ground elements in Operation Pegasus killed 350 enemy women in scattered contacts yesterday, while Second Division Marines killed 124 women communists..."

War The possibility at last exists that war may be defeated on the linguistic plane. If war is an extreme metaphor, we may defeat it by devising metaphors that are even more extreme.

X-ray Does the body still exist at all, in any but the most mundane sense? Its role has been steadily diminished, so that it seems little more than a ghostly shadow seen on the X-ray plate of our moral disapproval. We are now entering a colonialist phase in our attitudes to the body, full of paternalistic notions that conceal a ruthless exploitation. This brutish creature must be housed, sparingly nourished, restricted to the minimum of sexual activity needed to reproduce itself and submitted to every manner of enlightened and improving patronage. Will the body at last rebel, tip all those vitamins, douches and aerobics schedules into Boston harbor and throw off the colonialist oppressor?

Zipper This small but astute machine has found an elegant way of restraining and rediscovering all the lost enchantments of the flesh.

◆   ◆   ◆

WHAT I BELIEVE by J.G. Ballard

I believe in the power of the imagination to remake the world, to release the truth within us, to hold back the night, to transcend death, to charm motorways, to ingratiate ourselves with birds, to enlist the confidences of madmen.

I believe in my own obsessions, in the beauty of the car crash, in the peace of the submerged forest, in the excitements of the deserted holiday beach, in the elegance of automobile graveyards, in the mystery of multi-story car parks, in the poetry of abandoned hotels.

I believe in the forgotten runways of Wake Island, pointing towards the Pacifics of our imaginations.

I believe in the beauty of all women, in the treachery of their imaginations, so close to my heart; in the junction of their disenchanted bodies with the enchanted chromium rails of supermarket counters; in their warm tolerance of my own perversions.

I believe in the death of tomorrow, in the exhaustion of time, in our search for a new time within the smiles of auto-route waitresses and the tired eyes of air-traffic controllers at out-of-season airports.

I believe in madness, in the truth of the inexplicable, in the common sense of stones, in the lunacy of flowers, in the disease stored up for the human race by the Apollo astronauts.

I believe in nothing.

I believe in Max Ernst, Delvaux, Dali, Titian, Goya, Leonardo, Vermeer, Chirico, Magritte, Redon, Durer, Tanguy, the Facteur Cheval, the Watts Towers, Bocklin, Francis Bacon, and all the invisible artists within the psychiatric institutions of the planet.

I believe in the impossibility of existence, in the humor of mountains, in the absurdity of electromagnetism, in the farce of geometry, in the cruelty of arithmetic, in the murderous intent of logic.

I believe in adolescent women, in their corruption by their own leg stances, in the purity of their disheveled bodies, in the traces of the pudenda left in the bathrooms of shabby motels.

I believe in flight, in the beauty of the wing, and in the beauty of everything that has ever flown, in the stone thrown by a small child that carries with it the wisdom of statesmen and midwives.

I believe in the gentleness of the surgeon's knife, in the limitless geometry of the cinema screen, in the hidden universe within supermarkets, in the loneliness of the sun, in the garrulousness of planets, in the repetitiveness of ourselves, in the inexistence of the universe and the boredom of the atom.

I believe in the non-existence of the past, in the death of the future, and the infinite possibilities of the present.

I believe in the derangement of the senses: in Rimbaud, William Burroughs, Huysmans, Genet, Celine, Swift, Defoe, Carroll, Coleridge, Kafka.

I believe in the death of the emotions and the triumph of the imagination.

I believe in all children.

I believe all hallucinations.

I believe all mythologies, memories, lies, fantasies, evasions.

I believe in the mystery and melancholy of a hand, in the kindness of trees, in the wisdom of light.

[abridged, from RE/Search #8/9]

© ANA BARRADO

A WORLD OF ENDLESS SUMMER

J.G. Ballard's review of Mark Lynas's
  High Tide: News From A Warming World, 2004

Have exaggerated fears about the weather replaced our dread of nuclear war? Human beings seem to need something to fear, and catastrophic climate change taps into our deepest fantasies of world destruction.

I remember vividly how awful the British weather was 50 years ago, the summers that lasted a fortnight followed by an unending autumn drizzle and Arctic winters. We sniffled and grumbled, but our minds were on a different kind of weather, those manmade mushroom clouds that rose over Pacific atolls, leaning across the sky as if eager to make their way to Europe.

Today the nuclear threat lies in the past, and the English summer lasts from March to November. My passion flowers and forsythia are already in bloom, and at any moment the appetizing reek of barbecue briquettes will drift across my neighbors' patios and signal the unleashing of sun-loungers and [sunscreen]. The global warming of which I dreamed for so many years has at last come true.

But how foolish I am, as Mark Lynas makes clear in his powerful account of the threat posed by climatic change and increased carbon dioxide emissions. Melting ice-caps, coastal flooding and the creation of vast new deserts threaten our entire way of life.

In Britain there has been a huge increase in rainfall during the 1990s, a blessing one might think for our water supplies and for those not affected by flooding. But according to Lynas, this was the wrong kind of rain. Heavy deluges are less likely to soak usefully into farmland, and more likely to run off in destructive torrents that wash away the fertile topsoil.

Lynas paints a fearsome picture of the near future, an overlit landscape not without its attractions. During the endless summer months the sun will blaze down on a re-engineered Eden. The British gardener will mow his lawn all the year round. Our herbaceous borders will wither, and our gardens will be filled with tree-ferns, palms, bamboos and bananas. Exotic birds will hover above our heads—asylum-seekers from the scorched jungles of the tropics.

But, to anyone tempted by this vision, Lynas points out that Continental Europe has just endured its highest temperatures for 500 years, which set off devastating forest fires in France, Spain and Portugal. In France 15,000 people died in last year's heat wave, triggering what Lynas terms "a national crisis of guilt and soul-searching"—not evident to me, I must say, as I surveyed the beach-bound traffic jamming the auto route to the Cote d'Azur.

Lynas moves restlessly around the world, from the melting Arctic ice-cap to drowned Pacific islands, hunting down climate change with the zeal of a missionary rooting out infidelity. I suspect that he sees global warming as a symptom of our faithlessness to a long-suffering planet. Everywhere ecosystems are unraveling. The melt-water of the Greenland ice-sheet now equals the Nile's annual flow, but this water is in the wrong place, unable to irrigate the immense deserts appearing in Asia. Agriculture will suffer, and tropical diseases will spread towards the poles.

It's a harrowing prospect, brilliantly set out by Lynas. What should we do? First, ratify the Kyoto Protocol on climate change, and cut down on greenhouse gas emissions. Rein back industrial growth around the world, and stop all exploration of new oil, coal and gas reserves. Above all, target that implacable enemy which haunts the race-memory of ecologists like Lynas: the motor car ("for most city dwellers, cars are an unnecessary luxury").

For all Lynas's passion, his solution is even more apocalyptic than the problem. Most of us prefer our sunloungers and traffic jams, and will lie back contentedly until the [asphalt] begins to boil off our roads, gazing at our banana trees and thoroughly enjoying the direst warnings in well-intentioned but somehow overwrought books like this one. ◆

Photo: S.M. Gray

A GUIDE TO VIRTUAL DEATH

For reasons documented elsewhere, intelligent life on earth became extinct in the closing hours of the 20th Century. Among the clues left to us, the following schedule of a day's television programs transmitted to an unnamed city in the northern hemisphere on December 2, 1999, offers its own intriguing insight into the origins of the disaster.

6:00am Porno-Disco. Wake yourself up with his-and-her hardcore sex images played to a disco beat.

7:00 Weather Report. Today's expected micro-climates in the city's hotel atriums, shopping malls and office complexes. Hilton International promises an afternoon snow-shower as a Christmas appetizer.

7:15 News Roundup. What our newsmakers have planned for you. Maybe a small war, a synthetic earthquake or a famine-zone/charity tie-in.

7:45 Breakfast Time. Gourmet meals to watch as you eat your diet cellulose.

8:30 Commuter Special. The rush-hour game show. How many bottoms can you pinch, how many faces can you slap?

9:30 The Travel Show. Visit the world's greatest airports and underground car-parks.

10:30 Homemakers of Yesterday. Nostalgic scenes of old-fashioned housework. No. 7—The Vacuum Cleaner.

11:00 Office War. Long-running serial of office gang wars.

12:00 Newsflash. The networks promise either a new serial killer or a deadly food toxin.

1:00pm Live from Parliament. No. 12—The Alcoholic M.P.

1:30 The Nose-Pickers. Hygiene program for the kiddies.

2:00 Caress Me. Soft-porn for the siesta hour.

2:30 Your Favorite Commercials. Popular demand re-runs of golden-oldie TV ads.

3:00 Housewives' Choice. Rape, and how to psychologically prepare yourself.

4:00 Countdown. Game show in which contestants count backwards from one million.

5:00 Newsflash. Either an airliner crash or a bank collapse. Viewers express preference.

6:00 Today's Special. Virtual Reality TV presents "The Kennedy Assassination." The Virtual Reality headset takes you to Dallas, Texas on November 22, 1963. First you fire the assassin's rifle from the Book Depository window, and then you sit between Jackie and JFK in the Presidential limo as the bullet strikes. For premium subscribers only—feel the Presidential brain tissue spatter your face OR wipe Jackie's tears onto your handkerchief.

8:00 Dinner Time. More gourmet dishes to view with your evening diet-cellulose.

9:00 Science Now. Is there life after death? Micro-electrodes pick up ultra-faint impulses from long-dead brains. Relatives question the departed.

11:00 Today's Special. Tele-Orgasm. Virtual Reality TV takes you to an orgy. Have sex with the world's greatest movie stars. Tonight: Marilyn Monroe and Madonna OR Warren Beatty and Tom Cruise. For premium subscribers only—experience transsexualism, pedophilia, terminal syphilis, gang rape, and bestiality (choice: German Shepherd or Golden Retriever).

1:00am Newsflash. Tonight's surprise air crash.

2:00 The Religious Hour. Imagine being dead. Priests and neuroscientists construct a life-like mock-up of your death.

3:00 Night-Hunter. Will the TV Rapist come through your bedroom window?

4:15 Sex for Insomniacs. Soft porn to rock you to sleep.

5:00 The Charity Hour. Game show in which Third-World contestants beg for money.

—J.G. Ballard (originally printed in Interzone, 1992)

◆　　　◆　　　◆

NEW! FALL 2004

J. G. BALLARD: QUOTES
Does the Future Have a Future?

A collection of provocative quotes from J. G. Ballard's fiction and non-fiction, plus hard-to-find articles and interviews, edited by V. Vale assisted by Mike Ryan. Quotes are arranged by topic. Also included: four examples of Ballard's most formally-innovative short writings. Includes dozens of photos by Ana Barrado, Charles Gatewood and others. 416 pages, index, $5\frac{1}{4}$ x7", $19.99.

Limited, signed and numbered edition of only 250 copies, flexibind: $60.00. (Libraries, please call for unsigned, flexibind edition price.)

FORTHCOMING: SPRING 2005

J.G. BALLARD: INTERVIEWS
Real conversations 2

Interviews and conversations with the British visionary writer J.G. Ballard, with V. Vale, Mark Pauline and Graeme Revell. Plus an interview with Ballard's long-time archivist, David Pringle. Introduction by Joe Donohoe. Two *Sgt. Pepper*-style collages of Ballardian Icons by Eric Nordhauser. Includes photos by Ana Barrado, Charles Gatewood and others. 200 pages, $5\frac{1}{4}$x7", $14.99.

J.G. BALLARD

RE/Search 8/9: J.G. Ballard J.G. Ballard predicted the future better than anyone else! His classic, *CRASH* (made into a movie by David Cronenberg) was the first book to investigate the psychopathological implications of the car crash, uncovering our darkest sexual crevices. He accurately predicted our media-saturated, information-overloaded environment where our most intimate fantasies and dreams involve pop stars and other public figures. Also contains a wide selection of quotations. "Highly recommended as both an introduction and a tribute to this remarkable writer."—*Washington Post* "The most detailed, probing and comprehensive study of Ballard on the market."—*Boston Phoenix.* "Open it up anywhere and you'll find inspiration."—Eric, *Show Cave* 8½x11″, 176 pp, illus. PB. Last copies left. **$19.99**

Atrocity Exhibition A dangerous imaginary work; as William Burroughs put it, "This book stirs sexual depths untouched by the hardest-core illustrated porn." Amazingly perverse medical illustrations by Phoebe Gloeckner, and haunting "Ruins of the Space Age" photos by Ana Barrado. Our most beautiful book, now used in many "Futurology" college classes. 8½x11″, 136 pp, illus. PB **$17.50. LIMITED EDITION OF SIGNED HARDBACKS** w/dust jacket, only $50

HUMOR

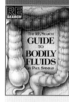

RE/Search GUIDE TO BODILY FLUIDS by Paul Spinrad. Everything you ever wanted to know about: Mucus, Menstruation, Saliva, Sweat, Vomit, Urine, Flatus, Feces, Earwax & more. Topics include: constipation (such as its relationship to cornflakes and graham crackers!); history and evolution of toilet paper; farting; smegma and more! Ideal bathroom reading! A perfect gift for that difficult-to-shop-for person! A scientific text; educational, yet fun. 8½x11″, 148 pp., PB only. Almost out-of-print. **$19.99**

RE/Search 11: PRANKS! A prank is a "trick, a mischievous act, a ludicrous act." Although not regarded as poetic or artistic acts, pranks constitute an art form and genre in themselves. Here pranksters such as Timothy Leary, Abbie Hoffman, Monte Cazazza, Jello Biafra, Earth First!, Joe Coleman, Karen Finley, John Waters, Henry Rollins and more challenge the sovereign authority of words, images and behavioral convention. This iconoclastic compendium will dazzle and delight all lovers of humor, satire and irony. *Pranks!* is a classic of the *rebel literature canon.* The  definitive treatment of the subject, offering extensive interviews with 36 contemporary tricksters . . . from the Underground's answer to Studs Terkel."—*Washington Post* "Pranks comes off as a statement of avant-garde philosophy–as a kind of wake-up call from an extended underground of Surrealist artists."—*S.F. Chronicle. PRANKS!* is V. Vale's favorite book. 8½x11″, 240 pp, 164 photos & illustrations, PB, **$19.99**

PUNK & D.I.Y.

PUNK '77: an inside look at the San Francisco rock n' roll scene, 1977 by James Stark

Covers the beginnings of the S.F. Punk Rock scene through the Sex Pistols' concert at Winterland in Jan., 1978, in interviews and photographs by James Stark. James was among the many artists involved in early punk. His photos were published in *New York Rocker, Search & Destroy* and *Slash*, among others. His posters for Crime are classics and highly prized collectors' items. Over 100 photos, including many behind-the-scenes looks at the bands who made things happen: Nuns, Avengers, Crime, Screamers, Negative Trend, Dils, Germs, UXA, etc. Interviews with the bands and people early on the scene give intimate, often darkly humorous glimpses of events in a *Please Kill Me* (Legs McNeil) style. "The photos themselves, a generous 115 of them, are richly satisfying. They're the kind of photos one wants to see..."—*Puncture*. "I would recommend this book not only for old-timers looking for nostalgia, but especially to young Punks who have no idea how this all got off the ground, who take today's Punk for granted, to see how precarious it was at birth, what a fluke it was, and to perhaps be able to get a fresh perspective on today's scene needs..."—*Maximum Rock'n'Roll* 7½x10¼", 98 pp, 100+ photos, on archival paper. Only a few left. **$19.99.**

ZINES! Vol. One & ZINES! Vol. 2: Incendiary Interviews with Independent Publishers

Making Zines [self-publications] is part of the Punk Tradition of Do-It-Yourself. Following the imperative: "Destroy the society that seeks to destroy you!", *ZINES!* #1 & 2 show how easy it is to express yourself, and thus change your world. Fascinating conversations reveal a host of inspiring ideas for empowering your personal creativity and firing up your imagination and righteous indignation. Vol.1: *Beer Frame, Crap Hound, Fat Girl, Thrift SCORE, Bunny Hop, Housewife Turned Assassin, Meat Hook, X-Ray &* more! Vol. 2: *Murder Can Be Fun, 8-Track Mind, McJob, Dishwasher, Temp Slave,* Bruno Richard. EACH: 8½x11", quotations, excerpts, zine directory, historical essay, index. Vol.1: 184 pp. PB, **$18.99;** Vol.2: 148 pp. PB, **$14.99.** **SPECIAL OFFER: Both for $20!**

RE/SEARCH #1, #2, #3—the shocking tabloid issues.

Deep into the heart of the Control Process; Creativity & Survival, past, present & future. ◆ **#1:** J.G. Ballard, Cabaret Voltaire, Julio Cortazar, Octavio Paz, Sun Ra, The Slits, Conspiracies, Throbbing Gristle. **#2:** DNA, James Blood Ulmer, Z'ev, Aboriginal Music, Surveillance, SRL, Monte Cazazza, Diane Di Prima, German Electronic Music Chart. **#3:** Fela, New Brain Research, The Rattlesnake Man, Sordide Sentimental, New Guinea, Kathy Acker, Pat Califia, Joe Dante, Johanna Went, SPK, Flipper, Physical Modification of Women. 11x17", Heavily illus. **$8 ea, all for $20** (Rare, not at stores, direct order only)

PUNK & D.I.Y.

SEARCH & DESTROY: The Complete Reprint (PUNK ROCK)
(in 2 big 10x15" PB volumes)

"The best punk publication ever"—Jello Biafra Facsimile editions (at 90% size) include all the interviews, articles, ads, illustrations and photos. Captures the enduring revolutionary spirit of punk rock, 1977-1979. Vol. 1 contains an abrasive intro-interview with Jello Biafra on the history and future of punk rock. Published by V. Vale before his RE/Search series, *Search & Destroy* is a definitive, first-hand documentation of the punk rock cultural revolution, printed as it happened! Patti Smith, Iggy Pop, Ramones, Sex Pistols, Clash, DEVO, Avengers, Mutants, Crime, Dead Kennedys, William S. Burroughs, J.G. Ballard, John Waters, Russ Meyer, David Lynch, etc. EACH 10x15" PB book, 148pp,
Vol. 1: $25, Vol. 2: $20. (extra shipping charge overseas)
Also available: SEARCH & DESTROY TABLOIDS #1-11 complete set $40

REAL CONVERSATIONS #1 with Henry Rollins, Jello Biafra, Lawrence Ferlinghetti & Billy Childish additional new material!

V. Vale interviews four counterculture stalwarts, each with a proven track record of integrity and commitment, despite the perils of celebrity. Fascinating conversations on the effects of the Internet, Global Corporatism, the population bomb, mind control, branding and advertising. Other topics: Beat history, literary censorship and the fascist mentality; sex and relationships; rare record collecting. Full of lists of recommended books, films, websites. "Like most RE/Search books, *Real Conversations #1* flies by."—*Maximum Rock'n'Roll.* "*Real Conversations #1* will stir something in the reader, be it creative juices or righteous indignation."—*Weekly Planet.* "Thought-provoking ideas and good stories"—*Activist Guide.* 5x7", 240pp, 30 photos. Only a few copies left **$12.95**

LOUDER FASTER SHORTER punk video by
Mindaugis Bagdon San Francisco, March 21, 1978. In the intense, original punk rock scene at the Mabuhay Gardens (the only club in town which would allow it), the AVENGERS, DILS, MUTANTS, SLEEPERS and UXA played a benefit for striking Kentucky coal miners ("Punks Against Oppression!").

One of the only surviving 16mm color documents of this short-lived era, *LOUDER FASTER SHORTER* captured the spirit and excitement of "punk rock" before revolt became style. Filmmaker Mindaugis Bagdon was a member of *Search & Destroy*, the publication which chronicled and catalyzed the Punk Rock Cultural Revolution of the '70s. "Exceptionally fine color photography, graphic design and editing."—*S.F. International Film Festival review, 1980.* 20 minute video in US NTSC VHS only. **$15.**

MUSIC: Read & Listen!

RE/Search #14 & 15: *Incredibly Strange Music* Vol. 1 & 2—BOOKS

These are the two books that launched the mad record-collecting fad of the '90s, inspiring publications like *Cool & Strange Music*. DJs, vinyl collectors and music lovers will greatly benefit by these illuminating books. Focus: "Easy listening," "exotica," and "celebrity" as well as recordings by (singing) cops and (polka-playing) priests, religious ventriloquists, astronauts, opera-singing parrots, and gospel by blind teenage girls with bouffant hairdos. EACH 8½x11", 220 pp, over 200 photos, PB. Vol. 1: **$19.99**, Vol. 2, only a few copies left: **$25**

Incredibly Strange Music

Incredibly Strange Music, Vol. 1 An amazing anthology of outstanding, hard-to-find musical/spoken word gems from LPs that are as scarce as hens' teeth. These tracks must be heard to be believed! Cassette with original artwork packaging, sealed, only **$12.**
Incredibly Strange Music, Vol. 2 Lucia Pamela's barnyard frenzy "Walking on the Moon"; "How to Speak Hip" by Del Close & John Brent; "Join the Gospel Express" by singing ventriloquist doll Little Marcy, and many more musical gems. Full liner notes. **CD $16**

Ken Nordine COLORS A kaleidoscope of riotous sound and imagery. The pioneer of "Word Jazz" delivers "good lines" which are as smooth as water, inviting the listener to embark upon a musical fantasy. Contains extra tracks not on original vinyl record. **CD $16**

The Essential Perrey & Kingsley Two fantastic, classic LPs (*In Sound from Way Out* and *Kaleidoscopic Vibrations*) combined on one hard-to-find CD. Contains all the tracks recorded by the Perrey-Kingsley duo. Sounds as fresh as tomorrow! **CD $16**

Jean-Jacques Perrey *CIRCUS OF LIFE* The latest from French electronic music pioneer Jean-Jacques Perrey. Entertaining, danceable, thought provoking and FUN! **CD $16**
CDs: **$16** each, cassette **$12**. (ALL 4 CDs + 1 cassette: **$55 plus shipping.**)

SWING! The New Retro Renaissance Rockabilly, swing, lounge and Vegas Show Acts PLUS MORE. Fads can come and go, but the music of Lavay Smith, Big Sandy, and Sam Butera will remain with us! Learn about *the life*: vintage clothes, hairdos, shoes, cars, books, movies. Photos of bands, aerial dancers, classic cars, hairstyles, clothes, shoes, ties, accessories, and interiors of homes. 8½x11", 224 pp, with hundreds of photographs; lists of recommended books, records and films; informative essays; movie reviews; index. PB. **$17.99.**

BODY MODIFICATION and S&M

RE/Search 12: MODERN PRIMITIVES [part of our S&M Library] The *New York Times* called this "the Bible of the underground tattooing and body piercing movement." *Modern Primitives* launched an entire '90s subculture. Crammed with illustrations & information, it's now considered a classic. The best texts on ancient human decoration practices such as tattooing, piercing, scarification and more. 279 eye-opening photos and graphics; 22 in-depth interviews with some of the most colorful people on the planet. "Dispassionate ethnography that lets people put their behavior in its own context."—*Voice Literary*

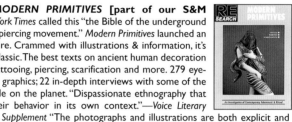

Supplement "The photographs and illustrations are both explicit and astounding . . . provides fascinating food for thought."—*Iron Horse* 8½x11″, 212 pp, 279 photos and illustrations. PB **$19.50**

SPECIAL OFFER: Modern Primitives book & T-shirt gift-pack—only $25

Modern Primitives T-shirt, beautiful design!
Multi-pastel colors on black 100% cotton T-shirt
Illustrations of 12 erotic piercings and implants.
Xtra Large only. Black, Purple, Red, Blue. $20.

MODERN PAGANS: A Sequel to MODERN PRIMITIVES. *Modern Primitives* restored to readers the right to symbolically decorate one's own body in accord with thousands of years of tradition. *Modern Pagans* restores the experience of poetic, Nature-based ritual celebration, especially important in child-raising. Children love the original "Easter" egg hunt and the Maypole. Charles Gatewood, Starhawk, Thorn Coyle, Isaac Bonewits, Oberon & Morning Glory, Sam Webster, and many others eloquently offer a vision of living counter to our bankrupt Western society which has lost its mythology and purpose. Densely informative about all aspects of Pagan cosmology, creativity, child-rearing, history, activism, ritual, ceremony, aesthetics, and sex magic. 8x10″, 212 pp., many photos, lists, guides, etc. **$19.95.**

BOB FLANAGAN: SUPERMASOCHIST [part of our S&M Library] Bob Flanagan grew up with Cystic Fibrosis. His childhood suffering was principally alleviated by masturbation, wherein pain and pleasure became linked, resulting in his lifelong practice of extreme masochism, branding, piercing, whipping, bondage and endurance trials. ". . . an eloquent tour through the psychic terrain of SM, discussing the most severe sexual diversions with the humorous detachment of a shy, clean living nerd. I came away from the book wanting to know this man."—*Details Magazine.* 8½x11″, 128 pp, 125 photos & illustrations. PB **$19.99.**

The Torture Garden by Octave Mirbeau This book was once described as the "most sickening work of art of the nineteenth century!" Long out of print, Octave Mirbeau's macabre classic (1899) features a corrupt Frenchman and an insatiably cruel Englishwoman who meet and then frequent a fantastic 19th century Chinese garden where torture is practiced as an art form. The fascinating, horrific narrative slithers deep into the human spirit, uncovering murderous proclivities and demented desires. "Hot with the fever of ecstatic, prohibited joys, as cruel as a thumbscrew and as luxuriant as an Oriental tapestry. Exotic, perverse . . . hailed by the critics."—Charles Hanson *Towne* 8½x11″, 120 pp, 21 mesmerizing photos. **Hardcover only** (edition of just 100 copies, with beautiful dust jacket) **$29**

MASOCHISM, FEMINISM

Confessions of Wanda von Sacher-Masoch Married for 10 years to Leopold von Sacher-Masoch (author: *Venus in Furs* & many other novels) whose whip-and-fur bedroom games spawned the term "masochism," Wanda's story is a feminist classic from 100 years ago. She was forced to play "sadistic" roles in Leopold's fantasies to ensure the survival of herself & their 3 children–games which called into question who was the Master and who the Slave. Besides being a compelling story of a woman's search for her own identity, strength and, ultimately, complete independence, this is a true-life adventure story–an odyssey through many lands peopled by amazing characters. Here is a woman's consistent unblinking investigation of the limits of morality and the deepest meanings of love. "Extravagantly designed in an illustrated, oversized edition that is a pleasure to hold. It is also exquisitely written, engaging and literary and turns our preconceptions upside down."—*L.A. Reader*

8½x11″, 136 pp, illustrated, PB. Only a few copies left: $19.99

RE/Search 13: Angry Women 16 cutting-edge performance artists discuss critical questions such as: How can revolutionary feminism encompass wild sex, humor, beauty, spirituality *plus* radical politics? How can a powerful movement for social change be *inclusionary?* Wide range of topics discussed *passionately.* **Included:** Karen Finley, Annie Sprinkle, bell hooks, Diamanda Galas, Kathy Acker, Susie Bright, Sapphire. Armed with contempt for dogma, stereotype & cliché, these visionaries probe into our social foundation of taboos, beliefs & totalitarian linguistic contradictions from whence spring (as well as thwart) theories, imaginings, behavior & dreams. "The view here is largely pro-sex, pro-porn, and pro-choice."—*Village Voice* "This book is a Bible—it hails the dawn of a new era–the era of an inclusive, fun, sexy feminism. Every interview contains brilliant moments of wisdom." *Am. Bk Review*
8½x11″, 240 pp, 135 illus. PB. RE/Search edition out-of-print, only a few copies left: **$19.99**

TWO BY DANIEL P. MANNIX

MEMOIRS OF A SWORD SWALLOWER Not for the faint-of-heart, this book will delight all lovers of sideshows & carnivals. "I probably never would have become America's leading fire-eater if Flamo the Great hadn't happened to explode that night . . ." So begins this true story of life with a traveling carnival, peopled by amazing characters—the Human Ostrich, the Human Salamander, Jolly Daisy, etc.—who commit outrageous feats of wizardry. This is one of the only *authentic* narratives revealing the "tricks" (or rather, painful skills) involved in a sideshow, .and is invaluable to those aspiring to this profession. OVER 50 RARE PHOTOS taken by Mannix in the 1930s and never before seen! Sideshow aficionados will delight in finally being able to see some of their favorite "stars" captured in candid moments. Rugged Individualist *Americana* history at its best. 8½x11″, 128 pp, 50+ photos, index, PB, **$15.99**
Rare, autographed (in 1997) copies of paperback available for only $30

FREAKS: We Who Are Not As Others

Amazing Photos! A fascinating, classic book, based on Mannix's personal acquaintance with sideshow stars such as the Alligator Man and the Monkey Woman. Read all about the notorious love affairs of midgets; the amazing story of the Elephant Boy; the unusual amours of Jolly Daisy, the fat woman; hermaphrodite love; the bulb-eating Human Ostrich, etc. 8½x11″, 124 pp, 88 wonderful, nostalgic yet shocking photos. PB. **$15.95**
Author died in 1997. **Autographed hardbounds (a few left) $50**

OUT-OF-PRINT

Wild Wives A classic of hard-boiled fiction, Willeford's *Wild Wives* is amoral, sexy, and brutal. Written in a sleazy San Francisco hotel in the early '50s while on leave from the Army, Willeford creates a tale of deception featuring the crooked detective Jacob C. Blake and his nemesis—a beautiful, insane young woman. Set in 50's San Francisco! 5x7″, 108 pp. PB. **$10.99**
ME & BIG JOE by Mike Bloomfield with Scott Summerville. Classic coming-of-age story with young Bloomfield meeting Chicago blues musicians, most scarily Big Joe Williams. Out-of-print, 5x7″, PB. **$8.**
BOB FLANAGAN: SUPER-MASOCHIST. Made into a movie. RE/Search's most hardcore-illustrated book, yet surprisingly engaging. A few copies left, 8.5x11." **$19.99**
SEARCH & DESTROY Tabloids #1-11 full set. 1977-1979. Classic punk. **only $40**
KATHY ACKER: *GREAT EXPECTATIONS.* RE/Search edition fabulously rare, PB **$50**
INCREDIBLY STRANGE MUSIC #1 **CD,** long out-of-print. Mint/sealed. **$32**
W. S. BURROUGHS & J.G. BALLARD interviews in *Search & Destroy #10* $6
SRL piece by **Mark Pauline** in **RE/Search #2 tabloid** (mint, from 1981) **only $8**
JOHN WATERS interview in *Search & Destroy #7* (from 1978!; mint) **$6**
HERE TO GO extremely rare R/S hardback by Brion Gysin, Burroughs (ed. 100) **$100**

W.S.Burroughs, I.S.Films, Industrial

R/S 4/5: WS Burroughs, Brion Gysin, Throbbing Gristle

A great, unknown Burroughs-Gysin treasure trove of radical ideas! Compilation of interviews, scarce fiction, essays: this is a manual of incendiary insights. Strikingly designed; filled with radical references. **Topics discussed**: biological warfare, utopias, con men, lost inventions, the JFK killing, Hassan I Sabbah, cloning, the cut-up theory, Moroccan trance music, the Dream Machine, Manson, the media control process, prostitution, and more. Includes part of *Revised Boy Scout Manual*. 8½x11″, 100 pp, 58 photos & illus. PB, **$19.99** Order Direct!

William S. Burroughs T-shirt! Black & red design on white, 100% cotton T-shirt.
"We intend to destroy all dogmatic verbal systems."—*WSB*. Original design hand-screened on 100% heavyweight cotton T-Shirt. **$20** XL only.

RE/Search 6/7: Industrial Culture Handbook

This book provided a radical education for many of the most subversive artists practicing today. The rich ideas of the *Industrial Culture* movement's performance artists and musicians are nakedly exposed: *Survival Research Laboratories, Throbbing Gristle, Cabaret Voltaire, SPK, Non, Monte Cazazza, Johanna Went, Sordide Sentimental, R&N,* & *Z'ev*. **Topics include:** brain research, forbidden medical texts & films, creative crime & *interesting* criminals, modern warfare & weaponry, neglected gore films & their directors, psychotic lyrics in past pop songs, and *art brut*. Many book lists, film lists, and record lists. 8½x11″, 140 pp, 179 photos & illust. PB, **$25**

RE/Search 10: INCREDIBLY STRANGE FILMS

First to champion Herschell Gordon Lewis, Russ Meyer, Larry Cohen, Ray Dennis Steckler, Ted V. Mikels, Doris Wishman & others who had been critically consigned to the ghettos of gore & sexploitation films, this book allowed artists to rationally explain how they made gripping dramas with zero budgets and overflowing imaginations. 13 interviews, A-Z of film personalities, "Favorite Films" list, quotations, bibliography, filmography, film synopses, & index. "Flicks like these are subversive alternatives to the mind control propagated by the mainstream media."—*Iron Horse* "The interviews are intelligent, enthusiastic and articulate."—*Small Press*. Has been used as textbook at UC Berkeley, etc. 8½x11″, 224 pp, 157 photos & illus. PB, last of this printing: **$19.99**

INDEX

◆   ◆   ◆